Booked on a Feeling

JAYCI LEE

D1313352

HEADLINE
ETERNAL

Published by arrangement with St. Martin's Griffin,
an imprint of St. Martin's Publishing Group

First published in Great Britain in 2022
by HEADLINE ETERNAL
An imprint of HEADLINE PUBLISHING GROUP

1

Cataloguing in Publication Data is available from the British Library

ISBN 978 1 4722 7713 8

Offset in 10.78/14.7 pt Electra LT Std by Jouve (UK), Milton Keynes

Printed and bound in Great Britain by Clays Ltd, Elcograf S.p.A.

MIX
Paper from
responsible sources
FSC® C104740

Headline's policy is to use papers that are natural, renewable and recyclable
products and made from wood grown in well-managed forests and other
controlled sources. The logging and manufacturing processes are expected
to conform to the environmental regulations of the country of origin.

HEADLINE PUBLISHING GROUP
An Hachette UK Company
Carmelite House
50 Victoria Embankment
London EC4Y 0DZ

www.headlineeternal.com
www.headline.co.uk
www.hachette.co.uk

Jayci Lee writes poignant, sexy, and laugh-out-loud romance every free second she can scavenge and is semi-retired from her fifteen-year career as a defense litigator. She loves food, wine, and travelling, and incidentally so do her characters in books like *The Dating Dare* and *A Sweet Mess*.

Jayci lives in sunny California with her tall, dark, and handsome husband, two amazing boys with boundless energy, and a fluffy rescue whose cuteness is a major distraction.

To find out more, visit her website: **jaycilee.com**, and find her on Facebook: **/authorjaycilee**, and Twitter and Instagram: **@authorjaycilee**.

Raves for Jayci's delicious rom-coms:

'A perfect balance of impeccable wit, laugh out loud hilarity, and off-the-charts chemistry. *A Sweet Mess* is a sinfully decadent romantic comedy!'
Helena Hunting, *New York Times* bestselling author

'A rich, vibrant romance that's a feast for all the senses!'
Lauren Blakely, *New York Times* bestselling author

'Readers will get lost in Aubrey's sugary creations while rooting for the characters to find their happily ever after'
Library Journal

'From the cute, witty bantering and downright naughty flirting to the fun dare between the hero and heroine, this was a diverse romance that left a huge smile on my face'
Harlequin Junkie

'Lee's lush romance is a delectable delight' *Booklist*

'A wonderful twist on a classic romance . . . this is a fun summer read that is best enjoyed poolside or at the beach'
Lit Up, Southern California News Group

By Jayci Lee

A Sweet Mess
The Dating Dare
Booked on a Feeling

To Oppa,
you will always be my Baymax

CHAPTER ONE

The slumbering city below held no answers for Lizzy Chung, but she nevertheless stared out her office window as she sipped her black coffee. The subtle shifts of color in the sky hinted at approaching dawn and painted downtown Los Angeles in muted gray tones, leaching the impressive city of its color and vitality.

Lizzy braked hard to stop her mind from comparing her own life to her reflections on the predawn city. Besides, color and vitality were overrated. Her life was fan-freaking-tastic. Five years out of law school, she was a senior counsel at Nelson Peters, one of the top law firms in the nation, and well on her way to making partner in two years. And she was trying a case as the lead trial counsel for the first time in her career, which happened to be the reason why she was at work at this godforsaken hour.

She brought her mug to her lips and wrinkled her nose. She hated black coffee, but her usual English breakfast tea with milk and sugar didn't seem badass enough for the day of her opening statement. The voir dire phase of the trial was over, and they had a decent set of jurors. Not perfect but workable. Juror numbers four and nine might be problematic. They were opinionated and didn't follow instructions well—which meant they might decide the case based on their common sense and life experiences rather than following the rule of law.

But a good trial attorney should be able to overcome that. She nodded, agreeing heartily with herself, then stopped mid-nod. How the hell was she supposed to know if she was any good? This was her first trial. She squeezed her eyes shut as a familiar tightness spread across her chest, constricting her breathing.

"Please let me be a good trial attorney," she whispered to the ceiling, hoping a higher power would hear her. Alas, no fairy godmother materialized out of thin air to offer her a dusting of awesome lawyer glitter. *Boo.*

Huffing out an impatient sigh, she turned her back on the window and her gnawing doubts. *I will be a good trial attorney because I have to be.* With stubborn determination, she walked to the kitchen and dumped out her coffee. There was no need for any black coffee or a fairy godmother. She was already plenty badass.

Lizzy marched to the small conference room they were using as the war room, armed with a warm mug of milk tea, and sat down at one end of the long oval table. She leaned her elbows on the table and massaged her temples as the headache she'd been fighting since 4:00 A.M. drilled a hole through her head. When that didn't help much, she took a sip of her tea and reached for the trial notebook and the exhibit binders. She knew the material inside out and upside down, but overpreparing calmed her nerves.

The sun at last completed its lazy ascent, and morning light streamed into the conference room. Reading over the documents had given her the distraction she'd needed, and her anxiety was under control—not gone but held at bay. She leaned back in her chair and stretched her arms over her head. The clock on the wall read a quarter till eight, and she frowned as she stood and strode out to the hallway. Her associate was fifteen minutes late, and punctuality mattered in the legal world. When she was a second-year attorney, she used to arrive at her destination thirty minutes early rather than be even a minute late.

"I'm so sorry I'm late." Right on cue, Katie ran down the hallway toward her, pulling a rattling cart piled high with three Bankers Boxes. Her hair was wet and twisted into a lopsided bun on top of her head. "I was up till two last night. I don't even remember hitting the snooze button."

Lizzy didn't have the heart to chew out her associate even though her younger self would've been masticated beyond recognition. Her law firm's culture could often be cutthroat, but that didn't mean she had to be. Besides, Katie was her second chair, and she didn't want to fry her nerves more than they already must be.

"Don't worry about it," Lizzy said briskly, walking back into the war room. "Let's just get to work."

"Of course. Absolutely." A relieved smile lit up Katie's face as she went about unloading the boxes. "I reread all three volumes of Steven Anderson's deposition transcript last night. I really think his testimony is strong."

"Make sure he reads them over as well. Thoroughly. The last thing we want are inconsistencies between his deposition testimony and his trial testimony," Lizzy said, more sharply than she'd intended, as her anxiety returned full force. Having their star witness bomb on the stand would be a nightmare of epic proportions. "I need you to start prepping him for trial. He won't take the stand for at least a couple of days, but I want you to have plenty of time to get him ready."

Katie sat up straighter at her tone. "He'll be here in ten minutes for his first session. I'll have two hours with him before we have to head over to the courthouse."

"Good. Be sure to drill him in the basics: Answer yes-or-no questions with a *yes* or *no*. Don't elaborate." She grabbed the war room's resident bottle of Tylenol and washed down two pills with the last of her tea. "If Plaintiff counsel's question is unclear, don't try to help her by answering with what he thinks she's asking. Request that she rephrase the question."

"Got it." Her associate scribbled down everything Lizzy rattled off even though she probably knew all that stuff already.

"Thanks, Katie." She stood and reached for her empty mug. "How are you getting to the court?"

"I'm driving over with one of the paralegals. They're bringing the extra set of trial exhibits Judge Reiner requested."

"Sounds good. I'll see you there."

She was almost at the door when Katie asked, "Are you ready for the opening statement?"

"Is this the part where I say, 'I was born ready'?" Lizzy grinned with more confidence than she felt, gripping the mug between her cold hands. She was as prepared as she would ever be, but that didn't mean she was *ready*. The ominous thump of her heart accentuated her uncertainty as a parade of what-ifs spun dizzyingly through her mind.

Katie laughed. "You're going to be amazing."

"Thank you." She had to be if she wanted to win this trial and increase her chances of making partner. Her headache tightened like a vise around her head.

The gloomy tint over downtown had lifted by the time Lizzy returned to her office, and the city below positively teemed with energy. Even so, the view from her sixty-second-floor office didn't capture her attention the way it used to when she was young and fresh out of law school. City life had a way of making a soul weary.

She closed her door and perched on the front of her desk, holding a printout of the bullet points for her opening statement. She didn't write out the entire statement, because she didn't want to come across to the jury as a smarmy, over-polished corporate lawyer with the perfect, practiced speech. She wanted her opening statement to be conversational and relatable.

It was a crucial opportunity to connect with the jurors. As the attorney for the corporate defendant in a gender discrimination case, she didn't want the jury to think she was playing for the Big Bad Wolf. She had to convince them that Defendant was a fair employer being targeted by a disgruntled former employee who was unqualified for the position she had held.

Lizzy inhaled through her nose and exhaled slowly through her mouth. Her client truly wasn't the Big Bad Wolf. They were a hardworking, midsize toy manufacturer who happened to have employed a supervisor with a blunt, abrasive personality. Fortunately for Defendant, the fact that the supervisor came across as a jerk wasn't a violation of the law. Especially since he was a jerk to everyone across the board *regardless* of gender. Unfortunately for Defendant, Plaintiff presented very well and seemed to genuinely believe that she had been discriminated against.

Another breath in and out. This case should've settled out of court months ago. Neither of the parties needed to waste time and money to be dragged into court. Lizzy laid the blame squarely on Plaintiff's counsel. She had dealt with many opposing counsels in her years as an attorney, but none had been as antagonistic and vicious as Carol Monty. She had made even the simplest of discovery exchanges into drawn-out court battles with motions and sanctions slapped on both parties.

Attorneys merely represent their clients' interests—they were both just doing their damn job—but Carol Monty constantly launched personal attacks on her. As much as Lizzy hated confrontations—yes, she was a conflict-averse lawyer—she hated losing even more, so their phone calls inevitably turned into heated arguments. She hoped Plaintiff's counsel would retain some civility during trial. These bullying sorts tended to behave better when they were in front of a judge and jury.

Lizzy ran through the opening statement twice before the clock struck ten. Trial convened in thirty minutes. Maybe Jack would be there for her opening statement. A spark of excitement coursed through her. Of course, she hadn't asked him to come, but he might come anyway because he was Jack—the kindest, most considerate friend a girl could ask for. A real smile lit up her face for the first time that morning. She lifted her black suit jacket from the back of her chair and shrugged into it, adjusting her pale blue blouse underneath it. After checking her makeup in her compact, she snapped it shut and dropped it into her purse.

The superior court was less than three miles from her office, but thanks to one-way streets and traffic, it was a solid ten-minute drive. She parked her white BMW 3 Series in her favorite structure, shelling out thirty dollars for all-day parking. It was across the street from a seldom-used entrance to the Stanley Mosk Courthouse, which allowed her to bypass the long line at the main entrance.

The side entrance led her directly to the fourth floor, so she only had to ride the escalator up one floor to where Judge Reiner's courtroom was located. It allowed her to avoid the cramped, dilapidated elevators altogether, which was key to getting anywhere on time at this courthouse. She smirked, feeling quite smug about having home-*court* advantage.

Her high heels clicked against the terrazzo floor, and their sharp staccato echoed down the long, nearly deserted hallway. The stone benches outside the courtrooms—because who doesn't want a cold ass to start the day off with—would've been filled with lawyers clad in black and gray suits just two hours ago. That was when the judges held their morning calendar, during which they dealt with the more day-to-day matters of the numerous cases assigned to them.

The few lawyers who remained in the hallway exuded the same vibe of exhaustion and adrenaline that sloshed through her. They were all in trial mode—similar to beast mode but infinitely less cool. Lizzy sighed. Poor souls.

She stepped into the courtroom with ten minutes to spare, pulling her briefcase close behind her. To her great annoyance, Carol Monty already sat at the plaintiff's table closer to the jury box with her perfectly highlighted blond head bent over a yellow legal pad. She didn't bother looking up when Lizzy sat down at the defendant's table.

Holding back an irritated sigh, Lizzy said, "Good morning, Carol."

Ever so slowly, Carol put down the pen she was holding and turned toward Lizzy, making it abundantly clear that she wasn't happy with the interruption. "Good morning, Counsel."

While most lawyers addressed one another by first name, Carol never called her *Lizzy*. Not even *Elizabeth*. It was either *Counsel* or *Ms. Chung*. God forbid there was even a hint of camaraderie between them. At this point, Lizzy would be grateful for a modicum of civility.

"Nice *pants* suit." Carol stared pointedly at Lizzy's slacks.

"Rumor has it that our esteemed judge finds female attorneys in pants unprofessional."

So much for her hopes for civility. The sad thing was Lizzy wasn't even shocked. Carol might very well be full of shit, but she wouldn't put it past the curmudgeonly judge to be flagrantly sexist. The point was her dear opposing counsel only shared that little tidbit to unnerve her before her opening statement. Lizzy didn't care what the judge thought about her slacks. Her audience today was the jury. What did make her blood pressure rise was Carol's unrelenting antagonism. She was just so sick of it.

"Good to know. Thanks for the tip, Carol," Lizzy said with a benign smile, deliberately using her first name again. She was rewarded with the tightening of Carol's lips. But it wasn't worth the brief flare of satisfaction. Her opponent was succeeding in bringing Lizzy down to her level. The realization left a bad taste in her mouth.

"God, I hate those elevators," Katie whispered as she settled down on the seat next to her. Her hair fell past her shoulders in lustrous waves. She was one of those people who could pull the pen out of their bun and shake their hair loose to achieve the perfect loose curls. *Lucky.* "Michael had those boxes of exhibits to bring, so we couldn't take the escalators."

"I hear you. I avoid those elevators at all costs." Lizzy waved at their paralegal, who was stacking up the Bankers Boxes against one of the walls.

She liked Michael. He did great work. She'd asked him to join their trial team as soon as she'd suspected the case wouldn't settle before another attorney could snatch him up. She also supplied him with a constant stream of chocolate from See's Candies so he would give her preferential treatment. Having competent support made an attorney's life so much easier.

Other than a couple of attorneys speaking with the court

clerk after the morning calendar, the courtroom had emptied out of any audiences. Lizzy pursed her lips as a strand of disappointment wound through her. Jack was four hours away in Weldon. She hadn't seriously expected him to drive all the way down to Los Angeles to watch her opening statement. But a small part of her had hoped he would come. She certainly could use the moral support.

Then she thought wistfully of her friend Ashley. If they had still been close, she would be there to support her. But there was a rift between them that she didn't know how to mend. They'd joined the firm at the same time, both fresh out of law school, and had connected instantly. Unfortunately, the firm culture and the drive to make partner inevitably pitted them against each other. Things hadn't been the same with Ashley since last year, when Lizzy made senior counsel first.

The bailiff opened the door to the deliberation room, and the jurors filed out to take their seats in the jury box. Lizzy dragged her attention back into the courtroom. Now was not the time to mull over her growing discontent with the firm culture and the ugly realities of climbing the corporate ladder. She had to focus on winning over the jury so she could win this damn trial.

Her heart pounded a relentless beat in her ears, and her palms grew slick with sweat. She poured herself a glass of water from the carafe on the table. As she brought the glass to her lips, she noticed her hands weren't quite steady. She needed to center herself. While this was her first trial, she was an experienced litigator with many court appearances under her belt. She'd argued and won multiple motions for summary judgment, which was like a mini trial where the judge decided the case based on a set of finite facts. The opening statement wasn't that much different from what she'd previously done.

Despite the sound logic of her mind, anxiety continued to climb its way up, and her breath quickened with her pulse. As her therapist said, becoming anxious about anxiety only made things worse. Lizzy could handle anxiety. She lived with it constantly. She breathed in five seconds through her nose and gently released it through her mouth for seven seconds. But even after multiple repetitions, her breathing technique wasn't slowing down her heart rate.

"All rise," the bailiff boomed. "The Honorable James Reiner presiding."

Lizzy got to her feet but grabbed the table in front of her when the room threatened to tilt. She felt Katie looking at her, but she kept her gaze focused straight ahead to will the dizziness away. Many of the superior court judges didn't require people to stand when they entered the room anymore, but Judge Reiner took his time settling into his seat and moving some files around before he said, "You may be seated."

She plopped back into her seat, her knees weaker than she would like. She envisioned waves crashing into the beach and receding and tried to allow her anxiety to wash over her. If she didn't fight it, it would run its course and move on.

"Ms. Chung, are you ready to make the opening statement for Defendant?" Judge Reiner asked, managing to sound both apathetic and patronizing. When she got to her feet, his glance flickered to her slacks, and the corners of his thin lips dove down.

"Yes, Your Honor." It felt as though her head were underwater, and her voice echoed in her head. Picking up her leather binder with her opening-statement bullet points, Lizzy made her way to the small podium by the jury box. She put her binder down and planted her palms on the podium to steady herself.

"Good morning, members of the jury. As you know, I'm Elizabeth Chung, counsel for Defendant Jubilee Toy Company."

Her body turned cold as though all the blood had drained out of it, and numbness spread to her fingertips. "Contrary to Ms. Monty's passionate monologue yesterday, this case isn't about gender discrimination. It's about hurt feelings and wounded pride taken way out of proportion . . ."

Darkness edged in from the corners of her vision, and suddenly, she couldn't get enough air into her lungs. *Oh, God. Not now.* Something squeezed at her skull as though she were a plush toy being gripped and carried in the air by a mechanical claw. She was shaking uncontrollably now, and her knees finally gave out. She thought she heard a lovely deep voice call out *Lizzy*, but the coldness of the hard floor met her body, then there was darkness everywhere.

~

"Lizzy!" Jack yelled.

His best friend fell to her knees just as he stepped through the courtroom door, then collapsed onto the thinly carpeted floor as he ran to her. He might have pushed someone out of the way, but Lizzy's head was cradled in the crook of his arm a moment later as he crouched on the floor beside her limp body.

"Lizzy," he said gently even as his heart beat the hell out of his rib cage. What was happening to her?

There was commotion all around him, and he vaguely noticed the pounding of a gavel. He normally would've gotten a kick out of that, but his entire attention was focused on the pale, heart-shaped face of his friend.

"Can you hear me?" He ran his thumb over her cheek, willing her to respond. His chest tightened a fraction more every minute Lizzy's expression remained blank.

"Is she okay? The bailiff wants to know if he should call an ambulance." A young woman knelt by his side. She was wearing a black suit and a worried expression on her face. She must have been one of Lizzy's colleagues.

Before he could answer, Lizzy stirred in his arms. "No, Katie. No ambulance."

"God, Lizzy." Jack gathered her against him, scrunching his eyes shut as relief rushed through him. "You scared the shit out of me."

"You're here," she said in a small voice, muffled against his chest. "I'm so happy you're here."

"Of course I'm here." He pulled away and grinned down at her, tucking a wayward strand of hair behind her ear. "I had to witness the great Elizabeth Chung's first opening statement."

"Oh, my God." She jerked into a sitting position. He wanted to kick himself for the rude reminder. "The opening statement . . . the trial . . ."

"Don't worry. The judge called a recess until one thirty," Katie said, putting a hand on Lizzy's shoulder. "But I think I should let Peter know what happened."

Jack didn't think it possible, but Lizzy's face paled even more, and his chest tightened with worry. He wrapped his arm around her waist in case she passed out again.

"You're right," she said grimly. "He's the supervising partner. He should be kept apprised of everything."

"And he'll know what we should do." Katie got to her feet.

"What we should do about what?" Lizzy's eyebrows furrowed above the bridge of her nose.

"You know"—she rummaged through her purse—"about what to do next."

"I know what to do next," Lizzy said with icy calm. Jack helped her struggle to her feet, holding her arms to steady her. He frowned when he felt tremors running through her. "I'm going to give my opening statement when the court reconvenes at one thirty."

"But . . ." Katie stared slack-jawed at Lizzy, hugging her cell phone to her chest.

"Are you sure you're well enough to do that?" Jack protested even though he recognized the stubborn determination in the jut of her chin.

Her narrowed eyes shot toward him, but he arched his brow and held her gaze. Nothing was going to stop her from resuming the trial. She always achieved her goals no matter what it took. But that didn't mean he had to like it. Sometimes she pushed herself too damn hard.

"I haven't eaten anything other than some peanut M&M's since yesterday afternoon," she said, turning back to her colleague. "Once I get some real food in me, I'll be good to go."

Jack wanted to call her bullshit when she swayed on her feet, but he just tightened his hold on her and watched as Katie rushed out of the courtroom with a dubious glance over her shoulder.

"You should sit down." He pulled out a chair for her with a resigned sigh. When Lizzy sank into it without argument, his concern grew stronger. Some color had returned to her lips, but her cheeks were still pale. "What really happened up here?"

"I . . ." She glanced around the courtroom. The bailiff was chatting with the court clerk at the front of the courtroom. There was no one else around them. "I had a panic attack."

"A panic attack?" He sat down in the chair next to her and leaned in closer. She was the most confident, unflappable person he knew. But maybe being strong all the time took a toll on her. "Has it ever happened before?"

"A few times," she said, her eyes sliding away from his. "But I've never passed out from it before."

"Lizzy." He waited until she looked at him. She'd been keeping things from him—a flash of hurt shot through him followed closely by guilt . . . he should've known—but that wasn't what mattered right now. "Do you think you can continue with the trial without it happening again?"

"I have anxiety medication. I didn't want to take it because it makes my head fuzzy, but maybe I'll take half a pill this afternoon." She wrung her hands in her lap. "I let my thoughts go down the rabbit hole, and my anxiety just snowballed. I know better than to let that happen. I have tools to deal with anxiety before it gets this bad, but sometimes I forget to actually use them."

"Hey, stop being so hard on yourself." He tugged her close with his hand behind her neck and pressed his forehead against hers. "This is your first trial. It's a fucking lot. Show yourself some grace."

"Thank you, Jack." She leaned into him for a second before she pulled back and smiled at him.

His breath caught in his throat. Even pale and drawn, she was so beautiful. He was staring, but he couldn't turn away. He couldn't even smile back like a normal person. If he didn't do or say something soon, she would be weirded out. And yet, his wordless staring continued. He wanted to drink in the sight of her. He hadn't seen her in close to three months.

"Sorry I took so long." Katie rushed into the courtroom, slightly out of breath. "I had to get out of the building to make the call. This courthouse is some sort of a signal-blocking fortress."

"What did Peter say?" Lizzy's face was placid, but Jack could see the strain in the corner of her eyes and the line of her lips. He fought against the impulse to pull her into his arms again. *She's got this.*

"He agreed that the trial should proceed as long as you're sure you can handle it," Katie said.

"I can handle it." Lizzy's expression hovered between confidence and arrogance.

There you are. He swiped his hand over his mouth to hide his smile.

Then she looked between him and her colleague. "Did I introduce you guys?"

"No, you were kind of busy being passed out and all," he joked even though he still wasn't over his shock of seeing her go down like that.

"Katie, this is my friend, Jack Park. And, Jack, this is my associate and second chair, Katie Douglas."

"Nice to meet you, Katie." He extended his hand to her.

"Same to you, Jack." Her gaze lingered on his face as though she were getting her first good look at him and liking what she saw. Other than an objective appreciation of her attractiveness, he didn't feel a similar interest. It probably had something to do with his dream girl standing right next to him. But he was flattered when Katie held his hand a second longer than necessary.

"Anyway." Lizzy stood abruptly from her chair. "I should go get something to eat."

"Definitely. I'll take you to lunch," he offered without hesitation. But he couldn't help wondering if he'd detected a hint of jealousy in Lizzy's demeanor. *Ha! Keep on dreaming, buddy.* She'd firmly relegated him to the friend zone twenty years ago. "Would you like to join us, Katie?"

"Thank you," she said with a rueful smile. "But I'm just going to grab a sandwich at the cafeteria and work on some cross-examination questions. You still want them by this evening, right?"

"Yes. That would be great." Lizzy picked up her purse, then hesitated. "Maybe I should join you at the cafeteria."

"No," he interjected, shooting her associate an apologetic

glance. Lizzy turned wide eyes to him, and he shrugged. "I'm getting you out of here for a couple of hours."

"I agree with Jack. You need a proper break," Katie said, and waved her hand around the courtroom. "This will all be waiting for you when you come back."

"Thanks, Katie." He smiled at her. "It was nice meeting you."

When Lizzy still looked unsure, Jack took a firm hold of her arm and tugged her toward the doors. She badly needed a break, and he wasn't taking no for an answer. But once they were out in the hallway, she walked beside him without the insistence of his hand.

"I feel so awful," she whispered.

"About us going out to lunch without Katie?" he teased, hoping to make her smile.

"That, too. I guess." One side of her mouth quirked up, but only for a second. "But mostly about having a panic attack in front of the jury during my opening statement."

"Yeah. I bet." False words of comfort wouldn't do her any good right now. What happened was a big deal, and he would feel awful, too. "But I think it's what you do from this point forward that matters the most. It'll be easy to stand before the jury after what happened and allow embarrassment and insecurity to rule you. They will probably expect that. But you should surprise them. Go up there with even more confidence and strength."

"You're right." She pivoted mid-step and wrapped her arms around his neck. His eyes slid shut as he held her close, and he did his damnedest not to breathe in the scent of her hair. "Thank you, Jack."

"For what?" He reluctantly dropped his arms to his sides when she stepped back.

"For being here," she said simply, her eyes wide and vulnerable.

His heart stuttered in his chest. In moments like these, he was almost content with just being her friend—someone she valued and trusted. Almost.

"I'll always be here for you," he promised, letting his gaze roam her face. Then he reached out and hooked his pinkie around hers—a gesture as old as their friendship.

"And I'll be here for you." Her lips curved softly as she wrapped her pinkie around his. Her smile warmed him down to his toes, and they walked out of the courthouse with their fingers still linked.

"Is there somewhere we can walk to?" He wanted to hold on to her a bit longer.

The city air smelled stale and musky, and the streets were congested with honking cars and people walking too fast, but the early-summer sun felt good against his face, and he was happy to be with Lizzy.

"There's a nice restaurant two blocks from here." She tugged him down the sidewalk by his pinkie. "It'll be my treat."

"I told you I'm taking you out to lunch." He lightly bumped her shoulder. "It's my treat to celebrate your first trial."

"After this morning's performance, it might turn out to be a disaster," she muttered, worry staining her words.

He stopped her in the middle of the sidewalk—undeterred by the annoyed glances of their fellow pedestrians—and turned her to face him, his hands firmly on her shoulders. "We both know you won't allow that to happen."

She searched his face and tears filled her eyes, but she quickly blinked them away. "No, I won't."

"You got this, Lizzy Chung." Jack gave her shoulders one last squeeze—wishing he could share the burden of her anxiety—

then started down the road again. The best he could do was take her mind off her worries for a couple of hours. "I have no idea where we're going, so lead the way."

"How was your drive to LA?" She turned at a corner, and he followed.

"It wasn't bad," he said with a shrug, not mentioning that he drove down the night before. He wasn't trying to keep his interview this morning a secret from her, but he didn't want to say anything until things were certain.

The interview had gone well as far as he could tell, but that didn't mean McBain Corporation would offer him the job. He was a thirty-year-old man applying for an entry-level business analyst position with no prior experience other than working at his family's microbrewery. He was no doubt competing against a slew of kids fresh out of college with their young, pliable minds. But given the chance, he would work his ass off to exceed everyone's expectations . . . even his own.

Lizzy would be excited at the prospect of him moving to Los Angeles and would support him no matter what, but talking about the interview would make things feel too real. He couldn't help but hang his hope on getting the job—for the chance to discover his latent potential and thrive—but if he didn't get it, it would be easier knowing he'd only disappointed himself.

"When are you driving back?" she asked a bit too casually.

He shot her an amused glance and answered her real question. "After I watch your opening statement."

She flashed him a grateful smile, which quickly turned mischievous. "Don't worry. It'll be worth the extra traffic. It's going to be better than *Law & Order.*"

"You don't say?" He raised a skeptical eyebrow, reining in his grin. He was relieved to see Lizzy's confidence restored even though she was probably putting on a brave face. Hopefully, she would be able to convince herself that she was going to kick ass by the end of their lunch.

"I do." She fluttered her fingers in a subtle version of jazz hands, and tender affection rushed through him. What should rightfully be cringeworthy was rendered adorable when committed by her. "Prepare to be dazzled."

Jack chuckled, darting a glance at her smiling face. Little did she know that she had always dazzled him.

CHAPTER TWO

Has the jury reached a verdict?" Judge Reiner swiveled his chair toward the jury box.

"Yes, Your Honor." The foreperson's voice rang with the excitement of someone who was nearly done with her jury duty.

Lizzy clenched and unclenched her hands beneath the table. Seven days of trial on less than four hours of sleep a night all came down to this single moment. She inhaled through her nose and subtly exhaled through her mouth. When she heard a small whimper from beside her, she snuck a quick peek at her associate, but Katie's expression remained calm and professional. Reassured that the younger attorney would retain her composure, she focused on her own.

Her blood was pounding in her ears, but she had taken a full dose of her anxiety medication this morning, so the walls refrained from closing in on her. Even so, she kept up with her deep breathing while she waited for the verdict to be delivered.

"The jury finds in favor of Defendant Jubilee Toy Company on all counts."

Heady relief filled Lizzy, and she took in a lungful of air that even her deep breathing couldn't quite achieve before. After a quick round of housekeeping, the trial was officially over. They had won. But the thrill of the win that the other trial lawyers spoke of wasn't there. Shouldn't she be doing cartwheels in her head? Maybe it hadn't sunk in yet. She did feel a bit numb.

Before the odd sense of disappointment could take root, Lizzy smiled at Katie and extended her hand to her. "Congratulations. You did an incredible job."

"Congratulations to you, too. You were amazing," her associate replied, pumping her hand enthusiastically.

"Please make sure Michael interviews as many of the jurors as he can," she said, holding back a wince. She didn't relish giving the younger attorney more work even before the high of the win wore off. "Let's find out what made them rule in our favor."

"He's already on it," Katie said with a deservedly smug smile.

Lizzy laughed lightly. "You're the best."

She turned toward the plaintiff's table, but her opposing counsel refused to meet her eyes. Keeping her head resolutely lowered to the table, Carol Monty haphazardly stacked her files and forced them into her briefcase with short, jerky movements. Lizzy watched her for a moment and came to a decision. She didn't want to end the trial on yet another antagonistic note. The solo practitioner did an admirable job on the trial. They didn't have to hug it out and become social media buddies, but she wasn't going to let her go without at least shaking her hand.

Carol at last shouldered her briefcase and headed past her. When Lizzy reached out a hand to stop her, her opposing counsel shot her a bitter glance and nearly snarled at her. "I'll see you at appeals."

"Ms. Monty," Lizzy called after her quickly retreating back, but Carol didn't bother turning around. So much for an amicable end to the trial.

"Don't let her get to you," Katie said, having witnessed the brief exchange. "Hopefully, we'll be seeing a lot less of her for a while."

"I know, but I just don't see the need for all the personal animosity. Being a lawyer is hard enough as it is." Lizzy sighed and gathered up her purse and rolling briefcase.

They walked out of the courthouse together into the warm summer afternoon. With the trial, she hadn't seen much sun in the last couple of weeks. She squinted against the cheery glare, resisting the urge to block the light with her hands like a vampire. She dug in her purse for her sunglasses and her cell phone.

"I'll call the client, and you call Peter," she said as they headed toward the parking structure. They had driven in together for the verdict. "They must be dying to hear from us."

"On it," Katie said.

When her associate was gesturing exuberantly with her free hand as she spoke into the phone, Lizzy snuck a moment to text Jack.

Lizzy: We won.

Jack: What? Where are the exclamation marks?

Jack: Congratulations!!!

Jack: I knew you'd win after that opening statement. Better than Law & Order.

Jack's texts arrived in quick succession, making her smile.

Lizzy: Thanks, Jack. I just wanted to let you know. Now I have to go and do lawyerly stuff.

Jack: Ok. I'm proud of you, Lizzy.

Her cheeks flushed with pleasure, and her heart pumped warmth through her. Sharing the news with her best friend made her happier than the actual win. Still smiling, she dialed the number for Jubilee Toy Company. Their HR director, Gloria, was supposed to be in court for the verdict, but she'd canceled at the last minute, saying the suspense would be too much for her. When Lizzy delivered the good news, Gloria was thrilled about the win, but she was more relieved than anything that the case was finally over. Lizzy couldn't agree more with the sentiment.

Even though they'd won, it still would've been better to settle the case months earlier. It didn't help that they had an unreasonable Plaintiff—who was fueled by an unreasonable Plaintiff's counsel—but her firm could've pushed a little harder for settlement. Alas, trials were what brought in the big bucks. The powers that be at her law firm didn't have the incentive to do more than what they'd already done.

Lizzy shook her head to disperse her bitter thoughts. The trial was over, and they'd won the damn thing. If anything, she should be ecstatic that she could finally get some sleep without jolting awake at three in the morning, thinking she forgot to file a crucial exhibit. Fun times.

"Peter wants to celebrate," Katie squealed. "He said to meet him at Skyline for drinks right now."

"It's barely two in the afternoon," Lizzy said, already thinking about all the work she had to catch up on. But she sighed when she saw her associate's wide, pleading eyes. *Way to be a wet blanket, Lizzy.* When had she become this boring workaholic? "No, scratch that. It's never too early for free alcohol. Let's go."

They crossed the street, dodging an SUV making an

aggressive right turn as soon as the WALK signal started blinking, and headed to the parking structure. She and Katie both forgot where they'd parked that morning, but they were in agreement that it was somewhere on the third level. Lizzy had to do that thing where she kept pushing the lock button on her key to find her car by sound. She liked her BMW, but playing Marco Polo was much more fun in a pool full of people.

Their drive back to the office took less time than locating her misplaced car. She pushed her sunglasses to the top of her head as she drove down to the underground parking. After handing her keys to the valet, she and Katie made their way to Skyline, a trendy bar and restaurant on the seventy-fourth floor of their office building.

A wistful smile lit Lizzy's face as they walked into the restaurant. The sharp, modern lines of the black-and-gray interior and the floor-to-ceiling windows with the panoramic view of Los Angeles made Skyline feel like a special destination even though it was only a few floors above her law firm. If she didn't have to eat lunch at her desk most days to meet her billable-hour requirement, she would probably come here more often.

Lizzy took a quick glance around as they stepped up to the hostess stand. It looked like they'd beat Peter to the restaurant.

"Hello, ladies," the hostess greeted them warmly. "Here for a late lunch?"

"That and for celebratory drinks," Katie said, bouncing on her heels.

"Wonderful. What's the occasion?" she asked, leading them to their table.

"We just won a trial." Her associate's excitement bubbled over, and she squeed a little.

"Shut the front door." The hostess's polish gave way to real surprise. "That is so exciting. Congratulations."

"Thank you," Katie gushed.

Lizzy smiled politely, feeling disquieted by her own lack of excitement. She was certainly glad they'd won the trial, but she should be bursting with pride. Well, she'd always been shy about tooting her own horn. "Peter from our office will be joining us."

"Of course. He's the tall gentleman with salt-and-pepper hair and horn-rimmed glasses, right?" When Lizzy nodded, the hostess said, "I'll show him to your table when he arrives."

They were seated at one of the coveted tables by the floor-to-ceiling windows. The air quality was actually decent today, so they were able to see all the way to the Hollywood sign. The expansive view was a welcome change after spending days in a windowless courtroom. Lizzy felt some of the tension from the trial draining out of her.

"Lizzy." Peter walked up to their table with his arms opened wide. She stood to receive his hug. "Fantastic job on the trial. Congratulations."

"Thank you," she said with a wide smile.

"And great job to you, too, Katie." He folded her into a quick hug as well.

Once all the hugs were meted out, he took a seat and signaled for a server. "Let's get the champagne flowing."

Other than the milk she'd added to her tea, Lizzy hadn't consumed anything with calories all day. So when the toasts were made and the champagne imbibed, the alcohol shot straight to her head. Before she could get tipsy, she put down her glass and bit into a bruschetta. The bright flavors of the fresh tomatoes and ribbons of basil burst in her mouth, making her realize how hungry she was. She reached eagerly for some fried calamari next. The salty, savory goodness drew a sigh out of her.

"Is it me, or does champagne make everything taste better?" she asked, piling her plate with more food.

"I think that's sweet victory you're tasting," Peter teased. "Are you ready for your walk of glory?"

News of their win had probably reached the entire law firm by now, so she and Katie would be showered with congratulations and praise when they returned to the office. Some of it might even be genuine. Lizzy intended to be gracious and appreciative, but she mostly wanted to get it out of the way. Other than the moment she'd had with Jack over text messages, an odd heaviness had hung over her since the verdict.

"I can follow you from behind, throwing confetti in the air," Katie chimed in, her cheeks rosy from the champagne.

"Not a chance," Lizzy scoffed, bringing her thoughts back to the celebration at hand. "You're walking right next to me. You deserve as much *glory* as I do."

The younger attorney's eyes widened when she saw that Lizzy was dead serious. Not many attorneys went out of their way to share the credit for a job well done. That wasn't how they made partner. The all-consuming climb toward partnership wasn't something Lizzy took lightly, but she also refused to be a glory hog. She wanted to retain at least a part of her soul in her quest for success.

Peter graciously paid the check, congratulating them once more, and told them to take their time going back to the office. Lizzy refrained from rolling her eyes. Just barely. When an equity partner hurried back to work, lowly associates didn't linger over finger foods. As they left the restaurant together, he placed a hand on her arm and let Katie walk a little ahead of them.

"This win certainly is a step in the right direction, but you need to be a rainmaker to be seriously considered for a partnership," he said in a low voice. "I want you to convince Jubilee Toy Company to sign a retainer with us. Since they are no doubt happy with the results of the case, you should be able to seal the deal with some savvy persuasion."

"Of course." Rainmakers brought in the clients—and the clients brought in the money. The muscles that had finally started relaxing on her shoulders bunched right back up. "Thank you so much for the advice."

"You know I'm on your side. I'm rooting for you to make partner. I just need you to go the extra mile to stack up the odds in your favor."

"I understand." Peter was a good mentor. She should take his advice to heart. But the past five years had been all about going the extra mile for her. What if she was like a car that puttered out when the mileage got too high?

The three of them rode the elevator down together, but Peter didn't get off at the main floor with her and Katie. "I'm going straight to my office. This is your moment."

"Thank you for celebrating with us," Lizzy said as the elevator doors closed.

"Congratulations," her assistant shouted from across the hallway. Maria wasn't purely motivated by excitement. She was announcing to everyone on the floor that the victors have returned.

"Woo-hoo!" Their receptionist shook her fists high above her head.

Attorneys and staff soon crowded the reception area to congratulate them on their win. Lizzy was already a bit light-headed from the champagne, and thanking and hugging all the well-wishers left her head swimming. Despite the overwhelming fanfare, she couldn't help noticing Ashley's conspicuous absence, and the sense of wrongness shadowing her grew darker.

When the crowd finally dispersed, she headed to her office, looking forward to some quiet after a whirlwind of a day. She was tempted to close her office door, but she didn't want to seem antisocial or snooty on the day of their win. Sinking into her chair, Lizzy leaned her head back and swiveled to face the window. She would eventually have to go through the hundreds of unread emails and play catch-up on all the other cases she'd had to neglect—just thinking about it made breathing a touch more difficult—but not yet. She'd earned a brief reprieve.

"Lizzy."

She spun her chair around at the sound of Ashley's voice coming from the doorway. Her heart fell seeing that the bright smile on her friend's face didn't quite reach her eyes.

"Congratulations. Not only did you try your first case but you won. What an accomplishment. The partners are sure to take notice."

"Thank you, Ashley," she said warily. She hated that they had to be this way. "It's only a matter of time before I'm congratulating you on the same."

She huffed a laugh that was jagged with bitterness. "Only if I'm as lucky as you are."

The not-so-subtle belittling of her hard work as *luck* stiffened Lizzy's spine. She hadn't realized Ashley had a mean streak in her. "What are you talking about?"

"This case would've been mine if I hadn't gone on leave for appendicitis." Ashley took a few more steps into her office and lowered her voice to a bristling whisper. "I would've gotten to work with Peter, who actually wants to support your career. Tracy is so preoccupied with her divorce that she couldn't care less about whether I made partner or not."

"I didn't *take* this case from you. It came in hot, and some-one had to jump in right away. That's why it was reassigned to me." Ashley's animosity bewildered Lizzy. Yes, they had been awkward and distant toward each other, but things had never gotten nasty. "I thought I was helping you out by taking the case off your plate while you were recovering."

"You could've given the case back to me when I returned," she accused.

"That wasn't my decision to make. And how could I have known you wanted this case back? You never asked." Lizzy spread out her hands, imploring her to be reasonable.

Ashley paused as though she was searching for a response. In the end, she scoffed, giving Lizzy a hostile glare. "Never mind. I knew you wouldn't understand."

Before Lizzy could respond to that last bit of unfair accusation, Ashley spun on her heels and stormed out of the office. Lizzy stared at her retreating back, trying to come to terms with the revelation. She had naively thought the mad dash to make partner had put a temporary strain on their friendship and that they could close the rift between them someday. She didn't know Ashley was filled with pent-up animosity and resentment toward her over a case she thought should've been hers. It hurt to think that their friendship was something that could be callously cast aside over a jealous grudge.

Carol Monty's angry snarl, Peter's well-meaning advice to go the extra mile, Ashley's hateful accusations . . . The events of the day crashed into Lizzy and sent her mind reeling. The familiar sensation of blood draining from her fingertips washed over her, and her heart rate kicked up several notches. She had to get out of there. Grabbing her cell phone and purse with shaky hands, she nearly stumbled out of her office.

"Heading home early?" the receptionist called out. "I don't blame you one bit."

Lizzy managed a small smile and waved weakly as she

passed the reception desk. Although it wouldn't make the elevator come any faster, she pressed the down button several times in quick succession. She didn't think she could manage a normal conversation if anyone were to catch her. Her breathing was uneven, and she was trembling from head to toe. Luckily, the doors opened to an empty elevator, and she stepped inside.

Once she made it to her car, she unlocked the door and slid into the driver's seat. She pressed her forehead against the steering wheel and breathed, letting her thoughts come and go like boxes chugging down a conveyor belt. Her thoughts couldn't hurt her if she didn't allow them to. She intentionally acknowledged them, accepted the accompanying emotions, and let them go.

She didn't know how long she sat in her car like that, but when her breathing evened out and her limbs felt solid, she started her car and maneuvered it onto the road. On a day like this, there was only one place she wanted to be.

～～

Accounting Fun Day meant Jack got to spend his entire morning holed up in his bedroom, which doubled as his office, and play with numbers. He typed the last amount into the accounting software and hit Enter. A satisfied smile stretched across his face, and he leaned back from the monitor with his fingers threaded behind his head. Weldon Brewery's accounting was done for the month, and the numbers looked good.

He sat back up and generated the pertinent financial reports, which confirmed that the brewery was indeed performing well. Numbers were his friends. They were infallible and infinite. Working with them made him feel warm and fuzzy, especially when they shared good news.

Too soon, his math-induced euphoria burst like a soap bubble. While numbers were infinite, his prospects were dismally finite . . . at least while he remained in Weldon. It was a lovely, small town in California, nestled in the outer edges of the Sierra Nevada. Their downtown thrived with eclectic independent stores, but none were in need of a business analyst with a math degree.

It wasn't that he disliked working at the brewery. Joining the family business had been exciting at first. His family had desperately needed his affinity for numbers and technology to wrangle in the financial aspect of the brewery. But Weldon Brewery was a well-oiled machine now, and he had to wear many hats—none that fit right—just to stay useful.

The walls of his bedroom seemed to close in on him. He hadn't heard anything back on his interview, but he wasn't ready to give up hope yet. He couldn't. The hope of getting that job was the only thing anchoring him these days. McBain did say it might be a while before they got back to him. He was one of the first people they interviewed, and they had a long list of candidates to interview after him. *Yeah, hope lives on.*

The job in Los Angeles was an entry-level position, but there was ample room for growth. He wanted to tap into his potential and see how high he could fly. The challenge called to him, and something heady buzzed through his veins. Excitement. He wondered how it would feel to wake up every morning, excited to work toward a goal all his own. Damn, he wanted that job.

And Lizzy was there. What would it be like to live close to her? So close they could bump into each other unexpectedly and one thing could lead to another. . . . When his pulse picked up pace, he corrected the course of his thoughts.

Jack knew she'd win the trial. Her opening statement had blown him away. She was articulate without being stuffy, intelligent without sounding arrogant, and wickedly funny at just the right moment. If he'd been on the jury, he would've believed everything she said. He was 98 percent sure that it wasn't his decades-long crush on her that colored his opinion.

Suddenly restless, he pushed away from his desk and got to his feet. Crush or no crush, Lizzy wasn't the reason he wanted to move to Los Angeles. He needed to do it for himself. Besides, she was too busy with her work and doing whatever else overachievers like her did—which probably included dating fellow overachievers—to spend much time with him.

He might as well go into the brewery early. Hopefully, there was something for him to fix or tinker with. He put on his handyman hat and grabbed his car keys. He was halfway to the brewery when his phone rang.

The screen read *MOM*. In all caps. Because his mom was the boss and deserved to be thought of in all caps.

He thumbed the answer button on his steering wheel. "Yes, Mother?"

"Where are you?" she asked without preamble.

"In my car. On my way to the brewery."

"Oh, good. Then you can go to market for me."

"Sure. What did you need?" He'd just passed the turn that would take him to the market, so he made a U-turn at the next street. He switched his handyman hat for the errand-boy hat. It was disquieting how relieved he was to have work to do.

"Your dad"—her words held a world of frustration—"got red onions instead of yellow onions."

"The yellow onions weren't fresh," his dad interjected from the background, loudly enough to be heard over the phone. "We can't serve the customers something that isn't fresh."

"I thought Dad was retired. What's he doing back in the kitchen?" Jack pulled into Nature Mart's parking lot.

"Driving me crazy," his mom muttered. "Can you imagine serving onion stacks made with red onions?"

"Don't worry, Mom," he said, holding back his laugh. "I'll pick up the yellow onions. How much do you need?"

"Just a box to hold us over," she said with a sigh, her ire sputtering out.

"Okay. I'll see you soon." He stepped out of his car and hurried inside the market. The sooner he delivered the onions, the sooner his parents would stop bickering.

He scanned the small market and found the person he was looking for. "Betty, please tell me you have an extra box of yellow onions in the back. I would hate to clean out your perfect display."

"An entire box?" The proud owner of Nature Mart hurried to the back of the store. "I'm sure we have one. Let me check to make sure."

"I appreciate it."

A minute later, she came out carrying a box of yellow onions.

"Whoa. Let me take that off your hands." Jack supported the bottom of the box to bear the brunt of the weight.

"You're so gallant." Betty chuckled, relinquishing her hold on the box of onions. "But I could carry three of these at once if I had to."

"I believe you. You're the fittest thirty-year-old I know." Jack grinned, putting down the onions at the register.

"Bite your tongue, boy." Betty, who wasn't a day under sixty, smiled coyly at him. "Or I might not charge you for the onions."

He left the store—after paying for the onions—and made his way to the brewery. The back door to the kitchen was propped open with a box of red onions, so he walked in without having to juggle the yellow onions in his arms.

"You got them?" His mom rushed toward him and expertly inspected the onions while he still held the box. "These look good. Thank you, Jack."

"You're welcome." He put the box down by the sink and glanced around the spotless kitchen. "Where's Dad?"

"Your dad needs a hobby," she said, not answering his question. She must have kicked him out for getting in her way. His parents loved each other, but they also loved to bicker.

"Do you need help with anything?" With the onion crisis averted, he needed something else to keep him busy.

"Not right now." She gave him a warm smile and a pat on the cheek. "Go and do what you came in to do."

And he was deftly dismissed from her domain. Jack at one point had tried to learn his way around the kitchen, wondering if he could someday inherit it from his mom. But the brief experiment was disastrous, and he was forever banned from using the fryer. He was lucky his mom didn't forbid him from entering the kitchen altogether.

There was a light at the corner of the dining hall that flickered. He should take a look at that. He grabbed his toolbox from the broom closet and headed to inspect the problem. The wiring for the light was connected with eight other lights in that area, so if it was an electrical issue, he was going to have to study a lot of YouTube videos to learn how to fix it. The prospect lifted his spirits as he tinkered with the light. But his hopes were soon dashed when it turned out to be a faulty light bulb.

He glumly returned his toolbox to its dark corner and trudged back into the hall. His shift didn't begin for another couple of hours, and his afternoon seemed to stretch out endlessly in front of him. He dragged his fingers through his hair and pondered which hat to put on next.

"You're in early," Alex said, coming out of the brewing area.

"Brother o' mine," Jack bellowed with relief, earning him a mildly alarmed look from his twin.

"Jack . . ." His brother finished approaching him with careful, measured steps. "How are you doing?"

"How am I doing?" He scoffed to cover up his embarrassment for his over-the-top greeting. "Dude, we live in the same house and work at the same place. You're acting as though we haven't seen each other for days."

"Riiight," Alex said, scrutinizing Jack like he was a peculiar insect. "Did you have a nice day hanging out with your beloved numbers?"

"Of course." Jack still enjoyed accounting days even though they weren't as exciting or rewarding as they'd been. But Alex hated math with a passion, and Jack's love of numbers bewildered him. "How about you? Did the brewing go well?"

"Yeah. Everything went smoothly." Enthusiasm lit up his brother's eyes. "But with a new recipe, you just don't know how it'll all come together until the tasting. I guess that's part of what makes brewing exciting."

Alex was born to be a brewer. Just like their younger sister, Tara. They were talented and passionate about what they did. Jack squelched the burst of envy inside him, but not before it made him feel small and bitter. How could he feel envious of his brother and sister? He wasn't in a healthy place. He needed to pour his pent-up drive and ambition into a goal of his own, and the job in Los Angeles would provide him with that goal.

"Is Tara still in the back?" he asked, glancing past his brother's shoulder. This batch was Alex's recipe, but they usually lent a hand to whoever was at the helm for the particular brew.

"She's out with Seth." Alex went behind the bar and poured himself a glass of water. "Something about a wedding venue they've been dying to see."

Jack smiled. He'd never seen his sister happier. Her fiancé, Seth Kim, was a good man, and he was head over heels for Tara. What more could he ask for in a brother-in-law?

"Let me know if you need an extra pair of hands for the brew," he offered casually. He didn't want to let on that he was desperate for some work.

"If you're free, I wouldn't mind having some help and company." Alex chugged down his water.

"Were you getting lonely all by yourself back there?" Jack said as he poured himself some water, too. Watching his brother drink made him thirsty. Alex had this strange talent for making everything he drank or ate look so good. Someday, when Weldon Brewery made it to the big leagues, they should use him for their beer commercials.

"You know I'm a social creature. Why do it alone when you can do it with someone?" Alex grinned and headed for the back door. "I'm going to take a walk to prevent vitamin D deficiency. I'll meet you back there in about half an hour."

"Go for it. I'll see you soon."

Some of the tension eased from Jack's shoulders. Having secured a task to keep himself busy for the remainder of the afternoon, killing thirty minutes wasn't so daunting. He could do that just checking the tables and chairs for wobbles.

He only got through a few sets of tables and chairs when he heard a *ding*. He pulled his cell phone out from his back pocket and glanced at the screen. His heart fluttered in a familiar dance, and the corners of his lips kicked up.

Lizzy: Guess where I am?

Jack: Somewhere hip and happening to celebrate your big win?

Lizzy: And I thought you knew me so well.

He prided himself in knowing her better than anyone else. *So think.* It was a bit early for a night of debauchery. And if she was indeed out partying somewhere, she wouldn't be texting him. His eyebrows drew together. He certainly hoped she wasn't holed up in the office. This was a special day for her. She should treat herself.

Of course. He chuckled, shaking his head. It was so obvious.

Jack: Not only can I guess where you are, but I can tell you which book you're skimming through.

Lizzy: No way.

Jack: You're at Hideaway Bookstore, reading through your favorite passages in Pride and Prejudice.

Lizzy: How did you know?

Jack: Because I know you, Elizabeth Chung.

And she was everything he wanted.

His smile turned wistful. He would never tell her that, of course. Not only was she way out of his league, but he didn't want to risk losing his best friend. He'd been content with their friendship for the last twenty years. Well, *content* might be an overstatement. Content, resigned. Po-tay-toes, po-tah-toes. The point was he had no plans to shake things up. He would take their friendship with a side of pining any day if it meant he would always have her in his life.

Besides, a little pining never hurt anyone.

CHAPTER THREE

*L*izzy smiled from her perch on the worn, floral couch nestled among the bookshelves and hugged *Pride and Prejudice* to her chest. Jack had guessed exactly where she was—Hideaway Bookstore. The small, idyllic shop was tucked between a wine bar and a Jamaican restaurant in the quaint, old-town street of Larchmont Village. The charming neighborhood was hidden in plain sight in central Los Angeles, just over five miles from her office. The only indication that she was still in the busy, sprawling city was the scarcity of street parking and the two-hour limit on the parking meters.

If it wasn't for said parking limit, Lizzy might have lived out her weekends at Hideaway. Warm, walnut bookshelves filled every wall space from floor to ceiling. And a mix of standalone bookshelves of every size cleverly lined the store, creating hidden nooks and crannies that were perfect places to hide away with a book. In a way, the bookstore felt more like home than her condo. It welcomed her with a feeling of cozy comfort that told her it was okay to put her hair down. She could count on it to center her.

But Jack's last text had made her heart skip a beat. Wondering why, she reread his message.

Jack: Because I know you, Elizabeth Chung.

She pressed the back of her hand against her warm cheek. She was being silly. Of course he knew her. They'd known each other since they were nine years old. He was her best friend. She shook her head and typed her belated response.

Lizzy: I guess that's why you're my best friend.

Jack didn't respond right away. He probably got pulled away for work. She sighed and dropped her phone back into her purse. It would've been nice to text with him a while longer. She felt . . . adrift and could've used his anchoring presence. She hated to admit it, but Hideaway Bookstore wasn't working its magic today.

"Lizzy," Beverly said with a wide smile, coming to sit beside her. She gathered her long silver hair over one shoulder. "I didn't see you come in."

"I snuck in while you were helping another customer." She grinned at Hideaway Bookstore's esteemed owner, who looked as stylish as ever in a pair of dark-wash jeans and a black flowy tunic. "Was he looking for a particular book?"

The older woman's sigh and the weary droop of her shoulders told Lizzy it was a bit more complicated than that. "More like a bookstore."

"What do you mean, Bev?" Unease prickled at the back of her neck.

"When you're young, your body feels like a natural extension of your mind." She chuckled at Lizzy's perplexed expression. "It's true. You think to yourself, *I should put this book away*, and your body does your bidding effortlessly."

"I never thought of it that way," Lizzy said slowly.

"At my age, you feel every bone, every muscle. You can't *not* be conscious of your every movement. Sometimes I feel like my mind is a puppeteer, trying to steer a clunky, creaky puppet to do the simplest tasks."

"That must be challenging." Lizzy didn't know what else to say without sounding supercilious. She couldn't claim to understand what it felt like to grow old.

"You must think I'm trying to scare you about the perils of old age." Beverly laughed again, waving a hand. "All I'm saying is that I can't do this forever."

"Do what forever?" Of course she knew what her friend meant, but she didn't want to contemplate the possibility. The bookstore wouldn't be the same without Bev. She wanted her favorite place in the world to stay suspended in time and always be there for her. But when the older woman leveled Lizzy with her bullshit-buster stare, she blushed, and her brief impulse to bury her head in the sand passed. "Are you . . . are you planning to sell Hideaway?"

"Eventually." Beverly gently squeezed her hand. "I'm not saying I'm going to retire next month, but I'm floating the idea around to test the waters."

"So that man you were talking to was interested in buying the bookstore?" Lizzy swallowed the lump of apprehension in her throat.

"Yes," she scoffed, clearly affronted, "but I think he was scoping out the space to turn it into yet another café."

Lizzy gasped, a hand fluttering to her mouth. "Hideaway won't be the same without you, Bev, but having it turned into something other than a bookstore is unthinkable."

The thought of losing both Beverly and Hideaway Bookstore devastated her. Without this safe haven, she would feel truly alone in this big city.

"Don't you worry. I'm holding out until I find someone who wants to take over the bookstore."

The cheery bell over the door jingled before Lizzy could ask more questions. After giving her a reassuring smile, Beverly pushed herself off the couch and headed to the front of the store.

Lizzy gathered up her purse and went to tuck *Pride and Prejudice* back in its rightful place. Then she wandered to the romance section to read the back covers of all the new releases. There were at least three that she was dying to read, but she promised herself not to buy any more books until she put a dent in her to-be-read pile. She didn't have much time to read for fun, but when she did, she always turned to her favorite genre—romance. Sure, it was a nice escape, but it was more than that. Those stories healed something inside her and made her feel less alone.

She pulled out her phone to see if Jack had responded to her last text. He had. He sent her a silly GIF of two animated bears holding hands and dancing in circles with the words *Best Friends Forever* blinking on the bottom. She giggled and put her phone away. Beverly was with the customer who'd just come in, so Lizzy caught her eyes and waved before she let herself out of the store.

The sun still hung low in the sky, and she turned up her face toward it. She would normally be in her office at this hour, but today wasn't just any other day. It was the day she'd won her first trial. She waited silently to *feel* something. But her heart beat on at its leisurely pace, and her cheek muscles stayed relaxed instead of pulling into a gigantic grin. The elusive thrill of the win continued to slip through her fingers.

She checked the parking meter before she slid into the driver's seat. Some lucky person was about to get fifteen minutes of free parking. She started her engine and contemplated going back into the office for a split second. Even that split second made her feel like a loser. *I mean, come on.* Did she really have nothing better to do on her big day than to go back into work? There was more to her life—more to *her*—than just her job. There had to be.

Lizzy put her game face on. She may not have been jumping for joy, but goddamn it, she was going to celebrate. She pulled out of the coveted Larchmont parking space with purpose and headed toward Koreatown.

With a tenacity true to her Korean American heritage, Lizzy refused to valet in front of her favorite restaurant and found street parking after twenty minutes. After she ordered bosam—braised pork belly with all the fixings for veggie-wrapped goodness—she walked down the block to a boba café and got herself a large milk tea with golden boba.

The awesome thing about Koreatown was that once you scored some street parking, you could find everything you needed within walking distance. So she headed next to a Korean-French bakery and bought herself an eight-inch strawberry cream cake. By the time she loaded her boba tea and cake in her car and walked back to the restaurant, her bosam platter was ready.

Her one-bedroom condo in downtown LA was only a couple of miles from the edge of Koreatown, so her dinner was still warm and her tea and cake were still cold when she let herself inside. She trudged straight for the kitchen to unload her bounty before she slipped off her court-day high heels.

After changing into her favorite retro Wonder Woman T-shirt and stretchy pants, she sat down at the dining table. Her face split into a gluttonous grin, and she dug into her bosam. She gently laid a piece of salted napa cabbage on her palm and lovingly put a slice of pork belly on top. Next came the shredded radish kimchi, salted shrimp sauce, and a piece of pickled jalapeño. After carefully folding in the front and end of the napa cabbage to make a pork belly bundle, she popped the whole thing into her mouth with gusto.

There was so much food in her mouth that she could hardly chew, but it was worth the effort. The harmony of the crunchy and chewy textures, the salty, savory flavor of the pork and shrimp sauce, and the kick of heat from the radish kimchi and jalapeño were a symphony in her mouth. It was perfection. No. Not yet. Still chewing, she ran to her fridge and grabbed a bottle of makgeolli, a fermented, unfiltered rice wine, and ran right back to her seat with a small bowl. She poured herself a generous amount and washed her bosam down with the cold makgeolli. Now it was perfection.

She hummed and danced in her seat as she built bundle after bundle of pork belly bosam until she couldn't eat another bite. She downed the last of the makgeolli and cleared the table. Happily buzzing, she grabbed her cake and boba tea from the fridge and set them down on the coffee table. She couldn't eat another bite of *savory* food, but she had a separate stomach for *sweets*.

And what was a solo celebration without some Netflix? The best movie pairing for dessert was a sweet movie. *To All the Boys I've Loved Before* it was. She'd watched it only six times before. With a contented sigh, she sat down on her cushy sofa and tucked her feet beneath her.

The cake tasted so good with the movie that Lizzy ate a third of it by the time the credits were rolling. Her buzz was wearing off, but it was replaced by a sugar high. This was much needed self-care—something she'd neglected to do in ages. When was the last time she'd left work early? She couldn't remember a single instance in the last year. When was the last time she'd pampered herself? If takeout sushi from Little Tokyo counted, then maybe a month ago. But does the fact that she ate it at her desk while working late nullify the pampering effect?

Refusing to allow these troubling reflections to ruin her self-care bonanza, she trotted to the bathroom and ran herself a mango-coconut bubble bath. She lit her favorite vanilla and jasmine votives and stripped naked. Catching a glimpse of herself in the mirror, she gave her body a quick scan. She shrugged and lowered herself into the slightly hot water. *Not bad for a thirty-year-old with not enough time to exercise.*

Not only did she not have enough time to exercise but her dating life had been nonexistent for the last six months. She could argue that the trial consumed three months of her life down to the last minute, but that wasn't the only reason for the dry spell. Her starry-eyed dream of finding romance and true love had grown jaded in the big-city dating scene. Well, big-city dating scene for a lawyer.

She mostly dated other attorneys since her social life consisted of mixers and networking events related to her work. Her last boyfriend had been a psychiatrist whom she'd met through a case. He was an expert witness for a co-counsel's firm. He was intelligent, successful, and handsome in a scholarly way. They lasted a year before they simply drifted apart. Honestly, they probably only lasted that long because they were too busy to see each other more than once a week, if that. Other than the intersection of their professional lives, they didn't have much in common. That seemed to be the story of her rather dismal love life.

She lifted her feet out of the water and wiggled her bubble-covered toes. In a sense, the only thing going well for her was her career. She certainly hoped it was going well considering the exorbitant time and energy she dedicated to her work. She'd just tried and won her first trial. Of course it was going well. But she felt no joy or excitement over the fact. Did she feel a sense of accomplishment? Maybe a little. That didn't seem enough, though.

Her stomach dipped with unease. If she couldn't find meaning in her career, what were all her sacrifices for? They couldn't have been for nothing. No, she refused to accept that. She was burned out to the core. That was what this was all about. If she just had some time to recharge, she would enjoy her job again. This called for bold, decisive action.

Lizzy quickly scrubbed herself clean and stepped out of the bath. She wrapped her long hair in a towel and cinched her bathrobe tightly around her waist. Snatching her laptop from her desk, she plopped down on her bed and leaned against the headrest. She opened up her work email and typed:

Dear Peter . . .

~~

His feet pounded on the ground as the wind rushed in his ears. This early in the morning, the tree-lined streets of his neighborhood stood empty, so Jack could run as fast as he wanted. He pushed himself until his lungs burned and he tasted iron in the back of his throat. He was fit from jogging every day, so he had to work hard to make his heart feel like it was about to burst. He ran flat out until he reached the edge of town. His muscles screamed from lactic acid–induced pain, and he gasped for air, bent at the waist with his hands on his thighs.

Still, the restlessness inside him refused to be silenced. All that pain and nothing gained. His sweat-soaked sleeveless

T-shirt clung uncomfortably to his back and chest, so he whipped it off in one impatient movement. Tucking his shirt into the back of his shorts, he headed home at a more leisurely pace. There was no need to kill himself when there was no payoff. He was within a block from his house when someone shot around the corner and cut him off.

"Whoa." He instinctively stopped in his tracks so he wouldn't crash into the back of the other runner.

It could've been an accident. It probably was an accident. Why else would she cut him off in the middle of an empty street? He resumed his jog but took it slow to create some space between them. He didn't want her to feel like he was chasing after her for payback or anything. But he couldn't help thinking that the jaunty ponytail swinging on her head was mocking him for being a sucker. Then the strangest thing happened. The woman started running backward. Was she *trying* to run him over?

"Hey, neighbor," she said gleefully, glancing over her shoulder.

"Lizzy?" He blinked several times to make sure he wasn't seeing things. What in the ever-loving hell? Why was she jogging in his neighborhood? And why was she trying to run him over?

They both slowed to a stop, Jack gaping and Lizzy grinning.

"Explain," he said, closing his mouth before a bug flew in.

"I decided to take some time off work." She shrugged as though it wasn't a big deal. He knew for a fact that she hadn't taken time off for at least two years. "I rented a little studio apartment over Sparrow Bookstore near Main Street. I found it on Vrbo. The place is absolutely adorable, by the way. The bookstore and the apartment. I got here yesterday evening, but I wanted to surprise you, so . . . surprise!"

Surprise? Damn right, he was surprised. Why was she taking time off? Was everything all right with her? Why Weldon? And how long did he get to keep her here? Lizzy. His Lizzy. Here. His heart pounded in his chest as though he were still running at breakneck speed.

"How did you manage this"—he pointed back and forth between them—"chance meeting?"

"You're not the only one who knows their best friend well. I know you, too, Jack Park," she said a smidgeon smugly.

Only if that were true. A familiar ache dug into the corner of his heart.

"I know your jogging schedule, and I figured if I hung out close by your house, I'd bump into you eventually."

"Let me get this straight." Joy tentatively bubbled up inside him, unsure if this was real. "You've been circling the block so you could jump out at me like a maniac?"

"Precisely. I only had to jog for about . . ." She checked her watch. "Twenty minutes."

She seemed slightly out of breath and had a sheen of perspiration on her forehead. While her boxy T-shirt hid part of her figure, her yoga pants highlighted her shapely legs. *Damn, she's beautiful.* Pushing away the impractical thought, he headed toward his house in a bit of a daze. Lizzy fell into step beside him.

"Aren't you . . . happy to see me?" She glanced at him a little uncertainly.

He screeched to a halt and stared at her as though she'd sprouted a second head. "Of course I'm happy to see you."

"Well, how am I supposed to know that when you have your Frowny McFrown face on?" She crossed her arms over her chest.

His frown deepened. *Shit.* He didn't mean to make her feel unwelcome. "That's what happens when you jump out at a man on a peaceful morning jog and nearly give him a heart attack."

"I wanted to surprise you." She pouted, and he gulped. It should be illegal for someone to be so adorable.

"I'm happy to see you. Okay? Ecstatic." A cheek-cramping grin overtook his face. There was no holding it back now. He couldn't believe Lizzy was standing in front of him. "I want to give you a hug to show you how happy I am, but I'm too sweaty."

Her eyes flicked to his bare chest and lingered for two seconds before they shot back up to his face. His body instinctively caught on fire. Was she blushing? He fought against his own blush.

"Good. I'm glad." She cleared her throat. "Not that you're sweaty but that you're happy to see me."

He chuckled, shaking his head. She hadn't been checking him out. That was ridiculous. "So how long are you here for?"

"I signed a deal with the devil to get three weeks off from work." She sounded equal parts excited and worried. "I've never taken such a long break before."

Was the heavenly choir singing? Lizzy was here for three weeks. Before he could sprout wings and fly, a thought grabbed him by the ankle and pulled him back to earth.

"Does this vacation have anything to do with your panic attack during your opening statement?" He pulled on his damp shirt with a grimace. This didn't feel like a conversation he should be having shirtless.

"Partly." She started walking down the street, and he joined her at her side. After a pause, she said, "But it mostly has to do with winning the trial."

"Winning the trial?" He stopped again to stare at her. At this rate, he would never make it home.

"It didn't make me happy. Not like it should have." She tugged on his arm to keep walking. "I realized it was because I was completely burned out."

"I get that." He nodded. She put in inhumane hours at that law firm. He was relieved she was taking a break. "Don't take this the wrong way—I'm psyched that you're here—but why did you decide on Weldon?"

"Well, *you're* here," she said sweetly, and his heart lurched with hope in spite of himself. *Stop it.* She didn't mean anything *like that.* "And I remembered how much I used to enjoy coming to Weldon to visit your family during the summer when we were kids. When I found that apartment above the bookstore, it felt like fate was calling."

His lips spread into another grin. It was finally sinking in. Missing Lizzy had become a part of his life, but he wouldn't need to for three whole weeks. "I know I'm sweaty, but I have to hug you."

With a squeal, she threw herself into his arms. He gathered her up, laughing, and swung her around in the air before he set her back down. When he found himself breathing in the scent of her hair, he let his arms fall to his sides and stepped back.

He felt a twinge of apprehension. Hiding his feelings for her when she lived a hundred fifty miles away was easy—they only got together a few times a year, so he managed not to spill his heart out to her. But could he handle having her around for three weeks? He didn't know the answer to that question, but it didn't matter. He wasn't about to let a little trepidation stop him from spending every minute he could with her.

They managed to walk the last few steps to his house without stopping, but he wasn't ready to let her go. "Do you want to come in for some breakfast?"

"I can't come to your house unannounced at eight in the morning." She crinkled her nose, giving him a sideways glance. "Let your parents know I'm here, and I'll visit you guys once they invite me over."

"Our families have been friends for years," he said. "There's no need for formalities."

"I insist. Tell Ajumma and Ajussi I said hello. Okay?"

"I will, but that doesn't solve the issue of breakfast." He wasn't giving up that easily. If he wasn't careful, the three weeks could fly by in a blink.

"I didn't know we had a breakfast issue," she said with a teasing light in her eyes.

"Oh, we most definitely do." He nodded mock solemnly and crossed his arms over his chest—he mostly did that so he wouldn't make a grab for her. When she looked at him like that, it was all he could do not to kiss her. "I'll tell you what. Give me half an hour to wash up and change, then we can meet for breakfast at the Pancake Hut."

"I'm going to need an hour, and where is this Pancake Hut?"

"Main Street. I'll just pick you up from Sparrow Bookstore in an hour."

"Sounds like a plan," she said brightly.

"Great." He gave her a thumbs-up like a huge dork because he was delirious with happiness. He stuffed the offending hand into his pocket and looked up and down the block to stop himself from staring at her. "Did you drive here?"

"Uh-huh. My car's right over there. Okay. I'll see you in an hour." She turned to go, then spun back to face him. "Oh, and please don't feel like you need to babysit me the whole time I'm here. I know you're busy with the brewery. The last thing I want to be is a bother."

He arched an eyebrow. "I'm not going to justify that with a response."

"I'm serious, Jack." She planted her fists on her hips.

"Look, I'm not going to play hooky to hang out with you," he leveled with her, "but you're delusional if you think I'm not going to take advantage of the situation and try to spend as much time with you as I can."

"I'd like that," she said with a soft smile that made him feel warm and toasty inside. "Just promise to tell me if you're getting sick of me."

He nearly laughed in her face. "Not possible."

"I think I made the right decision to come here." She wrapped her arms around his neck for a quick hug, then crossed the street to her car.

He watched her get in and drive away before he let himself into the house. He closed the door behind him and leaned back on it. His heart pounded against his ribs as though it were trying to break free.

The way he saw it, he had three choices here.

One: Maintain the status quo.

He could spend three amazing weeks with his best friend and help her recharge so she could return to her über-successful life . . . and date über-successful men, all the while pretending that he wasn't pining for her.

Two: Get over his crush on Lizzy.

He probably saw her best side, since they only got to spend a few days out of the year together. Maybe he would get to see all her annoying sides if he spent nearly every day with her for three weeks.

Three: Make her fall in love with him.

Which was fine and dandy, except he had no idea how. And there was the very real possibility that he just might end up losing his best friend.

Shit.

CHAPTER FOUR

*L*izzy locked the cheery red door to her apartment and trotted down the outdoor staircase tucked behind the bookstore building. Her three-week vacation was off to a great start. She giggled remembering Jack's expression when she'd ambushed him on his jog. She wished she'd taken a picture.

She was both happy and relieved that Jack wanted to spend as much time with her as she with him. She'd packed up and driven to Weldon with vague plans of sleeping in and catching up on her reading. But maybe what she really wanted was to not feel alone, and Jack was the first person she'd thought of . . . Well, he *was* her best friend.

After a quick glance at her watch, she walked along the narrow brick pathway that led to the front of the store. She had fifteen minutes to spare until Jack picked her up for breakfast, so she wanted to check out Sparrow. She'd arrived past nine o'clock the night before, so she hadn't seen the inside of the store yet. The anticipation of discovering a new bookstore put a spring in her steps.

Sparrow Bookstore stood on the corner of a quiet street about two blocks away from downtown Weldon. The two-story folk Victorian building could easily be mistaken for a residential property if it weren't for the store name written in flowing cursive on the shop window and the hanging store sign. Its modest size and white exterior with black trimmings gave it a homey, welcoming feel.

But the happy smile on her face fell at seeing the CLOSED sign on the door. What was she thinking? It wasn't even nine o'clock yet. Most bookstores didn't open till ten or eleven. As she turned to leave with a disappointed sigh, she saw a small red car parked in front of the store. Maybe Shannon—which was the owner's name, according to her Vrbo profile—came in early to prepare for the day. Lizzy didn't want to intrude, but she should say hello to her landlady, right?

She hesitantly pushed open the door, expecting a little bell to announce her arrival like Hideaway Bookstore, but all she heard was a slight squeaking of the hinges. *Wait.* She backed out and squinted at the storefront before stepping back in. The inside of the store definitely felt smaller than it looked from the outside. It was like the TARDIS, but flipped the other way around.

Tall, gray bookshelves lined the entire store, creating tight corridors between them. It reminded her of the reference section in a library. As much as she loved books, the sheer volume overwhelmed her. And other than a straight-backed wooden chair near the cashier stand, Lizzy didn't see a single cozy nook or corner to sit and read in.

"Hello?" she said as she took a tentative step forward. The store looked empty, but any number of people could be hiding behind the mountainous bookshelves. "Hello?"

"Just a minute," someone called out. It sounded as though the voice was coming from the back of the store.

"Take your time," Lizzy rushed to reassure. She stayed near the front of the store but craned her neck to peek at the rows of books.

A tall, attractive redhead in her late thirties or early forties walked up to her, wearing a friendly smile. "Hello there."

"Hi, I'm Lizzy Chung"—she held out her hand—"your tenant for the next three weeks."

"Sorry. Dusty." The other woman crinkled her nose and wiped her hands on the front of her jeans before shaking Lizzy's. "I was organizing some boxes in the back. I'm Shannon. It's lovely to meet you."

"Likewise." She immediately warmed to Shannon, her unaffected personality putting Lizzy at ease. "I got in late last evening, so I didn't get a chance to say hello. When I saw your car out front—I assumed the red car was yours—I thought I'd pop by and see if you were in."

"I'm glad you did. And yup, the red car is mine." Shannon strolled toward the cash register, where a cup of tea sat on the counter. "I usually come in around eight thirty, after I drop my son off at school."

"Oh, what grade is he in?" Lizzy followed her, her eyes busily taking in more of the store.

"Elliot is in fourth grade." Her features melted into a tender smile. "He's ten going on thirty-eight."

Lizzy laughed. "He sounds like a lot of fun."

"He is," she said with obvious pride and took a sip from her cup. "Do you want to take a look around the store?"

"You don't mind?" The store wasn't technically open, but Lizzy was curious to see what was hidden in its depths. "I don't want to keep you from what you were doing in the back."

"Don't worry about it." Shannon waved away Lizzy's concerns. "I want to finish my tea anyway."

"Thank you so much. I won't be long." She had less than ten minutes until Jack showed up. He was never late.

"Take as long as you need."

The bookshelves were neatly labeled into sections and were tightly packed with books. Nonfiction, literary fiction, fantasy, mystery/suspense . . . romance. Lizzy squealed, bouncing on her heels.

"Find something you like back there?" There was a smile in Shannon's voice.

"You have a romance section," she gushed. "Some bookstores don't carry romance at all."

"I can't imagine not having a romance section in my bookstore." Shannon joined her near the back. "Romance novels mean so much to so many people."

"I couldn't agree more." Lizzy ran her fingertips over the spines of the lovely books. She saw many of her recent favorites as well as some from her wish list. Despite her vow not to buy any more books—she could almost feel the accusing glare of her TBR stack back home—she predicted an overly enthusiastic book haul in her near future. "I think I would've run away from Los Angeles a lot sooner if it hadn't been for these books."

"It sounds like you really needed the escape." The bookstore owner gave her a speculative glance. "Is there something in particular you want to run away from? Or is it the city itself?"

Lizzy sucked in a sharp breath, her hand stilling over the books. *Is it the city itself?* The moment she'd arrived in Weldon, a tight, tangled knot in her chest had loosened and unraveled. She could breathe freely for the first time in what felt like years. The anxiety. The loneliness. Had it been Los Angeles all along?

It had always been her goal to become a partner in a top law firm in a major city. When she was still a child, dancing in circles and naming clouds, her parents had grabbed her firmly by the shoulders and planted her in that direction. The green flowering field of her childhood was replaced by a narrow concrete road. She had walked that road unquestioningly until now.

Her parents. She hadn't told them about her leave from work yet. The familiar weight of anxiety hovered over her, but she pushed it aside before it could take root. She didn't want to worry about disappointing her parents for now.

"I'm sorry if I'm prying—" Shannon began when Lizzy didn't answer right away.

"Oh, no. Not at all," Lizzy interrupted, placing a reassuring hand on her arm. "I never thought of it that way, but it could be Los Angeles itself. It's such a big, sprawling city. When you drive around, you're surrounded by countless cars, but everyone is isolated from one another in their own cocoon. And when you walk down the busy streets, a crowd of people mills around you, but they're just strangers passing by. You never really stop being alone."

"Wow. That's almost poetic," the bookstore owner said appreciatively, then sobered. "But it does sound very lonely."

Lizzy nodded. "It is. I think after a while, it sort of drains you."

"And I guess that's when romance novels came to the rescue."

"Definitely. They *saved* me." Her mind flitted back to the bookshelves in her condo, overflowing with romance novels. It all made so much sense. The deep human connection inherent in all romance novels was the antithesis to the life she was living. How was this the first time she'd made this connection? "And who doesn't love happily ever afters?"

"The cold, bitter people with shriveled raisins for hearts who disparage romance for being *formulaic*. That's who."

"Yeah. They suck." Lizzy's response was immediate and heartfelt.

Shannon burst out laughing. "There's no bond stronger than the one forged over bashing romance haters."

"That's very true. I hope we can be friends," Lizzy said earnestly, before she caught herself.

Was she coming on too strong, too fast? Lawyers were notorious for being socially awkward. Other than recharging and spending time with Jack, she hadn't thought much about what she wanted out of her three-week vacation. Making new friends certainly hadn't been a part of her plan, but she really liked Shannon and hoped she didn't mess it up.

"Aww, that's so sweet. Are you a hugger? Because I'm a huge hugger," Shannon said, opening her arms wide. "And I'm coming in for one right now."

"I love hugs." Lizzy squeezed her new friend tightly, relieved she didn't scare her off. And she did love hugs, but she didn't seem to get enough of them.

"I should get back to work, but please stay and browse all you want."

"Actually . . ." Her cell phone chimed in her purse at that exact moment. "My friend is here to pick me up for breakfast. Will it be all right if I come to visit again?"

"I'd be hurt if you didn't." Shannon walked her to the door. "The store isn't nearly as busy as I'd like, so I could use the company."

Lizzy's brows drew together in a frown. "Do you have a competitor in town?"

"Nope." Shannon breathed the sigh of the downtrodden. "But this is a conversation for another time. You'd better not keep your friend waiting."

"Okay. But I definitely want to hear more about it when I come back."

Lizzy loved independent bookstores. Each one had a distinct personality, showcasing the hopes and dreams of their owners. A bookstore was never just a business. They had souls filled with love, passion, and vulnerability. It broke her heart to hear that Sparrow wasn't thriving.

When she stepped out of the store, she spotted Jack leaning against the passenger door of his hybrid semi-compact. His eyes crinkled at the corners as his lips spread into a crooked grin, and an answering smile blossomed in her heart and spread across her face. His hair was still damp from his shower and a strand fell across his forehead, and her fingers twitched at her side with a sudden urge to brush it back. As her gaze dipped lower, she couldn't help noticing that his gray T-shirt did ridiculous things to his chest and arms. Maybe it was because she knew exactly what he looked like underneath. The image of his glistening, naked torso swept across her mind.

What in the literal hell? Was she undressing her best friend in her head? No, no, no. It was merely a passing thought. An objective observation. She was just a woman who *objectively* noticed *in passing* that Jack, a man, had an impressive physique. It was not a big deal.

"Hungry?" he asked, opening the passenger door for her.

"What?" *Oh, my God.* Had she been devouring him with her eyes? She looked everywhere but at him as she slid past him and into the car.

He closed her door and came around to get into the driver's seat. "I figured you must be hungry after the morning jog."

"Why, yes." She coughed into her fist, then loudly cleared her throat. "Yes, I am positively starving. For food."

For some good old-fashioned breakfast food. That was what she was hungry for. Nothing else. *Good Lord.* Why was it so hot in the car? She rolled down her window.

"Are you still warm from the run?" Jack glanced at her and lowered the AC by a couple of degrees.

"Maybe. I'm so out of shape. It's been hard to make time to

exercise. Busy, busy, busy." She snapped her mouth shut. She needed to chill.

"Well, we should make it a regular thing." He turned the corner and drove down Main Street.

"Make what a regular thing?" she asked absently, taking in Weldon's lovely downtown. The mom-and-pop stores spilled onto the tidy street with their cheery handwritten signs and carts filled with goodies. Brightly colored awnings dotted the storefronts of cafés and restaurants with inviting outdoor seating. She really liked it here.

"The morning run. You should join me every day while you're here." He pulled into a small parking lot and took one of the many spots.

Ooh . . . ample parking. It was so luxurious. But what was he saying about morning runs? The image of him shirtless flashed through her mind again. "Run? Every day?"

"Yeah. It'll help you recharge." He turned off the ignition and got out of the car.

"Maybe," she murmured, joining him outside. She wasn't at all sure if she could handle a shirtless Jack every day even if her observations were purely objective. "I'll think about it."

"You do that." He shot her a playful grin. "Just don't think I'll let you off the hook easily."

A sudden premonition told Lizzy that her stay in Weldon was going to be more eventful than she'd anticipated.

～

Jack fell into an easy pace so Lizzy could keep up with him. It took some convincing to get her out to jog this morning. She complained that she had five years of sleep to catch up on, but she capitulated when Jack reminded her that she could take naps. Her eyes had gone dreamy at the prospect of sleeping in the middle of the day. She called it the ultimate indulgence. She should take every opportunity to indulge in whatever her heart desired while she was in Weldon. She deserved it. Before he could fantasize about what other indulgences she desired, he focused on breathing in the fresh morning air and doing the opposite of mooning over her.

For the sake of his sanity, Jack decided on Option Two: Get over his crush on Lizzy. It was the safest, most logical choice—he could protect their friendship and stop the needless heartache of a one-sided crush. Over the many years they'd been friends— while only seeing each other a few times a year—he'd probably built her up as this impossibly perfect person in his head. But spending every free moment of the next three weeks with her was sure to shatter his fantasy. Then he would be able to see her as she saw him—just as an old and trusted friend.

"My mom wants you to come over for lunch today," he said, glancing to his right. Lizzy, who had been jogging beside him, wasn't there. He looked over his shoulder to find her lagging a few paces behind. He ran in place until she caught up with him and resumed jogging by her side. "Did you hear me?"

"Your legs . . . are . . . freakishly . . . long," she accused.

"What has that got to do with lunch with my family?" he asked, confused by her sudden animosity. He thought they were having a nice run. More than nice for him. Seeing Lizzy first thing in the morning felt amazing. Shit. He was mooning over her again. But there was no need to worry. It was bound to get old after a few days. This was all a part of his plan for carrying out Option Two.

"I have to . . . work . . . twice . . . as hard . . . to keep up." She glared menacingly at him as she wheezed for air.

"Sorry." He made a valiant effort to keep his face straight as he shortened his stride. "Is this better?"

She stared straight ahead and pressed her lips into a mutinous line as she kept pace with him. Her face was bright pink with blotches of red on her cheeks, and she huffed and puffed like an angry bull. She was too stubborn to admit that she needed a break. He bit the inside of his cheek to hold back his grin. She was too cute. No, wait. Being a blotchy, stubborn bull was *not* cute. It was very unattractive. Damn it, he wasn't buying his own lies. *Patience, Jack.*

He was tempted to see how long she would keep pushing herself, but he caved and slowed down so they were basically taking a brisk walk. Like a couple of spry senior citizens.

"That was quick." She was still out of breath, but her words held more sound than air this time.

"What was? Your near collapse after ten minutes of jogging?" he deadpanned.

"Har har." She stuck out her tongue at him. It wasn't cute at all. "The lunch invitation from your mom, dingus."

"When I told her you were here yesterday, she wanted to have you over right away." He smiled wryly. "If she wasn't in total denial about her daughter moving in with her fiancé, she probably would've asked you to come stay in Tara's room."

"Tara moved in with her fiancé?" Lizzy casually eased their brisk walk into a leisurely stroll.

He arched an eyebrow at her so she knew he was onto her. "Technically, no. She didn't have the heart to tell our parents that she was moving out before the wedding, so she comes home a couple of times a week to putter around and eat my mom's cooking. But every time she leaves, she takes more and more of her stuff to Seth's place."

"I can't believe Tara's getting married. She always seemed so much younger than us when we were growing up. What was she? Three grades behind us?"

"Yeah. She's only two years younger than us, but she has a late birthday."

"Two years is nothing now, but back then, she seemed like a baby."

"She'll always be my baby sister." He might have sniffed.

"Are you a little sad about her getting married?" Lizzy asked quietly.

"Not exactly sad. Just . . . wistful, I guess. She'll have a family of her own now." He cleared his throat. "I'm going to miss teasing her."

"You mean you'll miss *her* teasing *you*." Her eyes twinkled knowingly.

Jack grinned at her. She was right, of course. He was a sucker for his little sister. He didn't have the heart to mess around with her, but Tara had no problem teasing him mercilessly. Even so, he was going to miss that.

"Well, when you put it that way, I wouldn't mind getting the brat out of my hair," he said.

Lizzy laughed. "Yeah, right, you softy."

Did she see him as a soft, sentimental chump? Was that why she never saw him as anything more than a friend? Even if that were the case, it couldn't be helped. She had a way of chopping down his defenses and making him reveal his innermost thoughts and vulnerabilities. In some ways, he showed her more of himself than he did with anyone else—except his true feelings for her. He kept that buried deep inside him where even she couldn't unearth it.

But in three weeks, he wouldn't have anything to hide from her. He wouldn't have this dull ache in his heart anymore. Their friendship would become simple and uncomplicated. He swallowed. That was what he wanted.

"I'm the softy, eh?" He grabbed her hand and picked up

his pace. "Let's get this run back on track. We'll see who's soft then."

Lizzy groaned and dragged her feet for a moment or two before allowing him to tug her into a nice jog. She kept up with him admirably for a good ten minutes.

"I . . . I'm . . . soft. Okay? You . . . win. Go on . . . without . . . me." She stopped with her hands on her knees, her ponytail drooping toward the ground.

"Come on. You can do it. Just hang on for one more block, then I'll *walk* you back to your car." He planted his hands on her back and gently propelled her forward, ignoring the heat of her skin seeping through her T-shirt.

"Oh, my God. You're worse . . . than that spin . . . instructor I . . . had once," she panted as she shuffled forward. Apparently, she decided it was easier to keep moving than to stand her ground. Most likely because he was still pushing her from behind.

When she'd gathered enough momentum, he came to jog alongside her. "You never told me you took spin classes."

"I took *one* . . . class. Well, maybe . . . half a class . . . is more . . . accurate." She tripped over her own foot but recovered her balance before he needed to catch her. "Fine . . . A quarter."

He chuckled. She was being a trooper and kept jogging even though her legs had obviously turned into gelatin. She was adorable. He'd be happier if she took better care of herself and made time to exercise, but she was still cute as hell. Yes, he was mooning over her again. *What of it?* he thought petulantly. He couldn't expect his feelings for her to disappear on command. If it were that easy, he would've done it years ago.

They slowed to a stop at the end of the block, and he waited for her to catch her breath. She was pink all over and panting, her chest rising and falling rapidly under her T-shirt. And he imagined her like that, lying naked in bed after they'd made love. He blinked rapidly. He had a strict rule about imagining his best friend naked. *Don't.* He wasn't a glutton for punishment. It was bad enough he couldn't have her without torturing himself even more.

He coughed and used the hem of his shirt to wipe the sweat off his brows. But an odd, strangled sound came from Lizzy's direction, and he looked up in time to see her gaze flit away from his exposed stomach. He let his shirt drop back into place, heat building low in his gut. Having her eyes on him like that made his skin catch fire.

"Let's walk back," she said with an easy smile and headed down the quiet residential street toward his house.

Had he imagined that look? He caught up with her in two long strides. He did imagine it. That was the only logical explanation. But if she *had* looked at him with . . . awareness, would he dare switch to Option Three: Make her fall in love with him? Would he dare risk losing Lizzy? He didn't realize he hadn't said a single word on their way back until they reached her car. And neither had she.

"I'll see you at lunch, then." She put her hand on the door handle. "What time?"

"Noon should be fine." His voice sounded oddly husky to him.

He watched her car disappear from view, then sprinted off into a run. He'd hardly broken a sweat while jogging/strolling with Lizzy, and he needed to get in a workout to burn off some of his restless energy. If he didn't want to act weird around her, he had to forget the look in her eyes as they rested on his bare abs. Hadn't he decided he'd imagined it all? The goal was to get over her, not dream up heated, lingering looks from her.

He was soaked through with sweat when he let himself inside the house. Grabbing some clean clothes from his room, he headed to the bathroom for a shower. Not a cold shower. Because he didn't need one. Just a regular-temperature shower to clean himself off like a civilized human being.

Washed up and determinedly normal, Jack walked into the kitchen to see his mom chopping vegetables with fierce efficiency.

"You're already cooking lunch?" He reached from behind her and snagged a chunk of carrot off the cutting board. "It's not even nine."

"Galbi jjim takes a long time to make properly." She walked over to the sink to check on the beef short ribs soaking in cold water. "But it's Lizzy's favorite, so I got an early start."

"Ooh, galbi jjim. We should have her over more often. You haven't made that for us since New Year's Day."

"Like I said, it's a lot of work, so I only make it for special occasions." When he reached for one of the peeled raw chestnuts, his mom slapped his hand away. "That took your dad forever to peel, and we barely have enough for the galbi jjim."

"Can I help with anything?" He knew what her answer was going to be, but he still had to ask. He couldn't leave his mom to cook all by herself. She already worked too hard in the kitchen at the brewery.

"Just stop eating all the ingredients," she said as she turned the round disks of sliced carrots into little flowers. It actually looked pretty simple. She cut small wedges out of the disk until five petals formed.

"I can do that for you." The skepticism in her narrowed gaze stung a bit. "I know I can't be trusted with actual cooking, but I'm good with woodworking. And that looks an awful lot like whittling."

She nodded with pursed lips as she considered his words, then pushed the bowl of carrots to him. "I could use the help."

With a smile, he grabbed a paring knife and got to work. The first couple of carrots looked more like ragged weeds than flowers, but he gradually improved until he was making carrot flowers as pretty as his mom had made them. She obviously approved of his work, because she slid a bowl of Korean radish across the counter to him. She'd cut them into perfect one-inch cubes earlier.

"Trim off all the sharp edges from the mu," she instructed.

"So they're more approachable?" He grinned, happy to be entrusted with more cooking tasks than he'd ever been allowed before.

His mom tsked at his admittedly goofy joke and poured out the short ribs she'd parboiled into a colander. After rinsing the pot and the short ribs, she added the ribs back into the pot. He watched carefully as his mom added the ingredients for the sauce into a mixing bowl.

Maybe he could sneak his way into the kitchen at the brewery. He could always use the extra work. His smile waned and faded away. How long could he last like this? Scrounging for work to feel useful? He thought longingly of the job in Los Angeles. What was taking them so long?

"You've never been this interested in my cooking before." Her gaze turned sly. "Does it have anything to do with this being Lizzy's favorite food?"

"I've always been interested. It's just that you usually shoo me away because you're afraid I'll burn the kitchen down or something." He absolutely hadn't been daydreaming about making dinner for Lizzy while he waited for her to come home after a long day at work.

"If you say so," his mom said breezily.

He didn't trust her tone at all. What was she implying? She couldn't possibly know about his decades-long crush on Lizzy. Could she? The kitchen suddenly felt very warm. Not wanting to meet her gaze, Jack focused on turning the white cubes of mu into smooth, bite-size nuggets.

"All done." He thrust the bowl of stylized radish to her. "I have some work to catch up on."

"You've taken care of the most fiddly, time-consuming stuff for me. It makes the rest of my work a lot easier."

"Glad to help." He pecked his mom on the cheek and escaped to his room.

Contrary to his assertion (a.k.a. his bullshit excuse to get the hell out of the kitchen to avoid his mom's probing gaze), he didn't have any work to catch up on or otherwise. As he stood in the middle of his room with his hands in his pockets, he couldn't remember for the life of him what he usually did to keep himself busy. He couldn't remember what it felt like to have real purpose.

To avoid facing how hopelessly lost he was, he sat down at his desk and woke his computer. Maybe they finally got back to him with the interview results. Alas, his in-box was glaringly devoid of new email. Not even a promotional email from his favorite shave club.

He dropped his head into his hands. This was precisely why Option Two was the only way to go. How could someone as driven and successful as Lizzy want someone who had no idea what to do with his life?

Before he could despair further, a notification alert *bing-bong*ed from his computer. His stomach dropped to his feet. Maybe it was the email that was meant to change his life. He slowly lifted his gaze to the computer screen, and like sunlight piercing through a cloudy sky, a smile lit across his face.

CHAPTER FIVE

Lizzy stared in awe at the feast of Korean food laid out before her. "This is too much, Ajumma."

"It's nothing." Jack's mom waved away her protests like she hadn't stood at the stove for hours cooking all this for her. "Besides, what will your parents say if they found out I didn't feed you properly?"

"I'll be sure to tell them you nearly broke the table legs," Lizzy promised solemnly, referring to a Korean saying. Overstuffing one's guest was an important part of their culture. But before she told her parents how well she was fed, she needed to break the news of her three-week vacation to them. She pushed aside the panic that threatened to overshadow her joy at seeing the Park family.

"Good girl." Mrs. Park patted her cheek, and the easy affection warmed her heart.

"She's just flexing her culinary muscles to impress you," Alex quipped, strolling into the kitchen. "Just remember to gush over how good everything tastes."

"Alex." Lizzy laughed as a pair of strong arms enveloped her. "It's so good to see you."

"Same here." He released her from the hug and held her at arm's length. "You look great."

"So do you." And he did.

Alex was slightly shorter than his twin brother but was broader around the chest and shoulders. He was handsome in a blatantly masculine way with a cut jaw and sharp cheekbones. She might've had a crush on him for about two weeks when they were eleven. He was only twelve minutes older than Jack, but he had seemed so much more grown-up to her back then. *Had* being the operative word. Now he seemed more like a mischievous younger brother than anything.

Jack appeared in the doorway at that moment. His eyes briefly searched for something and landed on her as though he'd found what he was looking for. That sweet, crooked smile she loved spread across his face, and her answering smile was instinctive. His smooth, oval face and deep, wide eyes made him more beautiful than handsome but not any less masculine.

He stepped between her and Alex, dislodging his brother's hands from her arms, and hugged her as though they hadn't seen each other for years—rather than just a few hours ago. Her arms went around his waist, and she buried her face in his chest. Her dread over calling her mom faded into the background as she relaxed against him. He smelled clean, fresh, and warm like a sunny day in the mountains. When she felt him pulling back, her hands tightened around him for a split second before she caught herself. *Geez*. She must've been lonelier than she'd realized.

"Unni!"

It was Tara. And God, she was stunning. Tall with silky black hair that fell halfway down her back and features so symmetrical that she looked photoshopped. Damn, these Park siblings hit some kind of genetic jackpot. Lizzy suddenly felt intimidated in the presence of their gorgeousness with her just perfectly pleasant looks. It only took her a moment to snap out of her ridiculous self-consciousness, and she wrapped Tara into a bear hug.

"I haven't seen you for the longest time," Lizzy said, stepping back from her. "How do you get more beautiful every time I see you?"

Tara slouched her shoulders and blew a raspberry, dispelling the illusion of unapproachable perfection. "Don't be silly. So not true. You just always see the best in people."

"What are you doing here anyway?" Alex shot his little sister a what-gives look. "Did you smell the galbi jjim all the way from Seth's place?"

"What do you mean, what is she doing here?" Mrs. Park interjected slightly louder than necessary. "She lives here."

Tara turned an interesting shade of guilty and exasperated but plastered a determined smile on her face. "Do you need any help, Umma?"

"Umma? You only call me that when you do something wrong." The Park matriarch busily set out even more food, making certain not a single inch of the table's surface remained visible.

"I do not," Tara mumbled, making minute adjustments to the perfectly set dishes on the table.

Lizzy felt for her. It was never easy disappointing your parents no matter how unreasonable their expectations. But if she could choose between Mrs. Park's overprotective coddling and her mom's constant disapproval, she would choose the coddling in a hot second.

Jack, ever the peacekeeper, quickly changed the subject. "Where's Dad?"

"I sent him out to pick up some fruit," Jack's mom said distractedly. "We need to have dessert after lunch."

Lizzy smiled. Only Koreans would consider sliced fruit dessert. "You didn't need to go to so much trouble."

"Trouble?" Mr. Park joined them in the kitchen, bearing a bag of apples. "It's no trouble at all."

"Ajussi." Lizzy bowed at the waist. "You look well."

"Retirement and Ajumma's cooking have been fattening me up." He patted his perfectly flat belly.

"Speaking of Mom's cooking, can we eat now?" Alex grabbed the back of a chair and pulled it out but waited until his parents sat before sitting down himself.

"Where should I sit?" Lizzy whispered to Jack.

"Across from me." He went and took his seat so she would know where he meant.

There was no way to avoid looking like a glutton as she filled her plate with galbi jjim, japchae, and the countless banchan. It had been so long since she had home-cooked Korean food, she couldn't decide what to put in her mouth first.

"Here, have some jeon." Mrs. Park reached across the table to put some pan-fried fish fillets with egg batter on Lizzy's plate.

"Thank you, Ajumma." She had to swallow the bite-size jeon along with a lump of emotion. She'd been on her own for so long, she'd forgotten what it felt like to be taken care of. Suddenly, her life in Los Angeles seemed so empty. But she had a successful career. Shouldn't that be enough? *Apparently not.* She backed away from the thought as though it burned her. She quickly took another bite of the jeon and let the rich, savory goodness bring her out of her musings. "This is so good."

"You got the idea," Alex said, reaching for some japchae with his chopsticks. He was clearly better skilled at the proper usage of chopsticks than she was, because he managed to get a load of the glass noodles between them without it all slipping out in a tangled mess. "Next time, add a little more oomph in the compliment using words like *best* and *ever.*"

"Quiet, you." Mrs. Park shot Alex an unconvincing glare.

"Never a dull moment with a comedian in the house." Jack caught Lizzy's eyes, and they shared a grin. "You should take your act on the road."

"I most certainly will not." Alex sat up straight, looking credibly affronted. "I'm a serious brewer, I am."

Still smiling, Lizzy bit into the galbi jjim and almost moaned embarrassingly in front of Jack and his entire family. The tender, juicy meat melted off the bones, filling her mouth with the salty, slightly sweet flavors of soy sauce, garlic, sesame oil, and the essence of all the vegetables in the slow-cooked dish. Mrs. Park went all out with the onions, dried jujubes, shiitake mushrooms, chestnuts, and the decorative pieces of carrots and radish. The layers of flavors were complex and so damn good.

"This literally is the best galbi jjim I've ever had," Lizzy said with hushed reverence.

"Attagirl." Alex gave her two thumbs up.

Mrs. Park ignored her eldest son and smiled warmly at her. "I'm glad you like it."

The happy silence of a good meal settled around them as everyone dug into the delicious food. Lizzy didn't think she could eat another bite, but managed to stuff another chopstick full of japchae in her face. She couldn't get enough of the glass noodles sprinkled through with julienned vegetables and tender beef. It was such a mouthful of umami. Someone needed to stop her from eating herself sick.

"Did I mention that Lizzy won her first trial?" Jack announced, beaming at her from across the table with pride written all over his face.

Having him look at her that way made her feel like she was . . . enough. Something unfurled inside her—a need to have the man who made her feel that way. Suddenly flustered, she lowered her eyes to the table, then glanced at him from under her lashes a moment later. *Jack?*

"Wow. That's fantastic. Your parents must be so proud of you," Mr. Park boomed, drawing Lizzy out of her unsettling thoughts. "I bet your dad is going to talk my ear off about how wonderful you are the next time we chat. Not that he doesn't already."

"Thank you, Ajussi." She forced herself to smile. Avoiding telling her parents about her leave from work only exacerbated her anxiety. She wasn't looking forward to her mom's disappointment, but it would be better to get it over with. She wanted to settle into her time in Weldon without it hanging over her head.

Once everyone was fed to Mrs. Park's satisfaction, the twins cleared and wiped the table while Tara peeled and sliced some apples. She served the "dessert," fanned out on the plate like the top of a beautiful apple tart. If it had come with sugar and a buttery crust, Lizzy would've found room to eat more than a single slice. Thankfully for her stomach, she was able to say no to the natural goodness. But the sweet-and-tart citron tea was so good, she couldn't stop sipping at it. She was going to unbutton her jeans the minute she was alone.

"Thank you so much for the delicious meal," Lizzy said, feeling a food coma coming on. "Let me help with the dishes."

Mrs. Park literally laughed in her face. "You'll do no such thing. That's Mr. Park's job."

"That's right," Mr. Park said, pulling on a pair of red rubber gloves that went up to his elbows—a Korean household staple. "You just go and enjoy your vacation."

After the thank-yous and goodbyes were said with hugs all around, Jack walked her out to her car.

"It was so nice seeing everyone." Lizzy glanced across the car at Jack with her hand on the door handle. He stood on the sidewalk, his arms crossed over his chest. From a strictly objective standpoint, it did amazing things to his manly, veiny forearms. The skip in her heart was a perfectly natural reaction to her observation. "So I'll see you tomorrow morning?"

"Um . . . actually. I won't be able to join you tomorrow. I have . . . an errand to run." He looked with great interest at something above her head. "But you should still go for a job . . . I mean, a jog."

"Maybe." By which she meant, *probably not*. She wasn't at a point in her exercise regimen where she would voluntarily torture herself. Instead, she should sleep in, then try out that clawfoot tub. There was a peach Bellini bath bomb with her name on it in her luggage, which she should see about unpacking. She would get around to it when she got around to it. She was on vacation. "We should hang out later, then. Have lunch or something?"

"Maybe." He said it in the same way she had. She made a conscious effort not to chew on her bottom lip. She'd told him he didn't need to babysit her while she was in Weldon, so she had no right to feel disappointed.

"Well, okay. Bye." She opened her car door and quickly slipped inside.

He waved to her and stood, watching her drive away. As soon as he was out of view, she popped the button on her jeans and groaned with relief. But a moment later, a forlorn sigh slipped past her lips. The prospect of a day without Jack seemed to stretch out before her, dull and aimless. It was probably because she didn't know what to do with her free time. It was a pretty foreign concept, this free-time business. When she was in school, she was busy studying. When she became an attorney, she was busy working. She hadn't had a stretch of time to herself like this since her high school summer vacations.

There was only so much shopping, strolling, and idling away the time she could do. In all honesty, doing nothing made her anxious. When she stayed still and quiet, her thoughts got louder and louder. She needed to keep moving to stay out of her head. Everyone had different ways of recharging. For her, working on a hobby or a project was the best way to let go and relax. She needed to find something she could throw herself into. In the meantime, she was grateful to have Sparrow to lose herself in.

She parked in her designated spot in the back of the building and headed for the bookstore. Again, when she stepped inside, she had to adjust to the sensation that the interior of the store was inexplicably smaller than the exterior. Could the dark, towering bookcases lined up in the middle of the store be the cause of the shrinking effect?

It was the middle of the day, and the sign on the door definitely read OPEN, but the bookstore was as quiet as it had been when she'd dropped by yesterday morning. Maybe the customers were hidden behind the bookcases, being very, very quiet because of the library-esque atmosphere.

Lizzy walked along the aisles but didn't discover any customers silently browsing through the books. As a matter of fact, the store was empty. Was Shannon in the back again? She really should get a bell for the door.

"Hello?" The wall of books seemed to swallow up her voice.

She heard a series of shuffles, scrapes, and curses before Shannon shouted, "Be right there."

"No rush." She followed the sound of Shannon's voice and found a half-open door at the back of the store. "It's Lizzy. Do you need any help?"

Lizzy gingerly poked her head around the door, expecting to find a hopelessly cluttered storage room but was surprised to discover a neatly organized space with boxes lined up against the walls. One corner was set up as an office with a long wooden desk and a row of tidy filing cabinets. Quite honestly, she could understand why Shannon spent so much time back here. It was much more welcoming than the front of the store even with the dim lighting and one small window at the back wall.

"Hey, Lizzy. No, I'm good." Shannon straightened from sorting through a box and stretched her back with a soft *oof.* "This storage room used to be piled sky-high with boxes and boxes of books I inherited from the previous bookstore owner. It took me nearly two years, but I'm down to eight boxes to sort through."

"Oh, wow. Do you ever find anything good?" Lizzy crouched by the open box and flipped through the books.

"Oh yeah. I've found some gems." Shannon huffed something between a laugh and a sigh. "That's why I persisted in going through all of them."

"Ahh." That was how the storefront became crammed with so many books. "Now instead of piles of boxes in the storage room, you have sky-high bookshelves in the store."

"Exactly. It sort of . . . got out of hand." Again that laugh-sigh. "This wasn't how I envisioned my bookstore would be. I wanted it to be a cozy haven for fellow book lovers, not somewhere people came in as a last resort when they needed a book in a hurry. If things continue like this, I'm not sure how long I can keep Sparrow open."

"Maybe the townspeople don't know about the store yet," Lizzy suggested, her heart going out to her new friend. It must be so hard to watch her beloved bookstore barely limping along.

"This bookstore had been around for a decade before I took over a couple of years ago. People know it's here, but I don't blame them for not beating down the door. I'll be the first to admit that it's a mess. It could be so much more, but I've been overwhelmed with . . . life." Shannon pressed her hand against her forehead. "Oh, my gosh. I can't believe I'm unloading on you like this. I'm so sorry."

"I can help out at the store," Lizzy blurted before she'd thought it through. But as she did, she realized what a brilliant idea it was. "I have close to three weeks of free time that I don't know what to do with."

"The bookstore barely gets us by. I won't be able to pay you. . . ." Shannon let her words hang and looked at Lizzy with hopeful eyes.

"I'm *volunteering*."

This was it. Her project. This was exactly what she needed. And she would be helping an indie bookstore—something she loved above all else—get back on its feet. A thrill went through her—the kind of thrill that had been missing when she won the trial. But she brushed aside her unexpected reaction. Her time in Weldon must be making her feel better already.

"Helping you build your book haven will be reward enough," Lizzy said, meaning every word. "When do I start?"

~~~

Traffic added an hour to his drive home, but it didn't snuff out a single ounce of Jack's excitement. Hope was a dangerously intoxicating feeling, but he'd be damned if he didn't enjoy the high. It really might happen. He nailed the second interview *and* the lunch—which they insisted wasn't part of the interview but was definitely a part of the interview. He actually might become McBain Corporation's newest—and lowliest (but who the hell cared)—business analyst. The opportunity to spread his wings and grow was dizzying.

He was dying to tell Lizzy, but he couldn't. Not right now. First of all, there was nothing to tell her yet. He hadn't actually gotten the job. He could technically share that he'd applied to entry-level analyst positions at several top consulting firms and had gotten this far with one of them. But he would hate to disappoint her if he didn't get the job. He grimaced imagining her sad, sympathetic eyes. His professional life was already underwhelming compared to hers without adding a possible flop on top of it.

He wasn't in any way ashamed of his job at Weldon Brewery. If taking over the family business had been his dream, he would've been damn proud of what he'd accomplished and thrilled to plan the next goals to conquer. But it wasn't, and all he felt was stuck and lost. He wasn't proud of being a thirty-year-old man who had no idea where his life was headed. That had to change before he told Lizzy any of this.

More important, he needed to tell his family, which he definitely couldn't do until he got the job. The thought of breaking the news to them did what Los Angeles traffic couldn't. It sobered him right up. Growing the brewery wasn't his dream—it was Alex's and Tara's—but he was grateful they considered him a part of their team. The Park siblings versus the world.

What would they think if—no, when—he told them that he wanted to leave the brewery? Leave Weldon? Would they feel betrayed and abandoned? He wouldn't blame them if they did. But truth be told, *they* were what made Weldon Brewery what it was. Their passion, their vision. That was what propelled the brewery forward, not Jack's conscientious bookkeeping. Would he be able to convince them that they could accomplish everything they set out to do without him? That Weldon Brewery didn't need him? That *they* didn't need him?

Daylight was waning by the time he parked outside his family's home. That was another thing. Their parents were getting older, and ever since the three of them took over running the brewery, they had been paying for the mortgage on the house. Mom and Dad worked hard to take care of Alex, Tara, and him, so now it was the kids' turn to take care of their parents. Even if he moved to Los Angeles, he fully intended to pay for his third of the mortgage.

He shut off the engine and swiped his hand down his face. If he got the job offer, he wouldn't be moving away to leave his family but to find himself. And he hoped that once the initial shock wore off, his family would be at least a little proud of him for leaving what was safe and comfortable to go forge his own path.

As he unlatched his seat belt and reached for the door handle, his cell phone lit up on the center console. It was still set to silent from the interview, but a new text message had arrived. Based on his alerts, Lizzy had sent him ten texts during his four-hour drive back home. He hurriedly scrolled down, hoping everything was okay.

Lizzy: Hey, you. Done with your errand?

Lizzy: Ok. I said no babysitting, but ignoring me is going a bit far.

Lizzy: Seriously, where are you?

Lizzy: Have dinner with me.

Relief rolled through him when he realized she was all right. That panic attack she had the day of her opening statement still had him a little jumpy.

Lizzy: I'm wasting away in protest to your silence.

Lizzy: Shit. Are you still on your errand? Sorry!

Lizzy: What kind of errand takes like ten hours?

His lips quirked into a grin. Did all these texts mean that she missed him? She was most likely bored, but maybe she missed him a little, too. He tried to ignore how happy that made him, because he was supposed to be getting over her.

Lizzy: I'm going to gnaw on my left slipper to curb my hunger because everyone knows the left shoe is always tenderer.

Lizzy: Or was it the right shoe? I can't think straight. You know, cuz the hunger.

Lizzy: You suck.

He chuckled as he texted back.

Jack: It's the right shoe. Everyone knows that.

The ellipses started rolling within a second of him hitting Send. She really must be hungry.

Lizzy: Well, they're both gone now, so I'm full.

Lizzy: Which means I'm rescinding my dinner offer.

Jack: Save your lawyer lingo and meet me for dinner.

Lizzy: Are you offering me your right shoe?

Jack: Even better. Mexican food.

Lizzy: Apology accepted.

He looked down at himself. He'd hung his suit jacket on a hanger in the back seat, but he was still wearing a loosened tie, dress shirt, and slacks. He was a bit overdressed for Mexican food with his best friend. He'd better change.

Jack: I'll pick you up in 15 minutes.

Lizzy: See you soon.

He pulled up in front of Sparrow Bookstore ten minutes later, his heart thumping with anticipation. He still couldn't believe Lizzy was in Weldon—just a five-minute drive away from his house. Even though he was early, he couldn't wait to see her, so he walked around to the back and climbed the steps to her temporary abode. He knocked and stood back, trying not to fidget.

"Who is it?" a hesitant voice asked from behind the red door.

"Guess," he said dryly.

The door opened an inch and a suspicious eye peeked out, which promptly rolled up to the ceiling. She opened the door wide and stood with a hand on her hip. "You said fifteen minutes."

"I got here early, so I thought I'd check out your place. I've never been up here before." He stepped inside but kept his shoes on because Lizzy was slipping hers on. "I forgot for a second that you big-city folks complete a full-body scan before opening the front door."

"I'm a woman who lives alone in LA. I'm not going to fling

open the door for anyone who knocks," she said, fiddling with the tiny straps on her sandals.

"I guess you shouldn't get used to the way things are in Weldon since you're going back in a few weeks." And *he* shouldn't get used to having her so near because it was a little too wonderful.

Would it be like this if he were to move to Los Angeles? Would they make impromptu dinner plans? See each other every day? Not likely with her demanding career, but he would love to have a chance to find out. He wanted to cross his fingers and say a prayer. *Please let me get that job.* Instead, he scanned the studio apartment, reminding himself to focus on Option Two.

Waist-high, birch bookshelves lined the far corner of the buttercream-colored room. A blue-gray tufted armchair nestled between them, delineating a homey sitting area, which prevented the studio from looking like one big bedroom. The queen-size bed in the opposite corner was neatly made with soft floral-printed sheets, but he averted his eyes too quickly to make out what kind of flowers they were.

Instead, he let his gaze linger on the small kitchenette on the other end of the apartment. With a two-burner stove top, a sink, and a mini-fridge, it was tidy and functional. It reminded him of a play kitchen that Tara used to have when they were kids. He would groan and complain when she asked him to play with her, but he actually loved playing in that toy kitchen.

"Plus, I haven't been in Weldon long enough to know how things work here," she said, straightening up.

"True." He nodded, taking in the woodwork on the armoire and the dresser. "Nice place, by the way."

"Thanks. Isn't it absolutely charming?" She grabbed her purse from an owl-shaped hook by the door. "Ready? I'm starving."

"Yeah. Let's go." He stepped out onto the landing and waited for her to lock the door, then followed her down the stairs.

Like most things in Weldon, La Cabana was only a few minutes away. The local favorite was busy as usual, but they were able to snag a table in the corner without a wait. Suzie, the owner's daughter, dropped off the menus with a quick "Hey, Jack," and bustled off to take the orders at another table.

"Ooh, they have horchata." Lizzy had her nose buried in the floppy, laminated menu.

"I always get their tamarindo." So good. Tart and just the right amount of sweet. "They make all their drinks from scratch every morning."

"Yay," she cheered happily. "I can't decide. I want everything."

"If you feel like soup, I love their cocido. And I like anything drenched with their rojo sauce."

"Hmm." She tapped her plush bottom lip with her index finger, and he followed the movement as though hypnotized. "I'm going to have the beef rojo tacos, then."

"Good choice," he croaked, dragging his gaze back up to her eyes. "I'm getting the beef rojo wet burrito."

"That sounds so good. Now I want that, too." She pouted, looking torn.

"Then get it." He refused to stare at her pouty lips.

"I can't get the same thing you do." She drew back in outrage as though he'd suggested that she denounce her religion. "Then how are we going to share?"

He grinned, remembering how she loved to taste everything on his plate and insisted on him tasting all her food. "Who says I'm going to share my glorious wet burrito?"

"You wouldn't dare," she challenged, narrowing her eyes threateningly.

Knowing she was only *half* joking, he raised his hands in surrender. "Of course I wouldn't dare. I value my life too much. Why don't you get the beef rojo burrito, and I'll get the chicken verde tacos. That's really good, too."

"See. That wasn't so hard, was it? Compromises make the world a better place," she said serenely.

Suzie dropped off some salsa and tortilla chips—so fresh that the oil was still sizzling on the surface—and then took their order.

"So what was this errand that took you away from Weldon?" Lizzy crunched into a salsa-dipped chip.

"Just something for work. Had to meet some people . . ." He stuffed a chip into his mouth, hoping she wouldn't delve deeper.

"Guess what I did today?" She practically bounced on her seat.

"Ate a lot of sugar?" he said, eyeing her sideways.

"Shut up." It looked as though she was about to throw a tortilla chip at him, but she seemed to think better of it and bit into it instead. "I got a job."

"Which involves eating a lot of sugar?" A partially eaten chip bounced off his chest and landed on the table.

"No, dingus." She wrinkled her nose at him. "I got a job at the bookstore."

"The truckload of money you make as a lawyer not enough for you?" he joked, but he was really curious what the hell she was talking about. "Fine. Tell me all about it."

"You know Shannon, right?" She stirred her horchata with a straw and took a long sip.

"I know *of* her. She has a little son, right?" His brows drew together. "I think they moved here a couple of years ago."

"Yeah, but she needs help revitalizing her bookstore." Lizzy leaned forward, brimming with excitement. "She doesn't have the time to do it all on her own, and she can't afford to hire anyone, so I volunteered to help her while I'm here."

Her eyes were wide and sparkling, and Jack couldn't look away from her. She got this way every time she talked about books and bookstores. "I thought you were here to rest and recharge."

"My poor, weary soul needs the rest and all that"—she waved her hands around as though *rest* were some sort of hocus-pocus—"not my mind and body. I would've been bored silly if I didn't have this project. It's going to be so much fun."

"Can you imagine what your firm will think if they find out you're providing your services free of charge?"

"Oh, my God." She giggled into her hand. "It's going to be so liberating to work without thinking about billable hours. I told you how we have to keep track of our time in six-minute increments *every single day*."

"Yeah, you've mentioned it. Keeping track of your time alone sounds like a full-time job," he said with a sympathetic grimace.

"It is." Lizzy flopped her head down on the table as though just talking about billing was exhausting her.

But in reality, she looked anything but exhausted. Her cheeks were rosy, and her eyes twinkled with laughter. There was a vibrance to her that he hadn't seen in a long time. He was glad her time in Weldon was doing her some good.

"I have to write down the tiniest details." She squinted, bringing her thumb and index finger together until they were almost touching. "Like three minutes to make a call and leave a message. Two minutes to reply to a short email. I have sticky notes everywhere on my desk by the end of the day until I input everything into the billing system, and I have to start all over the next day. And of course, we have to use fancier wording for the actual billing: 0.1 hours—telephone conference with so and so about this and that; 0.1 hours—draft email correspondence to so and so about this and that. Ick."

"*Ick* about sums it up." He shook his head, appalled for her. "You never told me the nitty-gritty details of billing before."

"And waste the few times we get to see each other bitching about work? Hell no."

"Well, I'm glad you're getting a break from all of that."

"Me too." She smiled sweetly at him. "This is nice."

His heart tripped and face-planted itself against his ribs. The more time he spent with Lizzy, the less likely it seemed that he would be able to pull off Option Two. No, he couldn't get discouraged. She was bound to irritate him sooner or later.

"I bet you say that to all the guys who buy you Mexican food," he said to cover his sudden panic.

"Heyyyy," she protested, scowling with indignation, "I do not discriminate based on the cuisine."

He snorted.

"Besides, who said you were buying me dinner?" She munched on another chip. "You bought breakfast last time. This one's on me."

"Damn it. I should've ordered something more expensive." He made a show of looking around the restaurant for Suzie, then grinned at Lizzy. His beautiful Lizzy. He drank in the sight of her, happiness curling his toes—but in a very platonic, friend-like way. "I'm so glad you're here."

"I bet you say that to all the gals who buy you Mexican food." She fluttered her eyelashes.

Oh, God. She was just playing around, but the coy, flirtatious curve of her lips made him think very bad thoughts. He gulped down half his drink. There was no need to panic. He had almost three whole weeks to get over her. He could do this. Couldn't he?

CHAPTER SIX

Not to make herself sound like a holiday turkey, but dinner with Jack left Lizzy nicely stuffed and toasty warm inside. He was a wonderful listener—his eyes never glazed over even when she talked about her lawyering woes—but sometimes it was the things she didn't have to say that made spending time with him feel so good. She wanted to wrap the lovely feels all around her and snuggle under the covers with them. A smitten sigh escaped her as she slipped her shoes off. *Smitten? What? No.* It was just a happy sigh.

Unfortunately, the dreaded phone call to Korea hung over her head like a Charlie Brown cloud. Her monthly calls with her mom were never warm-and-fuzzy affairs. She spent most of it reassuring her mom that she was working hard and excelling at her job, listing every praise and accolade she could think of. And without fail, her mom would end the call sounding mildly disappointed in her.

There was going to be nothing mild about her disappointment when Lizzy told her about her time off from work. She trudged to the kitchen and poured herself an unsophisticated amount of red wine before sitting down at the two-person dining table. The straight-backed wooden chair gave her the illusion of having a backbone when it came to facing her parents.

Lizzy had been nine years old when her family immigrated to the United States. Her dad was assigned to the Los Angeles branch of Korean Air for a few years. Her parents thought it was a golden opportunity for their daughter to get the coveted American education. But once they came here, her dad was always working, and her mom found living in Los Angeles suffocating. It wasn't just the language barrier. Everyone drove everywhere in Southern California, but she couldn't drive—and was too afraid to learn—so she was *stuck* at home . . . with Lizzy.

At first, Lizzy's bringing home straight As and getting on the honor roll made her mom smile, but soon nothing she did seemed to be enough. When her dad was reassigned to the Seoul office—she had just started high school—her mom decided to return to Korea with him.

Lizzy had to stay behind for her American education.

Her attempt at a deep breath caught in her throat, and she felt mildly light-headed, a sure sign that anxiety was taking hold. This was getting out of hand. She was calling her mom, not walking to the guillotine. Yet there was something honest and blunt—figuratively speaking, because a literal blunt blade was probably way worse than a sharp one—about the guillotine that held a certain appeal. She should quit stalling and rip off the Band-Aid. *Off with her head!* She jabbed the Dial button with grim determination.

"Yeoboseyo?" Her mom picked up on the third ring and answered with a generic *hello* as though she didn't know who was calling.

"Umma, it's me," Lizzy said in Korean. Her voice came out

an octave higher than usual, making her sound like a ten-year-old.

"Saeyoon-ah. You're doing well?" She sounded perfectly pleasant if not overjoyed to hear from her only daughter. It was true they spoke at least once a month, but sometimes it would be nice to feel missed.

"Um . . . yeah. Mm-hmm." Which was true. She *was* doing well. Besides, she couldn't start off the conversation with *I'm taking three weeks off from work because I'm utterly burned out.* "You and Appa are good, too, right?"

"Appa is *so* busy with work as usual, and I have the house to take care of." Her mom sighed with the weight of her responsibilities. She had a live-in housekeeper, but she always managed to sound beleaguered.

"Is now an okay time to talk?" Lizzy asked, hearing the sound of cars and voices in the background.

"It's fine. I just had lunch with Mrs. Paek. You remember Mrs. Paek." *Nope. No idea.* "She got you that lovely Fendi brief-case when you graduated from law school."

Oh, *that* Mrs. Paek. Her parents had made sure she called and thanked her profusely at her graduation while her friends waited to take pictures with her. The sleek briefcase was much too slim for any practical use. She probably still had it somewhere in her closet.

"Of course I remember her. How is she doing?"

"She's doing great. Her daughter is a plastic surgeon, you know. She makes *very* good money." The slightest sharpening of her mom's voice told her this was a rebuke. Lizzy's annual income wasn't shabby, but it wasn't anywhere near what a successful plastic surgeon would earn in Korea. Her mother had comparing Lizzy to her friends' children down to an art.

"Mrs. Paek must be so proud." Long-honed self-control prevented sarcasm from bleeding into her words.

"Yes, very proud." Another forlorn sigh escaped her mom. Yes, her disappointment was vast. With her obligatory guilt-tripping out of the way, silence stretched on between them.

Lizzy was just prolonging the torture. She needed to spit it out. "I'm taking time off from work."

There was a surprised pause. "That must be . . . nice. Are you traveling?"

"Not exactly. I'm staying in Weldon . . . for three weeks." She held her breath.

"Three weeks? What are you thinking?" Her mom's voice dipped into a furious whisper. She never raised her voice. "Aren't the next two years crucial for you if you want to make partner?"

"I'm so tired, Umma." Her stomach clenched with nausea as her anxiety settled in for an extended stay. "I didn't tell you before because I didn't want you to worry, but I fainted during the trial."

"So you're just giving up? Do you *not* want to make partner?"

"No. Of course not. I just needed a break." Not even a cursory *Are you okay?* How could her mom care so little about her well-being? Lizzy bit her trembling lips. Why was she letting this hurt her when it was exactly what she'd expected? She was so tired of scrambling to meet her mom's expectations and failing. Always failing. "When I go back, I'll work harder than ever before. I promise you."

"What am I going to tell Appa?" Her mom's disappointment glinted like a sharp dagger poised to strike. Truth be told, if her dad had time to spare, he would understand better than her mom.

Even so, Lizzy shrank to the size of a thimble. "I'm sorry."

"I only want what's best for you," her mom said in a low, tired voice—let down once more by her ungrateful daughter.

"I know." And she shrank smaller yet. Would she ever be good enough for her mom?

Lizzy ended the call with a mumbled goodbye, and the tears she'd held at bay slid down her cheeks and fell onto her hands. She absently glanced down at them and discovered a full glass of wine in front of her, waiting to be imbibed. *Oh, joy.* After lifting the wine in a mocking toast, she chugged it all down in one breath. Alas, the last drop went down the wrong pipe and she coughed up her lungs. Almost.

She wiped her wet face with both hands and dried them on her jean-clad thighs. The tears of self-pity had receded—this type of conversation with her mom was much too routine for it to keep her down for long—to be replaced by tears from her coughing fit. At least her anxiety had backed off. There was that.

She cleared her throat raucously enough to make a crotchety old man slow clap. *Respect.* But it still felt scratchy from choking on the wine, so she poured herself another glass and took a careful, soothing sip. Whatever ill the wine had caused, the wine shall fix.

~~~

Evil, *evil* wine.

Lizzy gave the empty bottle of Shiraz a one-eyed glare, then promptly closed her eye. The big, east-facing window had been one of her favorite things about the apartment. But even with the curtains drawn, a small gap at the side let one piercing ray of sunlight shine directly onto her poor, hungover face.

"Curse you, wretched window," she mumbled, her dry lips stuck together on one side.

With her face squished to the pillow, she scooted her hips
to the edge of the bed and dropped one leg on the floor. Then
she tugged her other leg to join it, so her body was bent into an
inverted L shape—half on, half off the bed. She was prepared
to stay in the rather perilous position indefinitely to avoid lifting
her head, but her lower back and thighs soon burned in protest.
A cowardly whimper escaped her lips as she gingerly slid her
butt to the floor, letting gravity pull her head upright against
the side of the bed.

"Ow." She sat very still, hardly breathing, while the room
stopped spinning.

Bits and pieces of her conversation with her mom floated
into her mind, but she shoved them aside. There was no use
ruminating on it. It happened. It was over. Moping about it
wouldn't do her any good. Besides, she already did that last
night, and look where it had gotten her.

With fluid grace and utmost dignity, she crawled on all
fours to the kitchenette. She grabbed a pitcher of water from
the fridge, popped the lid off, and chugged the water straight
from the pitcher. Some dribbled down her chin and onto her
wrinkled T-shirt, but she was too invested in hydrating to care.

Feeling somewhat human, Lizzy struggled to her feet and
refilled the top of the pitcher to make more filtered water. Next
order of business: food. She opened one of the cupboards and
rummaged around its contents. Cereal, Oreos, potato chips,
and . . . *cup ramen*. She beamed at the instant noodles as she
cradled it adoringly between her hands. Past Lizzy was a smart
and wise woman.

When the ramen was ready, she poured a generous amount
of Tapatío into it and greedily drank the soup. Her churning
stomach welcomed the hot and spicy liquid and promptly began
behaving itself.

"Ahh." Sweet relief.

Korean hangover cures always involved steamy, hearty soup. There was even an actual dish called *the hangover soup*, which consisted of some variation of meat or bone broth, leafy veggies, and a generous helping of red pepper powder. Cup ramen with hot sauce hardly compared to haejangguk, but it worked like a charm in a pinch.

With the worst of her hangover symptoms cured, Lizzy lingered in the shower, luxuriating in the feel of the hot water running down her body. Back in Los Angeles, she used to shower in a mad rush as though someone were pounding on her bathroom door, screaming at her to get out. But today, the bathroom looked like a steam sauna by the time she came out. She wiped her hand across the fogged-up mirror and stared at her reflection. She lived her life as though she were running away from it. Maybe it was time she figured out why.

She deliberately took her time getting dressed in a pair of red capris and a white, short-sleeved blouse. She'd filled her suitcase with all the fun, casual clothes she couldn't wear to work. Attorney Elizabeth Chung was unavailable for the duration of her leave.

Her sunglasses firmly in place, she stepped into the sunny summer day and headed to the bookstore. She had butterflies in her stomach. Had she ever gone into her office with such joy and excitement before? Hmm . . . no matter. That was why she was taking this break—to recharge and rediscover her passion for her real job. For now, she would savor this incredible chance to work at a bookstore. A *bookstore*!

Despite the CLOSED sign, she pushed open the door with confidence—she worked there after all—then faltered at the silence. First things first. She needed to speak with her boss/ landlady—ooh, Boss Lady—about getting a bell for the entrance. It had such a welcoming sound. It was one of the many things she loved about Hideaway Bookstore. She headed straight for the back room and poked her head around the door. Shannon was sitting at her desk with her nose buried in a laptop.

"Knock, knock."

"Hey, Lizzy." Shannon looked up from the screen with a warm smile.

"Good morning." Lizzy pulled a wooden crate to the front of the desk and sat down on it. "Have you thought about getting a shopkeeper's bell for the door? Since you're back here so often, the bell will let you know when a customer walks in."

"I know." Shannon slumped in her seat. "It's been on my to-do list forever."

"A to-do list?" Lizzy closed her eyes and steadied her breath. "Is this a real list or a figurative list?"

"It's an actual list. A long one." Her friend stacked her hands a yard apart.

"Lists. Are. Everything." Lizzy might as well have said, *My precious*. It wasn't creepy at all.

"Not if they keep getting longer without anything getting checked off." Shannon sighed and sank farther into her chair, too dejected to notice Lizzy's brief transformation into Gollum.

"I can help you work through your list." She bolted up from the crate with such gusto that it scraped loudly against the concrete floor. "Can you print out the list for me while I run to buy a shopkeeper's bell?"

"Wow. You're going to buy the bell now?"

"Yeah. Why not?" Lizzy could always shop online, but that meant she would have to wait for the bell to be delivered. Two-day shipping sounded like an eternity. "It'll let us cross off an item from your list right away."

"Ms. Lizzy," Shannon said with a dazed smile, "you're a force of nature."

"Nah. I just like putting little check marks by list items. Almost as much as I like bullet points." Lizzy was already at the back room door when she realized she had no idea where she was headed. "Just one thing. Where can I buy a shopkeeper's bell?"

"Hmm. I would say your best bet is Arthur's Hardware or Nickel Antique Shop."

"Those stores can't be as adorable as they sound." She raised a skeptical eyebrow but sounded way too hopeful to pull it off.

"They are *so* adorable. You're going to die," Shannon said with undisguised glee.

"I'll die happy, then." With a jaunty wave at her friend, Lizzy merrily headed to her demise.

~

Jack walked around the brewery, listlessly jiggling tables and chairs to see if any of them wobbled. No luck so far. He considered himself a patient man, but waiting for an answer was a special kind of torture. It was filled with hope and dread—both sweet and bitter. As long as he waited, there was hope that the answer would be *yes*. And that hope filled him with optimism, fueled his dreams, and propelled him forward. Yet there were times when he wanted an answer even if it was a *no* just to be put out of his misery—because the uncertainty and the fear of *no* could feel worse than the actual *no*.

All his musings, however, were a bit premature since he went on his second interview the day before. Well, maybe not exactly premature. He'd been searching for a job for more than six months now. The guilt of keeping it a secret from his family and being in limbo over what came next had begun to take a toll on him. If this opportunity with McBain Corporation didn't pan out, should he continue searching for a new career or find a way to make things work at Weldon Brewery?

He suddenly felt claustrophobic standing inside the brewery and pushed his way out the front entrance. And there it was. His pride and joy. He crossed his arms over his chest and took in the resplendent outdoor seating area—it wasn't the Gardens of Versailles, but it was pretty damn great. Getting the green light from the city was a pain in the ass, but he'd doggedly pursued it until it happened and dedicated months of his life into building the patio.

The wraparound patio hugged the front and side of the brewery, which stood on the corner of the street. To echo the theme of the brick-and-wood interior, the patio was lined with wooden picnic tables, which he'd built himself. Sandy-beige triangular shade sails protected the customers from the elements without detracting from the feel of the California outdoors, and the crisscross of string lights gave the seating area a festive vibe. The black heat lamps dotting the patio, which reminded him of old-fashioned streetlamps, made it feel a touch rustic and homey.

Perhaps it had been a last-ditch effort on his part to feel like an essential part of Weldon Brewery. It had occupied every minute of his free time to finish, but once he was done . . . he was done. A week later, he began submitting résumés.

He blew out a long breath, his cheeks expanding from the force, and buried his fingers in his hair. With his future undecided, all he could do was wait. Resisting the urge to fist his hands, he dropped his arms back down to his sides. In the meantime, he should focus on doing his best for Weldon Brewery. He went from heat lamp to heat lamp, checking the propane tanks. A couple of them felt light. It was still summer, but soon the evenings would start cooling down.

Jack went back inside and stopped by the kitchen. "Mom, I'm going to the hardware store to pick up some propane tanks."

His mom was chopping what looked like her twentieth on-ion based on the small mountain beside her. When she looked up, she had tears in her eyes.

"Aww, there's no need for that," he said, patting her shoul-der. "I won't be gone that long."

With an exaggerated sniffle, she said, "Sorry. It's just that I'll miss you so very much."

He laughed as a surge of affection rushed through him. His mom was the world's best one-upper. "Do you need anything?"

"Not that I can think of. But isn't it a little early to be stock-ing up on propane?"

"Being prepared never hurt anyone." He hated the hint of defensiveness in his tone.

"Can't argue with that." Her eyes softened with understand-ing, making him wonder if his mom knew how lost he felt.

He was gripped by a desperate urge to spill everything to the woman who gave him life—how he felt like a third wheel at the brewery and how he believed that he could do so much more if he branched out on his own. But the urge fizzled out as swiftly as it had flared.

"Bye, Mom."

He reached his car with long, hurried strides and got into the driver's seat. Gripping the steering wheel, he forced himself to take a deep breath. Waiting to hear back from McBain was stressing the hell out of him and making him irrational. Tell-ing his mom right now would've only caused her unnecessary worry. Even if he got the job, he needed a plan before he shared the news with his family—he had to convince them Weldon Brewery would be fine without him. He huffed a humorless laugh. Little did they know, all they needed was a bookkeeper and a server to replace him.

He scrubbed his face with his hands, then started the engine.

He needed a distraction—something to keep him busy while he waited for McBain's decision. For the time being, shopping for propane would have to do.

After parking his car in a shared lot in the back, Jack walked into Arthur's Hardware Store. It was a cluttered mess with every available space, including the walls, covered with wares for sale, and yet, it was somehow utterly charming. Much of it probably had to do with Ol' Arthur. He always had a joke to share and knew the exact location of every nut and bolt in the store.

Ol' Arthur was actually a twenty-three-year-old recent college grad who had taken over the store when Li'l Arthur, his grandfather, retired about a year earlier. It wasn't a surprise to most townsfolk when Ol' Arthur became the new owner. As a kid, he'd spent all his summers *happily* working for his grandfather. Those of little faith predicted that he wouldn't come back once he left for college, but every summer without fail, he was back in Weldon at his grandfather's store. Arthur's Hardware was his calling—his passion. Jack envied him.

But at the present, the good owner was nowhere to be found. Puzzled, Jack roamed down an empty aisle when he heard a familiar laugh—a sound he would never have expected to hear at Weldon's premier hardware store . . . or any hardware store, for that matter. If she needed any frames hung up, she would wait months for him to visit Los Angeles to do it for her. She claimed she was traumatized by the one time she'd hung up a picture in her dormitory only to have it come crashing down the next day.

He followed the merry sound down two aisles to find Ol' Arthur leaning toward a laughing Lizzy, grinning like a dumbass. A muscle ticked in Jack's clenched jaws, and his nostrils flared. Logic dictated that his raging-bull impression was unwarranted, but the kid was standing much too close to her.

"Hey, Arthur. Where's my joke of the day?" he boomed, marching up to them.

"Jack?" Lizzy's smile widened.

"Umm . . . you guys know each other?" Arthur shifted from foot to foot under Jack's icy glare.

"Yeah. We've been friends forever," she offered helpfully before turning back to Jack. "What are you doing here?"

"I'm here to pick up a couple of propane tanks for the heat lamps." He cocked his head at the kid, stomping down on his irrational antagonism. He couldn't blame Arthur for being drawn to Lizzy. She just had that effect on people. Besides, Jack wasn't the flirtation police. "If you're done helping her, can you get those out for me?"

"Sure." Arthur recovered his good humor. "And I'll have that joke ready for you as well."

"Looking forward to it," Jack said before turning toward Lizzy. "And what brings *you* here?"

"Shannon needed a shopkeeper's bell for the front entrance." She held up the bell in her hands.

"Is this part of your volunteer work?" He reached out and tapped the bell. It made an impressive jingle.

"Yup." But there was more to it. She tugged her upper lip between her teeth and performed a variation of the gotta-go dance. Either she had to pee or she was dying to tell him something. Before he could tell her where the restroom was, she squealed, "Shehasatodolist."

"Good Lord." He swiped a hand down his mouth, half in dismay and half to cover his smile.

She once made him go through his entire summer reading list in two weeks. For *fun*. Because who needed sleep? To her credit, she read all the books with him, and they didn't run out of things to talk about for the rest of the summer. In short, Lizzy with a list was both a wonderous and infuriating thing.

"Is the bell on her list?" he said, understanding dawning on him.

"Mmm-hmm." She rocked back on her heels.

"I see." He nodded solemnly. He already knew the answer to his next question but asked anyway. "Do you get to check it off?"

"*Yes!*"

"Holy shit." He drew back and twisted his pinkie in his smarting ear. "You don't need to scream. I'm standing right in front of you."

"Sorry." She ran her hand up and down his arm with a sheepish smile.

He was wearing a T-shirt. Which had short sleeves. Thus— this was very important—his arms were *bare*. Her warm hand was caressing his bare skin. *Fuck*. Try as he might, he couldn't stop the goose bumps from spreading across his arms.

A deep furrow appeared between her brows, and the movement of her hand slowed and softened . . . but didn't stop. She looked down at his arm and tilted her head to the side. "Are you—"

And he tackled her. He folded himself in half, grabbed her by the waist, and lifted her onto his shoulder. Yeah, he did that.

A sound between a shriek and a laugh escaped from her. "Jack Park. What do you think you're doing?"

Think fast, genius.

In hindsight, if he'd let her finish her sentence, she probably would've said *cold* rather than *turned on*. Then he could've avoided any awkwardness with a generic, *Someone walked over my grave.* But tackling her worked, too . . .

"You need to be stopped," he said, carrying her to the cash register. It was true. Someone unused to the ball of energy known as Lizzy Chung with a list might get knocked down like a rack of bowling pins. "Shannon doesn't know what she's getting into. You're going to walk all over the poor woman until everything on her list is checked off."

"I would never." She clutched her figurative pearls.

He wasn't buying it. "Lizzy."

"Fine." He couldn't see her face but heard the pout in her voice. "I won't walk all over her."

"Do you promise?" This was an impromptu intervention, but it was important that he saw it through. For both Shannon's and Lizzy's sake. But he wasn't going to last much longer, carrying her like this.

Not that he ever thought tackling his best friend and throwing her over his shoulder was a good idea, but now the feel of her breasts against his back impressed upon him how *bad* the idea was. He needed to put some distance between his back and her breasts in the next eight seconds because his body's response to the current situation would be much more mortifying than goose bumps.

"Yes, I promise." She kicked her feet. "Now put me down."

He promptly complied and planted her in front of a gaping Arthur. "She's ready to pay for that."

Lizzy gave Jack a narrow-eyed glare, then smiled prettily at the store owner, handing him the bell. "Yes, please ring me up."

Was the kid actually blushing? Jack's annoyance quickly doused the last remnants of his arousal. "How did you get here?"

"I walked," she said without looking at him.

"Good. I'll give you a lift back."

"No, thank you. I'd rather walk." She handed Arthur her credit card.

"Fine." He shrugged. "I'll meet you at the bookstore, then."

She finally faced him. "Why?"

"To make sure you keep your promise," he said, deliberately baiting her. After the brief bout of awkwardness—all on his part—he was eager to resume their easy banter.

"You know Shannon might not even want your *protection*." She rolled her eyes before stepping aside to let Jack pay for his propane.

"You're just annoyed because I'm right. You've already made it your mission to get through her checklist while you're here, and you're going to hound her till you're done."

"Even so, she seems like a strong, independent woman who can take care of herself." Her expression turned wily. "Maybe you need to go undercover."

"Undercover?" He accepted the propane tanks from Arthur and nodded his thanks.

"Yeah. You should volunteer to help fix up Sparrow." Lizzy fiddled with the mini screwdriver set on the counter. "That way you could keep an eye on me without her suspecting that you're providing her with unsolicited protection."

"So you need my help with the bookstore?" He grinned at her transparent ploy.

"Who said I needed help?" She scoffed. "You're the one who wants to keep an eye on me."

As they walked out the store with their heads close together, Ol' Arthur called out, "Thank you. Come again."

"I'll be happy to lend a hand if you ask nicely," Jack pressed for the fun of it, even though he'd already decided to help out. For the sake of Option Two, of course. Lizzy would probably drive him up the wall with unreasonable demands in her quest to complete the to-do list. As an added bonus, the extra work should keep him busy enough to distract him from obsessing over the results of his job interview.

"You accused me of being a list bully. I don't want to ask

nicely." She followed him to his car, forgetting that she'd refused his offer to give her a ride.

"Hey, I wasn't calling you a bully. I was just reminding you that you could be a little overbearing when it comes to completing tasks and checking little boxes off."

"Not helping."

"Okay. I'm sorry."

"If you're sorry, you should help out at the bookstore."

"You're not even really mad, are you?" He shut the trunk after putting the propane tanks away.

She grinned as she slipped into the passenger seat. "I might be. You never know."

"Fine," he said ponderously as he got in the car. A quick glance at the rearview mirror confirmed that he was doing a piss-poor job of looking like someone who'd gotten suckered into a raw deal. He gave up and returned her smile. "I'll go undercover."

CHAPTER SEVEN

I brought reinforcements," Lizzy announced as she stepped into the bookstore with Jack in tow.

She glanced over her shoulder but whipped back around when he arched an eyebrow at her. Once the shock—or the thrill might be more accurate—of being thrown over his shoulder had worn off, she had trouble looking him in the eye.

She couldn't believe she'd pawed at his arm like that, but the mesmerizing juxtaposition of his smooth skin and hard muscles had made it impossible to stop touching him. Things had really gotten out of hand when her boobs were molded to his broad back and his aforementioned muscular arm was pressed against the backs of her thighs. Was she so hard up that some playful rough-housing between friends was enough to light a fire in her panties?

Instead of putting as much distance between them as possible while she got her libido in check, Lizzy had finagled Jack into helping her with her bookstore project. What was she thinking? She wasn't. Overthinking about what had happened would unnecessarily weird her out. She was right not to make a big deal out of her body's reaction to him. It had slipped her mind for a second that she only *objectively* thought he was gorgeous. She wasn't *attracted* to him or anything. It was a fluke. Nothing more.

"I thought you went to buy a bell for the door," Shannon said, coming around the cash register.

"I did." Lizzy raised the bell as evidence. "But we need someone to install it."

"I guess that's where I come in," Jack said, stepping forward with his hand outstretched. "Hi. I'm Jack."

"Lovely to meet you." Shannon's voice dipped shyly as she tucked her hand into his. "I'm Shannon."

"Anyway," Lizzy said louder than technically necessary and shoved the shopkeeper's bell at Jack, forcing him to release Shannon's hand. "In case you're worried, I didn't snatch a stranger off the street. Jack and I've been friends since we were nine, and his family runs the renowned Weldon Brewery."

"Weldon Brewery? I've heard such great things about it." Shannon kept her warm smile directed at Jack.

"You should come by sometime," he suggested right away in that kind, unaffected way he had.

Oh, look. They were hitting it off. How nice.

"The bell is made of real solid brass," Lizzy blurted. She grabbed the bell back from Jack and shook it in the air. "It makes such a pretty sound."

"That is pretty." Shannon finally turned to Lizzy. "I'm going to smile every time I hear it ring."

"I could install it for you now." Jack retrieved the bell and studied it for a minute. "Do you have an electric drill?"

"No, I'm afraid not." Shannon scrunched her lips to one side. "I might have some screwdrivers at home, though."

"Don't worry about it. I'll just go grab my toolbox." Jack placed the bell by the cash register and headed for the door.

"Hey, are you sure you have time to do this now?" Lizzy followed him, worrying on her lower lip. He was right. She was a list bully. "You must have work to do at the brewery."

"It won't take me long." He leaned close and said in her ear, "And you're dying to check it off the list."

A shiver ran down her spine. She wasn't sure if it was his hot breath against her sensitive skin or the anticipation of checking the bell off the list. "Well, if you're sure."

"Be back in ten." He grinned and tapped her on the nose, and she . . . blushed. Why was she blushing?

She watched him walk away, then continued to stare at the door after it shut behind him. If she didn't know better, she would think she was counting the seconds until he returned.

"Oh, I printed out that to-do list for you," Shannon said, startling Lizzy out of her stupor.

"That's great." Lizzy walked back over to her. "Thank you."

Shannon reached behind the counter and handed her the list. It was three pages long. With a happy sigh, Lizzy hugged it to her chest.

"Do you sell journals?" she asked, struck by inspiration. She needed to organize the hell out of this list.

"We sure do." Her friend pointed to a floating shelf on the wall behind the cash register. It held a tightly packed row of what she assumed were journals.

"Um . . . can I go behind the register to browse through them?"

"Absolutely," Shannon said with a wry smile.

Lizzy pulled out this journal and that, pleasantly surprised at how cute and unique they all were. It was a shame they weren't displayed more prominently.

"By the way," Shannon said after a few minutes, "look about halfway down page two of the list."

"Find a new place for the journals," Lizzy read out loud. "That's a very good idea because these are too adorable to keep hidden back here."

"I wanted you to know that I wasn't totally incompetent. Just overwhelmed."

"We'll have this all figured out soon." She folded Shannon into a tight hug, then stepped back. If she was serious about helping her friend, it was time to get down to business. "I'll take that llama journal and a pack of colored pens. I need them to reorganize the list and color coordinate the tasks based on how important they are and how fast we could get them done. Prioritization and maximum efficiency are key to getting shit done. I swear to you we'll complete this to-do list before I leave for LA."

"I'm so excited." Shannon's smile held a hint of a grimace. "Maybe a little intimidated, but mostly excited."

"Who's intimidated?" Jack walked in at that moment, carrying a professional-looking toolbox and a short stepladder.

"No one is intimidated," Lizzy said quickly, shooting Shannon an apologetic look. She couldn't have Jack thinking he was right about her being a list bully. Besides, she hadn't walked all over her friend. She'd merely suggested some color coordination and prioritizing. "It's just that we have a three-page to-do list to go through, and it's a little intimidating."

"Oh, crap. Elliot has a half day today." Shannon looked up from her watch. "I need to go pick him up. Do you mind watching the store for fifteen minutes?"

"Not at all. Don't worry about a thing." As soon as the words left her mouth, Lizzy realized that she had no idea how to use the cash register. *Shit.* Fortunately—or unfortunately—she hadn't seen many paying customers at the store when she'd visited.

"Thank you so much." After grabbing her purse from behind the counter, Shannon rushed out the door.

Lizzy and Jack suddenly found themselves alone, and an awkward silence descended between them. They never had awkward silences. She frowned, and he cleared his throat. What the hell?

"I guess I'll get started on the bell," he said, scratching the back of his head.

"Yes. Of course." She nodded repeatedly like a bobblehead. She made herself stop and planted her hands on her hips. *Hmm.* She shifted her weight from one foot to the other, trying to settle into the position, but it didn't feel right. So she crossed her arms instead. Then she dropped them to her sides. God, she had no idea what to do with her hands. Before she could start swinging them around in the air, she blurted, "Do you want me to hold the ladder for you?"

"It only has three steps." Jack's eyebrows burrowed down in confusion.

"Well, it could still wobble," she insisted, fighting an embarrassed blush. Why was she acting so weird?

"That's okay," he said with a crooked smile. "I'll be fine."

He took out his electric drill, then propped open the door with his toolbox. Then he opened up the annoyingly sturdy ladder and climbed to the top step. With two screws held between his lips, he drilled in the first screw.

"That can't be sanitary. I'll hold the screws for you." She walked up to the ladder and held out her hand.

Without answering, he drilled in the second screw, then the third in quick succession. He climbed down the ladder with a smug smirk. "No need."

"Show-off," she croaked.

The air in the bookstore turned stifling, and Lizzy tugged at her blouse, which suddenly felt a size too small. Something about Jack's competence with tools made her . . . hot. The movements of his hands were so sure and confident. She blew out a slow breath, resisting the urge to fan her face with the to-do list.

Her appreciation for his skills was blown way out of proportion. All he did was hang up a shopkeeper's bell, not build a bookshelf from scratch. But apparently, three screws were all it took to make her warm and achy. There was a dirty joke in there somewhere, but she was too flustered to appreciate the humor.

Now he was bending over to retrieve his toolbox from the doorway. His jeans clung to his perfectly sculpted ass, and his T-shirt rode up for a scintillating peek at his lower back. Oh, my God. She wanted to jump him. Jack. Her oldest and dearest friend. Something was very wrong with her. It had to be some hitherto undiscovered handyman fetish. It wasn't Jack she was attracted to. It was him as a handyman. This was good. Yes. Because Jack wasn't really a handyman. She buried her nose in the list just as he straightened up and turned to her.

"What's next on the list?" he asked.

"I'm not sure yet, but you should definitely put away your toolbox and ladder." *Please make Jack the Handyman go away.* "I don't think we'll be needing those."

"I'll keep them in that corner just in case."

"Whatever," she said with a nonchalance she didn't feel. But it should be okay as long as they weren't in his vicinity.

Lizzy could never see Jack with a tool in his hand again. Their friendship depended on it.

~~~

"By the way, where were you this morning?" Jack asked as he stacked a pile of nonfiction books into a box.

Based on some sort of internal algorithm, Lizzy decided the most productive and efficient task after installing the shopkeeper's bell was lining up the massive bookshelves, currently occupying the center of the store, against the walls. The end goal was to open up the space to make it more inviting for customers to browse. They decided to start with emptying the nonfiction books from the shelves.

"Oh, my gosh. Our jog. I'm so sorry." She spun around, finally meeting his eyes.

Relief rolled through him. He thought she was acting strangely around him because she'd noticed the goose bumps on his arms earlier in the hardware store. He must've imagined it. Thank God for that. This getting-over-her business was hard enough without Lizzy figuring out how he felt about her.

"I called my mom to tell her about my leave from work and—"

"She freaked," he finished her sentence with a soft grimace. His relief was replaced with a spurt of frustration. Mrs. Chung wasn't a bad person per se, but she had always been way too hard on Lizzy.

"It could've been worse." Her careless shrug made his heart ache. She wanted her mother's approval more than she let on. "But afterward, I got carried away with a bottle of Shiraz Shannon left in the apartment as a welcome gift."

"How carried away?"

"I finished the bottle," she said, tucking her chin in.

"Were you hungover?" He dipped his head to catch her expression.

"Yeah, but some cup ramen with Tapatío took care of it." She patted her stomach with a sheepish smile.

"Attagirl." Sometimes she was so adorable, he couldn't stand it.

Without thinking, he reached out and ran his thumb down her cheek, and her lips parted on a sharp indrawn breath. His heart hustled into a sprint as his brain came to a sluggish halt. Her skin couldn't really be that soft. As her wide eyes held him captive, his hand moved of its own accord and cupped her face. She immediately leaned into his touch as though it was the most natural thing to do. It really was. Soft. Her skin.

Her expression reflected the wonder and bewilderment he felt, but neither of them pulled away. The air between them sizzled and sparked, and their breathing quickened. An invisible rope of tension tightened around them and drew them closer together . . . and closer yet. The warmth of her breath fluttered against his lips, and a tremor racked through him.

The cheery tinkle of the recently installed brass bell rang out like a clap of thunder, and they jumped apart as though struck by lightning despite being hidden behind the bookshelves. Before more storm metaphors could cloud his mind, Jack bent to retrieve the pile of books that had just tumbled out of Lizzy's limp fingers.

"Sorry I took so long," Shannon said as the door closed behind her with another ring-a-ling. "I had to drop Elliot off at his friend's house for a playdate. He has a busier social calendar than I do. By far."

"No worries," Lizzy called out before kneeling down beside Jack.

While surreptitiously studying her downturned face, he reached for a book and ended up grabbing her hand. He practically threw it back at her as heat shot up his arm. "Sorry. I didn't mean to . . . I wasn't . . ."

A flush crept up her neck and stained her cheeks red. "Stop apologizing. It's not a big deal."

"Sorry," he croaked, and immediately wanted to smack his head.

Before he could apologize again for apologizing, he shot to his feet and slid more nonfictions off the shelf. When she said it wasn't a big deal, was she referring to him accidentally grabbing her hand or to whatever the hell happened before that? And what exactly happened? He would've kissed her if the bell hadn't rung. Holy shit. He would've kissed her. Jack inhaled deeply through his nose and exhaled a slow, furtive breath through his mouth. But he didn't actually kiss her, so arguably, nothing had happened. They were literally saved by the bell. Regret and relief warred inside him and tied his stomach into intricate sailing knots.

He'd kept his real feelings for her a secret for so long that the thought of being caught red-handed with hearts in his eyes made him feel a little naked and a lot vulnerable. Had she figured out he'd been hopelessly in love with her for two decades? Then a horrifying thought occurred to him. What if she was grossed out? He could almost hear her, *You're like a brother to me, and the thought of you thinking of me that way makes me feel—how do I put this delicately?—pukey.*

He might've dumped the next stack of books a bit forcefully into the box. Her startled eyes shot to him, then quickly skittered away. He made some apologetic noise. Had he blown it? Goddamn it. He would've had his feelings under control by the time she left for Los Angeles. He didn't want to lose her. Having some of her was better than not having her at all.

"Do you guys need help back there?" Shannon asked from one end of the aisle.

"No, thanks," Lizzy said with a forced smile—her eyes didn't quite crinkle enough. "We've got it. Go do your stuff."

"Thank you so much, guys. I hope you know how much this means to me." Shannon choked up and fanned her hands in front of her eyes. "Okay. I'm going to the back room before I start blubbering in earnest. Thank you again."

She stumbled away before he could say, *You're welcome.* He

turned in time to catch a genuine smile on Lizzy's face. "You're doing a good thing."

"You know as well as I do that it's for purely selfish reasons," she said, closing the top of a full box.

"Yes, you're diabolical," he agreed dryly.

She laughed as though she was delighted to have her sinister ways acknowledged. Chuckling under his breath, Jack hefted the finished box off the floor and carried it to the back corner of the store. Their shared laughter eased some of the tension that lingered between them.

When he came back, Lizzy stood with her hands on her hips, biting her poor bottom lip. The hint of a furrow between her eyebrows meant her mind was whirring. His heart seized up again. Was she brooding over their near kiss?

"With both of us working, do you think we could finish this task by tonight?" she asked.

He nearly sagged with relief. She was just obsessing over the to-do list. *That* he knew how to deal with. "Sorry to burst your bubble, but you don't get to boss me around all night long. That wasn't part of this undercover gig."

"Whaaat?" A splash of pink streaked her cheeks and the bridge of her nose. "Who said anything about all night long? I wasn't thinking anything like . . . that."

"I just meant that I have to go into work around five." Did he embarrass her by calling her bossy? Maybe she was still peeved about him accusing her of walking all over Shannon. "You know, because of my real job?"

"Oh." She turned a shade pinker. "Right. The brewery. I can't believe I forgot about that. I'm an asshole. Sorry."

"Hey, it's no big deal." He tugged on his earlobe. He felt bad for making her feel bad. "You're just so caught up on finishing the list that you've developed tunnel vision. Maybe you should slow down a little. This is your vacation after all."

"You know what? You're right." Even as she agreed with him, she returned her attention to boxing up the books. He followed her unspoken suggestion—*work while you talk*—with a wry smile. "I should enjoy the process more. I mean, it's a dream come true to help Shannon with her bookstore. I shouldn't make this all about ticking off the boxes."

"Now that you mention it, wasn't becoming a bookstore owner your dream once?" He knelt to close up another full box.

"Yes, it was," she whispered with a faraway look in her eyes. "I've always felt so at home in bookstores, especially the small, cozy ones."

"When you used to come to stay with us over the summer, you made all of us play bookstore with you." He smiled fondly at the memory.

"Oh, my gosh. I did, didn't I?" She covered her cheeks with her hands, giving an embarrassed shake of her head. "Even Alex used to join us because of my genuine enthusiasm."

"You mean because of your relentless insistence," he corrected her rose-colored recollection. "I guess you grew out of that dream when you became an attorney."

"Maybe, yeah." Something in her tone made him turn to her, but she shook her head again and grinned. "And you wanted to be an astronaut. You were a math whiz even back then."

It was his turn to feel a shade melancholy. "I guess I kind of veered off course when I became Weldon Brewery's bookkeeper."

"Bookkeeper? Is this some kind of false modesty?" Indignation tinged his best friend's voice. "You're the business mind behind the brewery. I know how hard you worked to help grow

Weldon Brewery into what it is today. Your family is proud of you. And so am I."

Is that what she really thought of him? Could she possibly see him as her equal in their respective careers? Even if he ended up staying in Weldon, maybe he could still make something out of himself—be worthy of her. Impatience slashed through him. His life goals weren't about being good enough for Lizzy.

Talk about developing tunnel vision. Having her in Weldon was making him think that his world revolved around her. Well, that had to stop. Moving to Los Angeles and starting a new career as a business analyst was about finding himself and realizing his highest potential. He had to do it for himself and no one else. And he shouldn't lose sight of the goal right in front of him, which was to get over her.

"Thank you," he said after overthinking her nice compliment.

"You're welcome, dingus." She still sounded mildly exasperated.

"Aww, now you're just trying to embarrass me." Sandwiching about ten books between his hands, he transferred them to yet another box. Then he straightened up and stretched his back. "You know what you said about enjoying the process?"

"You mean what I said about three minutes ago?"

"Yeah, smart-ass. That." He leaned against the bookshelf and crossed his arms over his chest. "Do you think you might even go as far as taking a lunch break?"

She snorted. "Let's just finish clearing this bookshelf first. I promise we'll break for lunch after that. It'll be my treat."

"Wow. I like this stop-and-smell-the-roses Lizzy."

"Whatever." She rolled her eyes. "You like the bossy-workaholic me, too."

She was right, of course. He liked every facet of her. A little too much for his own good.

CHAPTER EIGHT

*T*oo. Many. Muscles.

Lizzy didn't have a handyman fetish. She had a Jack fetish. There. She'd said it. Admitting the problem was half the solution.

He held one end of the bookshelf while Shannon and her son held the other. Lizzy was yelling out directions while trying not to get distracted by the rippling muscles in Jack's arms, chest, and back. *Gah.*

"A little to the right," she hollered. When three annoyed heads turned to her, she quickly clarified, "Okay. Shannon and Elliot are going to take a step forward, and Jack's going to take a step back. Ready?"

Once they mumbled, grumbled, and nodded their assent, she said, "Go!"

As the three moved to Lizzy's right, Elliot stumbled a little. For a heart-shrinking second, the shelf seemed to lean too far forward, but Jack stabilized it with a grunt. An oh-so-sexy grunt.

"Perfect," she murmured dreamily before she snapped herself out of it. "Now move up against the wall just like that."

With a collective sigh of relief, they lowered the last book-shelf to the ground. Jack and Shannon shook out their arms and pounded on their backs. Even Elliot made a show of stretching his back, mimicking the grimaces on the grown-ups' faces.

~~~

Shannon had closed the shop for a couple of days so they could relocate the bookshelves. After working their asses off all day, the tall bookshelves were lined up against the walls. Even so, Lizzy had to reassure herself they were *not* half a day behind schedule, and taking a lunch break yesterday had *not* been a waste of precious time. *Geez*. She was so uptight sometimes. In her defense, she had less than three weeks to work through a three-page to-do list.

It wasn't anxiety that plagued her, though. In fact, she hadn't struggled with anxiety since her call with her mom. The realization dawned on her like sunlight breaking through the clouds. Living with constant anxiety had become the norm for her, but . . . it didn't have to be. Look at her now. The only thing driving her to finish the to-do list was excitement. Well, excitement and impatience—she couldn't wait to see Sparrow transformed—but she had promised herself and Jack that she would enjoy the process.

A calm she hadn't felt in a long time—a feeling she hardly recognized—seeped into her and filled her. She was going to relax into the project ahead of her and savor every moment of it, because relaxing didn't make her feel anxious anymore. Had her short time in Weldon already changed her? Or had this been her all along—forgotten in the rat race that was her life in Los Angeles?

The four of them stepped back and took a moment to ad-mire the fruits of their labor. The center of the store was now bright, open, and filled with promise.

"This looks amazing," Shannon said, turning in a full circle.

"Yeah," her son agreed. "Who knew this place was so big?"

To prove his point, Elliot ran laps around the shop with his arms outstretched, letting his fingertips skim across the bookshelves they'd just relocated.

Lizzy walked over to the cash register and picked up the clipboard with the to-do list on it. Her heart rate kicked up a beat as she prepared to check off their latest accomplishment. Then she paused. "Shannon, do you want to check this off the list?"

"No, you go ahead." Her friend smiled with a knowing look in her eyes. "I know you're dying to do it."

"Here." Jack walked over to Lizzy, wearing a teasing grin. "Let me check it off."

"Stay back." She brandished her number 2 pencil like a weapon. It was recently sharpened. "I'm not afraid to use this."

He grabbed Elliot, who was running past him, and held him out like a shield. "Tell the scary lady she can do whatever she wants."

The boy looked between Lizzy and Jack for a moment with quiet curiosity. "You guys are weird."

Jack burst out laughing and released his hostage. Lizzy stuck her tongue out at him and checked the box off with a flowery twist of her wrist.

"There." She hugged the clipboard to her chest for a second.

"Mom," Elliot said, "you promised to help me with the science fair project."

"That's right." Shannon turned to Lizzy with an apologetic grimace. "I did promise."

"Go on," Lizzy said, shooing them away with her hands. "Jack and I'll put the books back."

"Thank you. I swear these school projects are more work for the parents than the kids." She hugged her son to her side and headed toward the back room. "Come on, kiddo. Let's go do some homework."

Lizzy watched them go with a smile. Jack draped a friendly arm around her shoulders and tugged her to his side. She returned his one-armed hug as casually as she could even though she wanted to melt against him.

"What do you say we take a lunch break?" he said.

"Lunch?" It was past three and she was starving, but their lunch break yesterday had taken an hour and a half out of their day. She wished there was a more efficient way to relax and savor the moment. "Sure . . ."

"You don't sound too sure," Jack said, his eyes crinkling at the corners.

Before she could answer, he stepped away from her, taking his warmth with him. She was briefly tempted to protest, but he'd already walked off. He picked up his backpack from the floor.

"Ta-da." He held up two brown paper bags with fanfare.

"What are those?"

"I packed our lunch to save us time. It's not good for you to skip meals."

"Aww, Jack." Her heart melted into a puddle, and she made grabby hands for her lunch. She was dying to see what he'd packed.

He handed her one of the paper bags, and they sat down cross-legged on the floor. She opened the bag and eagerly pulled out its contents. A peanut butter and jelly sandwich, cut into triangles. Some baby carrots. A box of apple juice. And . . . Oreos. Her eyes almost rolled back into her head. She *loved* Oreos.

"I hope I didn't get your hopes up." Jack rubbed the back of his neck. "It's just a boring sack lunch."

"Are you kidding? This is incredible." She took a giant bite out of her sandwich. "Oh, my God. How is this so good?"

"You're just hungry," he said, looking pleased nonetheless. He bit into his sandwich. "Damn. This *is* good."

"Did you use grape jelly?" She poked the straw into her juice box.

"Yeah. That's how my mom used to make them for us."

"Classic."

She chewed her second bite more slowly to enjoy the nostalgic flavors. The sticky saltiness of the peanut butter perfectly complemented the cool and tangy sweetness of the grape jelly. The soft, squishy white bread was the ideal conduit for the heavenly combination.

"Can we have this again tomorrow?" she asked.

Jack chuckled and finished off his sandwich in two more bites. A smudge of peanut butter and jelly clung to the corner of his lips. She reached across with her hand, wiped it neatly off, and stuck her finger into her mouth, licking it with a smack. Only when his eyes widened did she realize what she'd done.

Shit. What was she thinking? Well, she obviously wasn't. But they were best friends, for God's sake. What was the big deal? They'd eaten off each other's plates plenty of times. The problem was they had never eaten off each other's faces before.

Shit. Jack's shell-shocked expression didn't alter as he stared at her mouth. There was a glint in his eyes that looked a lot like . . . hunger. Desire burst into flames inside her body in response. But for him, it was probably because he was still hungry. For food.

Shit. She grabbed four baby carrots and stuffed them all into her mouth at the same time. Jack finally blinked—several times—before the hungry look disappeared to be replaced by amusement. A corner of his lips—the one she'd so nicely cleaned off for him—quirked into a lopsided grin.

She worked to chew the four pieces of carrots as they slipped around her mouth and jabbed into her cheeks. But, she was tenacious, and she at last swallowed. If it weren't for the Oreos, she would've claimed to be full and jumped back to work to avoid the awkwardness.

He watched her eat, munching on one baby carrot at a time like a sane person. She made an *eh* face—the careless shrug of facial expressions—and stuffed a whole Oreo in her mouth. That was how she always ate her Oreos—the whole thing in her mouth at once. Because who has the patience to carefully twist it apart, lick the cream off, and dip it in milk and shit? She didn't.

Lizzy still had no idea how to deal with the whole eating-off-his-face thing. She took a stealthy peek at Jack from under her lashes. He seemed completely recovered from his earlier shock.

"Back to work." She jumped to her feet and threw away the trash.

"Right." He followed suit after a stealthy peek at her of his own.

They worked side by side, pretending like nothing had happened. That was fine for the time being, but she wasn't planning on ignoring it. She needed to think through what the hell was going on with her when it came to Jack. Then she was going to do something about it, because ignoring it was not working.

~

Jack pulled up in front of the bookstore the next morning and stepped out of his car. He did some light stretches on the sidewalk as he waited for Lizzy to make her appearance. He finished his warm-ups and was about to check his watch when she trudged over from behind the building, covering a yawn.

A smile spread across his face. He liked seeing her first thing in the morning with her cheeks softly flushed and her eyes still fuzzy with sleep.

"Wasn't moving all those bookshelves yesterday enough exercise?" she grumbled. "We should take today off."

"You mostly exercised your vocal cords, telling the rest of us what to do." That *was* rather annoying, but truth be told, it did very little to further the progress of Option Two. Being bossy was a part of Lizzy—a part of her overall wonderfulness. "Besides, it's not good to spend all day inside the bookstore. We need some fresh air and sunlight."

"I have an idea." She brightened up. "We could have breakfast somewhere with an outdoor terrace."

"I'll make you a deal. We'll do our morning run, then have breakfast on a terrace."

"Talk about bossy." She crossed her arms over her chest. "Anyway, why are we meeting here today? Are we going to jog around downtown?"

"Nope. That's not a bad idea for next time, though." He opened the passenger door and motioned for her to get in. "I think you should enjoy all that Weldon has to offer while you're here."

"So we're going to drive somewhere just to go running?"

He got into the car and started the engine. "Save your judgment until you've experienced it."

"Care to share where we're going?" she asked as she buckled in.

"Not particularly."

Cheerfully ignoring her indignant huff, he drove them to his favorite hiking trail. Lizzy was stubbornly mute during their short drive, but he knew she wasn't sulking. She was just trying very hard not to badger him about where they were going. Even after they parked on the street and got out of the car, their final destination wasn't visible. She was ready to burst. He couldn't wait to see her reaction.

They walked through the woods for a few minutes until they came into a clearing. The sun cast its warm light across Kern River, and the sound of rushing water filled the quiet morning. He filled his lungs with the fresh, crisp air and felt his worries melt away.

"It's beautiful," she whispered, her face filled with wonder.

"Not feeling so judgy anymore, are you?" He smirked, feeling smug for putting that expression on her face. Well, the river was technically responsible, but he was the one who'd dragged her out here.

"Shove it," she murmured benignly, her eyes scanning the tree-lined hills hugging the water from both sides.

"You're welcome." He tugged her lightly by the arm. "Come on."

They walked in comfortable silence, listening to the river and soaking in their surroundings. None of the awkwardness and tension of the last few days plagued them. It almost felt as though things were back to normal. Where his feelings for her were buried so deep inside him that even he forgot sometimes.

But that was just wishful thinking. No matter how beautiful this morning was and how tranquil he felt, things were far from normal. His feelings rippled so close to the surface that she must've seen glimpses of them. How much he longed for her. How much he desired her. He couldn't forget the tense, heated moments between them. He'd turned them over in his mind a hundred times, and he was almost certain they weren't imagined.

Especially the peanut butter and jelly incident. That definitely happened. He could still feel the pressure of her finger swiping against his lips and hear the soft pop her mouth made when she pulled her finger out of it.

His breathing quickened. He stole a glance at Lizzy and hoped she would think it was from the exertion of the hike. She didn't seem to notice, though. She was busy keeping up with him—huffing and puffing. Lost in his thoughts, he'd picked up his pace without noticing. He immediately slowed down and turned to her.

"Do you want to take a water break?" he asked casually as though his heart weren't bruising his ribs. *Option Two. Option Two.* Goddamn it, Jack. *Option Two.*

She stopped walking and held up a finger. After a moment, she wheezed, "Yes."

He swung his backpack forward and handed her the extra water bottle he'd packed for her. He drank from his own bottle, then stowed it away.

"Thank you." She handed him her bottle. "You prepared for everything. You're like the room mom."

"Thanks?" Right. The room mom. So sexy. "We should head back if we're going to get breakfast."

"Let's hike a bit longer," she said to his surprise. "We can grab some muffins or something for breakfast."

"I'm impressed. Exercise grows on you, doesn't it?" If Lizzy could come to appreciate exercise, then anything seemed possible. Even Option Two.

"I need to burn off some excess energy," she mumbled, glancing away.

"What was that?" He must've misheard her, but his imagination still wanted to run wild with what she could've meant.

"Never mind. Let's keep going." She marched ahead and immediately stumbled.

"Whoa. Are you okay?" He caught her around the waist before she toppled sideways.

"Yeah—" She stopped short and blinked.

Their faces—and their lips—were mere inches from each other's, and their bodies were pressed together in what could only be called an intimate embrace. He felt the puffs of her quick breaths tickling his chin and the rise and fall of her breasts against his chest. She felt so fucking good in his arms. His fingers dug into her waist. The soft give of her skin nearly undid him. He should let go and step back. But he couldn't.

Any second now, she was going to bring up her hands and push him away. Then they would laugh it off.

Any second now.

The seconds ticked by, and she didn't push him away. And he didn't let her go. They just stood . . . pressed tightly against each other. She stared into his eyes, and he stared into hers. He watched in fascination as her eyelashes fluttered every few seconds. As long as his gaze didn't stray from her eyes, he would be fine. Maybe they could stay like this forever—blood boiling, nerves tingling.

His gaze dipped to her mouth.

Fuck.

He needed to taste her. She licked her lips as though the same hunger gripped her. He might have whimpered. Now staying still was torture. What harm could one small kiss do? *Oh, I don't know. Ruin twenty years of friendship, maybe?* But he loved her. He needed her. Was he trying to convince himself to kiss her or let her go? He could lose his best friend. Or he could gain someone who meant infinitely more. *What about Option Two?* Fuck Option Two.

His breaths came in short huffs. He was panting . . . really loudly. Why was he doing that? Lizzy's eyebrows drew together over the bridge of her nose. Then he heard a soft *ruff* followed by more panting. Okay. He might be panting—he *was* struggling to catch his breath—but he definitely did not bark.

Slowly, they turned their heads and looked down. A jolly golden retriever sat at their feet—panting with its big pink tongue drooping.

"Hello, sweetheart." Jack reached down and scratched behind the dog's ear. "Where did you come from?"

"It . . . no . . ." Lizzy tilted her head and inspected the golden retriever before she continued. "*She* looks thirsty."

He knelt in front of the dog and poured some water into his palm, cupping it the best he could. She lapped it up happily, tickling his hand. He laughed when she moved on to lick his face.

"What a good dog," Lizzy cooed, rubbing her back. Then she checked the tag on her collar. "Where's your owner, Zoe?"

"Is there a phone number on there?" He reached for his phone.

"I can hardly make it out." She scrunched her lips to the side, squinting at the tag.

"Zoe!" a voice called out from the distance.

The dog barked once and bounded off toward the sound. Jack and Lizzy ran after her. They found her with an elderly gentleman, who was securing a leash around her neck.

"We've talked about this, Zoe," he was saying. "You need to reach deep down for your self-control."

"Oh, good. You must be her owner," Lizzy said as they walked up to them. "We thought she was lost."

"Not lost. Just sidetracked." Zoe's owner smiled ruefully. "She spotted a squirrel before I leashed her, and she got away from me. But she knows this trail well and never wanders far."

"Well, I'm glad you found each other." Jack reached down to pat the sweet dog's head. "Have a nice hike."

"Thank you. Come on, girl." The old man led the dog down the path. "Remember. You control you. Not the squirrels."

They watched the pair walk away, then it was just the two of them again.

"Should we—"

"It's getting—"

They both broke off and paused awkwardly.

"You go—"

"You can—"

They stopped again. This time, Jack kept his mouth firmly shut until Lizzy spoke.

"It's getting late," she said briskly. "We should get back."

"Sure." He tried to match her business-as-usual tone. "I'll drop you off, then bring you a muffin when I get back to Sparrow."

"Awesome. I'll take a chocolate muffin." She headed back down the hiking trail, watching her step this time.

"You mean the chocolate cupcake without the frosting?" he teased as he followed her.

"Yup, the breakfast of champions." She glanced over her shoulder with a mischievous smile.

For a second—just for a split second, really—he wished she would trip again.

CHAPTER NINE

F or the love of God," Lizzy muttered, leaning back against a bookshelf.

She'd considered tripping again on their hike back. It was only for a split second, but the damage was done. *Oh, where art thou, self-respect?* She buried her face in her hands. This wasn't like her. She usually knew her own mind, but she didn't recognize the confused mess she'd become.

Jack was her best friend. For twenty years, he'd been her confidant, her cheerleader, and her sounding board. Her anchor. He was still all those things to her, but now there was something else. Her heart skipped a beat every time she saw him, and her pulse raced whenever he was near her. She caught herself staring at him countless times like he was a magnet for her eyeballs.

She dropped her hands from her face and sighed. It was attraction, pure and simple. Well, it was complicated and potent, but it was attraction nonetheless. For the first time, she was seeing Jack as a man, and it was freaking the hell out of her.

And said man walked into the bookstore looking fine as hell. *Thump, thump, thump.* There went her ridiculous heart. She wished she had a minute to compose herself, but the store was wide open without the tall bookshelves to hide behind.

"Hey. I brought one for Shannon, too." Jack held up a white paper bag with the name *Comfort Zone* printed in pretty, purple cursive. "Is she in the back?"

"No. She went to watch Elliot's school play." Which meant they were alone. *Thump, thump, thump.* "We'll save her one."

"Or we can eat that one, too, and get rid of the evidence." He wiggled his eyebrows.

"I like the way you think." She grinned, reassured by the reminder that he was still a dork. "Do you want some tea?"

"I'd kill for some coffee."

"No need to get homicidal about it." She was intent on keeping the dorkiness going. It was safer grounds than attraction. "I'll get you a cup."

They sat down at their usual corner and munched on their muffins. She had her clipboard on her lap so she would have something other than Jack to stare at while they ate.

"What's the game plan for today?" he asked, leaning over to look at the list.

"Umm . . ." She failed miserably at not sniffing him. He smelled so clean and woodsy. "Well, we need to finish putting away all the books. Then I want to go through the furniture Shannon has in the back room. See if we can bring some out to the front."

"I'm at your disposal all day, by the way." He took a sip of his coffee. "Today's my off day."

She glanced up from the list. "Your off day? Don't you have errands to run and stuff?"

"I'm willing to take one for the team and put off laundry for a few more days."

"I have no right to monopolize your time like this." She'd been selfish to drag him into her project. He had a life in Weldon—a life she had no place in except for this brief window of stolen time. He probably had things to do. People to see. Dates to go on. She nearly creamed her half-eaten muffin in her fist.

"Maybe you don't," he said quietly, "but I have every right to spend my time any way I want. And being with you . . . I mean, helping you help Shannon . . . is what I want."

"Oh." She wanted to tackle hug him for wanting to spend time with her rather than date random women. But since that would seem somewhat odd, she smiled into her muffin as she took a bite. "This muffin is phenomenal."

"Mm-hmm." He washed down his last morsel with his coffee. "Aubrey is an amazing baker."

"Tara's best friend, right?" She studied her muffin from different angles as though she could figure out its secret ingredient just by looking at it. "So Aubrey is magic with baked goods, and Tara is an incredible brewer. They must give each other freebies all the time. How awesome is that?"

"We're pretty awesome, too. I can give you free accounting advice or a refresher on calculus, and you can give me free legal advice."

"Thrilling." Lizzy rolled her eyes. "How can you even compare free beer and dessert to those things?"

"You're right." Jack chuckled. "Tara and Aubrey have it made."

As they worked side by side, reshelving the books, Lizzy couldn't deny how lucky she was to have a best friend like Jack. Her attraction to him had to be a fleeting reaction, which probably had a lot to do with the fact that she hadn't gotten laid in over six months. She would be over it soon enough—she had to be. She couldn't risk their friendship over some primal urges.

"Huh." Jack's bemusement snapped her out of her thoughts.

"What?"

He was staring down at a book in his hand as though he couldn't figure out what exactly he was looking at. She leaned over and recognized the iconic historical romance cover right away. She snatched the book out of his hand.

"Oh, my God," she whispered reverently. "I can't believe Shannon has a copy of this. It's so rare."

"I see," he said, sounding dubious. He obviously did not see.

"What? What are you thinking?"

"Nothing." He scratched the side of his nose. "It just seems a bit unrealistic."

"Two people who are passionate about each other is unrealistic?" She arched an eyebrow in challenge.

"No, it's not that." He gently retrieved the book from her and pointed down to the couple. "Look. Standing like that can't be very comfortable. He's holding her leg up to his armpit and has her bent over backward. That takes a whole lot of arm and core strength. And how is she even that flexible?"

"I am," she said mutinously, refusing to allow him to diss the gorgeous cover.

He slowly raised his head and met her eyes. "You are what?"

"Bendy. Super bendy."

His face went slack, and his eyes glazed over. Did he not believe her?

"Here." She grabbed the book out of his hand once more and put it face forward on the shelf. "We can totally pose like them."

"No, we can't," he said a bit huskily.

"Why not?" She planted her hands on her hips. "I've seen you lift these bookshelves without breaking a sweat. You're strong enough. And like I said, I'm flexible."

"Can you stop saying that?" he said in a strangled voice, clutching his head with both hands as though trying to keep it from exploding.

"Stop saying what?" She scrunched up her nose. He was acting weird. Wait. Was it because she said she was flexible? No . . . it couldn't be. He probably didn't want to be proven wrong.

"Never mind." He wiped a hand down his face. "You're not letting this go, are you?"

"Nope. We're going to do this, and then I'm going to say, 'I told you so.'" She could almost taste the words on her tongue. Like honey.

"Okay. Fine."

With a grim set of his lips, Jack wrapped an arm around her waist and pulled her flush against him. She gasped as shock waves of pleasure shot through her. Shit. Did she learn nothing from their hike this morning? Being in his arms meant losing her mind. She should've backed off. Why did she have to be right all the time? This was a bad idea, but it was too late for second thoughts.

Jack's big, rough hand wrapped around the inside of her bare knee—it was shorts weather—and tugged her leg up past his waist. He'd never touched her this way before. God, she loved it. She wanted to purr and rub herself against him. Moisture gathered between her legs, and her fingers dug into his taut arms. He paused to glare at her, a muscle jumping in his jaw, and her heart thudded a frantic beat. Then he tightened his grip on her knee and tilted her back into a deep dip.

Their harsh breathing filled the quiet of the store. Fire snapped in his eyes as they roamed her face and settled on her lips. She had never wanted anything as much as she wanted to kiss him right then—to wrap her arms around his neck and tug his head down. But she was so precariously balanced on one leg that she was afraid to move an inch.

"Goddamn it, Jack. Kiss me."

Her command jerked his gaze back up to her eyes, and he

blinked rapidly several times. After a long moment, he pressed his forehead against hers and took a ragged breath. Then he gently lifted her up to standing and released her leg. Her heart withered and drooped inside her. He didn't want to kiss her. She was too bereft with disappointment to even feel embarrassed at having thrown herself at him. She stared down at her feet, fighting hot tears.

It took her a few seconds to realize that even though he'd released her, he hadn't moved away from her. Still, she couldn't make herself look up at him. With a soft sigh, he lifted her chin with the crook of his finger and waited for her to meet his eyes. When she finally looked at him, the tenderness and yearning in his gaze took her breath away.

"Jack?"

"Shh." He placed a finger on her lips.

Lizzy stood still and silent, afraid of shattering the fragile balance of the moment. When the soft pressure of his finger left her mouth, she released a shaky sigh. They stood on the precipice of something neither of them fully understood, but it was achingly beautiful. She gazed steadily at him so he understood that she was ready to step off.

Jack brushed the pad of his thumb across her cheekbone, then smoothed it back and forth on her bottom lip. She couldn't help it. Her tongue flicked out to steal a taste of him. He sucked in a breath, and his eyes darkened. At long last, he lowered his head, and her eyelids fluttered closed.

His kiss was as light as a whisper, but the feel of his lips against hers spread through her like a drop of watercolor dissolving into clear water. It saturated her body from the top of her head to the tips of her toes. Delicious shivers ran down her spine, and heat gathered low in her stomach. She hummed in pleasure and wrapped her arms around his neck.

Digging his hand into her hair, he angled her head to the side and kissed her more fully with softly parted lips. It was so lovely that her toes curled in her shoes—but it wasn't enough. They were taking small, careful sips when she wanted nothing more than to take big, sloppy gulps. The taut lines of his body told her he was holding himself in check—as though he was afraid of what he might unleash—but she was growing impatient. She wanted more.

~

He was kissing Lizzy. And she was kissing him back. Fuck. She tasted good.

On the one hand, he'd been waiting for this moment for so long that he wanted to savor every second of it. On the other hand, he was fucking losing his mind trying to take this slow when all he wanted to do was fuck her mouth with his tongue. God, he didn't recognize himself. He had never wanted anyone like this before. It was heady and terrifying. Still, he kept his kiss sweet and gentle, and held on to his sanity for dear life.

Then she bit him. She bit his bottom lip, then licked the sting away with a flick of her tongue. An unfamiliar, almost feral growl escaped him, and he plunged his tongue into her hot, wet mouth. Holy hell. How could it feel this good? When she moaned and opened wide for him, he lost his last shred of control.

Jack grabbed her waist, pushed her against the bookshelf, and kissed her liked the starved man he was. Their teeth clacked, and their tongues tangled—rough, desperate, and oh so good. He was light-headed with lust, and he was so hard it hurt. He pulled her leg around his waist and almost passed out when she ground her hips against his erection.

She slid her hands down his chest and stomach, then reached around to grab his ass. His hips jerked forward into her softness, and he groaned deep in his throat, but his lips never left hers. He knew in the back of his mind that they needed to breathe, but that seemed so trivial compared to what they were doing.

He reached around her to pull her even tighter against him, and a bunch of books tumbled to the floor. His hand crept under her shirt, and her back felt like warm silk, but something was trying to register in his lust-fogged brain. There was something he needed to remember. Books. Something about books. Shit. They were making out like there was no tomorrow in a wide-open bookstore. Shannon or a customer could walk in on them at any moment.

"We can't do this," he panted, tearing his lips away from hers. Fuck it. He swooped down and kissed her hard—one last time—then he pulled away again.

"Why the hell not?" Lizzy—her chest heaving and face flushed pink—was all righteous indignation and sexual frustration.

"We're in a bookstore, for one thing." He frowned slightly, overcompensating for the smile that was fighting to surface. She was so adorable. And sexy as hell. But if he laughed right now, she would probably throttle him with her bare hands.

"Fine. That's one thing," she said grudgingly. "But you said that like there was more than one thing."

"Well, the other thing is . . ." He dragged his hand through his hair and blew out a rough breath. "I don't think I can handle much more."

"Wimp."

He didn't even try this time. He burst out laughing and pulled her into his arms in a rush of affection. "What am I going to do with you?"

"For one thing . . . ," she whispered into his ear.

A shiver traveled down his spine. If he held her for a second longer, he was going to kiss her again. Then he might not care that they were in a bookstore. The thought unnerved him enough to make him drop his arms and step away from her. What he had done—what he had wanted to do—began to really dawn on him. Shit.

"Jack . . ." A shadow flitted across her face as he withdrew into himself.

He wanted to chase away the darkness, but panic seeped into his bones, and he had no idea what to say to her. The reasons why he couldn't kiss her hadn't magically disappeared. He was still in love with her, and friendship might be the only way to have her in his life. From the way she'd responded to his kiss, she was attracted to him, but what would happen if they let their attraction take its natural course? It would fizzle out, and nothing would be the same between them. Hadn't he chosen Option Two precisely for those reasons?

The bell over the door tinkled brightly, and Shannon breezed into the store. "Thank you so much for holding down the fort."

Again, he was saved by the bell. He was embarrassed by how relieved he felt about the interruption, but he needed time to digest what had happened.

"No problem," Lizzy said with a tight smile on her face.

"How was the play?" he asked, picking up the books strewn across the floor. He needed to keep moving.

"It was adorable." Shannon laughed. "Elliot only had one line, but he got to scream his head off at the end. I felt a few of the parents jumping in their seats. He was so happy when I told him after the play."

"Way to go, Elliot." Lizzy smiled more easily this time and waved toward the bag from Comfort Zone. "Have you had breakfast? Jack brought us muffins."

"Wow, thanks, Jack. I'm starving." She smiled a little sheepishly. "I really should provide you guys with breakfast for everything you're doing for me."

"You're welcome, and don't worry about it," he said sincerely. "You're raising a kid and running this bookstore all by yourself. You deserve what little help we can give."

"He's right." Lizzy put her arm around Shannon and gave her a sideways hug. "Besides, I know I can get a little nutso with checking things off the to-do list, but I'm honestly having a great time. It feels amazing to work on something with my hands and see the changes come to life. It's nothing like writing and deleting things off a dull legal document all day long. This is so . . . rewarding."

"It's an odd way to spend your vacation, if you ask me, but knock yourself out, hon." Shannon hugged her back. "Though I have to agree, this work is doing you some good. You have more color in your face, and the dark circles under your eyes have all but disappeared. You looked so exhausted your first day here. I'm glad you're enjoying yourself, and the store is already looking fantastic—so much open space."

"Speaking of open space, Lizzy mentioned that you have some furniture we might be able to use out front." Jack was desperate for some busywork. It was impossible to take his mind off their kiss, especially since he could still taste her on his lips. "Can I take a look?"

"Sure," Shannon said, leading them to the back room. "But be forewarned, most of them are pretty old and worn."

A cluster of furniture sat together at one corner in the back. There were wooden chairs, small tables in different shapes and sizes, and a couple of bookshelves that came up to his chest. They were chipped and scratched with patches of paint peeling off, but they had good bones.

"Where did you get these?" he asked Shannon just as she

was taking a big bite out of her muffin. She held up a finger and chewed.

In the silence, he had to acknowledge that he and Lizzy hadn't spoken directly to each other since Shannon came back. His mind whirred. Could he still salvage their friendship? Or would everything unravel now that he'd given in and kissed her? No. It wasn't too late. Their friendship was strong enough to recover from one impulsive kiss.

He snuck a glance at Lizzy and got caught red-handed because she had been staring right at him. She arched an eyebrow and held his gaze. He looked away first.

"I inherited them from the old owner," Shannon finally said after swallowing. "Some came from the apartment upstairs, and some were in the bookstore."

"They're really great." He ran his hand over a chair with a curved back and spokes. Both women gave him dubious looks. "I'm serious. All we need to do is sand them down and stain or paint them."

"And that's easy?" Lizzy's eyebrows rose up high. "That sounds like a shitload of work."

"What she said." Shannon nodded in solidarity with her.

"If we work together, it shouldn't take us more than two days to refinish the ones you want to put out front." He rubbed his hands together, getting excited. He loved working on old furniture and seeing them turn out like new. "Let me run over to my house and grab some tools."

He thought he heard Lizzy whisper, *Please not that,* but when he glanced at her, she was busy picking out furniture with Shannon. This little project was a lifesaver. He planned to use an electric sander so they wouldn't be able to talk. He was a huge asshole.

CHAPTER TEN

Jack with tools makes Lizzy a very horny girl.

Goddamn it, he brought his tools. She couldn't think straight when Jack was in the presence of tools, which wasn't ideal since she was already dizzy with lust from their kiss. As she watched him sand a table—with his arm muscles flexing and manly veins bulging—it was all she could do not to jump him right there in the back lot of the bookstore. But she had her pride.

The bastard was acting like nothing happened between them. They were just two buddies refinishing some furniture under the warm sun. *La-di-da.* She also had a sneaking suspicion that he was using the electric sander to avoid talking to her about the kiss. She scowled at the innocent chair she was stripping and rubbed her palm-size sandpaper viciously against one of its spindles.

Lizzy belatedly noticed the blissful silence surrounding her. Jack had turned off the damn sander. A shadow fell across her chair.

"Just do the best you can on those," he said ever so kindly.

"You won't be able to get them perfectly sanded with all those curves and dips."

How could he stand there and give her helpful, practical advice? She sanded harder. She was huffing and puffing so much from the effort that she breathed in a lungful of wood dust and started coughing.

"Do you need a mask?" He knelt next to her and peered into her face. "Let me get you a mask."

How could he crouch there and be all considerate like that? She rubbed her eyes with the back of her hand and resumed sanding. He stood after a minute and came back with a disposable dust mask. She took the mask he held out without looking at him, put it on, and kept sanding. Condensation formed over the top of her lips, but it was better than breathing in wood dust.

"Are you giving me the silent treatment?" he asked after a stretch of silence.

She hadn't planned on it, but she had no interest in speaking to him at the moment. They'd kissed. It was incredible. Did it not mean anything to him?

"You're never quiet when you're mad," he said in a pained voice. "It usually kills you not to spit out what you're thinking."

If he knew her so well, then why was he doing this to her? How could he kiss her like that and try to sweep it under the rug like she was some dust bunny?

"I packed us bologna sandwiches for lunch."

Her hand stilled for a moment. The hopeful lilt in his words almost made her look up at him. She used to love bologna sandwiches. *Yum. Mystery meat.* But it wasn't enough to make her want to talk. She moved on to the next spindle. Jack sighed and walked away with heavy steps. She hardly felt guilty.

The annoying buzz of the electric sander filled the air once more, and she fumed in silence. She was freaking out about the kiss, too. They'd been best friends for two decades, and that kiss was definitely not a friend-zone thing. But was it the worst thing for them to be more than friends?

Sure, it was weird and unexpected, but it wasn't bad. At least, she didn't think so. It just hadn't happened before because they didn't see each other that way. Things were different now. Weren't they? They certainly were for her. She saw him as a man—someone she wanted. It wasn't something she could unsee. And after that kiss, she was pretty sure she didn't want to unsee it.

How would this work, though? She lived in Los Angeles, and he lived in Weldon. Did a four-hour drive make it a long-distance relationship? She had no idea. Besides, that was just logistics. They could figure that stuff out later. She only wanted him to acknowledge that something was happening between them and that it was kind of wonderful.

That was it. She was afraid to speak to him because he might not be as happy about the turn of events as she was. Why else would he pretend like everything was normal? He wanted to forget the kiss ever happened. Her lips quivered behind her mask. Was the thought of being with her so horrible? She blinked back tears.

She instinctively searched inside herself for anxiety to sprout its ugly head, but it didn't come. She was hurt and worried that he might regret their kiss—as she had every right to be—but anxiety had not taken control of her. She took a deep breath with ease.

Jack was right. There was no use torturing herself like this when they could talk it out. She got to her feet and dusted her hands. Then she wiped them on her shorts. Then she dusted off her shorts. When there was nothing else for her to dust to delay the talk, she walked over to him. The sander immediately went silent.

"You want to talk?" she said.

He pulled off his mask and smiled uncertainly at her. "Talking is definitely better than the silent treatment."

She went to sit at the bottom of the stairs that led up to her apartment. He sat down next to her. He was so close, she could feel his warmth against her skin. Awareness raised the hair on her arms, but she was also comforted by his nearness. He was still her Jack.

"Why are you pretending like nothing happened earlier?" She dived straight in and waited with her heart pounding.

He leaned forward with his elbows on his knees and looked down at his hands. "I needed time to process what happened."

"We kissed." It wasn't as simple as that, she knew. But did it have to be much more complicated?

"Yes, I realize that," he said with a wry curve of his lips.

"Do you . . . regret that it happened?" Her nails dug into the palm of her hands.

"I'm conflicted as hell, but no." He met her gaze and held it. "I don't regret it happening."

A knot unraveled in her chest and she puffed a sigh of relief. "I'm glad."

His eyes fell to his hands again, and he didn't say anything for a long moment. "Our friendship means a lot to me, Lizzy."

Her stomach sank. "It means a lot to me, too."

"We kissed, but that doesn't mean we have to do it again." One of his knees started bouncing. "It doesn't mean that anything has to change."

"What if I want us to kiss again?" She put her hand on his knee until he stilled. "And just because some things change doesn't mean that everything has to change."

"I don't want to lose you," he said with aching vulnerability.

"I don't think that's possible," Lizzy whispered. She didn't want to lose him, either. She wouldn't be able to bear it. "We're amazing as friends. Why would things be different just because we become . . . more?"

"That depends on how much *more* we become."

"Why are you being so sensible?" she said sullenly. He was right, of course. Things could get very complicated very quickly.

"Because it's you, Lizzy." His eyes were so dark, she could drown in their depths. "I can't rush headfirst into something just because I want you."

"I want you, too." She must've developed selective hearing, because that was all that stood out to her. "I don't think I can stop wanting you."

"You can't say things like that." He wrapped his hand around her neck and pressed his forehead against hers.

"Why not?" She breathed in the scent of him.

"Because I'm not strong enough to resist you."

"Really?" She hoped they were too close for him to notice that she was grinning from ear to ear. He was going to cave.

"It's not funny."

"I'm not laughing," she said with a burst of laughter. "Fine, I am, but I'm not laughing at you. I'm just so happy."

"I would do anything—*anything*—to make you happy," he said fervently.

"Then let's do this. Let's kiss again." She tilted her head so her lips were just a breath away from his. "Let's be more and see where this leads us."

He kissed her, sweet and lingering, but he pulled away much too quickly and got to his feet. "But we're taking this slowly."

"I can do slow." As a general rule, she wasn't the most patient person, but she would've agreed to anything right now. "We can think of the next couple of weeks as kind of a trial period. How about that?"

"I like that." He reached down to help her to her feet. "And if we feel like this isn't working, then we go back to the way things were. Go back to being best friends without being weird about it."

"Taking things slow with a fallback plan. Got it."

"You're being much too agreeable." He narrowed his eyes suspiciously.

Her smile was angelic. "You're just making a lot of sense at the moment."

"So . . ." He stuffed his hands in his shorts pockets and rocked back on his feet. "Are you free this evening?"

"I am, actually." Was she blushing? Why was she blushing? "Any particular reason you want to know?"

"Will you have dinner with me?" His grin was playful and sexy. Oh, mercy.

"Yes. I'd like that." Her heart was beating way too fast. Was she about to pass out? She might need to start carrying smelling salts if sexy Jack intended to make regular appearances.

"Say at seven o'clock?" Had his voice always been so low and rumbly? It traveled down her spine in a delicious tingle.

"Sounds good to me," she chirped. Like a dork.

"Okay. I'll pick you up then." He tapped her on the nose and walked back to the table he was working on. "Now go strip that chair."

"Bossy," she grumbled, trying and failing to hide her smile. She donned her mask and lovingly sanded the chair, anticipation coursing through her veins.

This was going to be so much fun.

～～～

Jack rolled up the sleeves of his white dress shirt and checked his reflection in the mirror. Option Two flew out the window the moment his lips touched Lizzy's. He was crap at getting over her anyway. But where did that leave him? He shied away from Option Three: Make her fall in love with him. It was too soon for that. They were taking things slowly. Option One: Maintain the status quo, was still a viable choice if things went south. He winced at the thought, though. He wasn't sure what it would mean for this to work out, but he hated the idea of it *not* working out.

And he couldn't deny that this new direction in their relationship made him even more desperate to hear back from McBain. Starting his career as a business analyst was about finding out what he was made of and following his own dream, but it would also mean moving to Los Angeles and being close to Lizzy.

He fidgeted with the collar before smoothing down the front of his charcoal-gray slacks. He was definitely overdressed. Probably. But he wanted to look nice for his first date with Lizzy.

His first date with Lizzy.

He wouldn't be surprised if he was tripping on some potent shit right now. How many times had he imagined taking her out on a date? They'd eaten together plenty of times, but it had never been a date. And a date was nothing like a meal with a friend.

Instead of talking comfortably with her and enjoying her company, he would have to worry about whether he was being the right amount of witty and intelligent—the wrong amount would make him look like an ass—and spend the whole dinner strategizing about the best ways to get a good-night kiss. And what if he got food stuck in his teeth? He should avoid ordering anything with green, leafy vegetables. At least they weren't having Korean food for dinner. There was gochugaru in everything, and those fine, red pepper flakes were masters at sticking to otherwise sparkling white teeth.

He was being absurd. But he didn't go on many dates, and none of them had mattered as much as this one. Unfortunately, that didn't make him any less absurd. He didn't have to worry about coming across as an ass. Lizzy already knew him. She might not think he was witty and intelligent, but she wouldn't be friends with him if she thought he was an ass. And if he got food stuck in his teeth, she would just point it out to him and vice versa. They wouldn't go the entire meal only to be horrified to discover later that they had a big chunk of something stuck in their teeth the entire night. Why was he obsessing over teeth anyway?

As for the good-night kiss . . . he couldn't even think about that. Kissing her in the bookstore had been intoxicating and scorching hot. He couldn't spend the entire dinner staring at her lips and drooling like some creep. *You know what?* He needed to take the whole good-night-kiss thing off the table for tonight. If he knew there wouldn't be a kiss at the end of the date, then he wouldn't have to worry about it. But he really wanted to kiss her again. . . . No. It was off the table. He didn't want to weird her out on their first date.

After grabbing his phone, wallet, and keys, he headed out the door and drove into downtown Weldon. He pulled up in front of the flower shop and checked the clock. He still had plenty of time.

"Hey, Rosie." He waved at the owner as he walked into the shop. "How's it going?"

"Jack." She came out from behind the counter. "I'm doing well. It's hard to complain when I spend my day surrounded by beautiful flowers. You?"

"Same. Except I'm surrounded by exceptional beer."

"You are indeed." She smiled widely. "Can I help you with anything?"

"I wanted to bring my date some flowers." He scratched the

side of his neck. Saying *date* out loud made butterflies flutter in his stomach. "Nothing over the top. Just something pretty that aren't clichéd like roses."

"How about some dahlias?" She motioned for him to follow her. "The deep red ones are my favorite."

"Nice. Can you make me a small bouquet with those?"

"Certainly. I'll add a tiny bit of white and green to spruce it up a bit."

"You're the expert." He cleared his throat. Why was he being so awkward?

Rosie didn't seem to notice. "Give me ten minutes."

"Take your time."

He strolled around the store, too restless to stand still, and spotted a simple vase. She was staying in a vacation rental, so she probably didn't have anywhere to put the flowers.

"Here it is." Rosie held up the bouquet proudly.

"It looks great." The spattering of white and green contrasted nicely with the red of the dahlia. He hoped Lizzy would like it. "Can you ring up this vase as well?"

"Oh, I love that one. I have several at home." She took the vase from him and put it in a simple brown bag, tying a white ribbon around the handles to match the one on the bouquet. "Your date's going to be very flattered."

"Thank you. I appreciate it," he said, his cheeks growing warm. Then sudden panic struck him. "Do these flowers have some kind of meaning?"

What if they meant undying love or soul mates or bountiful procreation? He couldn't give away how he felt about Lizzy. The moment his true feelings came to light, their chances of going back to being friends would be blown. How would she be able to treat him the way she used to knowing that he was head over heels for her? No, she couldn't find out.

"Don't quote me on this, but I think it means strength and power," Rosie said.

Sighing with relief, he paid for his purchases and headed to Sparrow Bookstore. He got there with three minutes to spare. If he took the stairs slowly, he would only be two minutes early. It wouldn't be too rude.

Once he rounded the building and reached the staircase, he bounded up the steps, taking two at a time. He suddenly didn't want to wait another minute to see her. He knocked on the red door and waited.

The door opened, and he forgot how to breathe. Lizzy stood just inside the doorway, wearing a shy smile and a fluttery yellow dress that fell to the top of her knees. She'd done something to her eyes to make them look wide and mesmerizing, and her lips were deep pink and glossy as though they'd been thoroughly kissed. It took him three tries to swallow.

"Here." He stuck out both his arms, one with the bouquet and the other with the vase.

She drew back a little in surprise—*Real smooth, Park*—then raised her hands to accept his offerings.

"These are beautiful, Jack," she said softly. She looked up from the flowers and beamed at him. "Thank you."

"You—" he wheezed. He coughed into his fist. "You're welcome."

"Do you want to come in for a minute? I want to put these in water."

"Sure?" He didn't mean to make it sound like a question. When Lizzy's brows drew together in confusion, he hastily stepped inside. "I mean, sure."

"This vase is so pretty," she said, filling it with water. She looked over her shoulder and scrunched her nose. "Why are you just standing there? You can come and sit down, you know."

"I'm fine here." He shifted from foot to foot. Maybe the flowers had been a mistake. He hadn't planned on being alone with her in her apartment . . . where there was a bed.

"You're making me feel rushed." She dried her hands on a towel and opened the refrigerator. "Here. Let me pour you a glass of wine. I have a bottle of sauvignon blanc chilling in the fridge."

"I'm not trying to rush you." He made no move to walk away from the entry. "Take your time."

She handed him the glass of sauvignon blanc and pointed at the love seat. "Sit."

He dutifully stepped out of his penny loafers and sat down on the couch as instructed. He could see the bed in his peripheral vision, but he didn't dare look directly at it. The sauvignon blanc was very refreshing—just dry enough with really nice white peach and berry notes. He didn't want to horrify his brother and sister, but he actually preferred wine over beer by a tiny margin. It was his deep, dark secret.

He sipped and watched as Lizzy lovingly arranged the dahlias in the vase. "You're really good at that."

"Thanks. I actually took a flower arrangement class once. It was very therapeutic." She turned the vase around this way and that before she put the last piece in. "Et voilà."

"Nice." He shot to his feet and placed his empty wineglass in the sink. He was getting a headache from studiously ignoring the bed. "Ready to go eat?"

"Yes, I'm starving."

He waited as she locked the door and followed her down the stairs.

"So where are we going?" she asked once he pulled away from the curb.

"There's this Himalayan restaurant the locals love." He

glanced at her quickly. "It's not fancy. I hope you don't mind. I promise you the food is fantastic."

"Ooh, I've never tried Himalayan before." She clapped her hands. "I heard momos are super yummy."

He laughed with relief and because she was . . . well . . . adorable. "This restaurant makes great ones."

Even though it was a weeknight, the restaurant was busy but not so busy that they had to wait for a table—just busy enough that it bustled with happy customers. It was what made eating out fun and first dates less awkward.

The drive over had been fine, but as soon as they were seated at their table, Jack wanted to hide his face behind the menu. It was a small table for two, and their knees brushed against each other's every time one of them moved. And they were close enough together that he wouldn't even have to lift his ass off his chair to lean over and kiss her. Not that he was going to kiss her. Because there wasn't going to be any kissing tonight.

He stared at her pink glistening lips exactly the way he wasn't supposed to. *Don't think about kissing her.* That worked about as well as telling someone who was about to pee their pants to not think about peeing their pants. Her lips moved, and he cocked his head to the side, fascinated by the way their shape changed with each syllable. Shit. She was talking to him.

"Sorry." His gaze flew to her eyes. "What was that?"

She reached across the table and gently unfurled his fingers from the tight fist they were in. "Remember what I said about some things changing but not everything having to change?"

"Yes, I remember."

"For example, I hadn't done this before." She curled her hand around his.

He gulped audibly but instinctively threaded his fingers through hers. "No, not quite like this."

"But we should be able to order some damn momos without being afraid to speak to each other," she said with a sweet smile. "You and I, we could always talk to each other. That should never change."

"Do you think I'm witty and intelligent?" he blurted.

"What?" She blinked.

"It's just that I've always been intimidated by that big, lawyer brain of yours." That came out wrong, so he rushed to clarify, "Not because I think I'm unintelligent—I know I'm smart—but it's hard to beat the speed and agility of a litigator's mind. I figured you sometimes humored me since I was your friend."

"Are you fishing for a compliment?" She rolled her eyes but humored him. "You are witty, intelligent, sensitive, and funny as hell. I love talking to you . . . dingus."

He snorted but sobered quickly. "I'm sorry for being weird."

"Don't worry about it. I'm nervous, too," she said, squeezing his hand. "Now, tell me more about this big, lawyer brain you think I have."

"Would it do to tell you that you're the smartest person I know? Or would you like me to recite a sonnet about how enormous your brain is?"

"You really think I'm the smartest person you know?"

"Of course I really think that. Why would I lie . . . doofus?"

"Shush. I'm no doofus. I'm the smartest person you know." She grinned and looked down at her menu, but she kept her hand where it was. "So are we going to get some momos or what?"

"We'll definitely get some momos and maybe even some yak meat, too."

He studied his menu with a smile, loving the contrast of their easy banter and the electricity traveling up his arm from where his fingers entwined with hers. Same but different.

CHAPTER ELEVEN

The momos were as fabulous as promised, but the food became a distant memory as Jack drove Lizzy to her apartment. Despite all her bravado that they shouldn't be nervous about talking to each other, she couldn't think of a single thing to say. Was their good-night kiss going to be as explosive as the kiss they'd shared this morning? If it was, would she want to stop kissing him when there was a bed right behind the door?

Oh, God. Sex. Sex with Jack. She couldn't even wrap her head around it. But she'd happily wrapped her leg around his waist earlier. She could hear the thumping of her heart in her ears and feel it in her throat. She fought to keep her breathing even. Why was she getting so worked up about a good-night kiss? Probably because she wanted more than a kiss.

Thankfully, the drive back to Sparrow was a short one, and she was able to hop out of Jack's car before she started hyperventilating. It had nothing to do with anxiety—it still pleasantly surprised her that her constant companion was so conspicuously absent these days—and all to do with lust. He came around to her side and stood smiling serenely at her. She couldn't spot a hint of nervousness on him. No fair. Unreasonably peeved by his ease, she spun on her heels and stomped her way to the back of the building. She heard him following from behind.

By the time she reached her door, her flash of annoyance was greatly outshadowed by anticipation and desire. Weird or not, she was horny. She wanted this man.

"This is me," she said inanely.

"Yes." He cleared his throat and leaned back on his heels, his hands deep in his pockets.

Maybe he wasn't as calm as he'd appeared. The thought eased some of her own nervousness. "I had a lovely time."

"Yes," he repeated. "I had a good time, too."

Should she invite him in for a drink and see where it led? Was she ready to go wherever it led? Her body screamed *yes*, but her mind said in a small voice, *This is Jack.* Of course she knew that. But maybe she wanted to invite him in so much *because* he was Jack. She drew an unsteady breath to ask him to come inside.

"Well, good night." He swiftly kissed her cheek and jogged down the steps as though he couldn't wait to get away from her.

She blinked and lifted her hand to cradle her tingling cheek. What the hell just happened? That was it? That was all she got? A peck on the cheek? She was getting her panties twisted into a knot—wondering if she was ready to sleep with him—when he wasn't even planning to kiss her good night? Well, she felt like a total asshat.

Lizzy let herself inside her apartment and got ready for bed. Alone. As some of her outrage subsided, she realized he was serious about taking things slowly. In all fairness, she had agreed to it, but she didn't know he'd meant glacial pace. Hmm. Whether something was slow or not was subjective. She couldn't help it if her definition of slow was much faster than his.

After sliding under the sheets, she clicked off the table lamp and hugged the comforter to her chest. She wasn't planning to seduce him—it wasn't about that at all—but the cheek-kissing nonsense was going to end. The point of this experiment was to see where their attraction led them. To see what it felt like to be *more*. That, by necessity, included kissing. Lots of kissing.

~

"Good morning," Jack said when Lizzy walked out from behind the building bright and early the next day.

"Good morning," she replied in a pleasant, cheery voice.

Without further ado, she stepped up close to him, rose on her tiptoes, and kissed him on his full, unsuspecting lips. She didn't stick her tongue into his mouth or anything, but it was a full-on, soft-mouthed, lingering kiss. Jack froze for two seconds. Just as his lips parted and he started returning her kiss, Lizzy stepped back from him, their lips separating with a satisfying kissy smack.

"Ah . . . good morning," Jack said with his gaze glued to her lips.

She licked them for good measure and watched his eyes glaze over. This was nice. She felt much better. "So we're going to jog through downtown today?"

"Uh . . . yes." A deep groove formed between his brows as though formulating those words took great effort. He was still staring at her lips.

"Well, show me the way. I'll just follow." She unzipped her sweatshirt and shrugged it off.

Jack's eyes almost popped out of their sockets. She hid her smile by pretending to do some hamstring stretches. She wasn't sure if his reaction was entirely warranted. Yes, she was only wearing a sports bra, but she was also wearing a pair of high-waisted tights, so only about three inches of her torso was visible.

He took off on a run before she could get too smug.

"Hey, wait up." She ran after him, which wasn't an easy feat considering he was eating up the sidewalk like some Olympic sprinter. When she thought she would never catch up with him, he finally slowed down enough for her to reach his side. "What was that about?"

He didn't answer, his lips pressed into a grim line, and continued jogging. Her body was adjusting to this cardio thing, but she was panting, trying to keep up with him. She stole a peek at Jack. He was staring straight ahead with a muscle jumping in his jaws. She was beginning to regret the sports bra ensemble a little. She just didn't like how laid-back he seemed when she was burning up for him.

She distracted herself from the niggling doubt inside her—and how her lungs were burning to a crisp—by studying her surroundings. At seven in the morning, Main Street was quiet with most shops still closed, but it was charming nonetheless with brightly colored storefronts and eclectic shop signs. She wished there were more neighborhoods like this in Los Angeles, where unique, independently owned stores dominated the streets.

It was on the tip of her tongue to apologize for her juvenile move when Jack whipped off his T-shirt. She faltered to a stop and became mesmerized by the movement of his ripped back as he jogged farther and farther away from her. He spun around to face her, while jogging backward.

She'd seen him shirtless her first day in Weldon when she'd surprised him on his run. She'd felt too shy to get a good look at him then, but now she took it all in. His smooth, sculpted pecs narrowed to ridiculously defined abs. It was too much, but she didn't look away. She couldn't. She wanted to put her hands and lips all over that.

"What's the matter, slowpoke?" He arched an eyebrow at her and grinned.

It was the smug grin that snapped her out of her paralysis. The fucker did it on purpose. It was payback for the sports bra. All because she showed three inches of bare midriff. She was suddenly incensed, and that somehow turned her on even more.

"Put your shirt back on," she spat through gritted teeth. She untied her jacket from her waist and shrugged into it. "If you don't, I'm taking you to that back alley behind you and jumping you so hard and fast, you won't even know what hit you."

He stopped in his tracks but didn't put his shirt back on. *Oh, God.* He was tempted to let her jump him in the back alley. The stark hunger on his face made her knees weak. She realized he wasn't calm. Not at all. He wanted her as desperately as she wanted him. He was just holding back for both of their sakes.

"Jack," she said softly and walked up to him. "I'm sorry about this morning. I'll stop playing games with you. We'll take things slow like you said."

The fire in his eyes dimmed to a simmer, then was replaced by tenderness. He reached out and tucked a strand of hair that had fallen out of her ponytail behind her ear. Then he cupped her face and kissed her sweetly and gently. With a sigh, she leaned into the kiss and placed her hands on his chest. Shit. He was still shirtless. She slid her palms up and down several times to confirm. His hot, naked skin felt so freaking fantastic that she nearly moaned.

She drew back with a gasp and hid her hands behind her back as though she'd stolen something. "Put your shirt back on."

"Sorry." He smiled sheepishly and tugged his T-shirt over his beautiful torso.

Regret flashed through her, but it was for the best. "Let's finish up so we can get to work."

They finished their run back to Sparrow at an even jog. She was out of breath, but she felt good. Exercise really was the best thing for burning off sexual frustration.

"That was a nice run," she said with an easy smile.

"It was. I'm glad you're starting to enjoy yourself." He closed the gap between them, making her tilt her head back to look up at him.

"I heard the *I told you so* between the lines," she whispered.

He chuckled softly as he leaned down to kiss her on one corner of her lips, then the other. His teeth gently scraped her bottom lip, and her mouth parted on a gasp. He deepened the kiss and groaned when her tongue eagerly tangled with his. But he lifted his head much too soon and planted a kiss on her forehead.

"I'll see you soon," he said, and got in his car.

She waved goodbye and watched the car disappear before she went to her apartment for a shower. A cold shower.

~

Lizzy promised no more games, and she always kept her word. Jack knew she wasn't playing any games. She merely chose a practical outfit for another day of refinishing furniture. A soft, worn T-shirt that hugged her breasts and showed him glimpses of her smooth stomach when she raised her arms, and a pair of shorts that did amazing things to her round ass. This was all him.

It was a good thing he wasn't working with any saws or even a nail gun, because he would've sawed off or impaled some digits by now considering how distracted he was. But he couldn't help himself knowing that this new road they had embarked on would allow him to *touch* her. He was grateful for his baggy cargo shorts, because he'd been sporting semi-wood all morning despite his freezing-cold shower.

"We're almost done here with the sanding, right?" Lizzy asked as she stretched her back, a pose that thrust her chest forward and revealed a tantalizing strip of her stomach.

Oh, God. He was going to jerk off tonight. In all his years of pining, he had never gotten off on thoughts of her. He didn't let himself cross that line. He couldn't let his fantasies take clear form. That was the only way he could be her friend and be near her without losing his sanity. But all bets were off now because he'd held her in his arms . . . kissed her. His fantasies were HD clear with fucking surround sound, because that humming noise she made when they kissed . . . Fuck.

As twisted as it sounded, he would be masturbating for both their sakes. It was the only way he could think of to take things slowly between them. If he touched her the way he really wanted to, there would be no going back for them. Once he had her, he wouldn't be able to let her go—he could never be content just being her friend. They would lose their fallback plan, and they would have to do this without a safety net. That wasn't a risk he was ready to take.

"Jack?" She dropped her hands from her lower back and cocked her head to the side.

"Yeah, we're about finished," he answered in a strangled voice. He coughed and waved his hands in front of his face as though the wood dust—and not his dirty thoughts—was bothering him.

"Then I should go to the hardware store to pick out the stains and paints," she said.

"I'll go with you." Was there such a thing as emotional whiplash? Because he just got one. He went from horny to jealous in a split second.

"Are you sure? I thought you wanted to finish up that little round table." She glanced around the back lot and pointed at the offending table when she spotted it.

"That won't take me long," he assured her. Lizzy hadn't seemed the least bit interested in Arthur the last time they were at the hardware store, but he still didn't like the thought of the kid mooning over her. "Besides, you might need my discerning taste to help you choose the colors."

"All right." She rolled her eyes but a smile peeped through. "You can come along."

They pulled into the parking lot of the hardware store five minutes later. Lizzy led the way inside, and Arthur's face split into a giant grin, which faltered when he caught sight of Jack's glare.

"Hey, folks," Ol' Arthur rallied with his signature charm. "How may I assist you today?"

"We're looking for some paint and—" Lizzy began.

"We know where to look," Jack cut in. "We'll let you know if we need anything."

"Umm . . . sure thing," Arthur said uncertainly, looking between Lizzy and Jack.

Jack took Lizzy by the arm and led her toward the paint section. She was studying him curiously.

"Do you and Arthur not get along?" she whispered.

"What?" He felt the tips of his ears grow hot. He was being a dick. Arthur was a good kid. "We get along great."

"Hmm," she said, pulling her lips to one side. "Okay. If you say so."

He was relieved she'd dropped it. He needed to get a handle

on this caveman possessiveness before she caught on. "So did you and Shannon discuss what paint colors you guys wanted?"

"We did." Her eyes lit up with excitement, and he couldn't hold back his grin. Her joie de vivre was one of the many things he loved about her. "We decided to go with several different shades. Shannon wants to give the store a burst of color."

"I couldn't help but overhear you folks discussing paint colors." Arthur walked down the aisle toward them.

It wasn't premeditated—he had no intention of doing it—but Jack wrapped his arm around Lizzy's waist, spreading his hand wide on her hip. He felt her eyes on him, but he didn't dare turn his head.

The other man's gaze flicked to Jack's hand before he fixed a friendly smile on his face. "I just wanted to let you know that I can mix whatever shade you need. I have a ton of color swatches up front. Do you want to take a look at them?"

"Yes, thank you. That would be so great," Lizzy said.

Arthur nodded and made his way back to retrieve the swatches. When he was far enough away, she pointedly cleared her throat, and Jack had no choice but to face her.

"Did you just pee on me?" She arched a perfect brow at him.

"What? I . . . What?" He knew exactly what she meant, but it sounded so much worse when she put it that way.

"Were you marking your territory for Arthur's benefit just now?" She stepped away from him and crossed her arms.

"I . . . That is . . ." He was an ass. The least he could do was own up to it. "Yes. I'm so sorry. I didn't know what I was thinking. Actually, I didn't think. I just did."

She narrowed her eyes and tapped her foot for a long moment as he waited for her wrath to rain down on him. But then . . . she smiled. "I think I'm going to let it pass this one time."

"You are?" he asked, not quite believing he was off the hook.

"Yes, but just this once." A soft blush rose to her cheeks. "I sort of liked it. I've never seen this side of you before. It's kind of sexy. Just don't make a habit of it."

"I won't. I promise." But he had more important things on his mind. He closed the distance between them and pulled her into his arms. "You think I'm sexy."

She blushed harder. "Figured that out all by yourself, Sherlock?"

"I like that," he said, his voice dipping low. He leaned down until their faces were only a few inches apart. "I really like that."

She sucked in a sharp breath and rose to her tiptoes, pressing her lips against his. He opened his mouth over hers and drank deeply from her. When she hummed, he wrapped his arms around her and pressed her flush against his body.

"Here we are . . . Oh, and there you are—" Arthur said, his voice cracking. Jack didn't bother lifting his head and just flapped his hand, shooing him away. "Well, then. I'll be at the counter if you need me."

Jack should have been more concerned about making out in the middle of the town's hardware store, but he couldn't have cared less. Lizzy was in his arms—*his* Lizzy—and she was kissing him as though she couldn't get enough of him. He ran his tongue along the bottom of her lips and drew another hum from her. He couldn't get enough of her—enough of this. He was in big trouble, and he liked it just fine.

CHAPTER TWELVE

Jack lifted his head, confiscating his lips from her. *The nerve.* Lizzy was about to protest when she realized she didn't have enough oxygen to speak, so she sucked in a lungful of air instead. Breathing slipped her mind whenever he kissed her. But he never seemed to forget to do silly things like breathe. In fact, he was always the one who broke off their kiss.

A part of her was peeved that he kept his head on so well when she could hardly remember her own name—when her need for him was all-consuming. But a part of her had to be grateful for his control. If it were up to her, they would be knocking over paint in the middle of Arthur's Hardware Store in their hurry to get each other naked.

"We should . . . uh . . . go look at those color swatches," she said, acting more nonchalant than she felt. In reality, she wanted to growl like a feral cat and launch herself at him.

"Yeah." He blew out a ragged breath and raked his fingers through his hair. "Let's do that."

So he wasn't as unaffected as she'd thought. *Hehe.* She bit her lip to keep her smug smile from surfacing and walked up to the front of the store.

"Hi, Arthur," she said. "We're ready to look at those swatches."

"Yes, of course." He didn't quite meet her eyes as he handed her the color booklet.

Did he see them making out in the paint aisle? His face did look a little blotchy. Geez. *Way to go, making the poor guy uncomfortable in his own store.* Lizzy studied the swatches intently to hide her embarrassment. She wasn't big on PDA, but she couldn't seem to help herself with Jack. They seemed to kiss regardless of where they were—the bookstore, the sidewalk, and now the hardware store. Where else would they end up kissing? She felt a flush rise up to the roots of her hair, but it had nothing to do with embarrassment.

She snuck a glance at Jack, who was grinning triumphantly at Arthur with his hand planted firmly on her back. With a slight shake of her head, she returned her gaze to the color booklet. He really couldn't seem to help himself. Despite her firm conviction that she would never be anyone's possession, she still thought he was adorable. He seemed like a kid who'd won first place in a pinewood derby. All because he was the guy who got to kiss her.

They chose shades in yellow, sky blue, coral, and light gray for the chairs and some warm, honey-colored wood stain for the tables. The coral and yellow would look great in Hideaway Bookstore, too. She should start a list of suggestions to share with Beverly for when she went back to Los Angeles. Her stomach sank at the thought. She would be leaving Weldon soon—too soon. She glanced at Jack, and he smiled at her, easing the sudden tension in her shoulders. She didn't want to think about leaving yet. She was just glad to be here now—with him.

After adding paintbrushes of various sizes to their loot, they headed back to Sparrow. She couldn't wait to show them to Shannon. They walked into the bookstore with a cheery jingle of the bell.

"Hi," Elliot said, from behind the counter—a sullen sigh behind his greeting.

"Hey, little man." Jack held out his fist, and the boy bumped it weakly with his. "What's gotten you so down today?"

"Mom's making me read a book. *For fun.*" His jaw dropped open to show how ridiculous he found the notion. "And she says comic books don't count. How else am I supposed to have fun reading?"

"Just to be clear," Shannon said, walking out of the back room with an armful of books. "I never said comic books didn't count. I only meant you couldn't read the ones you already read twenty times."

"But I don't have any new comic books," Elliot protested, pulling at his hair.

"I told you to think twice before you spent your birthday money on those computer game upgrades." Shannon shrugged with her head to one side. "The good news is you have a store full of books to choose from."

"I don't like any of these books." The inconsolable boy buried his head in his arms on the counter.

Lizzy couldn't hold back her gasp of dismay. "Elliot, I'm about to ask you a question. Please don't take it the wrong way if I'm way off, but . . . do you not like reading?"

The child responded with an eloquent gag and hid his face again.

"But . . . but . . ." She couldn't believe what she was hearing. Or seeing. He had this amazing wonderland of books at his disposal, and he didn't even want it. "What . . . How . . ."

"I know," Shannon said kindly, putting a consoling hand on Lizzy's shoulder. "For me to have a child who doesn't love reading is my life's biggest irony."

"Don't worry. I don't think I liked reading when I was your age." Jack tousled Elliot's hair. "But one day, you'll find a book that changes everything. Have you seen *The LEGO Movie*?"

"Of course." The boy lifted his head, suddenly interested in the conversation.

"You know how Emmet is totally clueless at the beginning of the movie, but at the end, he suddenly *sees everything*?" Jack asked.

"Yeah. It's so cool." Elliot twisted his hands like he was working a Rubik's Cube, making *swish-whoosh* sound effects. "All of a sudden, he could see what every piece was for and build all these awesome things in like a second."

"Well, finding *the* right book kind of feels like that. Once you read that book, a whole new world will open up for you. You'll take these incredible journeys through your imagination and find limitless possibilities with every new book. It only takes that one right book to change everything."

Elliot's eyes grew wide with wonder. "Whoa."

"Do you want to know which book did that for me? It's called *The Phantom Tollbooth*." Jack motioned for the kid to follow. "Let's see if your mom has it in the store."

Elliot scurried after Jack to the children's section. Lizzy's smile turned misty as memories fluttered through her like a warm breeze. She'd lent Jack her copy of *The Phantom Tollbooth* on her second visit to Weldon. They were both ten. He'd never told her that was the book that had turned him into an avid reader.

"You got yourself a wonderful man there," Shannon murmured, nudging her with her shoulder.

"He's not . . ." He wasn't, right? But he wasn't just her friend anymore, either. Maybe he wasn't quite *her* man, but she might want him to be. Yes . . . she would like that very much. "Thank you. He is wonderful."

"And a reader to boot. Only a true book lover could talk about reading the way he did." She sighed wistfully. "Elliot's dad never liked reading, and it annoyed him no end that I always had my nose stuck in a book. It doesn't matter to me anymore, but I don't think Elliot ever cracks open a book when he visits his dad in the summers."

"That's a shame," Lizzy said. She knew Shannon was divorced from Elliot's dad, but she didn't talk about her ex-husband very much. "Where does he live?"

"In Atlanta with his new family. His wife recently had a baby girl. Elliot is going to meet his little sister for the first time next month."

"He's going to be great with her." *Next month.* She would be back in Los Angeles by then.

"Yeah, he's pretty excited to meet her . . ." Shannon seemed to want to say more, but she hesitated.

"Are you worried about how things will change for him at his dad's?" Lizzy asked softly.

"I'm so happy that he has a sister now, but a part of me can't help but worry that he might feel like a third wheel there." Her friend shook her head and grinned. "Worrying and overthinking the hell out of things is what being a mom is all about."

"You're an awesome mom." Lizzy laughed, shushing the unkind thought that not all moms were so caring. Her mom cared, too. She just showed it by relentlessly pushing her to make partner.

"Aww. Thank you, hon." Shannon snapped her fingers. "Oh yeah. Did you have any luck finding the colors we talked about at the hardware store?"

"We did." Lizzy was so busy melting into a puddle watching

Jack interact with Elliot that she'd completely forgotten about the task at hand. What was she thinking? There were tiny boxes to check off. "We put the paint out back. Do you want to see it?"

"Heck yeah. I'm so excited." Shannon turned to her son. He was sitting on the floor with his head buried in a book. "Do you want to help us paint some furniture, buddy?"

"No, thanks," he said without looking up. "I want to read this."

Shannon turned rounded eyes from Lizzy to Jack to Elliot, then back to Lizzy. "I'm either in *The Twilight Zone* or Jack is a genius with children."

"I didn't do anything." Jack tugged on his earlobe, coming to stand beside Lizzy. "This is all on the kid. He was just ready to find his book."

"And he's humble, too. You lucky girl," Shannon stage-whispered to Lizzy.

Jack arched an eyebrow at Lizzy, and she shrugged. Based on what had happened this morning at the hardware store, it didn't seem like they were keeping their new dating status a secret. And if his grin was anything to go by, he didn't seem to mind Shannon knowing.

As the three of them walked around the building heading for the back lot, Jack leaned down close to her ear and drawled, "So do you think you're a lucky girl?"

A shiver zipped down her spine. They would become billionaires if they could bottle their chemistry. It was something rare and special. She certainly had never experienced it before. And she was impatient to experience more of it.

"Why do you ask?" She fluttered her eyelashes. "Am I getting lucky soon?"

"What was that, Shannon?" He cupped his hand against his ear. "Sorry. I think she needs something."

Lizzy watched in dismay as Jack ran ahead of her toward the back lot. Shannon hadn't so much as sneezed. He literally ran away from her to avoid talking about sex. Didn't he realize where all that kissing was leading them?

Maybe he had a no-sex-until-the-third-date rule or something. That sort of rule should be waived by virtue of them having known each other for twenty years. Well, if he wanted to be a stickler for such things, then she could go along with that. But since she only had a couple of weeks left in Weldon, she would just speed up the process by setting up back-to-back dates.

~~~

Jack stood behind the bar with a broad grin, shaving orange peels for garnish. The sweet tang of oranges reminded him of Lizzy for some reason—maybe it was because she tasted so sweet—and thinking about her made him happy. He'd left her earlier in the afternoon painting furniture with Shannon. She'd had sky-blue paint on the tip of her nose and looked absolutely beautiful. The brewery didn't open for another fifteen minutes, so he had plenty of time to daydream.

"Someone's in a good mood today." Alex walked out of the brewing room, wiping his hands on a kitchen towel. "Does it have anything to do with you spending every spare minute with Lizzy?"

"Yeah, it does." Jack took a deep breath. He hadn't really had a chance to talk to his brother the last couple of days—he *had* spent every spare minute with Lizzy—so now was as good a time as any to share the news with him. "We're seeing each other."

"I know." Alex joined him behind the bar and poured himself a glass of water.

"No, I mean we're *seeing* each other," he repeated meaningfully. His brother probably didn't understand because it was so unexpected. "Lizzy and I are dating."

"I know." There wasn't so much as a ripple on the serene surface of his twin's visage. "It's about time."

"How can you have known?" Jack deflated a little. "We went on our first date last night."

"You've been wearing that goofy grin on your face since yesterday afternoon."

"You can tell by my smile that I'm dating Lizzy?" He shook his head. "I'm calling bullshit on that one."

"Only a very special woman can produce a smile that ridiculous in a man." Alex sipped from his glass, every line of his posture screaming *smug*. "Like the woman you've been carrying a torch for since the tender young age of ten."

"That was a childish crush. I got over that in one summer." He thought he'd hidden his feelings so well from everyone. Thank God Lizzy didn't suspect anything. "This is a completely unexpected, *new* development."

"Of course it is." His brother's voice was soaked through with sarcasm. "I super believe you."

There was no use arguing—his twin knew him better than anyone else—so Jack quickly changed tactics and went on the offensive. "How can you be so nonchalant about the whole thing?"

"How else should I be?" Alex laughed.

"A little surprised at the very least. I mean, I'm shocked as hell that Lizzy and I are actually doing this."

"Okay. You want me to act surprised? I'll act surprised." His brother cleared his throat. "Holy shit. Are you fucking shitting me? No fucking way. I would never have guessed in a hundred billion years."

"Fuck you," Jack said, chuckling.

"I'm really happy for you guys." Alex took out another peeler from the drawer and grabbed an orange from the pile. "But I'm a little worried, too."

"Worried?" Jack's eyebrows furrowed above the bridge of his nose. "Worried how?"

"Well, Lizzy's going back to LA soon, and you'll be here. With both of you so busy with work, the long-distance thing won't be easy."

But Jack might be moving to Los Angeles, too. God, he hoped he got the job. He felt guilty as soon as the thought entered his head. Even his brother didn't know that he'd been interviewing for a new job. Alex thought they were a team. Jack didn't know how he would take it if he left Weldon Brewery to work in LA.

"We haven't thought that far ahead yet." Jack shrugged and resumed shaving orange peels. "Like I said, we've only gone on one date."

"Have you kissed her?" Alex playfully elbowed him in the ribs.

He lightly shoved his shoulder. "Maybe."

"Damn. That must be so weird after being friends for so long."

"Not as weird as you'd think." Jack grinned.

"Annnnd there is that absurd smile again."

"Shut up, asshole."

"Now, now, boys." Tara came out of the kitchen, tying an apron around her waist. "When are you guys going to learn how to get along?"

"*Asshole* is a term of endearment between us. Isn't that right, Alex?" Jack slung an arm around his brother's shoulders.

"Sure. Whatever you say, asshole."

Their little sister rolled her eyes at them and went to turn on the OPEN sign. When she came back to the bar, she cocked her head to the side and stared at Jack. "Why are you smiling like that?"

Alex spewed water out of his nose.

"What the hell is wrong with my smile?" Jack threw up his hands.

"You guys are acting really strange today," Tara observed. "Then again, that's nothing new."

"Jack and Lizzy are dating," his brother announced, sniffing loudly.

"It's about time," his sister murmured, tapping the menu into a neat stack. "I mean, you've had it bad for her since you were ten."

"You knew, too?" Jack stared bug-eyed at his siblings. "Did everyone expect this to happen except for me?"

"No, I don't think Lizzy had a clue," Tara said.

"Oh, God." He wanted to find a hole to hide in. "Do Mom and Dad know?"

"About your crush? Nah." His sister shook her head, saving Jack from having a heart attack. "Just some wishful thinking that one of you boys would snatch her up."

"*One* of us?" He glared at his twin.

"Whoa." Alex held up both his hands. "I can't help what Mom and Dad think. I never once thought about snatching her up."

"Besides, I think they gave up hope a long time ago," Tara added.

"That's good," Jack said, nodding. "And let's not rekindle their hope. I don't want to complicate things by having the parents involved. If Dad finds out, then so does Mr. Chung. And Mrs. Chung would probably get on Lizzy's case for dating someone beneath her."

"She wouldn't dare," Tara growled fiercely. "Lizzy is lucky to have you, Oppa."

"Quite frankly, Mrs. Chung is a piece of work." An outraged frown darkened Alex's face. "But even she wouldn't consider the mastermind behind Weldon Brewery *beneath* her daughter."

"It's your talent as brewers that's putting Weldon Brewery on the map." Jack was touched by their loyalty, but their thinking was biased. "I just do the numbers."

His brother and sister exchanged concerned glances.

"You can't possibly believe that," his sister whispered.

"Yeah, Jack." Alex put a hand on his shoulder. "You're taking the humility thing a bit too far."

Maybe he'd said too much. He didn't want to worry his siblings. "All right, all right. I'm awesome, and you two could beat up anyone who says otherwise."

"Damn right, we will." Tara cracked her knuckles.

"That's one ass-kicking I'll relish." Alex flashed a sinister grin.

Not wanting to linger on the subject, Jack tossed out a distraction. "Please don't be obnoxious to Lizzy about the whole dating thing. Like I said, we've only gone on one date."

"He's talking to you, Alex," his sister said dryly.

"Yeah, I'm talking to you, bro," Jack confirmed. "And *do not* under any circumstance tell her that I had a crush on her since elementary school. I don't want to weird her out."

"Are you serious?" When Jack and Tara nodded, Alex continued, "I'm going to adult the shit out of this situation and shock you both. I'll be so respectful and supportive that Lizzy will come to me for relationship advice."

Jack threw a piece of orange peel at him while Tara snorted eloquently. But when it came down to it, there was no one he trusted more than Alex. If he needed someone's shoulder to cry on, it would be his. Hopefully, he wouldn't have a reason to anytime soon.

CHAPTER THIRTEEN

I can't believe he's still reading," Shannon whispered, staring at her son sprawled out on the bookstore floor. "I'm not even sure if he has homework, but I don't want to ask him. I'm afraid if he stops reading, he'll go back to hating books."

Lizzy smiled and fanned out the cute journals on a small table near the front of the store. Customers could browse them much more easily than from their prior position behind the counter. Hideaway Bookstore sold journals, too, but Beverly could use an update on the selections. Lizzy should add that to her suggestions list.

Working at Sparrow reminded her of Hideaway, and thinking about Hideaway reminded her that she had to go back to Los Angeles soon. A part of her wanted to stop thinking about the LA bookstore, but her suggestions could make her favorite bookstore even more successful—so successful that no one would dare turn it into a trendy café.

"You have to feed the kid dinner at some point," Lizzy gently reminded her friend.

"He can eat while he reads." Shannon shrugged, arranging

colored pens into a pencil holder next to the journals. "Something easy like chicken nuggets."

"What about bedtime?" she pointed out for the sake of argument.

"Sleep is overrated." The book lover trumped the sensible mom in Shannon. "Reading is everything."

Lizzy burst out laughing. "Who am I to argue with such sound logic?"

When they returned to setting up the journal table, Lizzy's mind wandered. With Jack working most evenings, it was much harder to plan back-to-back dates than she'd thought. Maybe they could have lunch dates from now on. Eating sack lunches on the floor of the bookstore didn't count. Those were working lunches. They could go out to restaurants or have lunch on a park bench. Something romantic.

But lunch wasn't until tomorrow. Her shoulders sagged. She was impatient to move the dating thing forward so . . . *other things* could start.

"Hello?" Shannon waved a hand in front of her face.

"I'm sorry. What?" Her mind had stalled on *other things*.

"We finished moving the journal display. You can check that off now." Shannon handed her the to-do list and a pen.

"Ooh, yay." Lizzy drew a fancy check mark in the box. "We're really moving through this thing."

"Thanks to you and Jack." Shannon offered her a wobbly smile. "Moving here after the divorce and starting over . . . It hasn't been easy. Between Sparrow and Elliot, the only people I met in the last couple of years were customers and other parents in passing. Everyone in Weldon is so friendly, but I didn't really have any friends." She swiped away a wayward tear with the back of her hand. "Oh, geez. I'm just babbling. What I mean to say is I'm so grateful for you."

"I'm grateful for you, too." Lizzy wrapped her friend in a bear hug. "I don't have many friends, either. Being an attorney is such an all-consuming job—it's really isolating." She didn't realize how alone she had been until she came to Weldon. "It'll mean so much to me if we keep in touch after I go back to LA."

"I don't want to think about you going back yet. But yeah. We'll definitely keep in touch." Shannon pulled back from the hug. "Now. Tell me what has you so distracted that you forgot to cross off a to-do-list item the moment it was completed."

Lizzy hadn't had a girlfriend to confide in for so long that she forgot she could do that. Maybe Shannon could help her figure out how to move things along with Jack.

"How should I put this?" She lowered her voice so Elliot wouldn't hear. "Jack is a true gentleman."

"Isn't that a good thing?" Shannon crinkled her nose for a second, then her face cleared. "Ohhhh. Yeah, no. That isn't necessarily a good thing, especially for you guys."

"Especially for us? Why?"

"Oh, my God. The sexual tension between you two is so heavy that I have to wade through it with a machete to get around the store."

Lizzy couldn't even laugh at the imagery. She was so frustrated. "Help."

"Is he working at the brewery tonight?"

"Yup."

"What time does he get off?"

"I think he said ten o'clock."

"Hmm." Her friend tapped her lips with her index finger. "Why don't you visit him at the brewery?"

"I don't want to bother him at work," Lizzy said uncertainly.

"Girl, now isn't the time to be polite. Just listen. Get there close to ten and wait for him to finish up. Then you guys can go for a nightcap." A mischievous smile lit up Shannon's face. "Of course, you'll need to wear a dress that will make Jack have very ungentlemanly thoughts."

"Ooh, you're evil. I love it." Lizzy nibbled her bottom lip. "But I'm not sure I packed anything like that."

"Not to worry. I have the perfect dress for you."

~~~

The black body-con dress left *very* little to the imagination. Lizzy's boobs were pushed up to her chin, and the skirt barely covered her ass. But the sleek, simple design of the dress managed to make her look classy. It was perfect.

She walked into Weldon Brewery at nine thirty sharp. Several heads turned to watch her progress toward the bar, and she was tempted to jump behind the nearest wooden beam. She wanted Jack's attention—and ungentlemanly thoughts—not anyone else's. But she donned her badass lawyer persona to overcome her shyness and didn't let her steps falter.

"Whoa, Unni." Tara whistled when she sat down at the bar. "You look stunning. Do you have a hot date tonight?"

"Thank you," Lizzy said instead of giving in to the urge to say, *Oh, this old thing?* "I sure hope so."

"Intriguing." Tara arched her eyebrow but seemed to be fighting a smile.

Lizzy twisted around to scan the dining hall for Jack but was distracted by the high-pitched laughter of several women. When she turned toward the sound, she found the man she was looking for being fawned over by a tableful of women. Well, three women, but that was more than enough.

He murmured something wearing a crooked grin, and the women erupted into laughter again. *How dare he act so charm-*

ing. Lizzy had seen enough, so she spun back to the bar and said with a hint of acid, "Someone is earning his tip today."

"Jack is a favorite with the customers." Tara smiled while expertly filling mugs of beer.

"I can see that," Lizzy said sullenly while drawing little circles on the bar with her finger.

She gave up trying to ignore the scene behind her and glanced over her shoulder. Jack was walking toward the bar with the women staring after him. When one woman's eyes dipped to check out his ass, Lizzy understood for the first time what seeing red meant. She shot to her feet—with a vague plan to tackle someone—at the same moment Jack spotted her.

"Lizzy?" His face turned stark with hunger as he perused her body.

The red filter fell from her eyes as she witnessed her plan working. He wanted her, and she couldn't have cared less about those women. All they got was a measly crooked smile when she got this searing, wild-eyed stare from him. He reached her side in three long strides and planted his hand on her lower back as though he couldn't help but touch her.

"Hey, Jack." Her voice was husky and seductive, and she wasn't even trying. It was like a primal instinct. *Hot man. Must seduce.* "I was hoping we could go out for a drink when you get off."

Jack didn't answer. His eyes were glued to her girls, and his fingers dug into her back. She gently tipped his chin up so he would look at her. "Drinks? After work?"

"Yes," he growled.

"Oh, for chicken's sake," Tara said. "Go, Jack. Now. I'll cover your tables."

"No, that's okay." Lizzy tore her gaze away from him. "I can wait."

"Look at him. He's in no condition to work." Tara's cheeks were pink. "And I don't want to watch my older brother undress a woman with his eyes. Even if that woman is you, Unni. I'm really happy that he's your hot date, but you need to take him with you *now*. Seriously."

"Jack?" Lizzy prompted. His eyes had dropped to her cleavage again.

He raised them to her face with effort. "Yes?"

"Do you want to leave now?" She bit the inside of her cheeks to hold back her smile.

"Yes," he said, but made no move to leave her side.

"Do you need to get your keys or anything?"

"Yeah." He blinked rapidly. "I'll be right back. Thanks, Tara. I owe you one."

"Don't worry about it." Tara covered her face with both her hands. "Just go."

Jack grinned rakishly and winked at Lizzy before he hurried to the back of the brewery. Lizzy almost swooned.

"Is he gone? Is it safe to look?" Tara asked from behind her hands.

"It's safe." Lizzy laughed sheepishly when Tara looked up. "Sorry about that little display. We're still getting used to this dating thing."

"Don't worry about it. To be honest, I think it's adorable. Jack literally could not take his eyes off you."

Lizzy flushed with equal parts embarrassment and pleasure.

"Okay. Let's go." Suddenly, Jack was by her side, tugging her off the barstool. He saluted his younger sister as he marched Lizzy toward the exit. "Thanks, sis. You're the best."

Lizzy had to skip and run to keep up with him, but her happiness bubbled over at his exuberance. Being with her made him feel this way. It was gratifying and heady, and she felt so treasured. And being with him made her feel the same way. She couldn't contain the giddy laugh that escaped her, and his deep laughter joined hers. He held out his hand to her, and she linked her fingers through his.

When they reached his car, Jack pushed her up against the side and crushed his mouth against hers. She wrapped her arms around his neck and melted against him. She liked him like this. A little out of control. A little helpless. She swept her tongue inside his mouth, and he groaned low in his throat. It made her feel in control and more than a little powerful. She did this to him.

He shifted against her, and she felt the door handle dig into her butt. The slight discomfort brought her out of the moment enough to make her aware that they were making out in the middle of the parking lot—the one right outside his family's brewery. It was glorious, but they needed to stop. Before all rational thought flew out the window, she turned her head to the side. But Jack wasn't to be deterred. He seamlessly changed course and trailed kisses down her neck. *Gah.* It felt so good.

"Jack," she said breathlessly with the last of her willpower.

"Hmm?" He moved on to nibble on her earlobe.

"We need to go." She placed her hands on his chest—trying not to notice the hard muscles underneath—and pushed gently.

He drew back from her, looking dazed with lust. "Go where?"

"We're going out for drinks, remember?"

"Right." He rubbed his hand down his face. "Right."

"Do you want me to drive?" she asked innocently. Horny Jack was sexy as sin but pretty darn adorable, too. She couldn't help teasing him a little. "You seem kind of out of it. Do you have enough blood going to your head?"

"Not at the moment. Thanks to you and that dress." He

leaned in for a hard, fast kiss, leaving her a bit light-headed herself. "But I'm okay to drive. Did you have a place in mind, or do you want me to pick?"

"You choose. I'm easy." She cringed as soon as the words left her mouth. "That's not . . . I mean . . . I'm not picky."

"I know what you mean, doofus." He held open the passenger-side door for her.

Lizzy stuck her tongue out at him and got in the car. A giant smile spread across her face as excitement coursed through her. She liked the direction their second date was headed. Maybe one thing would lead to other things sooner than she'd thought.

~

It was karaoke night at the sushi sports bar.

Jack drove all the way over to the next town specifically to come to the most unromantic venue for their nightcap. He was so turned on that he wanted to drive them off to the side of the road and jump Lizzy. Because a back seat quickie would be the perfect culmination of decades-long yearning. Fuck. He badly needed to cool off, and watching Lizzy sing might be the only thing in the world that could help him do that tonight. She was a truly horrible singer, and she always—without fail—sang when she got tipsy.

"Don't fool yourself for a minute that I don't know what you're up to," Lizzy whisper-screamed at him as they walked into the restaurant.

"I haven't the faintest clue what you're talking about." He widened his eyes innocently.

"See." She pointed her finger so close to his face that he flinched a little. "There's the tell. You talk funny when you're lying. *I haven't the faintest clue.* Ha!"

"Come on." He placed his hand on her lower back and led her to a small table near the bar. "Let's sit and order some drinks."

"I'll stick to water. Thank you very much." She plopped down on the chair he pulled out for her and crossed her arms over her chest.

He quickly drew his eyes away from the tantalizing view and focused on the task at hand. "Are you sure? They have plum wine."

"Shit," she said succinctly. She loved plum wine.

"And lychee shochu," he tempted in a lilting voice.

"Bastard." She glared at him.

"I'm hurt." He put his hand to his chest. "I brought you here because they have your favorite drinks. How can you be mad at me for thinking of you?"

"Because . . ." Her pout turned into an edgy smile, and she brought her mouth close to his ear. "Sex."

He nearly jumped out of his seat. The forbidden word echoed in his mind as though his head were an empty, cavernous space. *Sex, sex, sex, sex . . .*

"Excuse me." He waved his hand frantically to get someone's—anyone's—attention and yelled across the restaurant, "We're ready to order."

"What's the matter, Park? You seem a little agitated," Lizzy cooed like a cat playing with a cornered mouse.

"I'm fine," he squeaked. He waved his hand faster, craning his neck to get noticed by a passing server.

"I'll be right with you," the server said with a friendly, unhurried smile, and disappeared behind the kitchen.

Jack gave up and sank into his chair, avoiding looking at Lizzy. When he heard a small sigh across the table, he finally met her eyes and said plaintively, "Let's just have some fun."

Her face fell in disappointment. "So you want to keep things . . . the same?"

"And different." He reached across the table to take ahold of her hand.

"This dress is different." She arched an eyebrow in challenge.

"Yes, it's very different." Without his permission, his gaze roamed her body, and heat flooded his veins again.

"In a good way?" she asked, her eyes skittering to the side.

"In a very good way." His heart wrenched at her uncertainty. "You're so beautiful. I can't breathe properly when I look at you."

"Then why do you want to watch me make an asshat out of myself?"

"Because breathing is an important aspect of a human being's life," he said with a dry smile.

"Didn't you get the memo? Breathing is overrated."

He pulled her hand close and kissed her knuckles. Her eyelashes fluttered, and a tremulous breath left her lips. *Holy shit.* He carefully placed her hand back on the table. "And I can't lose my head."

"Why not?" Her chin tipped up in challenge.

"Because you're you." How else could he explain that he couldn't risk losing her? That she was too important for him to rush into this?

"Well, being me is starting to sound like a drag," she grumbled.

"All right, folks. What can I get you started with?" At long last, the server materialized at their table and handed them the drink menu.

"I'll have the lemon shochu," Jack said, picking the first drink he saw on the menu. He glanced quickly at Lizzy. "And I think she's sticking with water."

"No, I'll have the lychee shochu," she corrected him, and smiled. "We're going to have some fun."

Once the server left with their orders, Jack laughed with

relief and gratitude. "You're not going to make an asshat out of yourself because I plan to be the biggest goofball this town has ever seen."

"Yeah, right." Lizzy rolled her eyes. "Every time you sing at karaoke, someone always comes up to you and tells you to go on *American Idol*."

"That's because they haven't seen me dancing." He winked at her and earned himself a twinkling laugh.

"Oh, please don't." She gave him an exaggerated cringe. "I don't want you to hurt yourself."

"If you can sing up there, then I can dance."

"Asshole," she said, reaching across the table to slap his shoulder. "Fine, boogie away."

"Ow." He rubbed his stinging shoulder. Lizzy had spicy hands. It was the Korean description for people whose slightest tap smarted like a son of a bitch. Spicy hands or not, he grinned like a fool at her. "Let's get this party started."

"I wonder which one of us will get us thrown out of here first," she murmured.

Sipping their shochu cocktails, they studied the songbook like they had a final exam on it the next day. He planned to crash and burn to take the heat off Lizzy and chose the perfect song for his public humiliation.

"I'm up," he said, and took one more gulp of his drink.

Jack faced the back of the small stage and shook his ass as a teaser. He heard a few catcalls and felt his ears grow hot, but he pushed on. When the distinctive intro blared from the speakers, he spun around to face the audience and started singing "Gangnam Style" in a low voice, holding the microphone close to his mouth.

Then he circled one fist by his head like he was swinging a lasso and reined his imaginary horse with his other hand, mimicking Psy's iconic choreography. That part wasn't too bad, but his damn legs refused to gallop, so he alternated between hopping and running in place. The dance itself was hilarious, but he was butchering it into the realm of the ridiculous. Not on purpose. He just had zero rhythm.

When Lizzy almost fell out of her chair laughing, he grinned and "danced" harder. He didn't mind that he probably looked like he was convulsing uncontrollably—several people were giving him concerned glances.

He sang his heart out. That part he couldn't help. He loved singing, and he wasn't half bad at it. That was probably why he wasn't booed off the stage. They forgave him for his hideous dancing thanks to his singing. When the song ended, he took a deep bow and came back to their table.

"I don't know how they do it," he huffed, collapsing onto his seat.

"You don't know how who does what?" Lizzy said, handing him his drink.

He threw aside the straw and drank deeply from his mug. "I don't know how those Korean idols sing and dance at the same time. It's seriously hard."

"Please, don't," Lizzy said, her expression deadly serious. "*Do not* compare what you just did up there to a Korean boy band performance."

"Harsh." He finished his drink in a few more gulps.

The server who had been so hard to track down a while ago appeared at his side in a magical instant. "Another?"

"Yes, please." Jack handed him the empty glass.

"I'll have another, too." Lizzy pointed at her nearly depleted mug.

With a gallant nod, the server left them.

"Did you pick your song yet?" Jack asked, leaning over to peek at the songbook.

"Yup." She nodded with a determined set of her lips. "I'm going with 'Can't Take My Eyes Off You.'"

"You're going to be awesome."

"Liar," she said affectionately.

When it was her turn, she graciously took the stage and held the mic with both hands. He could tell she wasn't quite tipsy enough to take the nervous edge off. *Shit.* His heart swooped to his stomach and slammed back up. She was doing this for him. She took his plea to *just have some fun* to heart and wanted to put him at ease.

His blood pounded in his ears as her voice cracked on the first note. He was falling. The ground was rushing up to meet him, but he didn't hit it. He kept falling. He'd been in love with Lizzy for so long that he didn't remember how it had happened. Loving her had always been a part of him. A quiet, tender ache. Something that could be contained inside him. But what he felt now was nothing like that.

Lizzy giggled into the microphone and renewed her efforts. Off-key and lovable, she charmed the crowd into cheering for her and singing along with her. He couldn't take his eyes off her. He was bewitched. Nothing about this was funny anymore. She was confident, courageous, and beautiful even when she laughed at herself. And he was falling for her in a way he'd never allowed himself to love her before.

His plan to cool down his longing for Lizzy had failed spectacularly. He had to stop the free fall. How else was he going to let her go if their venture into the dating sphere didn't work out? How else could he content himself with having only a piece of her if they went back to being just friends? But he had no idea how to stop himself from falling in love with Lizzy. How could he? He'd never fallen in love before. Not like this.

When she came back to their table flushed and smiling, he leaned across the table and kissed her because he couldn't not kiss her. She tasted like lychee and laughter, and he felt her smile against his lips. He wanted to capture this moment—capture this memory of her—and sear it into his mind. Even if he couldn't have her forever, this moment was his to keep. This sliver of her was his. He reluctantly drew back even though he wanted to go on kissing her until everything else disappeared.

"What was that for?" she asked with a shy blush staining her cheeks.

"Because you're you," he whispered.

"I guess being me isn't half bad," Lizzy said breathlessly.

Jack couldn't believe that the most perfect woman in the world was sitting across from him. He wanted to weep in gratitude for her existence. This was enough. He didn't want to be greedy for more, and he didn't want to lose how much he had. Just this much was enough for him.

CHAPTER FOURTEEN

Lizzy drank more lychee shochu and sang a ridiculous number of songs. Having fun with Jack was the best kind of fun. And she loved the secret flutter of her heart every time he touched her or looked at her just so.

"Last call for drinks and karaoke," the bartender shouted with his hands cupped over his mouth.

"Do you want another drink?" Jack asked.

"No, not if I'm going to get up bright and early for our morning run," Lizzy said.

"How about another song?"

"I'll pass on that, too." She gingerly placed the tips of her fingers on her throat. "I sang so much, I'm losing my voice."

"I think I'll sing one last song," he said, flipping through the songbook.

"Oh, God. I don't know if my sides can handle any more laughing." Her stomach muscles already felt sore from all the laughter. She was going to hurt like she'd done a hundred crunches tomorrow morning.

"I'll take it easy on you with this one." A corner of his lips lifted in a crooked smile that made her heart trip.

They were among the last customers left at the sushi sports bar, but everyone focused on the stage when Jack stepped up to the mic. Even his silly dancing theatrics couldn't detract from his smooth-as-butter voice. She'd always loved listening to him sing, but now it sent shivers of awareness down her spine.

As Jack sang, silence descended in the room. No one was ready—least of all her—for the seductive croon. She used to listen to John Legend's "All of Me" on repeat on those days she felt especially lonely. It spoke of a love so true and beautiful that it filled her with hope and determination to find it for herself one day.

Jack captured and held her eyes, and his voice vibrated through her body.

She knew the words coming out of his mouth weren't his. And she knew they weren't meant for her. But she wished . . . in that moment . . . oh, how she wished they were true. So she held her breath and listened and pretended that the words were his and they were meant for her. She let the warmth, the pain, and the beauty of the love fill her.

The thundering applause brought her out of her heart-wrenching dream. Her cheeks were wet with tears, and she quickly wiped them away before Jack approached the table. He had practically begged her to take things slowly, and here she was daydreaming about love and happily ever after. He would freak out if he found out.

"Thirty isn't too old to go on *American Idol*, is it?" she quipped while she got her wayward emotions under control.

"I'm not sure how to take that comment." Jack narrowed his

eyes at her. "It's like you're insulting me and complimenting me at the same time."

"I'm cautiously optimistic that you'll take my comment in the way most agreeable to you," she said, giving her most lawyerly nonanswer.

"Does talking straight shorten a lawyer's life span or something?"

"By big, hulking chunks."

"We can't have that." Jack chuckled and waved down their server. "Carry on with your word games, then."

Lizzy smiled in answer, neither denying nor confirming her intent to play word games.

"Oh, you're good," he said, wagging a finger at her. "No wonder you make the big bucks."

After paying the bill and tipping generously, they made their way to his car. Jack didn't push her up against it to kiss her this time. He just opened the car door for her like the gentleman he was, and she dropped into the passenger seat with a forlorn sigh. The effects of the dress seemed to have worn off.

Their drive to Weldon Brewery was quiet but not uncomfortable. She drummed her fingers on the door panel in rhythm with the song playing on the radio and reminisced about the eventful night. They pulled into the brewery's parking lot to find her car to be its only occupant. Jack parked right next to it and turned to her.

"I had fun tonight," he said, reaching over to tuck a strand of hair behind her ear.

She shivered at the slight touch. "That was the goal, right?"

"Fun is always a worthy goal to strive for." He drew close to her.

She leaned toward him as though pulled by a magnet. "Kissing should also be up there as far as life goals go."

"Way, way up there," he whispered.

She closed the remaining distance between them and kissed him with a little moan. She'd been dying to kiss him since he'd sung "All of Me." She wanted to kiss the lips that had formed those beautiful words—to feel the words on them . . . to absorb them into herself. But once their lips met, all she could think about was Jack and this moment. He tasted like lemons and smelled like those woods they had hiked through—fresh and masculine. And she wanted more.

She climbed over the center console and straddled Jack's lap, not once breaking their kiss. He groaned against her lips and buried a hand in her hair. She sucked in a sharp breath when his hand fisted and tugged her head back, and shuddered as his open mouth trailed down her exposed neck. His hands grasped her shoulders and pushed her away from him. Before she could protest, his lips found the soft mounds of her breasts, spilling above the low neckline. She whimpered and shifted on his lap. With a low growl, his tongue dipped below her dress and bra, and brushed against the top of her hardened nipples.

"Jack," she gasped as she brazenly thrust her chest into his face.

With rough, impatient hands, he unzipped her dress and pulled down her bodice and bra, and took her fully into his mouth. Her head rolled back, and her hips gyrated on his lap, desperately seeking friction. He pushed her back and sucked in her other nipple when the car horn blared into the quiet night.

They both froze to the spot, and the sound of their harsh breathing filled the car. Jack released her nipple from his mouth, and she shivered when the cool night air brushed against the sensitive tip. His hands were gentle as he restored her clothes to their rightful places, but she didn't like the grim set of his lips.

Desire still pulsed between her thighs, and she didn't want

the night to end like this. She wanted to finish what they had started. "Come home with me."

His hands stilled for a moment, then he zipped up her dress with swift finality. "Let's skip our run tomorrow. I don't want to be a walking zombie for the rest of the day."

She scrambled over the center console and crawled back to the passenger seat with as much dignity as she could muster— which wasn't much considering she was jutting her scantily clad ass into Jack's face. Once she was seated, she adjusted her dress to cover as much of herself as possible and smoothed a hand over her hair.

"You can't keep doing this," she said, nervous but resolute.

"I'm not going to make a habit out of skipping our morning runs—"

"Just shut up," she snapped, but her anger died as quickly as it had flared. They needed to talk this out once and for all. "I really want this to work, Jack."

"I do, too," he said with a fleeting glance her way.

"Then why do you keep pulling back?"

"Things got out of hand just now. I didn't mean for things to go so far." He massaged the back of his neck.

"You know I'm not just talking about tonight." She was getting tired of speaking to his profile.

He blew out a long breath and met her eyes at last. "I just want us to be certain that this is going to work out before we go too far."

"How would we know that if we don't give this a real try?" She gently unfurled his hand from the steering wheel and held it in her own. "I'm not just talking about sex. I understand that you want to take things slowly. But I feel like I cannonballed myself into this thing while you're just dipping your toes."

He chuckled under his breath. "If you only knew . . ."

"Then tell me. I want to know. I'm trying to understand."

Jack stared at her with an unreadable expression, then he looked away. "Our friendship means more to me than you can imagine. If we go too far, too fast, we won't be able to return to being friends if we realize this isn't going to work."

"How can we make this work when you're already preparing to fail?" Her whispered words were hardly audible. "We might as well not try."

She waited for him to contradict her—to tell her that he wanted this enough to risk everything. But he said nothing. Her heart cracked and splintered. She understood his silence only too well. He was trying to protect them from getting hurt before it was too late. Little did he know that she'd already come too far.

~~~~~

Jack had let her drive away without trying to stop her—without begging her not to give up on them. Then he'd spent half the night second-guessing himself. But it was for the best. No matter how hard he tried to hold back—to take things slowly—he couldn't stop himself from racing toward her. If things went any further, he would have risked everything to have all of her. He would have risked losing all of her.

It was better this way. Maybe if he repeated that enough times, he would believe it, and the hollow ache in his chest would go away. He had thrown away the brilliant vibrancy of the last few days—the alluring hope of something more, something wonderful. This morning, he had to look at Lizzy and only see his best friend—someone he loved in secret, someone he would never truly have.

He turned the doorknob to Sparrow and found it locked. His brows drew together as panic attempted to erupt inside him.

Just to make sure, he tried the door again. Locked. Maybe Lizzy forgot to leave the door unlocked for him. It wasn't store hours yet. So he knocked.

Shannon hurried to the door and opened it wide. "Good morning, Jack."

"Hey, Shannon." He peeked over her shoulder into the bookstore. "Is Lizzy in the back room?"

"Actually, she hasn't come down yet." She glanced at her watch and pursed her lips. "That's pretty unusual for her."

"It's probably because she got in late last night. We went out for drinks after I got off from work."

"Oh." Her smile turned wily. "Maybe you tired her out."

He cleared his throat loudly. "We did sing a lot of karaoke."

"Karaoke." Shannon blinked. "I see."

"Well, I'm going to run up and check on her," he said, already turning around. "See you in a bit."

"Sure," she said with a worried frown. "See you."

He climbed the stairs at a quick clip and raised his hand to knock but stopped before his knuckles met the door. She might not want to see him. But why would she not want to see him? She was the one who'd suggested they stopped trying. He leaned his forehead against the door. Who was he kidding? He'd all but told her they were doomed from the start. What else could she have said?

He had been so afraid of things not working out that he hadn't allowed himself to envision really being with her. It still terrified him to let hope take root in his heart, but Lizzy was finally seeing him in a new light and opening herself up to him. This might be his only chance to have her belong to him as he belonged to her. Was he seriously giving that up to hold on to their friendship?

Hell no.

He rapped his knuckles against the door. After a second, he did it again. He was going to knock until his knuckles were raw. He wouldn't quit until she let him in so he could grovel for another chance.

"Don't." The door swung open, and Lizzy held up a finger.

Her hair was damp, and she didn't have a scrap of makeup on her face. She was so beautiful that it felt like a punch in the gut. He felt himself free-falling again, but he wasn't going to let fear stop him from fighting for his chance to be with Lizzy. Even if it wasn't forever—even if it was just for two weeks.

"Cannonball," he whispered, his eyes imploring her to forgive him.

She gasped and searched his face. With a sound somewhere between a sob and a laugh, she threw herself at him. He had to widen his stance to keep from stumbling into the railing.

"Asshole," she said, burrowing into his chest.

He tightened his arms around her. "I know, right?"

"You hurt me." She leaned back to meet his gaze. "Don't do it again."

"I'm so sorry." He traced the back of his fingers down her cheek. "I had no idea I could hurt you. Not like this."

"You can. So don't." She held his hand against her cheek and turned his hand to kiss his palm. "I told you. I cannonballed into this. I'm soaking wet."

Her eyes grew wide, and her cheeks turned as red as a signal light. His dick knew exactly where her mind had gone and got hard fast enough to leave him dizzy. His brain caught up a beat late, and he smiled wolfishly. "Are you now?"

"I'm metaphorically wet. Meaning I'm committed to this thing . . ." She frantically waved her hand back and forth between them. "Like I'm all in. Like it's too late to try to keep my head above water because I'm soaked through."

She whimpered. How was she this adorable? While his hard-on throbbed a painful rhythm, he wanted to give her a break. "I'm all in, too. No more safety net. No more pulling away."

The brilliance of her smile almost made his heart stop. "That's all I want. I want us to have a real chance."

"A real chance," he murmured. He was a lucky bastard. How had he stumbled onto this golden chance to win Lizzy's love? "I like the sound of that."

"Well?" She arched an eyebrow.

"Uh . . ." Did he miss something while he was doing cartwheels in his head?

"Do I have to do everything around here?" She pushed onto her toes and pressed her lips against his.

He kissed her back with a heady sense of possession—he had every right to kiss her like this. It was a decadent and leisurely kiss—both of them secure in their newfound commitment. He tugged her flush against him and lifted her off her feet. When they broke apart, they were breathless and laughing.

"Are you ready to head down to the bookstore?" Jack asked, moving his hands up and down her soft arms. He wasn't ready to stop touching her. "Shannon must be getting worried."

"Oh no. I didn't mean to worry her. Let me just grab my keys."

They walked into Sparrow with their hands linked and were greeted by the now familiar jingle of the shopkeeper's bell.

"Jack?" Shannon called out from the back. "How's Lizzy?"

"I'm doing great," Lizzy yelled out with a quick squeeze of his hand.

Jack drew his shoulders back and stood a little taller, proud of himself for making her happy.

"Oh, thank goodness." Shannon rushed up to the front of

the store and wrapped Lizzy in a hug. "I was worried I gave out bad advice yesterday."

Jack looked between the two women. "What advice?"

"Let's just say Shannon was the one who lent me that dress." Lizzy grinned.

"Thank you." He turned to the shop owner and grabbed her hand in both of his. "Thank you and God bless you."

"Don't say I never did nothing for you." She winked. "So you two kids are all good?"

"Yes." He met Lizzy's gaze and smiled. "We're all good."

CHAPTER FIFTEEN

I want to live in this bookstore," Lizzy said, sinking into one of the refinished chairs in the new and improved Sparrow. The place was turning into a cheerful booklover's haven right before her eyes—it was beginning to rival Hideaway as her favorite spot in the world. All the hard work was so worth it.

"You already kind of do," Jack pointed out. "Downstairs during the day. Upstairs during the night."

"I know." She sighed dreamily. "Isn't life perfect?"

Her life in Weldon *was* perfect—at least since this morning when Jack whispered *cannonball* to her. Their budding romance, Sparrow, the pace of the small-town life . . . Everything felt so right. She hadn't felt this whole and content in such a long time. Would she be able to carry this feeling back to Los Angeles? Was it really just the burnout that had made her life back home so . . . empty?

Jack straddled one of their masterpieces and leaned a forearm across the back. Her eyes promptly fell to said forearm, and she lost her train of thought. She wanted to leave her comfy perch and go run her fingers over its fascinating grooves and ridges. What was holding her back? Nothing. Absolutely nothing.

She sashayed over to him and ran her hand over his forearm, reveling in its hard strength. He held himself still and watched her with hooded lids. Then he reached up with his free hand and tugged her down by her arm. She lowered her head without resistance, enthralled by the heat in his eyes.

"Wait." She drew away from him. "I'm all sweaty and gross from moving all this furniture."

"I don't mind," he said in a low, sexy voice and tugged her back.

Lizzy didn't mind that he was a little rumpled and sweaty, either. It was actually rather sexy. So she leaned down and nipped at his lips. He sat up taller and kissed her deeply, and she hummed as heat spread through her. But when he buried his hand in her hair, she pulled back again.

"Wait. Hang on." She was certain that her hair smelled.

Jack groaned and let his head fall against her stomach.

"Just let me go upstairs and shower really fast," she said.

He straightened up and glanced at his watch. "I should actually head out and get ready for work. I need to wash up, too."

"You can use my shower." The words were out before she could stop them, and images of them showering together rampaged through her head.

Jack stood to his full height and looked down at her with an intensity that made her heart stutter. He swooped down and kissed her thoroughly before releasing her.

"As tempting as that offer is"—his eyes roamed over her body—"I can't. I don't have any clean clothes, and I don't want to be late for work."

"Oh," she said, both embarrassed and disappointed.

He brought his mouth close to her ear and said in a low voice, "And I refuse to be rushed the first time I have you."

"Oh." Her knees wobbled.

"Will you wait up for me?" He trailed kisses along her jawline.

"Yes." The single word held more air than sound.

"Good." With one last kiss—a lingering promise—he stepped back. "See you later."

See you later as in he would see her later to make hot, sloppy love to her? Okay. Sure. She was good with that. *Gah.* She was soaking wet, and she didn't mean metaphorically.

"See you later." She waved weakly.

Now the question was: how was she going to survive until midnight without losing her shit? Washing, shaving, moisturizing, and dressing wouldn't occupy her for more than a couple of hours. She needed something to do to stay busy. *Hmm.* She picked up her trusty clipboard and searched for the next task to tackle.

"Window display." She nodded with approval. "Perfect."

But her eyebrows burrowed into a frown when she glanced at the front window. Well, not the actual window but the deep purple curtains that blocked it from sight. The checkout counter used to stand in front of the window, but they'd moved it to the back of the store when they'd brought the other furniture in. Now the space was occupied by a round table—they should totally showcase some new releases on there—and a bright, yellow chair.

She walked past the table and chair and pulled back the curtains with a sharp tug. She coughed and waved her hand in front of her face as dust clouds plumed around her. But once the offending curtains were pushed firmly to the sides, the soft hue of late-afternoon sunlight flooded the storefront. She stood for a moment enjoying the view of the tidy, residential street outside the bookstore.

The curtains definitely had to go. Not only would customers be able to peek inside from the sidewalk, the store itself felt a whole lot airier with the outside view. Even when they set up displays, the exposed window should open up the space and make the bookstore more welcoming inside and out. Excitement buzzed through her. This was going to work. They were going to make Sparrow a beloved local bookstore.

Lizzy moved the few boxes that were stashed on the display area to the back room. Dusty and sweaty again, she was glad she hadn't taken that shower—the one she'd originally planned on taking by herself to kiss Jack without worrying about her smelly hair. Not the one she'd imagined taking *with* him, where they were both slippery with soap, hot water streaming down his hard, naked body, and his hands were . . . Oh, my *God*. The back room grew sweltering under her deliciously naughty thoughts. She grasped the front of her shirt and fanned it vigorously. Midnight felt like eons away.

The doorbell jingled just as she came out from the back, dusting off her hands with her horniness under tenuous control.

"Wow," Elliot said, his wide eyes taking in the redecorated storefront. "Mom, can we live here?"

"I was thinking the exact same thing," Lizzy said, laughing. "We can be roomies."

"Cool. Roomies," the little boy crowed. Then he zipped to a rocking chair and proceeded to rock back and forth with enthusiasm.

"Can you believe he asked to be picked up early from his playdate so he could check out what we did today?" Shannon shook her head, wearing a fond smile. "Anyway, sorry for leaving you to watch the store again."

"You were gone for less than half an hour." Lizzy waved away her friend's apology. "Don't worry about it. But I'm think-

ing you should teach me how to use the cash register and what-
not in case a customer comes in while you're gone."

"Oh, my gosh. I can't put you to work like that. From now
on, I'm putting the BE RIGHT BACK sign up like I used to." Before
Lizzy could protest, Shannon turned her attention to the front
window. "So what's next on the list? I'm guessing the window
display?"

"Yup. It's going to be so much fun." Lizzy pinched a piece
of the purple curtain between her thumb and index finger.
"Would you mind terribly if we got rid of these curtains?"

"No, not at all. I had them up mostly so that I wouldn't be
reminded of the lack of a window display." Shannon grimaced
and lifted up one end of the curtain. "They're pretty hideous,
aren't they?"

"It's not that they're hideous," Lizzy said diplomatically—
another one of her lawyerly skills. This one was most often used
to gently inform her clients that they'd fucked up and needed
to clean up their act. "But taking them down will open up the
store so much."

"You're right." Shannon glanced around the store. "The space
does feel more open, and I love all the natural light we're getting."

"Awesome. It's down with the purple curtains, then." Lizzy
bounced a tiny bit on her heels.

"Down with the purple curtains!" Elliot roared as he ran
over to test-drive another chair.

"Crap. Sugar high," Shannon muttered under her breath.
"He snuck in cookies again. I can't really blame him, though.
They always have fresh-baked cookies at his friend's house. I
wouldn't be able to resist, either."

Between Lizzy, Shannon, and her sugar-pumped son, they
managed to take off the heavy curtains and dispose of them,
coughing and sneezing all the way. Lizzy was now sweaty,

dusty, and snotty. But she only considered Elliot's proposal to burn the curtains for a split second.

"What kind of window displays are you envisioning?" Lizzy asked Shannon as they both stared at the empty display area.

"You should put a life-size Iron Man suit up there," Elliot piped up from his perch on the rocking chair where he was engaging in his new favorite pastime—reading.

"We're not a comic book store," Shannon pointed out.

"It's not only for comic book stores." The boy put a finger in between the pages to mark his spot. "When I was visiting Dad, he took me to this shoe store at the mall, and they had the coolest Iron Man suit set up by the door. I totally thought it was real for a second."

"We don't sell shoes here, either," his mother said dryly.

Elliot shrugged and returned to his book, satisfied with contributing his two cents to the conversation.

"I just have some vague ideas about making it seasonal," Shannon belatedly answered Lizzy's question.

"Yeah. There are so many options." Lizzy squinted at the space, trying to visualize the perfect display. Of course, one of her favorites from Hideaway popped into mind. "You know what looks nice? I love it when stores have open books hanging from the ceiling like they're a flock of birds. Ooh, ours could be a flock of sparrows."

"I *love* it." Her friend clasped her hands in front of her chest. "So how would we do that? With fishing line?"

"Probably."

"I think that would look beautiful." Shannon turned to the front entrance when the shopkeeper's bell announced a new arrival. "Hi, Lisa. It's good to see you."

"Hi, Shannon." The customer's mouth dropped open as she looked around the bookstore. "Oh, my. Am I in the right store?"

"Do you like our new look?" Shannon chewed on her bottom lip nervously.

"I absolutely adore it," Lisa whispered, walking deeper into the store. "I have to come in here more often. And bring my girls. It's so bright and cheerful."

Lizzy felt such a sense of accomplishment and joy for the part she'd played in Sparrow's transformation. She bumped Shannon's shoulder, who beamed at her. Her friend's heart must have felt so full at seeing her store grow and flourish under her caring hands.

It was so different from spending her days arguing with her opposing counsels and appeasing her clients. With her job, the best-case scenario was a settlement where both parties walked away somewhat dissatisfied. One party felt like they paid too much, and the other party felt like they received too little. It wasn't ideal, but that was the nature of compromise. Trials weren't any better. Considering the drain on time, resources, and emotional reserve, the "winner" wasn't really a winner. In the end, all lawsuits were lose-lose situations.

But it was what she did. She didn't know how to do anything else. The only thing that gave meaning to her job was becoming the best one at it. At times, she resented her mom for pressuring her with her constant disapproval—driving Lizzy to push herself harder and harder yet. But it was her own choice, too, because if she didn't make partner, what was the point of it all? The thought left a hollow feeling in her chest.

~

"How are you doing back here, Mom?" Jack asked, walking into the kitchen. He was on his break, and he didn't want to spend it alone with his thoughts—thoughts about Lizzy and what was going to happen tonight.

"Our fry cook is out today, so I've got my hands full," she replied, stirring this and flipping that.

"And it's a busy night on top of that." He went to stand behind her and massaged her tight shoulders. "I wish I could help out, but I know I'll just get in the way."

His mom reached behind her and patted his hand. "You're needed on the floor. I've got it covered back here."

"You're Superwoman." He continued kneading her shoulders. It was the only way to make her take a breather.

"I prefer Wonder Woman." She swatted his hand away after a minute and returned to cooking. "Speaking of Wonder Woman, how is Lizzy doing?"

"Lizzy? Doing?" he stuttered, grateful that his mom's eyes were on the stove so she didn't see his blush. "Fine. She's doing fine. Why is she Wonder Woman?"

"She's living up to Mrs. Chung's expectations. That's not an easy feat." She glanced up briefly with a mischievous smile. "Besides, Lizzy has always been an overachiever."

"Yeah." He looked down and scuffed his shoe on the floor, fighting against the insecurities rising in him. Lizzy wanted him, not some fellow overachiever. "She's amazing."

His mom met his eyes and held on to them for long enough to make him fidget. It seemed like she was reading a word bubble over his head that spelled out his every thought in real time. But she dropped her eyes again without saying anything.

"I should get back out there," he said, pointing his thumb over his shoulder. "Do you want me to send Tara in as backup?"

"There's no need," she reassured him, sprinkling furikake over a basket of piping-hot fries. "This is ready. For table eight."

"Got it." He grabbed a tray and loaded the furikake fries on it. "Let us know if it gets too much."

The crowd didn't let up for most of the night, which was a

blessing for Jack. Between lust and nerves, he would've been a jittery mess if they hadn't been busy. But as the night neared the end, he was impatient to go to Lizzy. Not because of the prospect of sex—well, that, too—but mostly because he missed her.

He didn't know how he used to be able to go for months without seeing her. It probably had to do with this falling-in-love business. A person had very little control over themselves when they were free-falling. He could barely last eight hours without seeing her. He laughed under his breath, shaking his head, but his smile froze on his face a moment later.

What was he going to do when she went back to Los Angeles in less than two weeks? And how much harder would it be to let her go after he made love to her? A vise clamped around his heart and squeezed. He took a deep breath. He didn't have the capacity to worry about that right now. He would risk whatever heartache awaited him down the line to have her tonight—to make her his, even for a little while.

Besides, it was too soon to worry. McBain remained frustratingly silent, but no news meant there was still a chance of good news. He might be able to join her in LA. He felt a familiar mix of nerves, hope, and excitement churning in his stomach. He resisted the urge to check his email yet again. It was close to midnight. He doubted anyone would be working at this hour.

He changed out of his T-shirt into a button-down he'd brought to the brewery earlier. Midnight or not, this was a date, and he wanted to look nice for Lizzy. His hands shook as he buttoned his shirt. It was too late to pick up flowers. Should he stop by the liquor store to buy a bottle of wine? To hell with it. He had no time to waste. He needed to see her.

"Good night, Alex." He marched out of the brewery without giving his brother a chance to respond.

When he arrived at the bookstore, he jumped out of his car

and ran up the stairs to Lizzy's apartment, taking two steps at a time. He knocked without pausing. He was breathing hard, but it had very little to do with the trip up the stairs.

His beleaguered breathing stopped altogether when the door opened. Lizzy stood before him in a silky, cream cami set with her hair falling down her shoulders and her face scrubbed clean of makeup. God, she was fucking beautiful. He had to hold himself motionless so he wouldn't lunge at her.

Jack didn't exactly have a plan as to how the night was going to turn out when he rushed over to see her. He had vague ideas about watching a movie on the couch and slowly making his move if she still seemed into the idea. By her attire, he would guess that she was still into the idea, but maybe this was what she normally wore to bed. It was past midnight after all.

"Well, are you going to stand there all night?" she asked in a slightly breathless voice.

He responded by staring some more at her, rooted to the spot. With a small smile quirking her lips, Lizzy reached out to grab his hand and tugged him inside. On autopilot, he kicked off his shoes and let her lead him toward the couch.

"Do you want a glass of wine?" She turned to him before they sat down.

"No, thank you." Victory. He managed to form words.

"Okay." She sank down on the sofa, and he lowered himself beside her.

Without meaning to, he sat down so close to her that their hips and thighs were pressed together, then his hand developed a mind of its own and settled itself on her bare thigh. He could feel her gaze on the side of his face, but he stared straight ahead at the TV, which was turned off.

This was similar to his not-quite-formed plan. They were sitting on the couch, and he was staring at the TV, which was kind of like watching a movie. He ignored the voice that told him it was nothing like watching a movie and that he was being weird. Now all he had to do was scope out whether Lizzy really wanted to do this. If she did, he would make his move.

His fingers tightened on her thigh. She was so soft. Then his hand made another executive decision and began smoothing up and down the length of her thigh. A shiver ran through her. Or had he imagined it? Did this count as scoping her out, or was he just feeling her up? He snatched his hand away and laced his fingers tightly together over his knees, sitting up and away from Lizzy.

"Jack?" Her voice was timid—uncertain.

He turned and searched her face. Had he made her feel that way? But behind the uncertainty, he saw the softness of her gaze, the flush on her cheeks, and her parted lips. There was anticipation and . . . want. Still, he had to be sure because he had mush for brains at the moment.

"May I kiss you?" he asked in a husky rumble.

"Yes, please." A sweet smile replaced the uncertainty on her face.

He reached out with a trembling hand to cup her cheek and pressed his lips against hers in a featherlight kiss. His blood pounded in his ears, and he breathed roughly against her lips. Every time he kissed her, he could hardly believe it. This was Lizzy. He was kissing her. His heart clenched almost painfully at how precious this moment was. How could this beautiful, amazing woman be in his arms right now?

She slowly moved her lips over his and hummed softly. The need to possess her crashed over him with such force that he pulled back with a sharp gasp. Before worry could cloud her eyes, he pressed a kiss on her forehead, her temple, then the corner of her mouth. She wanted him, and there was no question he wanted her. But his need for her was too great to unleash. He didn't want to scare her away.

So with exquisite care, he traced his lips down her neck, lightly cradling her head in his hand. She squirmed a little beneath him, and he placed his other hand on her waist, gently restraining her. He needed to do this slowly and carefully; otherwise, he would lose control. He traveled back up her neck and claimed her mouth once more. This time, he parted his lips because he couldn't resist the urge to taste her.

Lizzy swept her tongue across the inside of his bottom lip, and he groaned. Helpless against her urging, he chased her tongue with his, flicking it in and out of her mouth in a tantalizing dance. Sweat sprang on his forehead as he fought to control himself. But he needed to touch her. He ran his hand down her hips and thighs, then he curled his fingers around the back of her knees. She sucked in a breath and wrapped her leg around his waist, brushing against his pounding cock in the process.

Every muscle in his body tensed, and he stopped breathing. This wasn't going to work. He couldn't hold back. With a feral growl he hardly recognized as his own, he grabbed her by the waist and hefted her onto his lap so that she fully straddled him. His head rolled back at the intense pleasure of her hot center pressing against his erection.

"God, Lizzy," he moaned. "I . . . I don't know if I can hang on. I can't . . . I can't hold back."

"Good," she said and swiveled her hips over him. "Now we're getting somewhere."

And this was how he was going to die.

CHAPTER SIXTEEN

Jack was holding back. Lizzy could feel it in the tautness of his body and his restrained touches. But even those tentative caresses had her burning up for more. She needed him to lose control because her control was already tenuously close to breaking, and when it did, she wanted him right beside her—or better yet, inside her.

She pulled her cami over her head and let it drop to the floor. When Jack's eyes fell to her breasts, she wanted to cover them with her arms, overcome with sudden shyness. But the dazed awe in his face stopped her, and she held still and waited. His hands left her waist and rose to cup her breasts. Her breath escaped her in a whoosh. His gaze shot to her face as his thumbs grazed over the hard tips of her breasts. Her head fell back, and she thrust her chest into his hands in a silent command for more.

He leaned her back and smoothed his lips on the side of her breast as his thumb traced the rounded bottom. A shiver ran through her, and she shifted impatiently on his lap.

"Fuck," he swore succinctly before he took one peak into his mouth and rolled it on his tongue.

She bit her lip and moaned as sharp pleasure shot to the juncture of her thighs. When he turned his attention to her other breast, she buried her fingers in his hair and held him tightly. He suddenly pulled her upright and crushed his lips against hers, kissing her with undisguised hunger. She kissed him back with equal intensity, glorying in the feel of wanting someone so desperately—and of being wanted back.

Lizzy needed to touch him. With trembling fingers, she unbuttoned his shirt and let out a whimper of frustration at her slow progress.

"Here," Jack said against her lips. "Let me."

When he undid the last button, she ripped his shirt apart and pushed it down his shoulders. She let him finish taking his shirt off the rest of the way because her hands were busy roaming over his hard, smooth chest. He tried to pull her back into his arms once he threw his shirt over the couch, but she held him back.

"I want to look at you," she said, her voice shaking. She ran her hands over his chest, then down to his ridiculous abs, letting her fingers dip in and out of the defined grooves. A laugh bubbled out of her. "I always thought you overdid it with your fitness routine, but I have to say I thoroughly approve if this is what results from it."

"I'm glad you approve." His lips quirked in a cocky grin, all his prior hesitancy gone. "Now I want to see the rest of you."

He crushed his lips against hers, and she caught fire again. When he stood from the sofa, she clung to him with her arms, legs, and lips. She felt the bed press against her back, and Jack drew away from her. She tightened her hold around him and buried her face against his neck. She was suddenly worried that he would be disappointed by her body. His was so breathtaking. She'd been perfectly happy with her soft body— even the rounded curve of her tummy—but for a brief moment, she wished she could be more beautiful for him. Then he made her forget all her foolish insecurities.

He carefully unwrapped her arms from his neck and drew back to look at her naked torso. Then he hooked his fingers in her shorts and panties and slowly tugged them down. She lifted her hips to help him, mesmerized by the intense wonder in his eyes.

"Jesus, Lizzy. I didn't think . . . I never thought . . ." His Adam's apple worked as he swallowed. "You're more beautiful than I'd ever imagined."

The corners of her mouth trembled as she smiled up at him. She had never felt more beautiful—more cherished—than she did in this moment. Still staring at her, Jack rose from the bed, unbuckled his jeans, and slid them down his hips. His thick, hard length pushed against his tight boxer briefs. She badly wanted to get her hands on him.

He climbed back on the bed and lay down on his side, holding himself up on his forearm. His eyes still devoured her as though he were starving for the sight of her, and his touch was almost reverent as he ran his hand down her arm, then up her waist to cup her breast. He leaned down and kissed her deeply, thoroughly, rolling her nipple between his thumb and index finger.

Hissing against his lips, she reached into his briefs and grabbed him tightly in her fist. He groaned as he jerked helplessly against her curious hand. He lifted his hips as she tugged down their last remaining barrier and kicked it off with his feet. She pulled back from their kiss to take a good look at him.

"Oh, my," she breathed. He was beautiful . . . and a little intimidating.

"We're going to fit perfectly," he said as though reading her thoughts.

Then he drew her back to him and kissed her until she didn't have room for any thoughts other than the need to have him inside her. He smoothed his hands down her stomach and her hips, then he looked into her eyes as he slowly pulled her legs up, his fingers digging into the soft flesh behind her knees.

"Open up for me," he said in a gravelly voice that sent a thrill down her spine.

He gently pushed her knees apart, and she complied wordlessly. His mouth fell open as he watched her. When his hand traveled between her thighs and touched her center, her hip jerked off the bed. With a low grunt of approval, he worked his fingers until she was writhing beside him. She was on the verge of tipping over into her climax when she clamped her thighs firmly over his hand.

"Not like this." She reached for him and pumped her hand up and down his length until he groaned. "I want you inside of me."

He climbed over her, and she pulled his head down to meet her eager lips. Their teeth clacked as their tongues tangled together—rough and clumsy in their need.

"Are you sure this is what you want?" He pushed up onto his elbows, and she felt him trembling against her as he held himself back. Sweat rolled down his jaw and onto her cheek. "If we do this, I can't go back to being friends with you. I won't be able to let you go."

His heated gaze held her captive, and she couldn't speak for a moment. But she knew what she wanted—what she needed.

"I don't want us to go back to being friends. I don't want you to let me go. I want you to . . ." She grabbed his ass and pulled him closer to her entrance. "Fuck. Me."

"No, Lizzy." His chuckle was a low timbre in his chest. "I'm going to make love to you. I'm going to make love to you until you fall apart in my arms and scream my name."

"Please," she whispered.

He rolled off her, and she cried in outrage. His lips quirked into a strained smile, and his eyes roamed over her naked body even as he reached for his pants on the floor. He grabbed his wallet and sheathed himself in a condom before he returned to her side.

"I'm going to make you mine now," he said with aching tenderness and yearning in his eyes.

"Please." She had no other words left to speak. She cupped his face and kissed him, pouring everything she felt into the kiss. How much she needed him. How much she wanted to be his. "Please."

He made her his, thoroughly and completely, until she screamed his name as promised—again and again.

~~~

One day at a time. Jack was going to cherish every moment he had with Lizzy before she returned to Los Angeles and reality set back in. Had she meant it when she said their time together in Weldon would be a trial period? What if she decided that she wanted to leave him and what happened in Weldon behind her when their time was up? He slammed the door on the thought. He couldn't worry about what would happen in a couple of weeks because he had to soak up the happiness he felt right now. There was no room for anything else.

She was sleeping soundly by his side, her body curved toward him and her hands tucked under her chin. He must've worn her out. His lips quirked into a smile. They'd reached for each other again in the middle of the night and earlier this morning. She caught fire in his arms every time he touched her, and he couldn't get enough of her.

He'd wondered what she would look like in her sleep. He used to tell himself that she probably snored and tangled up the blanket with restless limbs—and pushed whoever was sleeping beside her off the bed. He wasn't completely wrong. She snored a little and blew air out of her puckered lips like she was demolishing haphazardly built piggy houses in her dreams. It was ridiculously cute. But she hardly stirred while she slept, and he was in no danger of being kicked off the bed.

Waking up next to her and watching her sleeping face felt surreal. He never believed that he would be given the chance. He was awed and humbled that this kind, intelligent, and beautiful woman shared herself with him—made herself vulnerable to him. His heart expanded with joy and gratitude until he thought it would explode. Lizzy was his. For now.

Unable to hold back, he ran the back of his fingers down her cheek. Then, cupping her bare shoulder in his hand, he leaned down and placed a featherlight kiss on her parted lips. She stirred but didn't wake up. He smoothed away the hair that had fallen across her face and resumed watching her sleep.

He didn't know how much time had passed when her eyelashes fluttered and two beautiful, sleepy eyes peered at him. A slow, brilliant smile spread across her face. A second later, she bit her lip and buried her face against his chest in a rush of shyness. But she stilled against him and ran the tip of her nose against his bare skin in languid, luxurious sweeps, then planted a kiss in the hollow of his throat. A shiver ran through him.

"I forgot you were naked," she mumbled.

"Just so you know, so are you," he said with a grin. He ran his hand down her side to illustrate.

"But you look so good naked." Her hands roamed his chest,

and the morning wood he'd gotten under control rushed back with a vengeance.

"And you don't?" he asked, his jaws going slack with shock. Did she just really imply that she didn't look good naked?

"Not as good as you," she said.

"You've got to be kidding me." He flipped back the cover with a quick tug so her glorious nudity lay resplendent before his eyes.

"Eek," she squeaked, and grabbed for the sheets.

"No you don't." He grabbed her hands and trapped them above her head with one hand. "I want to look at you. I never want to stop looking at you. You are so beautiful, I want to weep."

"Crybaby," she teased, even as a blush spread across her cheeks.

"I guess I didn't do a proper job of showing you how beautiful you are last night." He lowered his head to kiss a trail down her neck. "And this morning."

"Yeah, that must be it." She tugged half-heartedly at her hands. "I assume you plan to remedy that."

"Immediately." He took a hardened peak of her breast into his mouth and suckled gently. She gasped and arched her torso off the bed. He rolled on top of her, pressing his hard length against her stomach. "Do you believe that you're beautiful?"

"I mean . . . I guess I'm kind of okay." Her eyes were sparkling with mischief . . . and raw heat.

With a low chuckle, he released her hands and made his way down her body. Her breathtaking, naked body. He lowered his head between her legs and murmured against her, "So beautiful."

He kissed her center and tasted her like he'd been dying to. She moaned and writhed against him, her hands buried in her hair. She didn't need to hold him in place because he had nowhere else he would rather be. He licked and laved her with his tongue, urged on by her sharp gasps and pleas until her hips arched off the bed and she shouted his name in a husky cry.

"Are you beautiful?" He made his way back up her body and looked down at her flushed face.

"Yes," she said breathlessly. "I'm a beautiful fucking goddess."

"That's more like it." Jack nibbled at her lips.

"And like many goddesses, I'm quite demanding." She reached down between them and took him in her hand.

"God, Lizzy," he groaned as she slid her fist up and down his length. "You're killing me."

"What? This?" she said coyly, squeezing her hand tightly around him until he growled. "But I plan to do so much more."

"Do it." Not his most eloquent moment, but he was proud of himself for stringing two words together.

With a wicked little smile, she carried out her plans with passion and generosity that wrecked him. His body was slick with sweat and heavy with satisfaction when she was done with him. Goddesses were indeed very demanding.

"We missed our morning run," Lizzy said around a yawn, nuzzling against his neck.

"I think it's safe to say that we got plenty of exercise between last night and this morning." He trailed his fingers down her spine and smiled when she shivered against him. He loved how responsive she was to his touch.

"We must've burned a lot of calories because I'm starving." Her stomach growled as though to bolster her statement.

"Why don't you go take a shower while I make us some breakfast?" He planted a kiss on the top of her head. She slipped off the covers and got to her feet, not at all self-conscious about her nudity. He must've done a good job of convincing her that she looked stunning naked. Lucky him.

"How about this?" she said. "Why don't *you* go take a shower while *I* make us some breakfast? I don't want to risk you starting a kitchen fire."

"Hey," he said, only a little hurt. "I can make toast without setting anything on fire. Or pour milk over cereal."

"You deserve some real sustenance." She grabbed his shirt off the floor and slipped into it. "Consider it an award for the many superior-quality orgasms you gave me. Or bribery for future orgasms."

He laughed and got out of bed. Her eyes immediately snapped to his body and roamed it greedily. He'd never thought much about his body. He exercised for his physical and mental health. But when Lizzy looked at him with wild-eyed desire, he was thrilled that he was in good shape.

"Neither of us are getting breakfast if you keep looking at me like that," he warned.

"Be gone, temptation." Lizzy waved her hand at him and turned to walk to the kitchen.

Jack grabbed his overnight bag from next to the sofa, where he'd tossed it the previous night, and made a beeline for the shower. By the time he came out of the bathroom, toweling his hair, Lizzy was pouring coffee into mugs. She'd already laid out two plates filled with scrambled eggs and toast.

"This looks fantastic." He grabbed the mugs and set them down on the table.

"I'm not exactly a great cook, either," she said, crinkling her nose. "But hopefully, the eggs are edible."

He took a bite of the scrambled eggs and smiled. She'd forgotten to salt them, but they were cooked well. Not too runny or dry. "It's delicious."

"Liar," she said after a taste. "It needs reinforcement. Do you want ketchup or hot sauce?"

"I don't need anything." He forked another mound of eggs into his mouth.

She brought a bottle of hot sauce along with a saltshaker and added both to her eggs. She nodded after another bite. "Much better."

He wasn't even tempted to reach for the salt. This was the first time she had cooked for him. It was pretty much the best meal of his life. A small smile lit her face when she saw him finish off his eggs just as she'd made them.

"Next time, I'll remember the salt," she promised.

Those words were music to his ears. *Next time.* Because there was going to be a next time. This wasn't some fluke. They were really together, and he got to make love to Lizzy again because that was what people did when they were together.

Before his happiness could reach dizzying heights, a small voice inside his head said, *This won't last forever.* His stomach dipped as though he were speeding down on a roller coaster. Their trial period would run its course in less than two weeks, and Lizzy would go back to her life in Los Angeles. He might follow if he got the job at McBain. Then what? Getting an entry-level position—even at a top consulting firm—wouldn't suddenly boost him into the overachiever stratosphere that Lizzy resided in.

But it would be a start. He forced aside his sense of fore-boding. No matter how hard he ran from his insecurities, they always seemed to catch up with him, but that didn't mean he had to let them rule him. Lizzy wanted him—even as he was now—and he would be hers as long as she wanted him.

CHAPTER SEVENTEEN

Lizzy snuck a peek at Jack from under her lashes. He was prepping the books that they were going to hang up as part of this month's display. She and Shannon decided that showcasing fun, un-put-downable beach reads would be fitting with summer here. He was working with fishing line to bind the books, carefully balancing them so they were close to horizontal to the floor when held up by the center string.

He was terribly good with his hands, tying delicate knots with nimble fingers. She tugged her bottom lip between her teeth. And those hands had been all over her only a few hours ago. A blush rushed up to her face, and she quickly looked away before he caught her staring at him with decidedly lecherous thoughts.

She and Shannon were picking out which beach reads would make it onto the window display, but there were just so many good books. They had to pare down more than thirty books to just about twelve to fifteen. It was such a lovely conundrum.

"This is hard, huh?" Lizzy turned to her friend. "But it's also kind of exciting that we have so many books to choose from."

Shannon slapped a hand over her mouth. But she was a second too late. The snort had already escaped.

"What?" Lizzy frowned.

"I don't think it's the books you find exciting," she said, cocking her head toward Jack. "Man, the looks you guys are giving each other . . . I feel like I should give you some privacy."

Lizzy flushed to the roots of her hair. "Oh, stop it. We're not that bad."

"No, no." Shannon shook her head, pursing her lips. "You two actually *are* that bad."

Had Jack been sneaking heated glances at her as well? Lizzy couldn't hold back her smile. Being in his arms had felt so liberating. So right. She didn't need to put on any armor around him, always ready to defend herself, because he would never make her feel cornered. She didn't have to *try* with him—like trying to fit the part of an ambitious lawyer or trying to meet her mom's insurmountable expectations. She could just *be* because he made her feel as though she was enough.

"See?" Shannon pointed at Lizzy's face. "That bad."

There was no use denying it. She had it bad for Jack. She'd always cared about him and thought he was an amazing human being. But now, seeing his generosity and kindness made her tear up—so grateful that he existed. His smile and touch made her heart pound and great flocks of birds—butterflies were too small to describe what she felt—take flight in her stomach. And knowing that they were together filled her with so much joy that she felt like it was going to ooze out of her.

Did he feel the same way? He'd been so reluctant to put their friendship at risk. If he felt the same way, would he have hesitated as much as he had? No, she wasn't going to wonder about that. He wanted to take things slowly, and she intended to give him the space he needed. Besides, it was too soon for her to feel this way—she refused to let the *L* word even take form in her mind. And it was much too soon to talk about the future or ask for promises. Especially since she'd practically bamboozled him into moving this relationship forward.

The bell above the door rang, and an attractive, older Asian woman walked into the store. She smiled when she saw Shannon. "Hi there. I need to replenish my book supply."

"Hey, Linda," Shannon said, walking up to the customer. "I can't believe you went through the last batch so fast."

"Well, I don't do much other than watch my granddaughter and spend time with my daughter and son-in-law." The lady shrugged and smiled a little wistfully. "I have plenty of time to read."

"Annyeonghaseyo." Jack walked up to the customer and bowed at the waist. "It's nice to see you, Mrs. Choi. Morgan must be getting big."

"Jack, I didn't see you back there." She smiled warmly at him. "Yes, she's officially a toddler. I feel like my life is in fast-forward mode when I measure it by how quickly Morgan is growing."

"This is Lizzy." He drew her into the conversation, placing a hand on her lower back. "Say hello to Aubrey's mother."

"Annyeonghaseyo," Lizzy said with a bow. Just the thought of Aubrey made her think back to the killer chocolate muffins Jack had brought her. Mrs. Choi deserved a medal for bringing the genius baker into this world. "Nice to meet you. I'm his . . ."

She stopped with a jolt of panic and shot a glance at Jack. She was his . . . what?

"She's my girlfriend," Jack smoothly interjected, pulling her closer to his side.

It felt as though her heart had sprouted wings and lifted her a few inches off the ground.

"Oh, isn't she just lovely," Mrs. Choi said, beaming at the two of them. "Nice to meet you, Lizzy."

"It sounds like you've been reading quite a bit," Lizzy said, bringing the topic back to the reason for Mrs. Choi's visit to the bookstore. Something the older woman said—there was a hint of loneliness in her words—had given Lizzy an idea.

"Yes, I have. I wish I can say it was purely for the love of reading, but some of it was to pass the time," the older woman said with a self-conscious laugh.

"Why don't you guys chat while I pick out some books for Linda." Shannon turned around and headed toward the fiction section.

"My mom enjoys your company," Jack said. "You guys should spend more time together."

"I already take up too much of her time." Mrs. Choi shook her head and waved aside the suggestion. "She's so busy with the brewery."

"Would you be interested in joining a book club?" Excitement fluttered in Lizzy's stomach. Hosting a book club would give Sparrow a presence in the community, and it would provide a wonderful way to meet people. Mrs. Choi wouldn't have to feel so lonely.

"A book club?" Jack and Mrs. Choi said at the same time.

"I have to confirm with Shannon, of course, but I think it'll be great if Sparrow started some book clubs for the community." Lizzy turned to the older woman and placed her hand on her arm. "You'll get to meet other avid readers and discuss interesting books with them. What could be more fun than that?"

"I would love to join a book club," Mrs. Choi said with a new glow in her face. "In fact, I must implore Shannon to get one together as soon as possible. I spend all day talking to a toddler. Stimulating adult conversation sounds like a dream."

She hurried over to Shannon, who was holding a pile of books in her arms.

"You know, I wouldn't mind joining a book club myself," Jack murmured.

"Really? I think that's a great idea . . . ," Lizzy began.

"Yeah, spending all day with you makes me miss stimulating adult conversation," he said with a shit-eating grin.

Her first impulse was to smack him on the back of his head, but then she got a much better idea. She pressed up against his side and said in a low, husky voice, "Stimulating adult conversation? Does this count? I want to take you upstairs and have you on the kitchen table. Twice."

Jack choked on his own spit and doubled over in a coughing fit.

"There, there." She patted his back, wearing a self-satisfied smile. When he straightened, she raised her eyebrow at him. "Stimulating enough for you?"

He had tears in his eyes from the coughing, but a wicked light came into them. He cast a quick glance toward the back of the store, where Shannon and Mrs. Choi were talking, and turned to her. His arms shot out and pulled her up against him.

"Here's what we're going to do," he said with a subtle pump of his hips.

God, he was already hard.

"We're going to wrap things up a little early here today," he continued in a gruff voice.

"Okay," she managed to squeak.

"I'll meet you upstairs." He gave her one last smoldering gaze, then projected his voice. "Bye, Mrs. Choi. See you later, Shannon."

Lizzy watched him walk out of the store with a swagger that was part attitude and part boner. Her hand fluttered to her chest, and she let out a Southern belle sigh. *Be still, my throbbing vagina.* She had to get the hell out of here.

"I think we should finish up the flying books tomorrow when we have better light." Her voice was an octave higher than usual. For a lawyer, she was a horrible liar. "It's a little overcast today."

"Okay. No problem." Shannon's face split into a Cheshire cat grin. "Go and enjoy the rest of the day."

"It was nice meeting you, Lizzy," Mrs. Choi said cheerfully.

Lizzy waved at them with a weak laugh, then bolted out the door. She took off toward her apartment. Her high school track teacher should see her now. She could've been his star sprinter. She screeched to a halt at the bottom of the staircase. Jack sat on the top step with his arm resting on a raised knee.

Her breath caught in her throat. It should be illegal for a man as handsome as Jack to have so much sex appeal. How were mortal women expected to keep their panties on? She took one step, then another, up the stairs. He watched her like a panther stalking its prey—all coiled muscles and strength.

It was a good thing she was not expected to keep her panties on.

～～

"Girlfriend, huh?" Lizzy said with her naked body draped over his.

"Yup. Problem?" Jack answered casually while he kept himself from tensing up under her. She lay satiated in his arms after he'd thoroughly ravished her. If she thought he was good enough for her, who was he to doubt it? To ease the sudden jolt of nerves, he swept his hand up and down her back, luxuriating in the feel of her soft skin. He might be addicted to touching her.

"No, none at all." She shifted her hips off him and entwined her leg between his, properly snuggling him.

Relief rushed through him, and his hands tightened around her. *Mine.* But they might actually face some problems ahead.

"I need to tell my parents about us. I'm already going to get an earful for telling Mrs. Choi before I told them." He paused, not sure how Lizzy would take the news. "So your parents will soon find out about us."

"My dad will be thrilled. As for my mom . . ." She sighed, a sound filled with exasperation and resignation.

"She . . . she'll think I'm not good enough for you," he said quietly. Lizzy wanted him. She thought he was good enough for her. That was what mattered even if he wasn't quite convinced he was.

"Well, she'll be way off the mark." She looked at him with a fierce gleam in her eyes. "My mom's not happy with anything I do, so I plan on not paying much attention to her."

Jack wrapped her in his arms and kissed her forehead. He didn't want to cause problems in her already strained relationship with her mother, but he had no intention of allowing Mrs. Chung to come between him and Lizzy. He might not be good enough for her now, but he could be soon. If he landed that job with McBain and worked his ass off, he would be pursuing his own dream instead of being an accessory to his brother's and sister's dream. He would be more than a glorified bookkeeper who didn't know where his life was headed. He would be his own man at last.

"You know what would be perfect right now?" She lifted herself onto an elbow.

He wanted to pull her back to him and hold on tightly. There was nothing more perfect than having her in his arms.

"What do you have in mind?" he said in a suggestive voice, nuzzling her neck.

"Hmm?" She tilted her head to give him better access.

"What would be perfect right now?" He made his way back up and nibbled on her earlobe.

"Not important. This . . ." She sighed. "This is perfect. Don't stop."

"Don't worry. I always finish what I start."

Every time he made love to her, he discovered something new—a hidden sensitive spot or a position that made her whimper and clench around him. He wanted to catalog all the different ways he could make her fall apart.

"I remember now," Lizzy said, her words slightly slurred as she lay limp beside him. "Cupcakes."

"Hmm?" He didn't know if he could articulate words yet.

"Some cupcakes would be perfect right now." Her stomach growled on cue. "We need to replenish all the calories we burned."

"Sex *and* cupcakes in one afternoon?" A lazy smile spread across his face as he imagined eating chocolate frosting off her navel.

"I know. How very hedonistic of me." She sounded quite pleased with herself.

He threw off the covers and got to his feet. If he lingered, he'd never leave Lizzy's bed. "Let's go, then."

"Are we going to Comfort Zone?" She bolted up from the bed and grabbed her clothes off the floor.

"Where else?" He pushed his arms through his T-shirt.

"Oh, my gosh. If Aubrey could make a muffin taste like heaven, I can't even imagine what her cupcakes are like."

"Foodgasmic," he described succinctly. Aubrey's desserts were sinfully good, and he couldn't wait for Lizzy to try them.

They parked in Comfort Zone's back lot and followed the tantalizing scent of something buttery and sweet into the store. It was crowded with locals as usual, giving it the perfect amount of bustling energy. He led Lizzy up to the display case and gave her time to gawk.

"You should've brought me here the moment I set foot in Weldon," she admonished while her eyes stayed glued to the array of desserts.

"How could I?" He chuckled. "You wouldn't even give me a lunch break."

"Whatever." She stuck out her tongue at him. "All because of you, I have less than two weeks to enjoy this heavenly oasis."

"Man, if this is your reaction now, I'm afraid of what you'll do after you actually taste some of those." He kept up the banter even though a knot of dread had formed in his chest. *Less than two weeks.* "Remember all our years of friendship before you do anything rash."

"Just hope that I'll be too busy foodgasming to notice your existence."

"I know exactly which one you have to eat, then." He turned to the server behind the counter. "Can you start us off with a slice of the black sesame and white chocolate cake? She'll be ordering the rest."

After they finished ordering, they settled into a plush, diner-style booth. Lizzy's eyes were still wide as she glanced around the bakery.

"This is kind of how I imagined Sparrow would feel like once we're finished," she said with a soft smile playing around her lips. "Not just a store but somewhere the community could gather together and be happy."

"I think we're getting there with Sparrow." He looked around Comfort Zone to see it from Lizzy's perspective. "We just need to get the word out."

"Shannon has social media on her to-do list," she said.

"Social media is important, but I was thinking something more immediate—local." He rested his chin on his fist and tapped the table with his fingers.

"The book club is a good start." She pursed her lips and narrowed her eyes. Her adorable thinking face. He could hear her brain whirring. *Wait for it . . . Wait for it . . .* Her eyes widened, and she snapped her fingers. "Events. Shannon needs to host events."

And there it was—and it was brilliant—but there was more, so he waited.

"Events that mean something to the community . . . about things that make Weldon special . . ." She slapped her palms flat on the table, and a slow grin spread across her face.

"Well? What is it?" he prompted.

She had a flare for the dramatic. It was part of what made her an effective trial attorney. He was literally sitting on the edge of his seat.

"Dessert and beer pairing." She pantomimed dropping the mic. "Highlight two of Weldon's beloved small businesses in a fun new way."

He laughed and fist-bumped her. What he really wanted to do was kiss the smarty-pants. Well, why the hell shouldn't he? As he lifted his ass to lean in for a kiss, plate after plate of desserts appeared on the table. He settled back on his seat and turned to find Aubrey standing by their booth, smiling ear to ear.

"Hi, Jack." Aubrey was barely holding back a squeal. Damn it. Tara must have told her about Lizzy. "So . . ."

"What?" he said like a grouch. He didn't mind that she knew, but she had awful timing. He could almost taste the kiss he had to postpone.

"Aren't you going to introduce us?" Aubrey pushed onto her toes, then dropped back down.

He shook his head and smiled wryly. Aubrey was like a little sister to him, and she was obviously happy to see him with someone. He couldn't stay annoyed at her, bad timing or not.

"Lizzy, this is Aubrey, the renowned chef and owner of Comfort Zone," he said with a bit of pomp and circumstance. Then he turned to Lizzy, and his heart skipped a beat. She looked so beautiful sitting across from him. "And this is Lizzy, my girlfriend."

"Oh, my gosh," Aubrey gushed. "It's so nice to meet you, Lizzy."

"It's nice to meet you, too. I've heard such wonderful things about you." His lovely girlfriend ogled the desserts with an unholy gleam in her eyes. "And look at all this. They're all so pretty. I almost don't want to eat them. Almost."

"Good," Aubrey laughed, "because they're meant to be eaten. Or sloppily devoured. I prefer the latter method. It makes me want to pat myself on the head for doing my job well."

"Consider it done," Lizzy said with a solemn nod.

"Well, I'll stop intruding on your date." Shielding one side of her mouth from him with her hand, she stage-whispered to Lizzy, "I fear the wrath of Jack."

He put on his most fearsome expression. The two women had a good laugh. There was nothing that felt better than making Lizzy laugh—maybe except for making her come. It was too close to call.

"Do you have a moment to sit with us?" Lizzy scooted to make room for Aubrey. "I wanted to talk to you about something."

Once Lizzy set her mind to something, she became a force of nature. She was just wonderful that way and in many other ways. Aubrey and Tara were as good as booked for the dessert-and-beer-pairing event.

CHAPTER EIGHTEEN

"Does this feel right?" Jack asked with a grunt.

Lizzy shifted positions and thought for a moment. "No, not quite."

"How about this?" A drop of sweat slid down the side of his jaw.

"We're close"—she bit her lip—"but . . . no. Just come down from there."

Jack clambered down the ladder and swiped his forearm across his brow. He carefully placed the book he'd been trying to hang on the floor.

"I can't hang off the ladder for hours on end for every book we put up." He rotated his right shoulder with a grimace.

"Hours on end?" Lizzy blustered even though she felt bad about making him work so hard. They'd been working on the window display all morning. She just wanted it to look perfect. How had Beverly done such a good job at Hideaway? It must've taken her forever and a day. "It takes thirty minutes, max, per book."

"We've been at this for over two hours, and there are only

three books up there," he pointed out, crossing his arms over his chest. It was a good look on him despite the fact that he was glaring at her.

He was right, so she stayed mutinously silent.

"All right, kids." Shannon stepped between them, waving her arms. "I'm officially kicking you out of my store."

"What?" Lizzy turned shocked eyes on her. "But there's work to be done."

"The work can wait. The book club won't start until next month. And the beer-and-dessert-pairing event isn't for another week," Shannon said in a soothing voice. "We have plenty of time to finish sprucing up the store."

"But—"

"No buts," her friend cut in firmly. "It's a beautiful day outside, and I want you to go and enjoy some of it. You've been stuck inside this store for your entire vacation so far. The key word being *vacation*. You're supposed to be relaxing."

"I like being stuck inside," Lizzy grumbled. She really didn't mind. She loved waking up in the morning knowing that she was going to work at Sparrow. Whereas, in Los Angeles, it felt as though she were putting on war paint and girding her loins for battle every morning. Working at the bookstore was a natural mood booster. "This is how I relax."

"Well, I'm tired of listening to the two of you bickering." Shannon took each of them by their arms and tugged them to the door. "Out you go."

"Thanks, Shannon." Jack grinned and grabbed Lizzy's hand. "I'll take it from here."

"You guys can't do this." Lizzy glanced wildly around for help. There were little boxes to check off, damn it.

"Consider this an intervention," he said, making Shannon cackle.

Lizzy glowered at them.

"I'll make it worth your while," he whispered against her ear.

That made her pause and weigh her options. *Hmm.* Orgasm or to-do list. Orgasm or to-do list.

"Fine," she succumbed at last, "but I'm holding you to it."

Jack chuckled and tugged her out of the store. She waved a quick goodbye to Shannon and skipped to keep up with him.

"If we hurry, I could give you the whole tour," he said once they were inside her apartment.

"I'm not sure I understand what that means, but I'm in." She whipped her shirt off and threw it on the ground.

"Good. You can wear your swimsuit under your clothes." He rummaged around her cupboards. "Did we eat all the granola bars? That's okay. We'll have to stop by my place to grab my swimming trunks anyway. I'll pack the snacks there."

"Umm." She paused in the middle of kicking off her shorts. "You want to see me in my swimsuit?"

Jack slowly turned to face her. "I bet you look fucking hot in a swimsuit, but I promise to behave."

Behave? Why? "Okay. Explain to me exactly what kind of tour you're planning on giving me."

"Didn't I do that already?" Two grooves appeared between his brows. "I'm going to take you white-water rafting. And if we have time, we can hike and swim for a bit."

"What? That's the *whole tour*?" She suddenly felt very underdressed. "Where is the orgasm?"

He finally seemed to notice that she was half-naked, and understanding filled his eyes. Understanding and hot, scorching lust. He took a step toward her with an expression that made her want to rip her panties off. But he jerked to a stop and clenched his fists by his sides.

"I'm not letting you leave Weldon without enjoying some of

the outdoors," he said with conviction—which was admirable, considering his gaze was glued to her lace-clad boobs. He finally met her eyes with some effort. "You spend every day inside your office in LA, and you've been spending all your time in the bookstore and this apartment since you got here. You need this."

Nature was supposed to do wonders for one's mental health—therapists actually prescribed time with nature to their patients—but Lizzy was doing incredibly well since she came to Weldon even being indoors all the time. In fact, she didn't remember having to take her anxiety medication once. Still, Jack wanted to do this for her, and it could only help her.

"Okay. It does sound like fun." She rose on her tiptoes and pecked him on the cheek. His hands tightened briefly around her arms as she drew back. She smiled. He wanted her as much as she wanted him, but the great outdoors awaited. "I'm going to change in the bathroom. Be back in a sec."

She only took two steps before he caught her wrist and pulled her flush against him, his lips meeting hers in a crushing kiss. She nearly stumbled when he pushed her away after a moment as though he didn't trust himself to hold on to her a second longer.

"I'll find time to fit in that orgasm during the tour," he promised, his chest heaving slightly.

"Oh, goodie," she said, flushing from head to toe.

She hadn't planned on going swimming but had packed her red bikini anyway. And she was glad she had. Not just because it came in handy for river rafting fun, but she looked freaking fantastic in it. Her boobs weren't big by any standards, but they were round and perky, and the halter-type bikini made them look voluptuous. She turned around to check out her ass in the mirror and nodded her approval.

If she walked out in her bikini, she was fairly certain that

Jack would rip it off before she could utter, *Behold my splendor.* Lizzy only hesitated for a few seconds before she pulled on a cropped T-shirt and a pair of shorts to hide away her deliciousness. Now that she'd adjusted her expectations, she was looking forward to spending the day outdoors.

"What? I don't get a sneak preview?" Jack complained when he saw that she was fully dressed.

"Trust me," she said with a cheeky grin. "You won't be able to handle it."

"This I have to see."

He stalked toward her, and she held out her hand. "Halt. Box those sexy thoughts to go. I was promised a day in the sun."

"Who even needs white-water rafting?" he grumbled as he followed her outside.

"Someone insisted *I* did." She trotted down the stairs, shouldering her tote bag.

"What an asshat." His footsteps fell heavily behind her.

The genuine regret in his voice did funny things to her stomach. She'd never felt so wanted before. Her previous relationships were about compatible career goals and similar social circles. They were convenient and practical. The passion and spontaneity of what she and Jack had was way out of her comfort zone. And she loved every moment of it. The insatiable desire, the heart palpitations, the laughter. All of it.

It.

Her heart shot to her throat, then dropped to her stomach. She knew what *it* was. The unexpected epiphany hit her like a runaway train, and she held out her hand to steady herself on the side of Jack's car.

"Hey." He peered into her face. "You okay?"

"Weird vertigo thing," she said with a nervous chuckle. "It passed."

She got in the car and buckled her seat belt. She hadn't exactly lied. It did feel a little like vertigo. No wonder people called *it* falling in love.

~~~

They pulled up in front of a dated log building befitting the adventure sports store it housed. Sierra Sporting Goods & River Adventures had been around for thirty-plus years. Jack had only been coming for about fifteen years and had been employed there on and off during his college days.

"Hey, Crystal." He waved at the tan, broad-shouldered lady behind the counter with permanent laugh lines around her eyes and mouth. His former boss.

"Jack, my boy." Crystal came around to grab him in a signature bear hug that never failed to knock the wind out of him. "It's about time you showed your handsome mug around here."

"Sorry. Busy with work," he wheezed. He continued when she released him with a booming laugh, "Is Nathan out on a tour?"

"No, he isn't," the man himself said, walking out of the back room.

Nathan came in for a bro hug that was as hearty as the hug his mother had just given Jack. After pounding his back to an inch of his life, his friend stepped back and allowed him to resume proper breathing.

"This is Lizzy, my girlfriend." Jack wrapped his arm around her shoulders and tugged her close. He loved the way that rolled off his tongue. "This is Crystal and her son, Nathan. They're the proud owners of Sierra River Adventures."

"It's so nice to meet you both," Lizzy said sweetly.

"She's a first timer, so I want to avoid R2 rafting," Jack said to his friend.

Nathan nodded. "That's probably a good idea."

"Do you happen to have room in any of your groups?"

"As a matter of fact, Steve just started his safety instructions. One group only has two people, so I'll take you guys out with them."

They went around back and joined the other groups. Jack nudged Lizzy to go listen to the safety instructions. Even while he and Nathan chatted quietly on the sidelines, his eyes kept drifting to her. She was listening intently to Steve, but her fingers were tapping impatiently against her thighs. Jack grinned at the sight. She was dying to take notes.

"Hey, do you mind if I borrow a pen and notepad?" he asked his friend.

"Go right ahead." Nathan raised an eyebrow but didn't ask any questions. "We have some under the cash register."

Jack ran into the store and came back out with his bounty. He walked up to Lizzy and handed the pen and notepad to her. She hugged them to her chest, looking at him with wide eyes. She mouthed, *Thank you*, then returned her attention to the instructor and took copious notes. No one person had a right to be this adorkable. He rejoined Nathan before he could grab and kiss her. She wouldn't be happy if he made her miss any of the instructions.

"She seems sweet," his friend said with a sidelong glance at him.

"She is." Jack did his best not to sound too besotted.

"Are things serious between you two?"

Panic slammed into him. *Serious* was a loaded word. He couldn't examine how much all this meant to him. This was his one and only chance at a forever with Lizzy, but he still had no idea how to make her fall in love with him. A part of him wanted to fit in a lifetime of happiness into these couple of weeks—into this trial period—because it might be all he would get. Emotions, questions, hopes, and fears were churning just beneath the surface. Touching it would feel like hitting a raw nerve. So he carefully and deliberately turned his back on it.

"We haven't been dating long." He shot for casual and missed it by miles.

"Right," Nathan said after a pause.

Once the safety instructions were complete, they were loaded into one of Sierra River Adventures' buses and headed for the river with a few other groups. Steve and Nathan kept a banter going for the benefit of their customers, but Jack appreciated it as well. Lizzy was lost in her own thoughts, and he needed a moment to regain his equilibrium. The other couple in their group snapped pictures nonstop on their phones the entire way. Jack had a feeling they were those people who let their food get cold so they could get the perfect picture to post on social media.

"I'm scared and excited," Lizzy said in a small voice. "I'm scarecited."

"You're going to love it." Jack kissed her forehead, running his hand up and down her back. "Nathan's a great guide, and I'm not exactly a novice, either. You're in good hands."

The bus pulled over, and the rafts were unloaded. Led by Nathan, their group hoisted the raft over their heads and tracked down to the river. Lizzy and Jack boarded the raft, sitting side by side. The other couple sat behind them, while Nathan took the back end. The first thirty minutes on the river was relatively calm, and they got to enjoy the view of the rocky terrain and trees as they got accustomed to rowing in sync.

"Cows," Lizzy squealed. Two black cows stood lazily by the river.

"Where? Where?" the other couple said simultaneously, reaching frantically for their phones.

"They're behind us now." Lizzy returned her attention to the river ahead of them.

"All right. I need everyone to pay attention," Nathan said when the couple continued swiveling in their seats. "We'll be hitting the rapids soon."

Jack saw it happen in slow motion. The man behind Lizzy lifted his ass off the raft to get a better shot of the rapids ahead of them, fumbled with his phone, and lost his balance. He used Lizzy to regain it, and she tumbled into the quickening water.

It wasn't until the cold water hit his body that Jack realized he'd gone in after her. His mind had gone blank with shock, and he did the one thing he shouldn't have done. Fuck. He located the chicken string around the raft and held on before he searched the water for her. Fear clutched his heart when he saw her head dip in and out of the water a few feet away.

"Lizzy," he screamed, and swallowed a mouthful of river.

She quickly got her bearings and swam toward him, keeping her feet out of the water and away from the jagged rocks beneath. *Good girl.* She remembered her safety training. He stretched one hand toward her while hanging on to the rope with the other. When her fingertips at last grazed his, he wrapped his hand around hers in an iron grip and hauled her to him. She reached his side with a gasp, and he guided her hands to the chicken rope.

"Hang tight," he yelled over the roar of the water.

They held on to the side of the raft with the water crashing over them until the river quieted around them. The woman watched the ordeal with a hand over her mouth, and the man sat looking miserable. Once the raft was stable, Nathan pulled Lizzy aboard with her kicking the water to assist in the process. She laughed breathlessly as she righted herself on the raft.

Jack felt like a monumental jackass as his friend hefted him out of the water next—especially since his logical side knew all along that Lizzy wasn't in any real danger. But he hadn't felt particularly coolheaded when she'd toppled into the river.

The thought of her getting hurt froze his blood in his veins. The whole ordeal had lasted less than five minutes, but it had stretched on like a nightmare until she was safely aboard the raft.

"Sorry, man," Jack said with a sheepish grimace. Whatever his reasons, jumping in after Lizzy hadn't been his finest moment.

Nathan just shook his head at him.

Jack turned his focus on Lizzy, saving his mortification for another time. "Are you okay?"

"I'm fine." Her eyes still twinkled with laughter, but there was something else there. Something that made Jack's heart thump with the force of a boulder dropping from a cliff. "I'll thank you later for coming in after me."

"I shouldn't have done that," he muttered.

"No shit." Her smile lit up her face brighter than sunshine. "I'll thank you nonetheless."

"Well, that was an adventure," Nathan said, putting on his guide voice, but he directed a stern gaze at the cell phone couple. "Let's *please* remember to respect the river and enjoy the rest of this trip *safely*."

Once the other couple apologized profusely to Lizzy and put away their phones at last, the trip indeed became more enjoyable. The serenity of the nature surrounding them and the exhilaration of the rapids helped Jack put the incident behind him . . . for the most part. The inescapable realization that he didn't know how to be sensible when it came to Lizzy stayed at the forefront of his mind.

He'd been fooling himself this entire time. He thought he could stop himself from falling in love with her if he convinced himself that they wouldn't last forever. He thought if he insisted on taking things slowly, then he could fall back to the comfortable norm of loving her from afar when things ended. All of that was nothing but wishful thinking.

Jack was in love with Lizzy. He had fallen hard for her. This was nothing like the amorphous infatuation he had carried with him for the last two decades. He'd loved Lizzy without hoping for anything in return. He didn't want. He didn't fear. He was safe in his secrecy. But now he wanted. God, how he wanted.

He wanted to love her with everything in him. And he wanted to win her love in return. He wanted more than these couple of weeks with her. He wanted to build a future where he was hers and she was his. He wanted forever.

And because he wanted, he was terrified. This wasn't the kind of love that he could hide away inside him. It burned too hot and bright—keeping it a secret would turn his heart into ashes. That meant he had to risk getting his heart broken. He had to risk losing her.

It was a risk he had no choice but to take. Nothing other than a lifetime with her would be enough anymore. If he couldn't love her with all his heart—the way she deserved to be loved—then his life would always be incomplete.

But not yet. It was too soon.

He'd told her he wanted to take things slowly. And she'd agreed. Lizzy had just begun to see him as a man—a man she desired. Confessing his love to her after a week of dating was the opposite of taking things slowly. It would probably freak her out. He needed to take his time and woo her properly. If he got the job with McBain—he *had* to get that job—he would have plenty of time to convince Lizzy that he was worthy of her love.

Besides, he wanted to cherish the rest of their "trial period" in Weldon. It was a slice of time removed from the real world—a sweet, warm cocoon. No matter what happened, he would always have this to remember. And he intended to make the most of it.

CHAPTER NINETEEN

W here do you want this?" Jack pushed the freshly painted three-tier rolling cart into the bookstore, looking mighty fine in his handyman mode. Then again, he always looked mighty fine.

"Right over there." Lizzy smiled up at him from her perch on the floor, surrounded by used-book candidates to go into the bright yellow cart.

"Are you almost done with that?" He walked over and peered down at her with his lips pursed. "You've been at it for hours."

"Shannon helped me narrow things down before she went to pick up Elliot." She rolled the stiffness out of her shoulders and creaked her neck left and right. "I think I'm about ready to start loading that baby up with these."

He stepped around and knelt behind her. Curious, she glanced back just as he placed his strong, warm hands on her shoulders and squeezed. She moaned as he gently kneaded her tight muscles. His thumb pressed down right on the spot that needed it most, and she hissed. He immediately eased the pressure.

"No, don't stop," she said, leaning into his hands. "That hurts so good."

Cupping her other shoulder to hold her steady, he pressed the heel of his hand into the knot just below the juncture of her neck and shoulder. Her head rolled back as tension released from her body. She sighed with a dreamy smile on her face.

"You're making an awful lot of noise over a shoulder massage," he growled into her ear, making a tremor run through her. "I find it very . . . distracting."

"Distracting you from what?" Her voice was embarrassingly breathless, considering he was just giving her an innocent massage on the floor of a bookstore.

"Distracting me from carrying out this selfless service without getting overly turned on." He placed a hot kiss behind her ear.

"Sorry. I'll be quiet." She bit her lip to stop a moan from escaping when his lips trailed down the side of her neck. "Carry on."

He continued his ministrations, but the movement became more languid, his hands shifting lower and lingering. His touch set off little sparks of electricity on her ultra-sensitized skin. She tried to turn around, but Jack stayed her with his hands on her shoulders, then squeezed her arms with firm pressure, traveling down, then back up.

"I want you to relax," he purred. "You've been working much too hard."

The massage wasn't innocent. It was obscene. His big hands grew rough on her body, and wetness seeped between her legs. Unable to sit still, she reached behind her and grabbed his ass, digging her fingers into the tight, round flesh. He groaned low in his chest. Their little game of shoulder massage was over.

When she turned her head to the side and lifted her face up, he leaned down and crushed his lips against hers—hot, wet, and a little out of control. Just her cup of tea. With a frustrated whimper, she spun around and wrapped her arms around his neck and let him taste a bit of her desperation. They were both on their knees, pressed from thigh to chest. Eschewing outdated notions such as breathing, they kissed as though their lives depended on it.

Sex with Jack was freaking amazing. But the kissing—just kissing—was lovely, too. The thrill of the first touch, the swell of emotions, and the breathless pleasure of it. With most of her common sense still intact, she could relish the fact that she was kissing the kind, generous, and wonderful man she was in love with.

In moments like these—when she felt cherished and adored in his arms and her heart swelled with joy—it was hard to hold back the words that clamored to be released. *I love you*. She could imagine what would happen if she said them out loud. He would stiffen and pull away, his eyes landing everywhere but on her. No. He wasn't ready for the words yet. But she told him in other ways. Through her kisses and her touch. With her eyes and her smile.

She felt Jack slowing down their kiss until he leaned back with a wistful smile. "I can't seem to be around you without kissing you."

"That's just the way this works," she quipped even though she was melting inside. "Accept it."

"Oh, I have." He swept in for a quick, hard kiss as though to make his point. "But I need to be mindful that this is Shannon's place of business."

"Fine. Be all responsible like that."

He laughed and got to his feet, then helped her up. "Only because I know how hard you and Shannon worked to turn things around for the bookstore."

"You were working right along with us." She linked her fingers through his and glanced around the store. "I can't believe how far we've come. Look at this place. I almost can't believe it's the same bookstore."

"And with social media and live events, it's only a matter of time before it becomes a town favorite."

"I can't wait for the beer-and-dessert-pairing night." She did a little happy dance. "Just a few more days."

"Tara says she and Aubrey are busting their asses to prepare for it"—his eyes crinkled at the corners—"even though it looks like they're just drinking a lot of beer and eating way too much dessert."

"Tell them their sacrifice will not go unnoticed."

"Speaking of beer, I need to go sell some." He tugged her to him and kissed her lightly on the lips. "I'll be back as soon as I get off."

"Well, don't let me keep you from your duties," she said, wrapping her arms around his waist. She wasn't letting go until she got a proper goodbye kiss.

With a knowing laugh, he kissed her thoroughly enough to make her dizzy, then firmly set her away from him.

"I'll see you soon." He walked backward toward the front entrance, holding her gaze.

"I'll miss you." She bit her lip, worried it was too much. But she couldn't help it. It just slipped out.

"I'll miss you, too," he said without hesitation. As though the words had already been on the tip of his tongue.

She almost sagged with relief, and warmth spread through her.

He was smiling so hard that he didn't pay attention to where he was going and backed into the door with a thud. Fumbling a little, he pulled open the door and waved at her before he finally turned around and walked out of the store.

True to her words, she missed him the moment he disappeared from view. Oh, she was in so much trouble. But maybe . . . not? Jack had been sweet—so sweet—with her. He brought her small, thoughtful presents like a piece of light, jiggly cheesecake from Comfort Zone or a quadruple-heat-level hot sauce from a local vendor. She would find little notes tucked into her current read or inside her favorite coffee mug that said things like, *The toenail on your pinkie toe is so itty-bitty. Just adorable.* Or *Your tongue peeps out between your lips just a tiny bit when you're concentrating. It makes me think very bad thoughts.* If she wasn't already in love with him, those notes would have done the job.

And he sometimes stared at her with this tender expression— like she was a sleepy baby goat or something equally lovable— when he thought she wasn't looking. It made her heart screech to a halt, then resume in a wild sprint. Because it made her think that maybe . . . just maybe . . . he was a little in love with her, too. She sighed. She should go hunt for some daisies to pluck. Being an honest, self-aware creature, she knew she would probably cheat so the last petal could fall on *he loves me.*

She'd suggested that their time together in Weldon would be a trial period—mainly to ease his worries about venturing out of the friend zone—but that time was running out much too quickly. Would everything change once she went back to Los Angeles? The thought of not seeing Jack every day brought tears to her eyes, but they could still make this work. They had to.

"Honey, we're home." Shannon walked into the store with Elliot in tow.

"Where's Jack?" Elliot said in lieu of a greeting.

"Sorry, bud." Lizzy squeezed the boy's shoulder. "He had to go to his real job."

"That sucks." He pouted. "I wanted to show him the new comic books my mom got me."

"You could show me," Lizzy suggested gently.

"You like comic books?" Elliot's eyes rounded.

"Heck yeah." Graphic novels counted as comic books, right?

"Cool," he said, brightening up. "And I can show Jack to-morrow."

"I bet he'll be thrilled," she said sincerely.

Once Elliot showed Lizzy his kick-ass comic books, she and Shannon finished loading up the used books cart. They would set it up outside starting tomorrow. Her work done for the day, Lizzy retired to her cozy apartment. As she wondered what to do about dinner, she heard the ominous strains of the theme from *Jaws* coming from somewhere. She briefly thought she was losing her mind before she realized it was her phone. Mother was call-ing. She must've changed the ringtone after her last call with her mom, which led her to empty a bottle of wine into her mouth.

"Umma," Lizzy answered, feeling guilty about the knot in her stomach. She shouldn't dread talking to her own mom.

"Are you out of your mind?" Her mom emphasized the harsh consonants in Korean, wielding her words like a swift slap.

"Ex . . . excuse me?" Lizzy stuttered as the blood drained from her face and a fine tremor started in her body.

"Mr. Park told us you're dating one of his *strapping* sons." Sarcasm dripped from her voice.

Lizzy tried to take a deep breath and failed. She'd known this was coming, but anxiety tightened her chest. "Jack. I'm dat-ing Jack."

"I don't care which one of them you're dating. They're both just pretty faces who work at a bar. You are going to stop this nonsense immediately."

"With all due respect, you don't dictate who I date." A part of her wanted to cower beneath her mom's fury, but she wasn't going to let her talk about Jack that way. "Jack is more than a pretty face. He's kind, generous, and brilliant. Did you know he's the business mind behind Weldon Brewery's success?"

"Baby, listen to yourself." Her mom smoothly changed tactics. "You've been working toward becoming a partner all these years. You can't afford to get distracted. It's your dream."

"No, it isn't." She spoke before she had a chance to think, but she knew it was the truth the moment the words left her mouth. "It's the path *you* chose for me. I merely followed it like an obedient daughter. I . . . I don't even know what my dream is . . ."

"So what? Are you planning to settle down in Weldon and become a barmaid?" All pretenses of caring seeped out of her mom's voice.

"I'm not going to stop seeing Jack," Lizzy said with steel in her voice even though she had to hold her phone with both hands because they were shaking so badly. "As for what I'm going to do about my future, it's about time I figured that out for myself. Goodbye, Mother."

She hung up before her mom could respond. She dug through her makeup bag for her anxiety medicine and swallowed one without water. Then she lay flat on her bed and did her breathing exercises to get back in control of her mind and body.

Lizzy wasn't sure what she wanted, but she knew what she *didn't* want. She didn't want to go back to Los Angeles. And she didn't want to work for a big law firm. Weldon had felt more like home these last couple of weeks than Los Angeles ever had. Maybe Weldon was just what she needed. A slower-paced life surrounded by a tight-knit community. She could find some-part time work at a small law firm in a neighboring town while she figured out what she really wanted.

And Jack. She could be with Jack. The thought warmed her to her toes, but that couldn't be why she chose to stay in

Weldon. It was time she decided what she wanted to do with her life on her own.

~~~

It was there right on the screen when Jack came out of the shower after his morning run with Lizzy. He'd been checking his email obsessively, refreshing it every couple of minutes, every chance he got. So he'd glanced at the screen out of habit without really expecting it to be there, but there it was.

He threw the towel he'd been using to dry his hair on the bed and sat down at his desk. Water dripped down his shoulders and back from his soaking hair, but he hardly noticed. It was a simple email. The HR director wanted to schedule a call at his earliest convenience. He shot back an email with his availability and sat staring at his computer as though a reply would come through immediately. He huffed out a laugh. People didn't even respond to text messages that quickly. He should dry off and get dressed.

Just as he was pushing himself off the chair, his computer dinged, announcing the arrival of a new email. He plopped back down on the seat with his heart pounding. She'd responded to his email. She would call him at two o'clock this afternoon. Of course, he knew what this meant. He'd gotten the job. They never delivered bad news over the phone. That was what emails were for in addition to doing mundane things like scheduling phone calls. But he scaled back his excitement just in case. He would know for sure at two o'clock.

Then guilt and anxiety rammed into him. Those weren't something he could hold back or temper. If he got the job, he had to tell his family. He had to tell Alex. *Shit*. He had given them absolutely no warning. He barely let on that he wasn't thoroughly happy with his life in Weldon. He realized how selfish he'd been in keeping it from them. They would've understood and supported him if he'd given them a chance.

Now he would be dropping a bombshell on them *and* leaving them in a lurch. Of course, he had planned everything so they would have a replacement bookkeeper when he left. And he would happily stay on as a business consultant if they would let him. But they had no time to prepare themselves—to adjust to the idea of him leaving.

His only excuse was that he'd been afraid. Not afraid that his family wouldn't support him—they would never do that—but afraid of failing. If he didn't tell anyone, the failure wouldn't feel as real. He'd made a mess of things, but he would set them right. He believed in his family, and they would accept his decision and support him no matter how badly he'd screwed up in not telling them.

Then a spark of joy and hope lit up in him. The conflicting emotions bombarding him were giving him whiplash, but he couldn't fight the smile that overtook his face. He was going to be with Lizzy. They didn't have to worry about a complicated long-distance relationship when her vacation was over.

A long-distance relationship would've meant that she would return to her successful life surrounded by other successful people while he was hours away in small-town Weldon. He was busy on the weekends with the brewery and busier when he had to attend beer festivals and competitions. And she worked more weekends than not herself. They would hardly get to see each other. It would've only been a matter of time before she realized how different their lives were—how he couldn't fit into her life.

But if the call this afternoon went the way he hoped, he would move to Los Angeles. Their relationship didn't have to end with the trial period. He would be by her side to show her how well they fit—to remind her that nothing else mattered but the way they made each other feel when they were together. He would be by her side until she was ready to accept his love—ready to give him a chance to win her love.

He had been planning to spend his off day with Lizzy anyway, but if he got the job, then he wanted to do something special with her. Neither of them had broached the topic of what would happen when she returned to Los Angeles. He couldn't talk to her while his job situation was in limbo.

And if he was honest with himself, a part of him had been afraid that she might say something to the effect of, *What happens in Weldon stays in Weldon*. But she wouldn't say that. Lizzy cared about him. She showed him every day just how much with her smile and her touch.

Tonight, he would tell her he didn't want what they had to end. He couldn't tell her he loved her yet, but he would tell her how much the last couple of weeks had meant to him. Then he would tell her that he was moving to Los Angeles and they could be together. His stomach clenched nervously. He had to believe she would be happy for him—and for them.

He would have to set the scene just right. A romantic dinner. He would make—*gulp*—dinner for her. He punched in *how to boil water* in Google as a droll joke about his cooking prowess, but he found perfectly serious YouTube videos on exactly how to boil water. He didn't feel so alone anymore.

When he leaned back in his chair laughing, he realized he was mostly naked and decided that if he wanted to take this cooking thing seriously, he should at least put some pants on. Then he would figure out how to make the perfect romantic dinner for two.

~

"Good morning." Jack rushed into the bookstore at close to eleven. "Sorry I'm late."

"Where were you?" Lizzy said, standing up on her tippy toes to give him a quick peck on the lips. "I was starting to get worried."

As always, a little bit of Lizzy made him want a lot more of her. He wanted to pull her back into his arms to give her a proper kiss, but there were customers in the store. In fact, there always seemed to be customers in the store now—which was great for Sparrow—but it meant he had to behave.

"I had some errands to run," he said vaguely.

"Hmm." Lizzy seemed a little distracted.

"Is everything all right?"

"I'm just tired." She smiled wanly. "You did keep me up last night."

"Try to be a little less irresistible tonight so I can let you sleep."

"Har." She rolled her eyes. "You think you're so charming, don't you?"

"I'm sorry if it's overwhelming, but it's not something I can turn off."

She elbowed him in his side and went back to arranging some new releases on one of the larger tables. Her long hair fell like a curtain to hide her face from him, and he frowned. Something seemed off last night, but he'd chalked it up to her being tired from waiting up for him. He would ask more when they were alone tonight.

Tonight. Right. He needed Shannon's help. He waited until she finished ringing up a customer, then approached her casually—he only needed to whistle to appear any more suspicious.

"Can I ask you for a favor?" he asked in a low whisper. He looked over his shoulder to make sure Lizzy was still busy at the table. She was staring off into space, worrying her poor bottom lip. Something wasn't right.

"Sure. You can ask for a hundred," Shannon said without hesitation. "Well . . . maybe we can start with ten."

He turned his attention back to her and smiled. "Just one will do. Can you try to keep Lizzy down here until seven tonight?"

"Not a problem. She's here until then most nights anyway." Shannon's eyes twinkled. "And why might you need such a favor?"

"I'm going to surprise her with a romantic dinner." Jack scratched the back of his head. "I need some time to cook and get it all ready."

"Aww, you guys are too cute. Do you need the spare keys to her apartment?"

"Yes, that would be great." He hadn't even thought about that part. It would've been awkward asking Lizzy for the keys without telling her why he needed them. "Thank you, Shannon."

"Anytime," she said with a wink.

~~~

Lizzy was still lost in thought when Jack returned to her side. She started a little when he put his hand on her back. He smoothed away the frown building between his brows. They would talk tonight.

"What's my assignment for the day?" he asked.

"Yes, your assignment." She brightened immediately. "Shannon and I want to use that space in front of the window as an event stage. She has the coolest rug we can use to mark off the stage area. But it needs a backdrop, so we need to put up some curtains behind the display case. We'll only close the curtains when we have events, since we love the natural light coming in."

"Nice." He glanced at the front window. "Then I'll need to install a curtain rod and some curtain holdbacks."

"We already picked up all the hardware and the curtains, so you can jump right in."

"Let me just grab my stepladder and toolbox from my car." He paused mid-step when she touched his arm.

"Did you bring your tool belt?" she said with a husky note in her voice.

His eyebrows drew down. "Yeah, but I probably won't need it."

"No, you really should wear it." A slightly unhinged light came into her eyes.

"Why, Lizzy?" A slow grin spread across his face. "Do you like seeing me in a tool belt?"

He saw a battle of lust and pride stampede across her lovely face. Lust won.

"Yes." She put her hand on his chest and leaned in close. "Put it on for me?"

All his cockiness drained away as heat spread through him. He swallowed after several attempts. "Anything for you."

With his tool belt slung low on his hips, he installed the curtain rod brackets with Lizzy's hungry eyes on him. The only reason he was able to avoid a full-blown hard-on was because he was preoccupied with his call with McBain's HR.

After he drilled in the final bracket, he climbed down the stepladder and made a beeline for Lizzy, who was pretending to rearrange some literary fiction on the bookshelves along the back wall. Her eyes widened and dropped to his tool belt—or crotch—when she saw him approach.

"Eyes up here," he said in a strained voice.

Her gaze made a slow ascent to his face, and it felt like licks of fire against his skin. The wicked smile that curled her lips was completely unrepentant. "My apologies."

His hands curled and uncurled by his side as he fought the urge to push her up against the bookshelves and bury himself inside her. But the murmurs of customers around him brought reason back into his lust-fogged brain. "Later. You'll pay for this later."

"Promises, promises." Lizzy bit the tip of her index finger and stared at him with naked hunger.

"Okay." He closed his eyes and filled his lungs with air. "I'm going to go to my car and put away my tool belt—"

"No . . ." She pouted with displeasure.

"I'm going to put away my tool belt and take some time to cool off. And when I come back, you're going to behave yourself"—he held up his finger to stop her protests—"because I can't take you upstairs and leave the project half-finished."

"You mean we should act like responsible adults?" Her shoulders drooped.

"Exactly. I'm actually shocked that I need to remind you of this, but once the curtains go up, you'll get to check off another box."

Lizzy leaned close and said in a low whisper, "Don't tell anyone this, but sex with you is better than checking off a to-do item."

"That is the nicest thing anyone has ever said to me." Jack chuckled and tugged her into a hug. He quickly set her away from him when her hands skimmed his waist under his T-shirt. "My car. Going. Now."

He rushed out of the bookstore and headed to his car. He popped open the trunk and threw in his tool belt, blowing out a long breath through his mouth. Leaning against the side of his car, he pulled out his phone. In less than two hours, his future would be decided—fear and anticipation clashed inside him, but hope bloomed . . . the hope that Lizzy would be a part of it.

CHAPTER TWENTY

Lizzy had hoped that Jack would spend his day off with her, but he'd left earlier in the afternoon with some mumbled excuses about important errands. She'd promptly squashed the disappointment that rose inside her—she had no right to monopolize his time—but she was feeling oddly out of sorts.

Jack had provided a nice distraction to keep her from mulling over what the hell she wanted to do with her life. She'd mostly daydreamed about being close to him and avoided thinking about tendering her resignation at her firm and finding herself a new position somewhere near Weldon. The logistics were a nightmare—uprooting her whole life and career goal to move to a small town—but the big-city life had left her lonely and empty.

Everything moved so quickly in Los Angeles that she hadn't had time to pause and figure out if she was happy with where her life was going. It was only when she slowed down that she realized everything wasn't perfect—far from it. Well, it was time to build a life she was happy with.

She wasn't sure how Jack would react to her announcement

that she intended to move to Weldon, but she felt hopeful that he would be happy about it. They had something special, and while they hadn't talked about the future, being close to each other felt right. She couldn't imagine having a long-distance relationship with him—only seeing him once or twice a month. She rubbed her chest with the heel of her palm. The thought of not seeing him every day hurt.

"I'm glad we went with the white curtains," Shannon said, coming over to stand beside her. "It looks so clean and crisp."

"It's perfect." Lizzy glanced around the store, filled with pride at what they had accomplished in such a short time.

Sparrow was now a welcoming haven with a seating area in the center of the store with reading nooks and bookish goodies in every corner. It had become a place where she would love to idle away her weekend, just like she had at Hideaway Bookstore.

"I'm dying for a cup of tea. Would you like some tea? I'll get you a cup of tea." Shannon hurried to the back room before Lizzy could say anything.

She was hoping to call it a day. She had some important decisions to make, and she wanted time to think things through. But that would have to wait for a bit. She was having tea with her dear friend.

They ended up talking until long after their cups were empty. Lizzy only left the store when her stomach was growling too loudly for them to continue their conversation. As she made her way to the back of the building, she went through the contents of her refrigerator in her head. Eggs, milk, butter, and cheese—breakfast items, basically. She'd gotten into the habit of making Jack breakfast. She enjoyed doing something for him—even something as simple as making him some scrambled eggs. And it warmed her heart when he cleaned his plate, wearing a huge-ass smile on his face.

A forlorn sigh escaped her. She missed him. He hadn't told her if he was coming over tonight. She could survive one night without him. She had a lot of thinking and planning to do. But the thing was, she didn't want to survive the night without him. She was going to ask him over. She didn't care about appearing needy or clingy. Besides, Jack would never think that of her. She was in love with the man, and she wanted him in her bed tonight.

She unlocked the door and stepped into her apartment. She noticed several things at once. A delicious, mouthwatering scent assailed her. There were candles flickering on the table. And Jack was wearing an apron. She continued to stand glued to the spot, holding on to the door handle.

"Welcome home, honey," he said with a crooked grin.

"Nice apron." She meant to sink a dose of sarcasm into her words, but instead, her voice came out breathy with awe. How a man wearing a frilly yellow apron with red polka dots could look so frigging hot was a mystery.

"Oh, this old thing?" He reached behind him to loosen the knot and pulled the apron over his head. It was like a striptease. He wore a navy polo shirt underneath that clung ever so slightly to his sculpted pecs and showed off his biceps beautifully.

God, she was so turned on. Had she always been this weird? It was her turn to say something, but she had nothing. She just stared at the man in front of her like she wanted to devour him.

Jack raised an eyebrow but didn't comment on being ogled like a piece of meat. "You're a bit early, but dinner is almost ready."

"Dinner?" she managed to say.

He gently unwrapped her fingers from the door handle and closed the door behind her. "Why don't you have a seat and I'll pour you some beer."

"Did you make me dinner?" All evidence pointed toward the fact, but Jack couldn't cook.

"I did." He took out a growler from the fridge and poured her a glass of amber-colored beer. "The plan was to make you a *romantic* dinner, but it didn't quite work out that way."

"This *is* romantic, Jack." Her pounding heart was proof of how romantic she thought he was being.

"I didn't want to risk setting fire to the bookstore, so I had to cook something I could throw together in an Instant Pot." He blushed adorably, and she didn't think she could love him any more than she did at that moment. "So instead of fancy pasta and wine, you get turkey chili and beer."

"Chili and beer should be the new gold standard for a romantic dinner," she said with a firm nod.

Jack laughed and leaned down to kiss her soundly on her lips. "Well, I am kind of proud of this part."

He brought a platter of small bowls and placed it on the center of the table.

"Ooh, fixings," she said, rubbing her hands together.

"That's right. We have sour cream, cheddar cheese, scallions, and"—he wiggled his eyebrows—"crushed Flamin' Hot Cheetos."

"Must. Eat. Now." Saliva pooled in her mouth, and she swallowed. Drooling definitely wasn't romantic.

After placing piping-hot bowls of chili on the table, he took a seat across from her and watched her top her chili with way too much sour cream and all the other toppings. She built a perfect spoonful and took her first bite. Her eyes fluttered closed.

"Oh, my God," she moaned. "This is so good."

He huffed a sigh of relief before a giant grin overtook his face. "You like it?"

"I love it," she said over another mouthful. It was crack

chili. She couldn't stop stuffing her face. And it was spicy. She reached for her beer and took a big gulp. "Oh, this is good, too. From the brewery?"

"Yeah, it's No Joke, Tara's amber lager."

"What's no joke?" She paused with the spoon in front of her mouth.

"That's the name of the lager. No Joke." He grinned at her. "As in, it's really that good. No joke."

She burst out laughing. "I don't know which I like better—the beer or the name."

"Tara's equally proud of both."

And she could tell he was very proud of his little sister. "You guys are doing amazing things with the brewery."

"Alex and Tara are incredible brewers," he said matter-of-factly. "They're the beating heart behind Weldon Brewery."

"You're incredible, too." Her eyebrows pulled together. She didn't know why he always shortchanged himself when it came to the brewery. "All your ideas and innovations helped put Weldon Brewery on the map."

"Maybe." He shrugged. "But it's their talent that's going to take the brewery the rest of the way."

"I don't like it when you talk like this." She put her spoon down. "You talk as though you have nothing to contribute to the business."

"Because I don't," he said with a shrug. "At least nothing that can't be provided by a part-time bookkeeper and a server."

"That's not true."

"It is." He reached across the table and took her hand in his. "I was going to wait until we finished dinner to tell you this, but . . . I got a job in LA."

"Wait . . . you what?" she said louder than she'd intended.

"I got a job as a business analyst with McBain Corporation.

It's an entry-level position, but it's a start . . ." He frowned and faltered when she withdrew her hand from his grasp.

"A start to what, Jack?" She was confused and angry. She didn't have time to reflect on why she was angry. She just reacted.

"To start living my life and chasing my own dreams instead of"—he swiped his hand down his mouth—"piggybacking on my brother's and sister's dream."

Piggybacking? Her heart ached at the way he described his life. Had he always felt that way? *My poor Jack.* Too many questions and feelings chased one another inside her. A part of her wanted to pull him into her arms and tell him that she was sorry he felt like a supporting actor in Alex's and Tara's lives. Tell him she was so proud of him for pursuing his own dreams.

But he was moving to Los Angeles. She was moving to Weldon. How was this happening? And how had she not known? He must have been applying for jobs and interviewing for a while to have received an offer. Sympathy, pride, betrayal, anger, and hurt swirled into a pool of anxiety. She was lost.

"And you didn't think to tell me any of this before?" she snapped, pushing up from her chair.

"I haven't told anyone." He got to his feet, holding out his hands. "I didn't know if I would get the job. I . . . I didn't want to disappoint everyone."

She paced toward the couch, then spun around to face him. "I would never be disappointed in you."

"I'm so sorry for not telling you sooner. But just think for a minute. I'm moving to LA," he said, gently grasping her arms. "We can be together."

Her first instinct was to forget her decision to leave her firm and move to Weldon. It would be so much easier to maintain the status quo *and* have Jack by her side. But she had already spent too many years of her life doing what someone else wanted of her. She needed to live her life the way she thought was best for her. She didn't have everything figured out, but going back to a life she didn't want just to be with Jack wasn't the answer.

"No, Jack. We won't be together." She shook his hands off her arm. "Because I'm moving to Weldon."

~~~

Jack laughed weakly. He must've misheard her. "You're joking, right?"

"No, not at all," she said quietly.

"You can't move to Weldon." He still wore a dismayed smile. "What about your job?"

"I'm leaving the firm." Her eyes narrowed slightly, and her chin tilted up a notch.

"Leaving the firm?" He didn't understand. "Your job is your life. I've never seen anyone work with such single-minded focus to achieve something. Making partner is your dream."

"It's not my dream. It's my mom's dream for me. And I thought the only way to live my life was to make my parents proud no matter how unhappy it made me." The sadness that swept across her face made him want to enfold her in his arms, but the expression vanished in a blink to be replaced by determination. "But now I know better. It's time I figured out what *I* want to do with my life."

"How does moving to Weldon have anything to do with that?" He dragged his fingers through his hair. He couldn't believe this was happening.

"I don't like living in LA. Even with the therapy and medication, I was constantly overcome with anxiety. I felt scared and alone *all the time*." She started pacing in the small space that marked the sitting area. "I don't feel like that here. Other than my phone calls with my mom, I haven't had to deal with anxiety once."

"You've been in Weldon less than three weeks. On a *vacation*. You have no idea what real life is like here." He sounded patronizing, but he couldn't stop himself as frustration filled him to the brim. Couldn't she see how rashly she was behaving? He was so close to being with her. He had waited so very long for her. She couldn't do this. Not now. "Why can't you just go back to LA?"

"I can ask you the same thing. Why can't you just stay in Weldon?" Her voice rose to a near shout, but her eyes entreated him.

A part of him wanted to stay. With Lizzy by his side, maybe he could be happy with his life in Weldon. He wouldn't have to disappoint his family. But *damn it*, he would be disappointed in himself. He needed to know he was following his own dreams— striving to become his best self. With his new job, he was on his way. If he didn't do this, he would always feel like he gave up on himself.

He grew desperate as he realized this was really happening. He would be moving to Los Angeles, but Lizzy wouldn't be there. He made a feeble, last-ditch effort to change her mind. "How could you abandon everything you've worked for?"

"Don't," she spat with clipped anger, "tell me how to live my life."

"I'm not . . . I'm not trying to tell you how to live your life." He rubbed his hands down his face. "I'm just trying to make you see reason."

"Oh, is that what you're trying to do? Because I'm incapable of being reasonable without your assistance?" Her lips curled in a bitter mockery of a smile. "Why don't I also be helpful and try to enlighten *you*. How is some entry-level position better than being your own boss? Do you think you'll be more valued at McBain than you are by your own family?"

Jack fought and lost to keep his insecurities in check. At the very least, he thought she would be proud of him for venturing out of his comfort zone to start a new chapter in his life. He never thought she would mock him for taking an entry-level position. His anger and frustration drained away. He'd always thought his feelings of inadequacy were his own problem. He'd had no idea that Lizzy could think so little of him and his choices.

"It might not seem like much to you, but it's the start of my dream," he said with cold detachment even as his heart cracked down the middle.

"Jack, I . . ." Her lips quivered, but she bit down on it until it stiffened into a grim line. "And if you think I'm throwing my life away when all I'm trying to do is figure out the life *I* want to live, I don't think you know me at all."

Don't know her at all? Her words gutted him. He knew her like he knew himself. He might not be handling himself well right now, but she must know how much he cared about her. Or maybe that was just wishful thinking on his part.

"It's a good thing we were taking things slowly and our emotions aren't involved." He heard the words as though someone else were speaking them. He hardly recognized his own voice. "Because if we can't even agree on the basics, this thing between us was never going to work anyway."

Lizzy sucked in a sharp breath, and hurt clouded her expression. But her voice was steady and calm as she said, "You might be right. Maybe it's for the best that we end this now."

No. Everything in him screamed, *No.* But hadn't he always expected this to happen? He'd always been afraid that he wasn't good enough for her. Now he knew that she agreed with him.

He felt hollowed out, and he welcomed the numbness. The pain would follow. He had no doubt about that. But for the time being, he could function enough to get himself home before his world finished crashing down around his head.

"Do you want me to help clean all this up before I leave?" He waved his hand toward the table and their half-eaten bowls of chili.

"No," she said in a whisper so soft he hardly heard her. "No, that's okay. I'll take care of it."

"Okay. Thank you." How polite and courteous they sounded. The sheer absurdity of it made Jack smile drunkenly. "I'll let myself out."

"Okay." She didn't move from her spot by the couch.

"Bye, Lizzy." He waved at her, still wearing the off-kilter smile as though he would see her tomorrow—when in reality, he was walking out of her life. Walking away from their decades-long friendship. Away from the love of his life.

"Goodbye, Jack."

The finality of her words wiped the smile off his face at last. This really wasn't funny at all. Nothing would ever be funny again. With a nod, he stepped out of her apartment and carefully closed the door behind him.

CHAPTER TWENTY-ONE

Shannon had been worried that no one would show up at their inaugural community event other than their guests, Tara and Aubrey. And being the supportive friend she was, Lizzy told her she was being a big ol' worrywart. And of course, Lizzy was right.

It was ten minutes until start time, and they had to scavenge for extra chairs to bring out. Soon it would be standing room only for the stragglers. The Weldon community was flat-out amazing. They came together for one another with such enthusiasm and joy. The interest in the monthly book club Shannon and Linda were putting together was busting through the roof, so they decided to create several book clubs for different genres to keep the numbers intimate.

Aubrey and Tara were definite town favorites, but the townspeople were here to support Shannon and Sparrow Bookstore, too. They oohed and aahed over the changes they'd made in the store, and they browsed through the bestsellers table and beach reads table, stacking books into their arms.

With her eyes everywhere, Shannon quickly replenished the

books and came back to stand beside Lizzy. She leaned in to be heard over the crowd and said with certainty, "He'll be here."

Lizzy looked at her friend and didn't even try to feign ignorance. "I hope so. He worked so hard to help make this happen. He deserves to be here."

She and Jack hadn't talked to each other—much less seen each other—since their horrible fight a few days ago. She picked up her phone every five minutes to call him, but then she would remember what he'd said. *It's a good thing we were taking things slowly and our emotions aren't involved.* She'd been nothing more than a friend with benefits to him.

No, that wasn't fair to him. He'd been so kind and good to her. It hadn't been a purely physical relationship for him, either—even if he insisted his emotions weren't involved. How could it have been? They were best friends. They had already cared deeply for each other. That part had never changed. And he'd wanted to be with her in Los Angeles. He had wanted this to work as much as she had.

But . . . he didn't love her. At least, not in the way that she needed him to love her. No matter how hard she'd pushed him to give them a real chance, he hadn't strayed far from the friend zone. Maybe if they'd had more time together, he might have grown to love her as she loved him, but what he felt for her now was lust and affection. That was why he was able to walk away from her.

Lizzy breathed through the ache in her chest. She hadn't allowed herself to feel the full ramifications of their fight. If she did, she would crack and crumble—turn to dust and be blown away by the wind. She couldn't let that happen. Shannon needed her. She hadn't taken on this project to abandon it unfinished. Lizzy had a couple of days left before she headed back to Los Angeles to give her two weeks' notice, so she had plenty of time to check off the few remaining tasks on the to-do list. She just had to keep it together until then.

She knew he was there without having to look. The bell jingled differently when it was announcing Jack's arrival. It was a softer, more melodic chime because he always took care with everything he handled.

He'd come. Of course he'd come. It was his sister's event after all. But that wasn't the only reason he'd come. No matter how uncomfortable he felt about seeing Lizzy, he wanted to come and support Shannon. He cared about her, her little boy, and Sparrow Bookstore. And Jack would never let his friends down.

No matter how many times Lizzy had let him down—canceling at the last minute because of a work emergency, forgetting his birthday, unfairly snapping at him because she was stressed—Jack had never let her down. And he hadn't let her down this time, either. He had figured out a way for them to be together. It wasn't his fault that she had chosen to go a different way.

She was still hurt that he'd never discussed how unhappy he was working at the brewery and that he was applying for jobs in Los Angeles. But she logically understood why he'd kept it to himself. He hadn't even told his family about it because he was afraid he wouldn't get the job he wanted. If she'd known, she would've told him that was nonsense. He was one of the smartest people she knew and so hardworking. McBain would have been blind not to hire him.

But maybe it was better that she hadn't known he was job searching in Los Angeles. If she'd known, then she might not have made the decision to leave the sprawling city and move to Weldon. She might have convinced herself that she was content with the life she had there. But sooner or later, she would've realized that living in Los Angeles wasn't right for her. What would they have done then? Maybe it really was better this way. It certainly didn't feel like it, but given some time, she would feel relieved that this happened now.

"Hi, Shannon," Jack said, coming to stand in front of them. "Look at all these people. You should be proud of putting this together."

"So should you." Shannon stepped up to him and wrapped him in a tight hug. "Thank you so much for everything you've done."

"My pleasure," he murmured.

"Well, I'm going to introduce the ladies to the crowd and get this party started," Shannon said, clasping her hands in front of her chest. "Wish me luck."

"Break a leg," Lizzy said with an encouraging smile. When Shannon nervously stood in place, Lizzy gave her a friendly shove toward the stage and watched her make her way up to the mic.

"Hello, Lizzy," Jack said quietly by her side.

The low timbre of his voice sent a shiver of awareness down her spine. Despite what happened, her body and heart recognized him as the man she loved—as the man she would never stop loving.

"Hi there." She made an effort to sound chipper. It fell way, way flat.

That was all the time they had to talk before the program started. She wouldn't have known what else to say to him anyway.

"I'm sure I speak for everyone when I say that the new and improved Sparrow is an absolute dream." Tara smiled brightly as the audience hooted and applauded. "Well, we are honored to host the first community event—the first of many, I hope— here tonight. In case any of you are wondering who the heck we are"—she pointed a thumb at herself then at her cohost—"let me introduce you to Aubrey Kim, Weldon's own celebrity chef and owner of Comfort Zone."

"Being a guest chef on one cooking show doesn't make me a celebrity," Aubrey muttered, turning a becoming shade of pink. "At any rate, let *me* introduce you to Tara Park—soon to be Tara Kim when she marries my brother-in-law in a few months . . . *Oh, my God.* I just realized we're going to be sisters soon."

"Oh, my glitter bomb." Tara's hand fluttered to her chest. "Bree, we're going to be *sisters*."

The two best friends hugged each other and swayed back and forth. The store full of locals laughed and clapped—not at all minding that the regularly scheduled program was delayed to accommodate the tender moment.

Lizzy stole a glance at Jack, who stood an arm's length away from her. The respectable distance between them made her heart clench with loneliness. She missed his warmth. She missed him. What would happen if she reached out her hand and took ahold of his? Would his fingers link through hers as though it were as natural as breathing to him—as it was to her?

She focused her attention back toward the stage. Aubrey and Tara had broken apart to proceed with their event.

"As I was saying," Aubrey said with an affectionate glance at her best friend, "Tara is an award-winning brewer and part owner of the incomparable Weldon Brewery. We're here tonight to share a bit about beer-and-dessert pairings."

"Some of you look dubious." Tara playfully narrowed her eyes at the audience, then smiled. "I can't say I blame you, but Aubrey and I put in many hours of research to present these truly awesome pairings to you."

"It was grueling work, but somebody had to do it," Aubrey deadpanned to delighted laughter.

"No one can call themselves a true Weldonian unless they've tried Comfort Zone's pretzel bread pudding," Tara said, holding up a plate of the famed dessert. "But have you ever tried it with Weldon Brewery's Smarty-Pants Ale, our coffee blond ale?"

IPA with carrot cake. Lambic beer with cheesecake. Imperial stout with brownies. The delicious pairings soon filled up the presentation table.

"And what would a beer-and-dessert-pairing presentation be without a tasting?" Aubrey said coyly. Everyone in the store burst out in cheers and crowded the table.

Shannon quickly joined the guest speakers on the stage to help set out bite-size pieces of the desserts they'd cut up earlier and pour plastic shot glasses with the award-winning brews. Lizzy took a step forward to lend an extra pair of hands when Jack's voice stopped her.

"Are you . . . Will you be staying at the apartment upstairs when you move to Weldon?"

"No, I'm afraid not," Lizzy said with her heart pounding—ridiculously happy to talk to him about anything. "It's already booked up for the rest of the summer. I'll need to find a place to lease."

"You can stay with my family," he blurted. When her mouth dropped open, Jack rushed to add, "I'll . . . I'll be gone by the time you come back in two weeks, and I won't be coming home for a while. I need time to get settled in LA."

"Jack, I can't . . ." She couldn't stay with his family. She would be reminded of him everywhere she looked.

"You can use Tara's room. She finally *officially* moved out. My parents could use the company," he said with a pleading look in his eyes. "You're going to be swamped, wrapping up your old job and taking care of your condo in LA. It'll be one less thing to worry about until you have some time to find a place here."

He was looking out for her like he always had. Hot tears prickled her eyes. Her sweet, kind Jack. She took a deep breath and opened her mouth.

"Please don't say no," he said before she could speak. "Just think about it."

"Okay." She couldn't refuse when he looked at her like that. "I'll think about it."

"Thank you." Relief washed across his features.

"I think I'm the one who's supposed to say that." She offered him a small smile, then quickly glanced away. She didn't think she could handle seeing his beautiful smile without falling at his feet and begging him to take her back. "I should go and help."

She walked off without another word—without looking back—because she was afraid to say goodbye. If she didn't say it, maybe this wouldn't really be goodbye.

~

Jack made chili again. This time to butter his family up before he broke the news that he was moving to Los Angeles. Not only because he didn't know how to make anything else but because he wanted to avoid granting chili the significance of being *the breakup meal*. He could imagine himself sobbing his heart out every time he sat in front of a bowl of chili, and it wasn't pretty. But even as he cooked it for his family—telling himself it was just some fucking chili—it felt as though his Adam's apple had tripled in size, and he struggled to swallow his rising emotions.

Lizzy had looked beautiful but sad the other night at Sparrow. He had felt like Atlas bearing the weight of the heavens on his back as he fought against his instinct to pull her into his arms. At the time, he'd believed it was for the best. The way they'd left things off . . . It didn't seem like there was anything he could've done to fix things between them. But now that she'd gone back to Los Angeles, he cursed himself for not taking the opportunity to hold her one last time.

In a couple of weeks, they would switch places—she would come back to Weldon, and he would go to Los Angeles. He huffed a humorless laugh at the irony. He'd thought the job with McBain would bring him closer to Lizzy. Even if they had only been friends, being closer to her would have made him so happy. They would've been close enough that they might even have run into each other by chance. The idea had seemed ridiculously romantic at the time.

Now—after all the things they'd ended up saying to each other—he couldn't even hope for friendship. At least, not for a very long time. Besides, he was the fool who fell in love with her. He didn't know if he could handle going back to being her friend. Not when he wanted her so much. It would bleed him dry to watch her move on from what they had together and date other men. To watch her fall in love and marry someone else. He couldn't do that anymore. It was better that he would be out of her life.

The onions he was chopping stung his eyes and made tears drip down his face. But why did his chest burn, too? He scraped the onions into a bowl and rinsed off the cutting board and knife. And since he didn't have an excuse to weep in the kitchen anymore, he wiped his face on the sleeve of his T-shirt.

"Dude, are you crying?" Alex said, walking into the kitchen.

"Onions," Jack said.

His twin gave him a worried glance but didn't push it. "So why have you called this family lunch meeting?"

"Can't a guy cook for his family without a motive?"

"That would be a fair question if you were a guy who could

cook." Alex peeked over Jack's shoulder suspiciously as he poured out some shredded cheese into a bowl. "I can't help but think you're climbing this insurmountable mountain because you want to butter us up."

"Butter us up for what?" Tara joined them in the kitchen.

Jack sighed ponderously. "I have something to tell you, but I want to do it when Mom and Dad are here."

"We're here," his mom said with his dad right behind her.

"Well, I made chili, so I'll tell you after we've all had a nice lunch together."

"Is he trying to butter us up for something?" his dad asked Tara.

Four pairs of suspicious eyes turned to Jack, and he threw his hands up. "Just sit down and eat, for Christ's sake."

"Language." His mom narrowed her eyes at him.

"Sorry." Jack took a deep breath. "Let's all have some chili, for *goodness*' sake. You guys like chili, don't you?"

"I love chili," Alex said, and sat down at the table.

Jack shot his brother a grateful smile as everyone followed his example and sat around the dining table. Warmth spread through his chest as he glanced at his family digging into the chili. Everyone was quiet, which was the best compliment they could give his cooking.

"I need to tell you guys something." He stirred some sour cream and cheese into his chili.

"Obviously," Tara said, gulping down some water. "Man, this has a kick."

"You called a family meeting *and* cooked lunch for us," Alex added. "I'm guessing it's not good news."

"That depends on how you look at it." Jack wiped his damp hands on his thighs. "I'm hoping you'll think of it as good news. Mostly."

"Well, let's hear it, then," his dad said.

Jack wanted to run out of the kitchen and go hide under his bed, but he would have to come out eventually. *Just tell them.* "I got a job in LA."

The silence around the table this time was not a good sign.

"But you have a job *here*." Tara's eyebrows furrowed together. "What do you mean you got a job in LA?"

"I got a job as a business analyst at McBain Corporation." This was even harder than he'd thought it would be. "I have someone lined up to take over the brewery's bookkeeping, and we can start running ads in the local paper for a server."

"Jack," Tara said sharply.

His mom put a hand on his sister's arm before she could continue and asked, "Are you happy you got the job?"

"Yes," Jack said.

His answer was simple in its truth. He lost Lizzy. He was letting his family down. Despite it all, Jack was glad he was following his own dream at last.

"Then your mom and I are happy for you," his dad said after exchanging a glance with his mom. "We'll figure everything else out."

"Thank you," Jack said quietly.

He was acutely aware that Alex hadn't said a single word during the entire conversation. His brother's uncharacteristic silence and stoic expression made it hard for him to breathe.

Then Alex suddenly pushed back from the table and got to his feet. "Jack and I are going to the brewery."

Jack stood, too. He wasn't about to argue. They needed to talk. His parents and Tara understood.

"Go," his sister said. "I'll see you guys tonight."

The car ride to the brewery was encased in icy silence. Jack clenched and unclenched his hands as he sat in the passenger seat. His twin didn't utter a single word until they walked into Weldon Brewery, then he spun to face Jack.

"The brewery is our *dream*."

"No." Anger Jack didn't know he felt surged to the surface. "It's *your* dream. Tara's and your dream. Not mine."

"I don't understand." Alex looked as though Jack had struck him.

The anger drained from Jack as suddenly as it filled him. "You assumed—no, everyone assumed—I wanted what you wanted."

"If this wasn't what you wanted, then why didn't you just tell me?"

"I didn't want to disappoint you and the rest of our family." Jack shrugged. "Besides, I was happy to help build Weldon Brewery. I was thrilled to watch you and Tara sweep all those beer awards and to see the business take off."

"Then why are you leaving?" His brother walked behind the bar and poured two glasses of beer, passing one to Jack.

He slid into a barstool and took a long sip. "I was happy to be here while I was needed, but it's been a while since I've felt that way."

"But we do need you."

"Only to a certain extent," Jack said. "Like I said, the book-keeping and serving can easily be outsourced, but I'd be happy to have you retain me as a business consultant. Weldon Brewery is a well-oiled machine, and as long as you and Tara keep brewing those fantastic beers, the brewery is going to thrive. But you might need some advice from time to time, and I'll be there for you when you do."

His twin emptied his glass. "How long have you known that you didn't want to work for Weldon Brewery forever and ever?"

Jack laughed, relieved to see his brother acting more like

himself. "For about a year now. I had to work so hard to make myself useful."

"You should've told me how you felt." It sounded like an apology.

"I wasn't sure myself. I wanted to figure everything out before I dropped this on you."

"You didn't need to do it alone." Alex dragged a hand through his hair. "I'm your twin, for fuck's sake."

"Language," Jack said with a broad grin.

"Fuck you, asshole."

"I love you, too, man."

When Alex chuckled, something loosened in Jack's chest. Everything was all right between them. He'd distanced himself from his family—kept his unhappiness a secret from them—because of his own insecurities and doubts. They would never be disappointed in him. The only person he disappointed was him by not believing in himself.

He was good enough. Everyone who mattered to him already knew that. It was about time he stopped doubting himself.

CHAPTER TWENTY-TWO

ere. A present," Lizzy said as she handed Katie her prized stapler from her bare desk. With her personal belongings packed away, her office looked cold and sterile. How had she worked such long hours here? "Now you can stop borrowing it."

"Oh, my gosh. Thank you." She petted the black stapler like it was a sweet, mewling kitten. "I have coveted this for so long."

"I'm going to miss it." Lizzy laughed. "I'll miss you, too, Katie. You're an amazing attorney, and it was a pleasure working with you."

Her associate's face crumpled. "I can't believe you're really leaving. Everyone here knew that you were going to make partner in the next couple of years. All that hard work. I still don't understand how you can walk away from it."

"I can't stay knowing that this isn't the life I want." Big-city lawyer wasn't who she was anymore. But who was she, then? That was what she planned on figuring out. "I need to change course while I can."

"I always knew you were brave," Katie said with a bittersweet smile. "Do you need help taking your stuff to your car?"

"No need." Lizzy patted the lone Bankers Box sitting on her desk. "This is it. I can't believe five years of my life fits into one box."

"Isn't that ficus plant yours, too?" Katie pointed toward a tall, leafy plant in the corner of the office.

"That's a ficus plant? I had no idea." Lizzy shook her head. "That's definitely not mine. The only reason it's still green and healthy is because my black thumb has never once touched it. You know the office manager can get you plants for your office, right?"

"What? How come no one's ever told me that? I always assumed you guys brought your own." Katie walked over to the plant. "Can I have this one?"

"Be my guest." Lizzy smiled. "The plant lady comes and waters it, so you don't have to worry about killing it. The firm doesn't want attorneys distracted from billable hours to water plants."

Katie crinkled her nose. "Speaking of billable hours, I'm behind on my time sheets."

"Well, go and get that done. I'll see myself out."

"I'll miss you, Lizzy." Her associate gave her a tight hug. "Please keep in touch. I mean it."

"I will." Lizzy hugged her back, realizing maybe she did have a friend in the firm. "Thank you."

After saying goodbye to Katie, Lizzy walked over to Peter's office and rapped lightly on his open door.

"There she is," he said, looking away from his computer. "What are you standing there for? Come sit down."

She planted herself in one of two guest chairs in front of his massive mahogany desk. She had sat on the chair countless times with a yellow notepad in hand to discuss her many cases with him. It felt strange to sit there empty-handed, preparing to say goodbye.

"Are you working on the Doheny trial?" she asked, catching a glimpse of the motions on his desk.

"Yes." He swiped a hand down his face. "This fucking case should've settled two weeks ago, but when both parties are unreasonable assholes . . ."

He didn't need to finish the sentence. Been there. Done that. Too many times. "Well, it's good for the firm, right?"

"Right," he said with a dry smile. "So are you ready to start your new job next week?"

"Yes. Thank you so much for the referral," she said. "I still can't believe you know a law office near Weldon."

"Robert used to practice in LA years ago at one of the boutique firms until he moved up there to branch out on his own. He did well for himself. I think he's up to three associates with you joining his practice."

"Well, I'll only be working part-time for now."

She hoped being at a small firm in a small town would make her happier, but she wasn't quite sure how she felt about it yet. Wasn't it what she wanted? Being an attorney was all she knew how to do . . . It was probably because none of it felt real yet. She just needed time to adjust to her new life.

"You'll figure it all out soon enough," Peter said, seeming to sense her disquiet. "I wish you the best of luck. You are a damn fine attorney."

"Thank you, Peter. You've been an amazing mentor." With one last hug, she left his office.

As she walked down the hallway, Lizzy thought about visiting Ashley for old times' sake, but she decided to save herself the trouble. She didn't want to endure her fake solicitude or ill-disguised glee. Instead, she said a silent goodbye to the law firm that had been the center of her life for the past five years and left without looking back.

Once she got to her car, she loaded her box in the trunk and slid into the driver's seat. It finally hit her that this was the last time she would be driving out of this parking structure—this building. She'd really done it. She had given her two weeks' notice and left Nelson Peters. When she'd told her mom about her decision to leave the firm, her rage had been palpable from across the ocean. But Lizzy was done living her life to earn her mom's approval. She deserved to choose the life she wanted to live. She deserved to be happy. That didn't make any of this easier, though.

It was just past six o'clock when she pulled out onto the street, and the sun was still shining brilliantly over downtown Los Angeles. The thought of going home to her empty condo suddenly filled her with dread. To avoid the loneliness and doubts threatening to overwhelm her, she changed course and headed to her safe place.

Hideaway Bookstore was warm and welcoming as ever when she walked into the familiar space, but the ring of the shop-keeper's bell made her heart flutter. For weeks, it had been her favorite sound in the world, because it often announced the arrival of her favorite person. Tears filled her eyes, and the book-store blurred in front of her.

"Lizzy?" Beverly came and put a hand on her arm. "What's wrong? Are you okay?"

She shook her head and forced a watery smile. "Sorry. It's nothing. I . . . I'm moving, and I'm really going to miss this place."

"Oh, my dear." The shop owner gave her a hug. "Where are you moving to?"

"To Weldon, a small town on the southern edge of the Sierra Nevada," Lizzy said, fighting back more tears. "It's . . . it's really beautiful there."

"That sounds lovely."

"It really is." Weldon had made her feel safe and content. Why was she blubbering like this? She couldn't understand herself. "Well, I'm going to have a look around and say farewell to my favorite bookstore."

"Take your time," Beverly said with a pat on Lizzy's back.

She meandered through the store, not knowing where to settle. She eventually ended up at the literature section and reached for *Pride and Prejudice*, but she couldn't open it. Last time she was at Hideaway Bookstore, Jack had known exactly where she was and what she was reading. Even though she had been "celebrating" her trial victory on her own, she hadn't been alone. But today—she took a shuddering breath and braced herself against the bookshelf—she was truly alone.

Even Hideaway couldn't offer her the solace that she so desperately needed, and she succumbed to the anxiety crashing into her. Darkness crowded into the edges of her vision, and dizziness swept through her. She couldn't get enough air in her lungs, and her legs shook with the effort to hold herself up. *Jack.* Was he still in Weldon? Or had he come to Los Angeles?

It was wrong—so wrong—to be without him. But she was lost. She didn't know how to find her way back to him.

~

Life without Lizzy was bleached of color and vibrancy. It was as though Jack's life went from high-definition TV to black and white. Even his move to Los Angeles—where everything was bigger, brighter, and louder—failed to stir any excitement in him. He still moved and talked because he couldn't stop living, but the world around him was cast in a dull gray light, and everything sounded like static.

Determination was the only thing propelling him forward.

Jack owed it to everyone who believed in him to give his new career everything he had. He had to thrive. He couldn't succumb to lethargy and apathy even though they tried to weigh him down like stones in his pockets. Monday was his first day at work. He hoped to drum up some excitement about it over the weekend, while settling into his new apartment.

Sitting on the floor with his back against the wall, he glanced around the living room without taking any of it in. Well, there wasn't much to take in since his apartment was pretty much empty. His desk and bed were the only furniture he'd brought from home. Everything else he would buy or build when he had time.

There was plenty of food, though. His mom had packed him enough banchan to last him a month. All he had to do was make some rice in his smart rice cooker—a housewarming gift from his parents—and he was set for dinner. Except food didn't interest him. Nothing interested him.

He missed Lizzy so much that it made him feel off-kilter. Did the last two weeks at her firm go well? Was she excited about moving to Weldon? Did she find a new job? He knew nothing. He couldn't stand it, but that was the way it had to be.

Jack changed into his workout clothes and pulled on his running shoes. He needed to do something to get out of his head. The sun had begun to set behind the tall buildings of LA's Koreatown as he blindly left his apartment. He ran down unfamiliar streets with unfamiliar sights, not paying attention to anything but the reassuring feel of his feet hitting the sidewalk and the burning in his chest from his unforgiving pace.

Lizzy. He pushed himself harder until sweat dripped down his face and stung his eyes. He wanted to run all the way to her, wherever she was, but he couldn't. The thought gutted him, and he nearly stumbled.

It had taken him much too long to realize that he was enough, and now he might have lost her. He swiped at his eyes and ran on. His insecurities had been his own all along and not a reflection on who Lizzy was. It didn't matter that she was a successful, driven attorney. It didn't matter what *type* of men she dated. It had always been about his feelings of inadequacy.

And he didn't feel inadequate because he was a bookkeeper for his family's business. If that had been what he'd wanted, then that would've been enough. Dedicating nearly a decade of his life to the brewery hadn't been about accepting his responsibilities to his family and sacrificing his dreams for them. Going along with what everyone expected of him had been the simplest route for him to take. He did it because it was easy and didn't stop to think about what he really wanted. It was on him.

He had held himself back from confessing his love to Lizzy because he hadn't known what he wanted from life. It had never been about losing her friendship or because it was *too soon*. Those were just excuses he'd made to himself to avoid facing the truth. He had been so lost that he'd convinced himself that he wasn't good enough for her.

What he hadn't understood was that he had to be good enough for himself before he could be free of his fears and insecurities. Now that he had taken his first steps on the path that he'd chosen for himself, he finally knew who he was. He knew he was *enough*. For himself and for her.

Jack knew Lizzy, understood her, and loved her more than anyone else in this world. If given the chance, he would love her the way she deserved to be loved. He would make her happy. He would be good enough for her. But would she still want him after what he'd said that night? How could he tell her that he didn't feel anything for her? It had been a blatant lie. He had never loved anyone more than he loved her. She was it for him. She had always been it for him.

He wanted nothing more than to beg for her forgiveness and tell her he loved her. Every beat of his heart told him to win her back. But he couldn't. Not because he was afraid that she would reject him. He would risk everything if it meant he could have a chance at forever with her. It was because she was as lost as he had been.

Becoming a partner in a national firm had driven her for all her adult life. But she'd said that wasn't her dream. It was her mother's dream for her. She wanted to move to Weldon and figure out what *she* wanted with her life. It was her turn to find herself. He couldn't hinder that all-important process by confessing his undying love for her. He couldn't cloud her judgment. Telling her now wouldn't be an act of love but one of selfishness and possessiveness.

Waiting for her to find her own way was the best way he could love her now. No matter how much he missed her. No matter how much he wanted her. He would love her by waiting. He had to trust her. Once she figured everything out, she would come to him. If not to be his love, then to be his friend. Then he would tell her. He would tell her everything. How much she meant to him. How he had loved her in secret for twenty years. How he had fallen in love with her for what felt like the first time during her three weeks in Weldon. But for now, he would wait.

It was dark by the time he slowed down to take in his surroundings. He had no idea where he was. With a huff of dumbfounded laughter, he pulled out his phone and opened his map app. This was the first time he didn't know how to find his way home. His fingers hovered over his phone and he squeezed his eyes shut. He prayed Lizzy would know how to find her way home to him when the time came.

CHAPTER TWENTY-THREE

In the end, Lizzy moved in with the Parks. Just temporarily—just as Jack had asked her to—while she looked for her own place in Weldon. It hurt to be reminded of him everywhere she looked, but she would rather hurt and feel closer to him than feel the distance between them like a jagged chasm in her heart.

Jack's parents had been wonderful and hadn't pried into what had happened between their son and her. But they knew something happened because they've been feeding her nonstop since she moved in. That was how Korean elders showed they cared. Busy? Eat to keep your strength up. Sick? Eat to fight off whatever ails you. Heartbroken? Eat to fill the hollowness inside you.

Surprisingly, the food really did help, and she felt marginally better, which was fortunate since she was heading into her first day at work. It was in a neighboring town, and the commute took only about half an hour. The law office was located in what appeared to be a converted single-family home, painted in a somber gray—perhaps to reflect the seriousness of the business.

At any rate, after she climbed up the porch steps, she nearly knocked because she felt like she was visiting someone's house. Remembering that she worked there now, she pushed open the door and walked inside.

The receptionist glanced up and smiled at her. "May I help you?"

"I'm Elizabeth Chung. I'm the new attorney starting today," Lizzy said, extending her hand.

"Nice to meet you." The receptionist came around the desk and shook her hand. "I'm Margaret. Let me show you to Robert's office. He's expecting you."

His office was down the short hallway in the back corner of the building. He was typing furiously on his keyboard with his two index fingers when Margaret rapped on the door.

"Robert, this is Elizabeth Chung," she said.

He grunted and jutted his chin toward one of the guest chairs. Guessing that was her cue to have a seat, Lizzy sat down. The receptionist headed back to her station with a wave. Lizzy crossed her legs and looked around the office. It was small and cluttered with stacks of accordion folders teetering on every available space.

"So you're Elizabeth Chung," Robert said at last, leaning back in his chair.

"Please call me Lizzy."

"Peter speaks highly of you," he continued as though she hadn't spoken, "which means I have high expectations from you. I hope you can meet them."

Lizzy blinked, slightly taken aback by his abrasive manner. "I hope so, too."

"You're going to be sharing an office with one of our associates. You have to earn your own office." He got to his feet and headed for the door. Lizzy assumed she was meant to follow.

"Trisha, this is your new office mate," he said, walking into a smaller office across from his. "Hand over the Stewart case to her."

"Hi, I'm Lizzy," she said to her new office mate.

"Hi. Let me get that file together for you," Trisha said with a hint of frustration. "I'm trying to get a motion to compel out the door right now, so bear with me."

"You can spare five minutes to hand over the file to her," Robert barked. "She's not here to sit around. She needs to start billing."

He stalked back to his office without waiting for Trisha's reply. Her office mate offered her a half-apologetic smile. "He always gets touchy when he's preparing for trial. He's normally more tolerable."

"That's okay," Lizzy replied automatically.

Robert's reference to billing five minutes into her first day made her stomach clench with nerves. One of the reasons she wanted to work part-time was to reduce her billable hours requirement. She didn't want to be a slave to her job and had expected a smaller firm to be somewhat more relaxed than her old firm had been.

"Here's the Stewart file. It's a standard breach of contract case, and we represent Defendant, Stewart Corporation." Trisha handed her a thick accordion folder. "The complaint is pretty self-explanatory. The written discovery and Plaintiff's deposition are done. Robert will probably want you to draft a motion for summary judgment."

"Are the undisputed facts that clear-cut?" Lizzy arched an eyebrow in surprise. "Enough to get the case dismissed without a jury trial?"

Trisha gave her a wary look. "When we're representing a defendant and billing by the hour, Robert always pushes for a motion for summary judgment."

Lizzy bit back her protest and sat at her desk, facing the side wall. It seemed all law firms, big and small, couldn't resist the chunk of change brought in by bringing a motion for summary judgment. A familiar tremor started deep inside her and spread into her limbs. Her hands shook as she pulled out the complaint. Tension gripped her neck and shoulders, and a headache flared behind her eyes. She tried to breathe through her anxiety and review the allegations in the complaint. She distracted herself from her panicked thoughts by analyzing the evidence in the written discovery and deposition transcript. Focusing on her logic helped slow her pulse to normal, and some of her tension left her body.

She had a decent grasp of the case within three hours. As she'd feared, she saw no basis for a summary judgment motion. Most of the key facts were disputed by the parties, so Plaintiff's claims were entitled to a jury trial.

"How's the motion to compel going?" Lizzy asked, coming up for air. It was past noon, and Trisha hadn't moved from her desk either.

"I'm done. I just need to read through it once before it goes out the door," her office mate said. "Then we can go to lunch to celebrate your first day, and I'll introduce you to the other associate."

"That's fine. Take your time."

Lunch was a simple affair at a nearby diner. Phil, the other associate, was friendly enough, but the entire lunch conversation consisted of him and Trisha venting about their workload and the terrible opposing counsels they were dealing with. Lizzy fought off another bout of anxiety by working through a mountain of french fries and listened to her coworkers' tirade with only half an ear.

They returned to their desks in less than an hour, and Lizzy decided there was no point in putting off the inevitable. She knocked on Robert's door, holding the Stewart complaint and a yellow notepad in her hand.

"Robert, do you have a minute?" she said when he didn't look up from his desk.

"Come in. What is it?" he asked impatiently.

"Trisha mentioned that I should prepare a summary judgment motion for the Stewart case."

"Yes. She's been with me for a couple of years. She knows how I like to do things."

"But this case isn't a good candidate for a motion for summary judgment." Lizzy got straight to her point. If he was busy, then it was best she didn't waste any of his time. "Plaintiff could raise a number of material issues of fact to bar the motion from being granted."

Robert narrowed his eyes at her. "A summary judgment motion is not only filed when you're certain of its success. It could also be used to pressure Plaintiff into a reasonable settlement."

"That only works when we have a strong enough motion to cause Plaintiff concern that they might lose their chance for a jury trial," she said, her frustration rising. "Filing a summary judgment motion in this case is almost frivolous."

"What are you? The ethics committee?" he snarled. "We are litigators, and this is what we do."

Why was she making such a big deal out of this? How many motions for summary judgment had she written knowing that she was going to lose? Too many to count. But she thought that was part of the big-firm culture. She thought things would be different in a smaller firm. She now realized that she had absolutely no grounds for believing that other than wishful thinking.

She couldn't escape it. The conflict, the antagonism, the constant reminders of the bottom line. Like Robert said, that was what litigators did. They fought for a living, day in and day out. The bigger the fight, the better it was for the bottom line. That was how they earned their keep. Well, she *could* escape it. All she had to do was stop being a litigator.

"Well, it isn't what *I* do." Lizzy stood from her seat.

"Sit down." Robert's eyes bugged out. "We aren't finished."

"No, I think we're done here," she said evenly. "Thank you for the opportunity. I'll show myself out."

"You're quitting on your first day?" he sputtered.

"Yes, I am."

Lizzy walked out of the law office both thrilled and terrified. Once she got in her car, she released the breath that she'd been holding and waited for the panic attack to hit. She'd quit her new job on the first day. Not only that, she'd decided to walk away from the only profession she'd known. She was unemployed for the first time in her life, and she had no idea what to do next.

But the panic attack never came. Instead, a weight lifted off her chest as she found brilliant clarity. She had taken the long way around, but she'd finally figured it out. She smiled and turned on the ignition, looking forward to her drive back to Weldon. It really was a lovely town, but it wasn't the place for her. She saw that now.

It wasn't the big city or the big firm that had made her unhappy but her profession in its entirety. She'd been too afraid to let go of the one thing she knew she was good at. Even as she'd claimed that she wanted to live her life for herself, she'd been too afraid to acknowledge which part of her life really needed changing. For years, being a successful attorney was her identity—it was what gave her a sense of self-worth—but it had never been who she truly was.

She hated being an attorney. Whoever heard of a conflict-averse lawyer? She was not made to practice law. She wasn't sure what she *was* made for, but she was crossing out *attorney* from her list. Her mom was going to be disappointed in her—she might never forgive her—but Lizzy needed to be at peace with that. Because she was done living the life she was expected to live.

If anyone had told her two months ago that she would be an unemployed thirty-year-old without a profession, she would have laughed in their faces. Oh, the bliss of ignorance. But she preferred the turmoil of knowing—knowing that she didn't know anything. It was the first step toward discovering the life she wanted to create for herself.

Even when faced with the knowledge that she didn't know who she was or what she wanted in life, she was certain of one thing. She loved Jack. The truth of her love would never falter or change. That love anchored her. As for everything else, she would figure it out in time.

CHAPTER TWENTY-FOUR

*L*izzy had moved back to Los Angeles from Weldon a couple of months earlier. During her brief stay, she'd helped out Shannon at Sparrow to keep herself from falling apart piece by piece—she missed Jack so much—and did some serious soul-searching to figure out what she wanted to do with her life. But the more she worked at the bookstore, the less she needed to search her soul.

It was so obvious. The answer had been waving its hands in front of her face, shouting *hellllo*, since she'd first walked into Sparrow and offered her assistance. Working through the to-do list and seeing the bookstore flourish had been deeply fulfilling—as though her soul was being injected with joie de vivre. It had made her happier than she'd ever been while practicing law. But she'd been too stuck being who she thought she ought to be to understand what it had all meant.

Owning a bookstore—being surrounded by books—was all Lizzy had ever wanted. The dream she had as a child wasn't a silly pipe dream. She might have been little, but her dream hadn't been. And when she searched deep inside her, she found that the dream had lived on as big and brightly as ever.

Being a bookseller meant helping people find their moments of escape or enlightenment—helping people fill a void in themselves to find a sense of wholeness and happiness. It could be through discovering new knowledge, being carried away by adventure, or having a good fright over a horror story. It could be something as simple as curing someone of mind-numbing boredom. There was a right book for everyone whenever they needed it.

Lizzy wanted to be there for those readers to help them find their way. And as always, books would be her friend and teacher. At this stage in her life, romance novels were still the right books for her but for slightly different reasons. She didn't need them so much to feel the human connection anymore but to help her hang on to hope. She needed to be reminded that everyone made mistakes—pretty awful ones sometimes—but there would always be a happy ending.

She had messed up big-time. She'd lashed out and hurt her best friend—the man she loved with all her heart. She'd belittled his dream and disparaged the courage it took for him to follow it. All because *she* was lost and frightened. She wished she could turn back time and unsay those words. It gutted her to think how much she must've hurt him. The radio silence from him for the last few months was indisputable evidence of how badly she'd messed up. Even so, she had to believe that there would be a happily ever after for her and Jack.

Weldon had felt like home because Jack had been there. He was her home. Her insistence that she had to move there to live the life she wanted was foolish and misguided. She'd wanted to convince herself that living in a small town would fix all her problems when she knew deep inside that her unhappiness would follow her wherever she went as long as she didn't follow her dream. It was hard to accept that she wasn't who she thought she was. But the identity she'd held on to for so long was an ill-fitting mask that hid who she really was. She wasn't someone who belonged in a courtroom. She was someone who belonged in a bookstore.

"Bev," Lizzy called out, "should we put this week's new releases on this table up front? I want to lay them out front-facing, and the new release shelf is getting kind of crowded."

"You're the boss. Do what you think is best," Beverly said from the other end of the store. "But that does sound like a good idea."

"Awesome. Thank you."

As soon as she'd returned to Los Angeles, she'd visited Bev at Hideaway and made an offer on her favorite bookstore. And . . . drumroll, please . . . *Beverly had accepted the offer*! Meanwhile, she'd asked the veteran bookseller to stay on as an employee for as long as she liked because Lizzy had a lot to learn about being a bookstore owner.

Hugging a stack of new releases to her chest, Lizzy sighed dreamily. A *bookstore owner*. Even two months later, she could hardly believe it. She woke up every morning excited to go into work because work was a freaking bookstore. Best. Job. Ever.

Her smiled waned and disappeared. She had finally figured out the life she wanted to live, but it would never be complete without Jack. She wanted to be brave and win him back, but she didn't want to be his friend with benefits. She cringed remembering what he'd said during their fight. *It's a good thing . . . our emotions aren't involved.* But her emotions had been very much involved. She'd gone and fallen in love with him. In her weakest moments, she thought she wanted him back any way she could have him, but that wasn't true. She wanted all of him. She deserved to be loved.

But she had far from given up. She was developing a strategy to make him fall hopelessly in love with her. That was also where the romance novels came in handy. Lizzy and Jack fit into the friends-to-lovers and second-chance romance tropes. Losing him had broken her heart, but how could there be a second-chance romance between them if she hadn't lost him? She huffed a frustrated sigh. Honestly, she wouldn't have minded skipping the whole second-chance romance thing, but what happened had happened. She had to work with what she'd gotten.

Often in second-chance romance novels, the hero or heroine returns to the town they had left because their life takes one horrible turn or another. For her, it was walking away from her job and profession in one fell swoop on her first day of work. But it really wasn't very horrible since she'd rediscovered and claimed her dream because of it.

The next step would be running into Jack by pure chance. He would realize he never stopped wanting her, and passion would explode. In the books, the hero and heroine would resist each other because something—a painful past, guilt, or mistrust—always held them back. But that was when real life would diverge from the romance novels. Lizzy had no intention of pushing him away or letting her fears hold her back. She refused to engage in the one-step-forward, two-steps-back lovers' dance. When he walked back into her life, she would hold on to him with all her strength—with all her love—and hope to high hell that he would someday love her back.

The problem was she had no idea how to orchestrate a chance meeting with him. If she planned it and went to stand around at his office lobby every day, then it wouldn't be a chance meeting. That would sort of be like cheating. Then again, she wasn't above a little cheating if it meant she got to see Jack sooner. The problem was she wouldn't even have a decent excuse for why she just happened to be at the lobby. If she were still an attorney, she could've said that she had a meeting or a deposition in the same building. But no matter how convenient the excuse might be, she had zero regrets about not being a lawyer.

She knew she was just going to have to suck it up and call him. This was their life, not a romance novel. She couldn't wait for chance to bring them together. Every second he wasn't in her life felt like a drop of blood falling from the crack in her heart. She couldn't let life hemorrhage out of her. God, she missed him. She squeezed her eyes shut for a second as a wave of pain and longing crashed into her.

Lizzy turned to the door when the shopkeeper's bell rang and froze to the spot. And the customer stopped in his tracks with his hand still on the door. Time resumed when her body forced out the breath she'd been holding and her heart remembered to beat again. It overcompensated for its brief pause by pounding extra fast. She pressed her hand against her chest to make sure that it didn't pop out of her.

"Lizzy." Her name left Jack's lips in a whoosh of breath.

He stepped into the store and let the door close behind him. The bell jingled quietly as though it didn't want to intrude in their private moment. He came to stand on the other side of the table she was stocking. It was a small table. If she reached out her arm, she would be able to touch him. She wanted to touch him—possibly jump him. So badly. But all she did was stare, drinking in the sight of him. And he stared back at her as though reassuring himself that she was real.

"What are you doing here?" he asked at last.

For some reason, she felt shy about telling him that she was the new owner of Hideaway Bookstore, so she asked back, "What are *you* doing here? It's the middle of the day."

Jack's eyebrows drew down in confusion. "Yes, it is the middle of the day . . ."

When he didn't continue, she prompted, "Shouldn't you be at work?"

"It's Saturday."

"Is it?" she said like she had wool for brains. She didn't notice the weekends so much anymore because the bookstore was open all week long. That was the life of a small business owner.

"I actually *was* at work for a few hours," he added, "but I left to stop by here."

They had gone full circle. "So what are you doing here?"

"I'm here to . . . buy a book," he said, rubbing the back of his neck.

"I see." That made perfect sense. Why else would he be here?

Oh, my God. This was the coincidental meeting she had been dreaming of, and she was bungling it all up. Didn't she have a plan for what to do next? Her mind had gone blank. She could . . . she could . . .

"Oops." She reached out and swept some of the new releases off the table.

Jack, being the gentleman he was, quickly knelt and began picking up the books even as his eyebrows furrowed in confusion. She crouched next to him, planning to pick up the same book he was reaching for, so their hands could accidentally brush against each other. But she hadn't knocked enough books off the table, and he had already collected all of them. She had no choice but to admit failure and stand when he got to his feet.

"Here you go." He handed her the books.

With a mumbled *thank you*, she reached for the books and accidentally brushed her fingers against his. She sucked in a sharp breath, and his eyes shot up to hers—fire burning in them. The accidental hand brushing actually happened. This was her chance. She should kiss him so passion could engulf them.

Lizzy burst into tears instead.

She'd missed him so much. She didn't know how she'd survived the last few months without him. Without hearing his voice. Without seeing his face. She was so happy he was there that it almost hurt.

Suddenly, she was in Jack's arms, and he cradled her head against his chest. "I'm sorry, Lizzy. I'm so sorry."

And she cried harder. She howled and slobbered. He just held her, smoothing his hand down her hair until she quieted against him.

"I'm—" she hiccupped, "I'm p . . . proud of you, Jack. I'm so proud of you for stepping out of your comfort zone and chasing after the life you want. The folks at McBain are probably patting themselves on the back right now for making the best decision they've ever made."

It had haunted her—her snide remark about his entry-level position. The shame of it had clawed at her insides every night. No matter what, she wanted him to know that she was proud of him.

"Thank you, Lizzy," he said against her hair. "You don't know how much that means to me."

She'd gotten into the habit of carrying around a couple of pieces of tissue in her pocket lately because she was prone to unexpected bouts of crying. She pulled one out now and stepped back from Jack to wipe her face and blow her nose. Once she was done, she cleared her throat, feeling self-conscious. Did they just make up? As friends? Were they back to being friends? *God, no. Not the friend zone.*

"Tell me about your work," she said, tossing the tissue in a trash can. Awkward or not, she wanted to know everything. She didn't want to miss a single moment in Jack's life. "Is it what you'd hoped for?"

"It's hard work, but I love the challenge of it." His eyes sparked with excitement.

"That makes me so happy." He deserved a job he loved to go into every morning. Just like she did.

He took her hand in his and looked around the store. For a moment, she said nothing as she registered that they were holding hands. Was it a sign that he still wanted to be more than friends? Or was it a friendly type of hand-holding?

"What is it?" she finally asked when Jack continued to look a little lost.

"I wanted to find somewhere for us to sit." He turned back to her, something sweet stealing into his expression. "There's so much to talk about."

"This way." She gently tugged his hand and led him to a love seat between two bookshelves. "Is this good?"

"It's perfect," he said.

They sat down still holding hands—she decided to take it as a good sign—and the worn springs on the sofa dipped to bring them closer together. It suddenly felt surreal that Jack was sitting beside her. Before she could stop herself, she ran her fingers down his cheek to make sure that he was really there. He was real and warm, and . . . he leaned into her touch. It was all she could do to stop herself from kissing him.

"Tell me about you. What have you been doing?" He looked intently at her as though his life depended on her answer.

"You must've heard from your parents that I left Weldon after a few weeks with them."

He nodded.

"I came back to LA because I finally figured out what I wanted to do with my life."

He sat so still she wasn't sure if he was breathing.

"Welcome to my bookstore, Jack." She got straight to the point. They could talk later about how it all happened. For the time being, she wanted to make sure he resumed breathing.

His eyes rounded, and his mouth dropped open. "Your bookstore?"

"Yes, mine," Lizzy said with pride filling her heart. "When I took time to dig deep, I found my childhood dream exactly where I'd left it."

"This . . . this is what you want?"

"Yes, this is what I want." She smiled softly, confident in knowing exactly what she wanted in life—this bookstore and Jack.

"I thought you hated LA." His eyes darted around her face.

"It wasn't LA that I hated," she explained. "I hated being an attorney. It was suffocating my soul."

"God, Lizzy. I'm so sorry." He squeezed her hand and swept his thumb across her knuckles.

A shiver of awareness traveled down her back even as his sympathy warmed her heart. "That's okay. I know where I belong now."

"But . . . you love Weldon."

"It isn't Weldon that I love." She breathed in deep. She promised herself she wouldn't let anything stop her from holding onto him once he walked back into her life. *Cannonball.* "I love you. I don't care where I live as long as I'm with you. You're my home, Jack."

Relief, wonder, and joy swam across his face in quick succession before he lunged for her. The force of his kiss pushed her against the arm of the sofa. She didn't mind. She kissed him back with as much desperation and hunger, tugging him closer. But he suddenly set her away from him.

"What the hell, Jack?" She tried to pull him back, but he held her away by her arms. She growled like a feral animal.

He tilted his head back and laughed. He looked so happy that she decided to stop snarling at him. When he looked at her again, there was laughter in his eyes and something else . . . a tenderness that made her heart wrench.

"I love you, Elizabeth Chung," he said, his voice deep and resonant.

Her eyelashes fluttered against her cheeks. "But you said your feelings weren't involved."

"That was *the* biggest lie I've ever told." Jacked pushed her hair off her forehead and planted a kiss there. "I'm so sorry. I thought you didn't think I was good enough for you."

"That's not true. I didn't mean what I said—"

"I know," he said, stopping the words tumbling out of her. "I know you believe in me. I know you're proud of me. But I was so lost that I let my own insecurities hold me back from you."

"You *are* good enough for me." She wanted him to know that he was her everything. "If anything, you're too good for me."

"Never too good for you." He swiped the back of his finger down her cheek. He couldn't seem to stop touching her. She liked it just fine. "But I know now that I *am* good enough for you, because no one knows you like I do. No one can ever love you as much as I do."

His words finally sank in. He loved her. Happiness, blinding in its brilliance, burst through her. *Jack loves me.*

"I've loved you since we were ten," he said.

"Wait." She put her fingers on his lips, and he kissed them, distracting her for a moment. "Since we were ten?"

"Give or take a year." He shrugged like loving someone for twenty years was no biggie.

"I can't believe you never said anything all these years." Fresh tears welled in her eyes. She was so grateful and humbled by his devotion.

"You had me squarely pegged as a friend. I didn't think you could ever see me as anything more."

"I was too young and foolish to see what I was missing out on." She ran her hand down his arm with a coy smile, and heat sparked in his eyes. "Now I know better."

"I'm glad." A husky note crept into his voice. "I've loved you for twenty years, but I truly fell in love with you when you belted out 'Can't Take My Eyes Off You' like a warrior that one night."

"I think I knew then, too." She laughed as happy tears streamed down her cheeks. He wiped them away with his thumbs. "When you sang 'All of Me,' I so wished you were saying those words to me."

"I was. I couldn't hold them inside anymore, so I sang them to you."

She leaned in and kissed him softly on the lips. "Why did you stay away all these months?"

"I wanted to give you the space to find yourself—to discover what you wanted from your life without interference from me. I just hoped that the life you chose will include me," he said. "I wasn't going to say anything today if you'd still been searching . . . but thank God, you have everything figured out. Because I didn't know where to find the strength to walk away from you."

"Oh, Jack," she said in a choked whisper. Even though it nearly broke her not to see him for so long, she had needed to figure out what she wanted on her own. And, of course, he had understood that. "Thank you for waiting for me. Through it all, you were the only thing I was certain of. Whatever life I imagined myself in, you were always in it."

"Good"—he punctuated his simple statement with a kiss on her wrist—"because I have no intention of leaving your side ever again."

Her heart fluttered in her chest, and she resisted the urge to pinch herself. Was this really happening? She linked her fingers through his, and the gentle pressure of his hand assured her this was real.

"I was going to win you back, you know," she confessed, looking down at their hands. "I was developing a strategy."

"A strategy? That sounds serious," he teased. "Did you make a list?"

"As a matter of fact, I did." She grinned, thinking of the pink journal on her desk at home. "It says, *Win Jack back*."

"Well, it's your lucky day because you can check that right off. You have won me back. But you never lost me in the first place. I came to Hideaway today because I was desperate to feel close to you. Staying away from you was the hardest thing I've ever done." His hand tightened around hers, and a glimmer of remembered pain flared behind his eyes—pain she understood only too well. To remind him that it was finally behind them—that they were together again—she caught his gaze and held it until a crooked smile tilted his lips. "Just so you know, I could never stop loving you. That's like telling my heart to stop beating."

"We can't have that." She slowly shook her head, wearing a tremulous smile. "You absolutely must love me forever, then."

"You say that like I have a choice," he said, making her heart melt into a puddle. "I love you. I've loved you since I was ten, and I'll love you until I'm one hundred and ten."

"I better start exercising as much as you do if we're going to live until we're a hundred and ten." Laughter bubbled out of her.

"Jogging buddies forever."

"Best friends forever," she said, her eyes roaming over his beautiful face. "I love you, Jack."

"I need you to say that again." His voice was so low it was nearly a growl.

"I love you."

"Again."

"I love you," she happily obliged. "I love you so much."

"I've been waiting twenty years to hear you say those words." He leaned his forehead against hers. "God, I love you, Lizzy."

"I love you, too," she said again because he had waited so long—and so patiently—for her.

He sighed as though he was releasing a long-held breath. "Do you think we'll ever get sick of hearing that?"

"Not a chance."

"Even if we live until we're—"

"One hundred and ten?" She laughed. "Not even then."

He tilted her chin and placed a lingering kiss on her lips— first sweetly, then inevitably with hunger, making sparks of passion jump across her skin. She climbed onto his lap and kissed him back even as the shopkeeper's bell announced the arrival of new customers. Reality could wait for a few minutes. She was busy living her dream with her love . . . her best friend . . . her forever.

EPILOGUE

"How far apart are the contractions?" Jack asked.

"About fifteen minutes," Lizzy said after a brief glance at her phone.

"When do you start pushing?" He wasn't quite hyperventilating . . . yet.

She cast a worried glance his way. "When the contractions are about five minutes apart, I think."

"Shit. We're not going to make it."

"Yes, we are," she assured him.

"Are you sure you don't want me to drive?" he asked for the tenth time in as many minutes.

"No." She scoffed. "You are in no condition to drive."

"I'm not the one who's having a baby," he practically shouted. "My sister is."

"Well, you're still in no condition to drive, Uncle Jack."

"Oh, my God. I'm going to be an uncle."

Just as Jack went into a shocked stupor and quieted for

the first time in nearly four hours, they crossed the city line into Weldon. Lizzy smiled as she drove through the beloved town—on their way to meet a new member for their family. Her sister-in-law had sounded happy and confident when they'd spoken a few hours earlier, but poor Jack was still worried about his little sister. Fortunately, Lizzy pulled into the parking lot of Weldon's one and only medical center before long.

The waiting room was filled with every Park and Kim in Weldon. Her in-laws and Seth's mom were huddled close together in the corner, talking and laughing quietly. Alex was sitting at the opposite corner, rocking back and forth. Landon, Seth's older brother and Aubrey's husband, was pacing the room at whirlwind speed, while Aubrey sat reading calmly to their adorable toddler, occasionally glancing up at her husband with an indulgent smile.

Lizzy went first to her in-laws and Mrs. Kim to say hello. Jack followed close behind her, relatively calm but fidgety. As they were checking in with the rest of the gang, Seth walked into the waiting room.

Landon rushed over to him and put a hand on his shoulder. "Everything is going to be fine."

"I know," Seth said evenly.

"I've done this before. Trust me," Landon persisted, and Aubrey snorted from her seat.

"I know, Hyung," Seth repeated. "I just came out to make sure you and Alex were okay."

"Of course we're okay. Why wouldn't we be okay?" Landon wheezed.

"Well, you guys seemed pretty freaked out when you first came to the hospital." Seth watched Alex muttering to himself in the corner with a frown.

"Seth, how is Tara doing?" Lizzy asked after giving him a hug.

"Oh, you know. Being her usual amazing self." Seth's smile was a little dreamy. "She wants to build an altar for epidurals and make sacrificial beer offerings."

"I'll be sure to offer up some sweets as well," Aubrey chimed in. "That stuff is the best."

"Take care of the big guy for me?" Seth asked his sister-in-law.

"Yup. Don't worry about a thing." Aubrey gave him a thumbs-up.

"Thank you. Well, I should go back in." Seth looked around the room. "Wish us luck. Tara's going to start pushing soon."

"Oh, God," Jack said weakly beside Lizzy. She reached over and squeezed his hand.

When Seth went back into the delivery room, Lizzy's mother-in-law came over to them and said in a low voice, "Alex has been rocking back and forth in that chair and hasn't made eye contact with anyone for the last hour. I've never seen him like this."

"Don't worry. We'll check on him." Tugging Jack along beside her, Lizzy said, "You need to pull yourself together, honey. Your brother needs you."

"Alex?" Jack's eyebrows rose as his gaze landed on his brother's stooped form. "Whoa. He's a mess."

Lizzy bit back her smile. "Yes, go calm him down."

Jack went to sit next to his brother and put his arm around his shoulder. Alex stopped rocking and glanced at him. They didn't say anything to each other, but soon, twin smiles spread across their faces. They were going to be just fine.

"Hey, Aubrey," Lizzy said, settling down next to her.

"It's so good to see you." Aubrey leaned in and gave her a hug. "How was the drive up? Did you hit a lot of traffic?"

"No more than usual. Other than my dear husband hyperventilating a tiny bit, the drive was fine."

"Landon has been solemnly reassuring everyone that everything will be okay this whole time." Aubrey laughed, crinkling her nose. "I think he's adorable for caring so much, but everyone else is probably tired of him."

"No, we all think he's adorable." Lizzy grinned and turned to the little girl on Aubrey's lap. "Hi, Morgan."

"Hi." She waved with her little hand. "I can sing the alphabet song. Do you want me to sing it for you?"

"I sure do," Lizzy said.

Morgan hopped down from her mom's lap and climbed onto Lizzy's before performing the alphabet song in a clear, ringing voice. Everyone in the waiting room clapped enthusiastically when she finished.

"I'm going to sing 'Twinkle, Twinkle, Little Star' now," the little girl announced. Once she finished singing, she turned to Lizzy with an expectant look in her eyes. "Do you get it?"

"Get what?" Lizzy's brows furrowed as she studied the toddler's upturned face. "Did I miss something?"

"The songs, silly." Morgan giggled behind her hands, kicking her feet in excitement. "Do you want to know?"

"Yes, please tell me."

"They're the same song. Different words. Same song." The little girl clapped at Lizzy's astounded expression. She was right. The alphabet song and "Twinkle, Twinkle, Little Star" had the same melody. Mind. Blown.

After regaling Lizzy with her encyclopedic knowledge of dinosaurs, Morgan wiggled off Lizzy's lap to give her daddy a hug and a kiss. Landon picked her up off the ground and planted twenty kisses on her face, and the sound of the toddler's laughter cut through the tension in the room.

Seth walked back into the waiting room about an hour later, wearing a smile that seemed almost too big for his face. Everyone shot to their feet.

"Conner Park-Kim is here," he said with his arms wide open, ready for the group hug coming his way. "Come meet him."

Tara looked spent, but she beamed at everyone when they trooped into her room. She held a baby wrapped like a burrito in her arms. The grandparents got to hold the tiny bundle first. Then the aunts and uncles. When it was her turn, Lizzy carefully lifted Conner into her arms and cradled him against her chest. He was beautiful—she leaned down to sniff his little head—and smelled warm and fuzzy. Jack stood by her side and smiled down at his nephew.

"This was excellent practice," Lizzy said to her husband once she returned the baby to Tara. "I'm going to check it off the to-do list."

"What to-do list?" Jack asked, his eyes still lingering on the newborn.

"For when our baby comes," she whispered into his ear—even though everyone was too busy fawning over the baby to overhear them. "We still have seven months, but I have everything all planned out."

"You . . . but . . ." Jack attempted to make words, frowning really hard.

"That's okay, honey." Lizzy patted his cheek. "Take your time."

She pulled out her cell phone and opened up her list app. She checked off *Do a practice run* and *Tell my husband I'm pregnant* from the list.

"Jack, you okay?" She rubbed his back in soothing circles.

"I was going to tell you tonight, but Tara went into labor, and it just felt right to tell you now."

The smile that dawned on his face was more brilliant than the sunrise. She squealed when he lifted her off her feet and spun her around. And in front of everyone in the hospital room, he kissed her—with tongue. *Oh, what the hell.* She kissed him back with equal enthusiasm.

"I love you," he said against her lips.

"I love you, too."

Jack kissed her again, holding her face in his hands despite the delicate and the not-so-delicate coughs piping up around them. In that moment, Lizzy's happiness was so complete that she didn't have room to feel embarrassed. Besides, they had to learn to grow thick skins. They were going to be parents soon.

ACKNOWLEDGMENTS

Some books are hard—really hard—to write, while some books seem to write themselves. *Booked on a Feeling* was an absolute delight to write. Something about Lizzy and Jack's story just got me carried away, and the words flowed through my fingers. I was wearing a goofy grin half the time I was writing this book. Maybe it was because I got to write about books and bookstores. Or maybe it was because I was finally writing about an attorney who left her profession for bookish reasons—like yours truly. Whatever the reason, I love this book.

To my agent, Sarah Younger, and my editor, Mara Delgado Sánchez, thank you so much for hopping online to help me brainstorm for this book. It was the most productive and fun video chat ever, and look what came out of it! Thank you, Mara, for all your hard work to make *Booked on a Feeling* the best book it can be. And Sarah, . . . what can I say? I don't know what I would do without you.

To my publicist, Sara LaCotti, and my marketing manager, Beatrice Jason, thank you for shouting from the rooftops about my little book. I'm so happy you're bringing *Booked on a Feeling* to more and more readers. And to the amazing team at St. Martin's Griffin, your support and dedication mean the world to me—you have never once made me feel small or unimportant. It makes me want to work even harder to reach my full potential.

To my bookstore muse, Jhoanna Belfer of Bel Canto Books, thank you for sharing your expertise about what it takes to own and run a successful bookstore. I have dispersed the many nuggets of wisdom you shared with me to revitalize Sparrow Bookstore in *Booked on a Feeling*. To my dear friend and critique partner, Gwen Hernandez, thank you for your insights and sound advice. It is so wonderful having someone I can trust to never lead me astray.

To my boys, thank you for going back to school (just kidding!) and staying healthy, so I could focus on writing Lizzy and Jack's story. To my husband, thank you for not distracting me *too much*, so I could meet my deadline. You guys are my reason for being. Your love and support mean everything to me.

To my parents and my brother, I am so proud to call you my family. I am who I am because of you.

To my dear readers, it still amazes me that you choose to read my books, and nothing makes me happier than hearing that you enjoyed reading them. I hope with all my heart that you love *Booked on a Feeling* as much as I do. Thank you, thank you, thank you.